inued . . .

An Unforgettable Lady

"Sensational romantic suspense." — *Romantic Times*

"I anxiously await her next book."
— The Romance Readers Connection

"Exhilarating romantic suspense." — The Best Reviews

By J. R. Ward

The Black Dagger Brotherhood Series
Dark Lover
Lover Eternal
Lover Awakened
Lover Revealed
Lover Unbound
Lover Enshrined
The Black Dagger Brotherhood: An Insider's Guide
Lover Avenged
Lover Mine
Lover Unleashed
Lover Reborn

Novels of the Fallen Angels
Covet
Crave
Envy

Writing as Jessica Bird
Heart of Gold
Leaping Hearts
An Unforgettable Lady
An Irresistible Bachelor

LEAPING
HEARTS

J. R. WARD
Writing as Jessica Bird

A SIGNET BOOK

SIGNET
Published by New American Library, a division of
Penguin Group (USA) Inc., 375 Hudson Street,
New York, New York 10014, USA
Penguin Group (Canada), 90 Eglinton Avenue East, Suite 700, Toronto,
Ontario M4P 2Y3, Canada (a division of Pearson Penguin Canada Inc.)
Penguin Books Ltd., 80 Strand, London WC2R 0RL, England
Penguin Ireland, 25 St. Stephen's Green, Dublin 2,
Ireland (a division of Penguin Books Ltd.)
Penguin Group (Australia), 250 Camberwell Road, Camberwell, Victoria 3124,
Australia (a division of Pearson Australia Group Pty. Ltd.)
Penguin Books India Pvt. Ltd., 11 Community Centre, Panchsheel Park,
New Delhi - 110 017, India
Penguin Group (NZ), 67 Apollo Drive, Rosedale, Auckland 0632,
New Zealand (a division of Pearson New Zealand Ltd.)
Penguin Books (South Africa) (Pty.) Ltd., 24 Sturdee Avenue,
Rosebank, Johannesburg 2196, South Africa

Penguin Books Ltd., Registered Offices:
80 Strand, London WC2R 0RL, England

Published by Signet, an imprint of New American Library, a division of Penguin
Group (USA) Inc. Previously published in an Ivy Books edition. Published by ar-
rangement with the author.

First Signet Printing, July 2012
10 9 8 7 6 5 4 3 2 1

For my husband, for my mother and my father,
but also for Ben.

Dear Reader:

Leaping Hearts is my first-ever-published book, and so not surprisingly, it's close to my heart—always will be. This is where everything started for me: I got "the call" that I was going to get a publisher on its manuscript; I got to be professionally edited for the first time; I got to hold a bound set of pages with my words on them in my hands; and I got to drive to a bookstore in Quincy, Massachusetts, to actually see my work on the shelves for sale.

I can pretty much trace everything that's in the story back to two teenage passions: approximately six liquor boxes full of about five hundred Harlequin Presents, and the fact that, like every girl where I'm from in New York, I loved horseback riding. Of course, both are now in my past. Those wonderful white-covered novels with the gold swirls and the circle pictures of couples on the front have long been given away—and I don't ride anymore (gravity tends to get a harder pull on you as you age) ... but that intersection between falling in love and Thoroughbreds was what led me to this wonderful book.

Here's how it all came together: throughout prep school and college and law school, I'd always written stories— some I finished, some I abandoned, but everything I put to the page was about two people falling in love. It's just what came out of my head—and not a shocker, considering all those Harlequins I'd devoured. After I got out of all that schooling, and started working in corporate America, I kept up with the noodling and the typing and the thinking—until I finally, after so many years of missteps and half-assed stuff, got to a "The End" that really worked.

Ironically, it was right about then that my boyfriend (now my wonderful husband) and I were going down to Cape Cod to visit my mother for the weekend. The road we took once we got off Route 6 always brought us by this fenced-in field that had horses in it. For some reason, on that particular day, I looked to the right, saw a Thoroughbred cantering around and BAM! the story that became *Leaping Hearts* took off in my head.

Always a seat-of-the-pantser back then (I'm now all about outlines,) I actually jotted down some things about the story, instead of throwing myself in at Chapter 1 with no clue what I was doing. I also took a steno book (still have it) to a horse show and jotted down notes to refresh my memories about hunter/jumping competitions. And then it was off to the races—or over the oxers, as the case was. I wrote the thing fairly fast, and by the time it was finished, I was making the trip to New York City to meet my first agent for the first time.

Over lunch at a French bistro, I told her I had something better than the manuscript she had on her desk, and she agreed to wait to see my new project before sending anything out. About a month or so later, I FedExed it to her— and then promptly took a trip to meet my future in-laws (not that any of us knew that was in the cards at this point).

Cue Sue Grafton. Yup, THAT Sue Grafton. While I was down there, my husband's father learned that I was dallying around with the whole writing thing and offered to introduce me to her. (He knows a lot about guns and ammunition and stuff like that, and he'd provided her with some info for one of her books.) I'll never forget walking into Sue's house for that initial time. She and her amazing husband had just bought this wonderful old home and were doing the interior-decorating bit. First thing she asked me was what I thought about a carpet sample.

She and I chatted (while I tried to keep my cool—I mean, not only was this A Real Writer, but Sue-frickin'-Grafton.) She offered to read the first fifty pages of my manuscript, but warned me she was really tough and brutally honest. I said please and thank you (and considered throwing up.) Two days later she called me and gave me, in the space of five minutes, the advice I now impart to every newbie who approaches me about their work (I don't read anyone else's manuscripts, but these three little ditties have never not been right): 1) take out your goddamn adverbs (the "goddamn" here is my addition, not Sue's.) Literally, do a word search with -ly and rip 'em out. Most newbies push too hard to make sure every nuance is on the page, not trusting their dialogue or descriptions to go far enough with the readers; 2) get rid of dumb-ass dialogue tags (the "dumb-ass" here is my addition, not Sue's). No "she exclaimed," "he derided," "she demurred," "he intoned." He said, she said. That's it; 3) cut the frickin' drama (um, yeah, the "frickin'" is my word, not hers). Most people don't emote at a high-pitched frequency all the time, flapping their arms and jumping around like monkeys. Yes, this is fiction, and as such, you don't want everyone acting like boring tax attorneys, but this isn't a silent movie, either.

It was like someone had shown me the path out of the jungle. (She also told me I "could actually write"—something she seemed to be a little surprised about. Frankly, so was I. In spite of all the time I'd spent plugging away, I still wasn't sure I could do it.) As soon as I hung up with her, I called my agent in New York, and told her to Stop!

The thing was, my agent had liked *Leaping Hearts* much more than the other manuscript and was ready to send it to editors at the big publishing houses. She'd actually made the copies, done her letter, gotten on the phone with people—it was about to happen. And here I was, a not-yet, maybe-never, unpub'd idiot telling her her business? But then I told her I'd gotten Sue Grafton to read part of it: "How in the *hell* did you do that?" "Long story. Just don't send it out yet!"

(I'm thinking at this moment of the scene in the movie *Wall Street* when Bud Fox gets the call from the big fish he's been courting—and the guy next to him whispers in awe, "Gekkkkkkkko." Just imagine, "Graffffffffton," and you get the gist of my agent's and my conversation that day.)

While I was still "on vacation," I went through that manuscript from start to finish, doing everything Sue said to. It was amazing—I saw exactly what she was talking about. The story was there, but my word choices and insecurities were getting in the way, the heavy veil of adverbs and stock phrases and yelling and screaming blocking the reader from the people.

Long story/short (too late,) the book was bought and it made it to the shelves and I got to write three more of these single titles (and then Wrath came along and everything changed!) Devlin McCloud is a classic, romance hero type with his dark past, his injury, his gruff exterior. And A. J. Sutherland is a lot like me, focused on her goals to the exclusion (almost) of everything else. And Sabbath—well, he's the horse my teenage self would have loved to own and ride . . . and win with.

I hope you adore the three of them as much as I do. This was the beginning of the ride for me, on so many levels, and along with *Dark Lover*, one of the best things that has ever happened to me. Thank you, thank you, thank you for your support, and as always . . .

Happy Reading!

J. R. Ward
December 2011

1

A. J. SUTHERLAND was captivated by the stallion from the moment she saw him. And she wasn't the only one. Like believers in front of a hypnotist, the whole audience was under a spell and had the dreamlike eyes of zombies. Called by the master to come forward, the crowd moved like a glacier, pushing its way toward the auctioneer's stand and bulging out of the cordoned-off area where the horse was displayed.

A.J. did her best to get through the throng but others were doing the same. A bottleneck formed and elbows were used like hockey sticks as people fought to come forward. Being no slouch, especially when it came to getting things she wanted, she mounted pointy defenses of her own until she made it to the front. Wrapping her arms around herself, she released her breath in a rush as she got an unobstructed view of the black stallion.

She'd seen a lot of good Thoroughbreds in Virginia but nothing like him.

Head held high, the horse stared out at the crowd with hostile uninterest. He was the king; he ruled the world. Everyone else just took up space.

Under the lights, his coat glistened with flashes of black and navy and his tail whipped back and forth impatiently. Dark hooves stamped the dirt as he threw his head against the halter and lead line that tied him to his handlers. With his powerful body dwarfing the men around him, he was the one in control despite being outnumbered by the five grooms who'd been assigned to try to hold him. The men around him circled cautiously, tense.

Like the crowd, they knew his reputation. It wasn't a good one.

A.J.'s eyes feasted on the stallion. In every move he made, there was a promise of strength and agility that was both athletic and poetic. And, behind his disdain, she sensed a fierce intelligence and an iron will.

At the head of the crush of people, she made up her mind. He was the most magnificent thing she'd ever seen. And she was going to have him.

"We're opening the bidding at ten thousand dollars," the auctioneer said.

Her hand flew up.

It was an outrageously low price considering the horse's bloodlines, high if you thought about his penchant for trouble.

"That's ten thousand dollars. Do I have eleven?"

Somewhere in the crowd another hand was raised. A ripple of speculation went through the arena. Many had come to get a look at him up close; few had come with the idea of buying. Everyone wanted to know who was going to take him.

"That's eleven. Do I hear twelve?"

She nodded.

The other bidder countered at thirteen and she immediately raised the price to fourteen. There was a pause and then the price came back at $15,000.

"Do I have sixteen?" The auctioneer looked her way. She inclined her head without hesitation.

Just then, her arm was grabbed by her stepbrother.

"What are you doing?" Peter Conrad's eyes were bulging.

"What does it look like I'm doing?"

"Like you're making another rash decision. Throwing yourself heedlessly into another mess that I'm going to have to pay for." As the price continued to climb, he escalated the argument along with it. "Have you heard about that thing's reputation?"

"Excuse me," A.J. said, moving around him. The two did a cramped box step, trading places.

"We are at twenty-two thousand dollars," the auctioneer said.

A.J. reestablished eye contact with the gavel man and nodded. The crowd's murmuring elevated, surging in waves with the bidding.

"Stop this," Peter hissed.

A.J. paid no attention to him. Her focus was on the other bidder. Like a train slowing down, her competition was losing steam but wasn't out of the game yet. There was a long pause and then the price was raised again. Without blinking, she tacked on another thousand.

"Don't you dare buy that animal!" Peter demanded. Turning toward the auctioneer, he started shaking his head and drawing his hand across his neck to dispute her authority.

When the bid came back, A.J. fixed her stepbrother with fierce blue eyes and spoke up loudly over the crowd. "I'll pay thirty thousand for the stallion."

The audience gasped in surprise and the auctioneer looked amazed at his good fortune. And her recklessness.

Peter began to sputter, overwhelmed by her audacity.

"Er, I have thirty thousand dollars," the auctioneer said, looking into the crowd at the other bidder. "That's thirty thousand going once."

"You're crazy!" her stepbrother said. He tried frantically to get the auctioneer to stop but the man shook his head at Peter's theatrics. It was a valid bid and everyone knew it.

"Going twice."

Rebuffed, Peter curled his fists in frustration and then tried a different tactic, assuming an air of haughty scorn.

"I won't be responsible for the trouble you're creating," he told A.J. "I've cleaned up the results of your enthusiasm one too many times. If you do this, you're on your own."

He straightened his cashmere jacket with a curt tug at the cuffs. The tan color was played off by his silk pants and cream turtleneck but did little for his pale complexion. He was a study in bland tones. The only bright spike in the outfit was a jaunty red handkerchief in his breast pocket. It looked like a pimiento that had fallen into a bowl of oat-meal.

A.J. looked down at her own clothes. Scruffy but clean blue jeans, a polo shirt and barn jacket, leather boots. She had on a Sutherland Stables baseball cap, which was controlling the top half of her mane of auburn curls. The bottom half was reeled in by a tie at the base of her neck. Practical, comfortable. Unremarkable.

"Going three times."

"You *will* regret this," Peter announced.

It was a promise A.J. had heard before from him. What it meant was, if something bad didn't flow naturally from her impulse, he'd make sure he took up the slack.

"I'd only regret it if I didn't get him," she murmured.

"Sold," the auctioneer called out. "Lot number 421, a four-year-old Thoroughbred stallion, Sabbath, to Sutherland Stables."

Peter's frustration came back as the gavel hit wood. "When the hell is this going to stop! When are you going to grow up and stop behaving so rashly?"

A.J. watched his face grow tight with rage as he went into a full snit.

It went further than the partial snit, she reflected, which merely involved foot stamping and huffing, or the half snit, which was the partial with verbal backup. She saw that beads of sweat, highly characteristic of the full snit, had formed at his temples and across his forehead. With a detachment she found amusing, she noted that forehead seemed to be getting more pronounced every year, courtesy of his receding hairline.

"Peter, take a breath, will you," she said in a calm voice. "Everything's going to be fine."

"Fine! You just paid thirty thousand dollars for a horse no one can ride!"

"He's magnificent. Even you should be able to see that. And his bloodlines are impeccable."

"Being distantly related to nobility hasn't made him a gentleman."

"He can clear any jump you put in front of him."

"And usually without his rider! That personality of his is

better suited for the rodeo than show jumping. Even better, put him in a ring with a red cape and he'd give any matador a run for his money."

People were starting to gather around them, fascinated by her outrageous bid and the ensuing argument. A.J. didn't care but it irked her to watch Peter get more flamboyant as their audience grew. He loved attention, and seeing him bloom under the eyes of strangers made her remember the one toothpaste commercial he'd been in as a child. He'd paraded around for months afterward like he'd won an Oscar, and the thirty-second spot had led him to believe he was destined for stardom. The afterglow of speaking the words *Minty-fresh, Mommy!* into a camera had lasted twenty years.

"You're overreacting," she told him, trying to get one more look at the stallion as the stable hands began to lead the horse away.

"And you're out of control! I run a stable of winners. Some of the best bloodlines in the country are under our roof and I won't let you bring a beast like that into their midst."

"He's not a beast—"

"That thing tossed his rider, ran out of the ring and trampled half the crowd at the Oak Bluff Jumper Classic."

"That's in the past."

"That was last week."

"He's going to be a champion. You'll see."

"The stallion's dangerous and unpredictable. What makes you think he's suddenly going to turn into a winner?"

"Because I'm going to be riding him."

Peter snorted. "I doubt you could hang on to him long enough to get both feet into the stirrups."

A mix of bravado and frustration made A.J.'s voice louder than she'd meant it to be when she replied, "You'll see. I'm going to take him into the Qualifier two months from now."

People around them gasped.

At that moment, a shout of alarm rang out from up front. When she turned around, she saw several stable hands bolting in different directions, diving for cover. Then, just as suddenly, everyone in the crowd was scrambling for safety. The stallion had broken free from his handlers, leapt into the cordoned-off area where the crowd had watched the auction and burst into the throng of people, scattering them like marbles across a floor.

Not again, A.J. thought, sparing Peter a glance as they both ran for it. His face was vacillating between a self-satisfied I-told-you-so look and one of naked fear as the horse charged toward them with thundering hooves.

Most people, being of sound mind, ran out of the ring, but a few brave souls rushed forward, spreading their arms wide in a semicircle around the animal. They were going to try to corral the horse through an open gate that led into an unoccupied paddock, but the stallion seemed to know what they were after. The horse made a beeline at the men instead of falling for their ploy, and they fell aside, trying not to get trampled.

Mission accomplished, the stallion raced on, ready for more action, his lead line streaming behind him like a banner. Chaos reigned as people shouted and cursed and it dawned on A.J. that the horse looked delighted at all the trouble he was causing. He'd broken free of his captors, terrified the crowd and was enjoying himself thoroughly by chasing after stragglers.

If he were human, he'd be laughing, she thought.

Peter's voice was furious in her ear. "I can't believe you want to bring this demon home!"

She smiled as the stallion galloped by, a black blur. He was limber and graceful, with the strength of steel in his muscles. "Look at him go."

"Straight to hell if I get to pick where to send him."

After another ten minutes of people trying to get control of the horse and failing, A.J. tugged her baseball cap down tight and stepped into the ring. She caught the stallion's eye immediately. Pegging her with a dark look, he rushed at her, only to come to a screeching halt a few yards away when she refused to move. Dirt kicked up around him in a cloud and he pawed the ground in warning, throwing his head up and down.

Instead of showing fear, A.J. put her hands into the pockets of her jeans. A silence fell over the crowd.

She could see the horse mulling over his options. Someone standing their ground in front of him was something new and he seemed confused.

"All right, you've had your fun," A.J. said in a low voice. "Now it's time to behave yourself."

As if he understood her, he shook his magnificent head and whinnied a loud denial. He was breathing heavily, his nostrils flaring widely, but she knew it was more for drama than from exertion. Even after bolting around the ring like a madman running from sanity, he hadn't broken a sweat across his gleaming black coat.

While they squared off, A.J. was looking at him with a calm disregard, as if he were a temperamental two-year-old. Inside, however, her instincts were sharp. She tracked every movement he made, noting the subtle twitching in the muscle fibers of his deep barrel chest and the beat of his heart in the veins just under his slick coat. She was searching for any advance warning that he was going to lunge at her, any hint as to what his next move might be.

After all, she might be daring but she wasn't stupid. It didn't take her years of experience with horses to know she had to be extremely careful when staring down an animal like Sabbath. A half ton of stallion backed by the personality of a pro wrestler didn't make for safety. It was a dangerous situation. And a thrilling one.

"You know, you may have missed your calling." She took a step forward, continuing to talk. "You'd make an excellent steamroller."

Sabbath snorted and reared up on his haunches for show.

"I'll make a deal with you," she said, stopping when she was only a couple of feet from him. "You calm down and come with me and I'll help you put all that energy to more constructive use."

She smiled at her own words, thinking it was probably like asking a rugby player to turn in his cleats for a pair of tap shoes.

While the horse seemed to be considering her proposal,

A.J. pictured herself saddling him up and mounting him for the first time.

"It's going to be a long way to the ground if you throw me," she said softly. "Fortunately, I tend to bounce."

Sabbath let out another ferocious roar. Her smile deepened.

"So do I take that as a yes? Are you ready to try a little tap dancing?"

Suspiciously, the horse moved his head forward, putting his black muzzle up to her face. He took in a huge lungful of air, drawing her scent through his nose. Then he blew it back at her, sending her baseball cap flying.

A.J. shook her head. "If you want to impress me, you're going to have to do more than play bowling ball to a crowd of people and knock off my hat."

Sabbath reared again, his mane streaking through the air, hooves pawing the space between them. Then, looking bored, he abruptly dropped his neck, lowering his head.

After a moment, A.J. cautiously reached forward and took his lead in her slender hand. When the stallion tolerated it with only a flick of his ears, she moved to the side and went forward. Together, they started to walk out of the arena.

One of the stable hands approached tentatively. Without words, he pointed out where the stallion had been housed and then scurried away. Left to handle the horse alone, A.J. led the way into the stable area and approached the stall Sabbath had been in.

"You don't know this yet," she whispered, leading him inside, "but you and I are going to make a great team."

Still watching him closely, she took off his halter and then shut the half door, leaning on it.

As he bent down and nipped at some hay in the corner, A.J. sighed. "We're just going to have to teach you some manners first."

From the fringes of the crowd, Devlin McCloud watched the scene unravel with cynical eyes. He'd known exactly when the horse was going to bolt. The stallion's massive haunches had tensed hard before the animal sprang forward and he picked the perfect time to make his move. At that exact moment, the groom holding the lead had let his attention lapse, looking in the opposite direction and laughing at someone behind him. Like a flash, the horse took off and, courtesy of his distraction, the young hand had been dragged through the dirt and almost trampled. By the time the kid let go of the lead, he looked like a breaded cutlet.

All around, people started scrambling to get out of the way, but Devlin, with his bad leg, wasn't able to move as fast as the rest of the crowd. Relying on his cane, he made his way to the edge of the ring in the awkward gait he despised, all the while keeping his eye on the horse.

He didn't stare just because he wanted to avoid getting run over. He was captivated. The stallion moved with a grace and force Devlin hadn't seen in a long time. It reminded him of—

He blocked the thought of Mercy. It had been almost a year since the accident, nearly a year since he'd had to put her down, but the pain was still unbearable. Once more, he wondered how long it was going to take to get over his grief, and feared the ache in his chest, like the one in his leg, was never going to go away.

When he finally reached the rail, he ducked out of the ring and then watched as order disintegrated. The crowd was still milling about like lemmings looking for water and he watched with amusement as several men tried to corral the horse.

The stallion's too smart for that trick, he thought, not at all surprised when the animal bolted at the men.

Devlin shook his head.

If someone could get a handle on that horse and channel all that energy, they'd have a hot ticket on their hands, he decided. It'd be like harnessing nuclear fission but the potential locked in the beast might just make the risk of getting burned worth it.

The stallion flashed by him, head held high, tail cocked and billowing in his wake.

Devlin thought about the horse's new owners. He hoped Sutherland Stables knew what they'd signed on for but doubted they were up to the task. The stable had a lot of money, great-looking tack and a swimming pool to play in, but he knew more about their toys than their feats of training. He had a feeling the stallion was going to put them to the test.

With an echo of remembered passion for his career, he thought how much he wished he could tackle the beast. As envy burned in his veins, he looked down at his leg with disgust. He was used to being in the ring, not at ringside. The distance between the two was vast and, after a year, he was still an uneasy traveler of the stretch of emptiness that separated where he'd been and where he was.

His gaze shifted back to the chaos and then sharpened as he watched a young woman step into the ring and approach the horse. She was tall and thin but her body was strong and he forgot all about the stallion. He couldn't see her face so he moved to try to get a better look. He wondered who she was. A groom? One of the auction's hands? He knew if he'd seen her before, he'd remember. There was something about the way she moved that was unforgettable.

Devlin watched as she walked toward the stallion with confidence, her hips swaying, her long legs carrying her across the ring. He felt like he'd been kneed in the gut as a strange ache settled into his body. He couldn't look away from the woman and his hand gripped his cane as she stopped in front of the stallion. Unlike the stable hand, her focus on the animal was unwavering and she was calm as she put her hands in her pockets.

Atta girl, Devlin thought with approval. Nice and slow. No big movements.

He watched the horse and the woman size each other up. The contrast between the two was striking. The animal, dark and fierce. The woman, slender and steady. Still, as she talked to the great black beast, it was immediately apparent there was something special happening between them. And then the stallion blew off her hat, clearly fishing for some sort of reaction, and, when he got none, dropped his head. It wasn't a surrender, more like an accommodation that was freely revocable. The instant her hand took the lead, Devlin, like the rest of the crowd, let out a sigh of relief.

He was really impressed. Like all daredevil feats, it had taken courage and stupidity for her to get that close to the stallion. Granted, she'd been smart in the way she did it, showing the kind of sense a person gets only after they spend a lifetime around unpredictable animals. The danger had been there all along, however, and Devlin was glad she hadn't been hurt.

And then the real miracle happened.

The stallion let her lead him. Feigning boredom, so he didn't appear to be giving in, the giant horse had let her take him from the ring. It was a small pledge of trust.

As the crowd dispersed, Devlin limped out to the center of the ring. Bending down, he picked up the woman's hat. The stately logo of Sutherland Stables, two Ss intertwined with ivy, was embroidered on the front.

He went in search of the woman.

"I'm not going to let you bring him back to the stables," Peter was saying to A.J. as they stood in front of the stallion's stall.

While her stepbrother continued yelling at her, she was absorbed by Sabbath, who had his head out in the aisle. The stallion seemed to be regarding Peter with the same level of interest she was. Which wasn't much.

"For heaven's sake," she finally broke in. "Sabbath is coming home and everything is going to be fine as soon as you drop this nonsense and get out of my way."

"That horse is not boarding at the stables."

"What are you suggesting—I bring him to the house? Your mother will hate the hoofprints all over those Persian carpets she insisted on buying. And besides, I don't think they make an equine equivalent of a doggie door."

She and Peter had been back living at her father's mansion since they'd both graduated from college. It created an awkward situation because of the strain between them but the location was conveniently close to the stables for her and luxurious enough to satisfy Peter. She knew her father wanted them home but his second wife was less magnanimous. Regina Conrad, Peter's mother and Garrett Sutherland's wife for the past eighteen years, always wanted her son close by but was less than enthusiastic about A.J.'s presence in the elegant home.

Peter pushed his chin forward. "I'm not going to argue about this. I warned you not to buy him. I've tried to be reasonable with you but, as usual, I'm getting nowhere."

A.J. was beginning to lose composure as frustration got the better of her. Struggling not to lose her temper, she brought a hand to her throat where a diamond solitaire dangled from a slender chain. It was the one thing she had of her own mother's, and as she rubbed the glittering stone between her thumb and forefinger, she tried to calm down.

"Peter, trust me. I can turn him around. I'm going to work with him, one-on-one."

"Not if I refuse to pay for him, you won't."

She turned her focus on Peter. "You can't be serious."

"One phone call to the office here and you're off the charge account."

"You can't do that."

"Try me."

"Well, then I'll just write a check from my personal account."

Peter paused, weighing his next move. "Your father isn't going to let you ride that stallion."

"He never interferes with my training."

"I'll bet that changes when I tell him all about your little friend's reputation for throwing riders. Not to mention his skills at crowd control."

"Look, you don't have to blow this out of proportion." A.J. let the stone fall back against the skin of her throat. "He'll be one horse out of fifty at the stables. You'll barely know he's there."

"It's not the ratio that bothers me. This animal is malevolent and dangerous. I don't want a mass exodus out of the barns. I have to protect my business."

"Let me remind you: Sutherland Stables is half mine."

"You do the riding part. I handle the business. And that's thirty thousand dollars of money I'm in charge of that you just threw out a window."

"In stud fees alone, this stallion will make thirty grand look like couch change."

"For what? The dubious pleasure of his company? I doubt it."

"When he's a champion, you can bet he'll be profitable."

"You don't know if that horse can compete in anything other than a bowling tournament. Knocking down people seems to be his forte, not jumping fences."

"He's been shown before."

"Only to be a horror in the ring. That's hardly a recommendation for a stud."

"It's in him."

"She's right."

A J. turned to see who had agreed with her and found herself looking at a legend.

Her breath caught in her throat as her body temperature soared. With her cap in one hand, Devlin McCloud was standing close enough for her to see the flecks of green in his hazel eyes. Her heart started to pound as she responded to an electric current that flared when they looked at each other.

Although she knew his face well from all the press he'd received throughout his career, it was the first time she'd ever been up close to the man, and she was stunned. If the champion was devastatingly handsome staring out of the cover of a magazine, he was downright mesmerizing in person. Her body began to tingle.

My God, he's beautiful, she thought.

The man was just over six feet tall, with broad shoulders, strong arms and a stance that was tough and confident. He looked out on the world from a pair of deep-set, highly intelligent eyes which were at the moment trained on her like searchlights. His hair was dark and brushed off his forehead, thanks to a cowlick that was in just the right place, and his skin was tanned from time in the sun. Unlike Peter, he was dressed as she was, in blue jeans and a work shirt, but with the command he held himself, he could have been wearing a dishrag and he'd have looked like he owned the place.

It really was *the* Devlin McCloud.

There were few in the equestrian world who didn't know him. He was a maverick, a national sports presence, the former captain of the Olympic Equestrian Team, a multiple gold medal winner and one of the best show jumpers the country had ever produced. And if he hadn't been known because of his accomplishments, his tragedy would have sealed the buzz on him. A.J.'s eyes flickered over his legs and she saw his flash of annoyance as he caught the glance.

"I believe this is yours." He held out her cap.

His voice was deep and sensuous and had a kind of gravel in it that reverberated through her ears and down into her spine. Although he'd been interviewed on national TV and radio numerous times, it was the first time she'd heard him speak live. Even though she knew so much about him, and his private stable was not far from the Sutherland compound, she'd never spoken with him before. That wasn't unusual. The man let few people get near him.

Aware she was staring, A.J. took the hat and confronted Peter. "You see? If anyone is likely to know a champion, it's him."

"I didn't say he was going to be a champion."

She turned back around in surprise. "But you agreed with me."

"I think he's got jumping in his blood. Being a champion is something else entirely."

That voice of his sounded delicious and she found herself preoccupied with the way his lips moved over the words. They were perfectly molded lips, she decided, the lower one more full, the upper curling over straight white teeth. She struggled to keep her train of thought.

"Er—but if he has the innate talent, then he can win."

"What's the use of the best foundation in the world if you can't raise the roof because the walls are unsteady?"

"My point exactly," Peter said.

"Well, you're both wrong. I'm going to turn him into a champion."

"You'd have a better result if you turned him into dog food," Peter muttered.

Standing in front of the woman who'd captivated him, Devlin shifted his weight and changed the position of his cane. He saw her eyes flash downward again as she tracked the movement, and hated that his physical weakness was so obvious to her.

Seeing her up close, he realized that he recognized her after all. She was the daughter of Garrett Sutherland, the incredibly wealthy engineer, and a newcomer on the professional circuit. In her middle twenties, she was just cutting her teeth in the big leagues but showed some real promise as a competitor. The guy with her had to be Peter Conrad, the one who ran the stables.

Ignoring Peter, Devlin kept looking at the woman and decided she was damn beautiful. Her features were strong, her chin determined, and her startling blue eyes met his head-on. He liked all of that. She also had the glow of someone who spent a lot of time outdoors and carried herself with the physical poise that comes from being an athlete. The fact that she filled out her jeans like they were a test she had all the right answers to didn't hurt, either. He found himself wondering what she looked like with that auburn hair free around her shoulders.

"I have faith in him," she was saying, "and I'm going to start by riding him in the Qualifier."

"You'll be the laughingstock of the circuit," her stepbrother countered.

"Or maybe he and I will win."

In two months, the best jumpers in the country would be competing for spots on a team destined to face the top riders in Europe. At the end of the competition, whoever won the most points got to be the captain of the team headed across the ocean and, because the whole sport was looking forward to the Olympics in another year, that rider would be considered the heir apparent to lead the American contenders for a shot at gold. The Qualifier was a prestigious event, held at the incomparable Borealis Hunt and Polo Club, and the open roster meant that anyone could compete even if they didn't have a ranking.

It was a competition Devlin knew well. He'd won it many times. It was also the very event that had cost him his career.

"You can't do this." Peter was shifting back and forth in his Italian loafers, a nervous metronome. "You simply can't. You're going to make a fool out of us."

"Thanks for all the support," she replied dryly, and then looked into Devlin's eyes.

Meeting her gaze, Devlin caught on to the insecurity she tried to hide.

She's right to worry, he thought. The stallion was going to need a lot of work and, even then, there'd be no telling what would come of the investment. Time and her inexperience were likewise working against her. Two months would be a stretch for any rider and new mount to forge a relationship, even if the rider was working with a compliant horse and had years of competing under her belt.

"I'm warning you," Peter said to her before turning to go. "Don't try to bring that horse into my stables."

"Our stables," she corrected.

But the man had already started walking away, delicately sidestepping a pile of hay in front of another stall and then yelping as a curious muzzle reached out to him.

"Damn animals," he muttered.

A.J. turned to Devlin and, as her eyes traveled across his wide shoulders, she momentarily forgot her frustration. She noted that his hair just brushed the top of his collar, the silky waves breaking against the flannel, and she wondered what it would feel like. Her fingers curled the baseball cap into a ball and her heart began to pound with a crazy anticipation.

Aware her cheeks were flushing, she cleared her throat and said, "Don't you think it can be done?"

Devlin regarded the hope in her face with nostalgia. Thinking back, he could dimly recall the emotion in himself. He was less than ten years older than she but felt ancient looking into the crystal blue of her eyes.

What color is that? he wondered. Sky blue?

He felt a stirring in the boiler room of his body and had to look away from her face to somewhere safer. Watching her fiddle with the hat, he caught a glimpse of the logo and frowned.

Devlin had always had an aversion to the kind of moneyed, restless people who were sometimes attracted to the horse world. Although all of the wealthy elites weren't bad, he couldn't abide the ones who played at the sport just because they thought it was glamorous. That was the way horses got mistreated or injured.

And, however unassuming the woman in front of him looked in her blue jeans and barn jacket, he knew more about the wealth of her family than about her riding skills. Watching that logo twist and turn in her hands, he was more than tempted to brush her off and walk away. Her father's greenbacks aside, the last thing he wanted was to comment on the hopes and dreams of another rider. He'd had a bad enough year trying to deal with losing his own.

In the end, Devlin got caught again in her eyes and couldn't deny her an answer. Looking into that blue, he found that something inexplicable happened to him. He felt cleansed, somehow. Less cynical, less tired of life. It made him want to get closer to her.

"I don't know you or the horse well enough to say," he answered cautiously. "Hard work and training will probably get you both over the fences, assuming he doesn't throw you just for the fun of it. But winning? That takes teamwork and you can't teach it. In horses or people."

Her face registered trepidation but then switched to optimism.

"I need a trainer," she declared.

Devlin felt a physical shock as he figured out where she was heading. "With what you can afford, you'll find one, I'm sure."

"I want you."

"No, you don't."

"But you're the best and I want—"

"You want a miracle worker. And I ran out of miracles at last year's Qualifier."

She reached out, touching his arm. He was stunned at how the soft touch affected him. It was like getting burned except he liked it. He pulled away sharply, even as he was curious about the sensation.

"Please, I can pay—"

"Money doesn't solve everything," he said.

Before he lost his wits again, he turned and walked away, his limp more pronounced than usual.

Standing in front of Sabbath's stall, A.J. let him go, feeling bad. She'd clearly offended him, which was the last thing she'd intended. It had seemed like a really good idea, though. Who could be better than he to help her turn the horse around?

She leaned back against the stall door and remembered McCloud's story. About ten years ago, out of nowhere, he'd erupted onto the jumping scene, becoming an overnight success. Even though he was in his early twenties, he quickly became known for being a hard-nosed, unflappable competitor with an instinct for horses that was unrivaled. After winning a string of events on mounts that were good under the bit for other people but spectacular with him on their backs, he'd found his perfect match in a pale gray, dappled mare. He and this horse, Mercy, went on to dominate the sport for so long, most couldn't remember a time when the two weren't on top.

Whether it was in the ring or out over a cross-country course, they were unbeatable and the crowds loved them. It wasn't just because the pair won. They were beautiful together, man and animal moving as one, connected, not separated, by the saddle. With his special mare and all his talent, it had seemed like Devlin McCloud's reign as king of the sport of kings was going to last forever.

But tragically, that didn't turn out to be the case.

People got hurt in competitive jumping. So did horses. It was the dangerous underbelly of the sport and, for some, maybe those risks were part of the thrill. In most cases, the fallen walked away with bumps and bruises, but not all. Tragically, Devlin and Mercy weren't that fortunate in an early-morning warm-up before the Qualifier. Devlin had to be taken out of the ring on a stretcher. Mercy had to be put down, right where she lay.

News of the accident had spread throughout the riding community within the hour. Immediately, the whole sport went into mourning and wanted to share their sympathy with Devlin. But, no matter how many people tried to reach out to help him, he rebuffed all kindness. With his reputation for being a loner, his retreat afterward wasn't a surprise to anyone. Shunning the support of the horse community, he turned in on his pain and shut out the world. Rumors circulated that he'd left the area, moved out of Virginia and would never be seen again but A.J. had known that wasn't true. Every once in a while, she'd be pulling in or out of the winding drive of Sutherland Stables and she'd see him, behind the wheel of a pickup truck, looking dark and preoccupied.

She sighed with resignation, feeling sad at all that he had lost. He was an enigma. A startlingly handsome, devastatingly sexy man who in five minutes of conversation made her feel like she'd swallowed a pint of moonshine. And that voice of his . . . She found herself wondering what his lips would feel like pressed against hers.

"Maybe it's for the best," she said out loud, feeling her face flush. Her palms felt ice-cold as she brought them to her cheeks.

After all, did she really want a trainer who affected her the way Devlin McCloud did? She could barely be in his presence for a moment or two before she felt like she was losing her composure. Considering the way the stallion behaved, it was going to be hard enough to make it to the Qualifier in one piece without complicating the workouts with a coach she was interested in getting physical with.

"So it is you with the horse, *non?*" A heavily accented voice broke through her reverie.

A.J. turned and had to smother a grimace as Philippe Marceau approached. He was widely known as a better rider than human being and it was like seeing someone with a bad head cold coming at her. She just wanted to run in the other direction.

As he strutted down the aisle, he reminded her a lot of Peter. He was likewise overdressed, wearing a pale silk suit, and a pastel shirt and tie that were a startling pink color. As the man sidled up to A.J. and the stallion, he straightened that glaring tie theatrically, pinkies cocked like gun hammers. She thought he looked like a lounge singer who'd gotten lost on his way to work and decided she'd be more than happy to redirect him to anywhere else on the planet.

"It is a good buy," he said, nodding to the stallion. "If one is looking for a busting bronc."

"Nice suit you got there. You headlining somewhere tonight?"

"Always with the comeback, you are. Pity that a woman as beautiful as you wastes her looks on tomboy clothes and her lovely lips on bad humor."

Sabbath, who'd gone back to eating after Devlin left, lifted his head at the new scent. Giving Philippe the once-over, he flattened his ears.

"So tell me," Philippe said as he moved in closer, the smell of his cologne overwhelming her. "When will we have that dinner together? A good French meal, some wine, some conversation. Perhaps something more . . ."

A.J. thought she'd rather eat tin cans with a billy goat. And as for the something more, she was the last person who'd fall for his continental lothario act. She knew the man's attentions were thrown around with the discretion of someone seeding a lawn and, even if she liked short men who were tall on conceit, she wasn't about to become another name at the end of what was a surprisingly long list.

"Thanks for the invite, Philippe, but I don't date."

"So I have heard. The ice queen living in her father's castle."

"Better to discriminate than be in bad company."

"*C'est vrai,* when that is the best you are able to attract."

A.J. held her tongue, about to remind him how he'd just propositioned her.

She said instead, "I'm going to be too busy getting Sabbath ready for the Qualifier."

"You are riding this thing in the Qualifier? Have you forgotten? It is two months from now, *cherie.* You will need another horse or an eternity before you can compete at that level."

"Well, then you can certainly understand why I'm not going to have dinner with you."

"*C'est dommage,*" he said, running his eyes over her. "You are foolish to attempt such an event on the back of this worthless horse, but then, no one would expect you to win anyway. When you fail, there will be no surprise and so you have nothing to lose. In this, you are lucky."

A.J. would have given him an earful about how seriously she took competing except he was already launching into his favorite subject. His dramatic sigh was like a singer warming up vocal cords.

"You cannot understand the burden of being a champion. The pressure to perform, to excel. Myself, I face this every time I go into the ring, even to practice.'"

The man had the same conversation with anyone unfortunate enough to get pulled into his orbit. People had been known to back themselves into rakes in hopes of getting free, and A.J., having been the audience herself a few times, was willing to bet that a whack in the head was less painful than listening to the man drone on.

As he continued, she watched Sabbath's head emerge from his stall. Philippe, however, was too self-absorbed to notice as the stallion inched his muzzle forward. She had a feeling the horse was up to no good but gave him the benefit of the doubt. There was plenty of time to step in, she reassured herself, as she watched Sabbath get closer to Philippe. Surely the stallion had had enough fun for one day.

It turned out she was wrong on both accounts. In a black flash, the stallion lunged forward, grabbed ahold of Philippe's sleeve and gave it a sturdy tug. The man tottered in his platform shoes and then fell over like a sack of grain, collapsing against the door of the stall.

Philippe's face ran an indignant red and he brushed off his suit with hands that shook. A.J. figured the torrent of words leaving the man's lips were probably curses. Even though they were in French and she couldn't understand a thing, she had a feeling it wasn't a list of the virtues of falling on his butt.

When the man was sufficiently recovered, he switched back to English. "This horse will never be a champion. He has the manners of a common donkey and I wouldn't expect him to perform over fences any more than I would hold my breath to see him walk upright. He is stupid and so are you for paying more than a dime for him."

The word was pronounced *stoo-peed*.

In an indignant huff, Philippe marched off, still trying to clean off his suit.

Turning to the stallion, A.J. shot Sabbath a dry look.

"That wasn't very nice. Although I have to say, we've all wanted to knock him off that pedestal at one time or another."

2

It was getting dark by the time A.J. gathered Sabbath's meager things from his former stable. Her conversation with the stallion's latest owner had been brief, as if he was afraid she'd change her mind, and the man handed over the registry papers like he was getting rid of a lit stick of dynamite.

The last thing she had to do before leaving was settle the balance due with the auction house's office. As she walked through the crowd, her stepbrother's words drifted back to her. Hearing him refer to Sutherland Stables as *his* made her stop to think. She'd always been so busy training and competing that she'd never given the business end of Sutherland's much thought.

Aside from the horses she trained on, the Sutherland compound housed some fifty other jumpers, which were boarded by their riders or trainers. Thanks to the hefty fees they paid, every conceivable training resource was available, including a pool for the horses to work out in. They also had a wide number of arenas, trails and jumping courses as well as multiple paddocks and lunging rings. It was a big business that brought in a lot of money.

It hadn't started out that way. When A.J.'s mother and father moved into their estate as newlyweds, Garrett had built a barn and a ring for his beloved wife's horses. A.J.'s fondest memories of her mother were of the two of them together working with the animals, and after her mother died, she'd become even more attached to riding. As her skills and interest grew, so did the compound, and A.J. knew her father had gotten a special pleasure out of watching both thrive. She'd certainly enjoyed seeing the new buildings rise up and having new faces come and join what became for her an extended family. In her heart, Sutherland's was more than a business; it was her mother's legacy as well as a community where A.J. felt accepted. The place was more home than the mansion she lived in.

Her stepbrother had a different take on it. Peter had become involved on the business end of things after college because his mother demanded that he make himself useful while he tried to become an actor. Figuring he'd be away a lot on callbacks, and would soon be a Hollywood star, he'd agreed to take on managing the books and quickly displayed a knack for finances. Unfortunately, his fiscal successes didn't impress him and he viewed time at the stables as a reminder of theatrical failure. After many years of auditioning, it appeared as if that one toothpaste commercial might be the national nadir of his acting career.

Though they fought about money, and just about everything else, A.J. had to admit Peter was good at managing the place. He had a flair for numbers even if his people skills were deplorable, and she knew Sutherland's wouldn't be the success it was without him. Sadly, though, he hated going to the stables and made sure everyone knew it. He didn't like the way the place smelled and the way hay and horse hair clung to his clothes. He hated the mud in the springtime, the bugs in the summer and the cold in the fall and winter. And no matter what the season was, he detested his office. Originally, the room had been a grain storage area and it still smelled like old sweet feed when it rained, no matter how many times he shampooed the rug he'd installed.

The only thing he did like was making money, and he liked for it to accumulate in accounts. Every time A.J. wanted to buy something for the stables, she had to go like a beggar and throw herself at him. She hated the begging. To her, money was all about utility. It gave people the ability to pursue their dreams, and her dreams were expensive.

Where money came from had never been of interest to A.J. She was always too busy picking out hooves, carting around bales of hay and bags of grain and giving worm shots. Wasting a moment to worry about how much she was spending on something she needed or waiting to see if a better price came along struck her as pointless.

Courtesy of the two different philosophies coexisting in the same business, there'd been a lot of battles, and the fights didn't stay at the compound. With both living at home, whatever blowup had occurred at the stables followed Peter and her up the hill to the mansion and was served with dinner. Regina would take Peter's side, and A.J.'s father, who got gassy in the face of conflict of any kind, would plead for everyone to keep a cool head and a quiet tongue.

Garrett took a lot of antacids.

With her and her stepbrother in their midtwenties, A.J. knew it was high time they moved out but she was too busy training to go look for a place of her own and she knew Peter thrived on all the amenities available to him at the mansion. She also suspected he'd need to be surgically removed from his mother's influence. Regina Conrad, now Sutherland, was a domineering woman with an insatiable need for approval. As a consequence, she had a burning desire to prove that everything about her and her son was superlative. To A.J.'s mind, the constant barrage of propaganda was hard to be around and she didn't know how Peter could stand being the subject of so much hot air.

The consolation prize, she guessed, was one hell of a mother fixation.

To her, the pair seemed like expensive pieces of matching baggage but Garrett appeared content. His happiness was the reason she kept trying to make things work with her stepbrother and Regina. It wasn't easy.

Coming to the auction office, A.J. opened a door, which creaked in the friendly way farm doors do, and stepped inside. Margaret Mead, an Irish widow of sixty, looked up from behind the counter and smiled. The two had known each other for years.

"Ah now, A.J., you should be lookin' happier this day."

"You must not have heard what I've volunteered for."

"I've heard, all right."

"So are you going to jump on the bandwagon and tell me I'm crazy, too?" A.J. put her knapsack on the counter and leaned across it.

"Is that what they been sayin' to you?"

A.J.'s look was dry.

"Just ignore them," Margaret said as she brought out a folder. "You followed your instincts on that horse. People only get into serious trouble when they think the pitch of other voices is more true than their own. The stallion is yours now and the slate is clean. You start fresh with him."

Margaret passed some paperwork across the counter and retrieved a pen out of a coffee mug full of various and sundry writing utensils. A.J. reviewed the documents, picked up the Bic and was about to scrawl her name on the bottom when she looked at the top of the charge slip. It read *Sutherland Stables, c/o Peter Conrad.*

On impulse, she ripped it up.

"I'm going to write a personal check instead," A.J. said, taking out her wallet.

She wasn't sure what she was doing but the decision came out of the same place that made her bid on the stallion. Postdating the check, so she could get enough money in the account before it cleared, she choked as she filled in all the zeros. It was a monstrous stretch of her savings but instinct told her it was better to make the investment than have any chance of Peter refusing payment while they fought over her right to buy the horse.

As she ripped her check free and handed it to Margaret, she wondered if she'd lost her mind. Over the years, she'd managed to save up a nest egg from excess money her father had given her. It was a symbol of independence she'd never seen fit to use before, and now she was wiping it out.

Maybe Peter had a point about financial prudence, she thought, getting a sense for the first time of how finite money could be. She found it hard to believe that she'd just sunk all her net worth into a four-legged, maladjusted frat boy with hooves.

Margaret took the check. "Don't look so worried. The pit

you feel in your belly's just buyer's remorse. A couple of deep breaths will get you through it—they will."

A.J. tried to swallow her shock. There'd always been money around and there'd be more of it, she told herself. And, if Sabbath turned out to be a champion, she could probably sell some of her interest in him to the stables and recoup the cash while still having him as her horse.

By the time she returned to Sabbath's stall, she was feeling a little better. The fact that the stallion seemed happy to see her helped. As soon as he caught her scent, he nickered and reached forward, letting her stroke the velvet of his muzzle.

"Well, it's legal now. We're in this together," she told him. "So whaddya say, you want to blow this Popsicle stand?"

It took her a half hour to get him ready to travel the hundred miles back to Sutherland Stables. She wrapped his legs, put a blanket across his sleek back and then went outside and brought around the eighteen-wheeler that was one of Sutherland's fleet of horse trailers. When she led the stallion onto the ramp, she was vigilant in case he decided to bolt, but he didn't seem interested in acting up.

When there's no stage, there's no performance, she thought, as she loaded him into one of the tight stalls. Satisfied the stallion was safe, she shut the rear doors and climbed into the cab, starting the mammoth diesel engine with the twist of a tiny key. As she left the grounds, she found herself thrilled by all the possibilities ahead of them.

While the highway miles passed and night started to fall, her mind drifted back to Devlin McCloud. She could recall the gravel sound of his voice, the way his handsome face had looked up close, every flash of those hazel eyes. Her body responded as if he were sitting beside her, the images making her feel like she'd been put under a heat lamp.

What was so intoxicating about him? There was something in his confidence and intelligence, in those hooded eyes, in that powerful way he carried himself, that body. . . .

"You can stop now," she said out loud. "He's a man, not a fantasy."

But A.J. let herself dream on. In the netherland between the auction house and the stables, she fantasized about ways to run into him again. They were hard to conjure up considering his reclusive nature but her favorite, and the only one that was a remote probability, was the daydream where she had a flat tire on the stretch of road, right in front of his driveway. He would come by with the truck; they would talk as he loosened lug nuts, maybe agree to have dinner. And a movie. Then he'd take her home and kiss her in the dark. . . .

Of course, it was all a complete and utter fabrication. She wasn't the kind of woman men asked out on dates, and she'd have found it hard to pull off the whole save-me-you-big-man thing. And anyway, Devlin McCloud didn't strike her as the kind who'd waste time on movies.

So what would he do with a woman, she wondered. Was he a cook-in-and-stay-home type? She didn't think he'd go for Monster Truck rallies. Formal dining at a five-star restaurant? Picnic on a mountain? Riding through wooded trails with lingering glances passing back and forth? It was the afterward she was especially interested in. How would he be as a lover? Soft and slow or with a raging lust? She thought it probably depended on whom he was with and how much he wanted her.

She frowned, disturbed by her train of thought. Her preoccupations typically ran toward the practical, not the romantic. And certainly not the erotic. She was more accustomed to getting lost in dreams of finding the perfect blacksmith or a vet that would come cheerfully to a cold stable at two a.m. Then again, she'd never met anyone like him before and she couldn't decide whether she was dying to see him or grateful that she wasn't likely to. He'd had a profound effect on her and, as thrilling as it had been to be in his orbit, she felt like she was on dangerous footing.

The reality check, and the fact that she'd arrived at Sutherland's, made her think of the stallion. As she pulled between the majestic white pillars that marked the drive to the stables' compound, she wondered how Sabbath was going to like his new home.

As it turned out, his hooves didn't even get a chance to touch the ground.

When she halted the eighteen-wheeler in front of the

clapboard expanse of a stable building, Peter and her father emerged from the office. Their expressions told her she was in for it. Peter was looking serious and her father wore the pained grimace he always did when he was going to deny her something.

Without stopping to greet them, A.J. got down from the cab and wrenched open the side door to the trailer so she could check on the stallion. They followed her inside.

"That horse has got to go," Peter said. "Your father agrees with me."

"Arlington, darling," Garrett urged, "please be sensible."

A.J. let out an exasperated breath. "Look, I don't have the time to argue with both of you. My first priority is getting this poor horse out of the shoe box he's been in for the last hour and a half."

"You're not bringing that stallion into the stables," Peter said.

"Doesn't look like you have much choice, does it?"

"You're the one who's out of choices. I've found a buyer for him."

"What!" She wheeled around. "You've no right to sell any of our horses without my permission!"

"Tell her, Garrett."

"Tell me what?" Fingers, shaking from anger, sought out her diamond.

"Well, dear, I—"

"There's been a little change in paperwork," Peter said. "Courtesy of your stunt, I'm now president of the corporation that owns Sutherland Stables."

"And what exactly does that mean?"

"Now I can run the business freely without worrying about your spending habits. I've got veto power. I can streamline operations, maybe even diversify. And I can send this demon as far away from here as I want."

"He's not a demon!"

"Then your definition of the word and mine are different. One thing I do know is that buying that stallion is another example of your inability to think things through or see financial realities."

"Financial realities! I'm talking about a champion. I'm

talking about winning. What we need at this stable are winners, not bean counters."

"You paid way over market value for him."

"He's worth every penny."

"He's worth half what you paid."

"How would you know?"

"Because that's what I sold him for."

A.J. looked at Garrett, stunned. "You can't be serious
about all this."

"Peter is right," he said with a pleading tone. "The horse
is dangerous and you probably paid too much for him."

"So you're giving him the stables?"

"He would never abuse—"

"What would you call unilaterally deciding to sell a
horse I have every intention of competing on?" She
watched as her father fumbled through his pockets, looking
for Rolaids. As he downed two and chewed desperately, she
said, "This is ridiculous. It's unnecessary."

"Arlington, I'm worried about your safety."

"I understand, but it takes risk to succeed."

"Calculated risk," Peter pointed out.

"I've made the calculations. I'm taking the risk."

"But you've got to learn to accept authority," Garrett
said. "You can't keep running around, acting on a whim and
explaining later. This is a big business now. There are other
people involved. It's not just a family hobby anymore."

With a stiff spine, she began to check Sabbath's fastenings. "I know all that."

"Don't bother getting him out of the trailer," Peter told
her. "The new owner wants him delivered tonight."

A.J. was about to take her stepbrother on when she remembered writing out all those zeros. What had started out
as yet another impulsive move had just proved to be a
stroke of genius.

When she faced them again, she was smiling. "You're
looking at his new owner."

"Don't be flippant," Peter said, turning away. "Just leave
him here in the trailer—"

"*I* own him, not the stables. So you can take your fancy
new corporate title and stick it up your—"

"You're lying."

She pulled out the receipt. "Got the paperwork right here."

Peter took the documents from her hand, lips tightening as he reviewed them: "Well, good for you. But you can't board him here."

"What do you mean?" A.J. looked over to her father for help.

"Now, Peter," Garrett hedged, "we can't just—"

"I'm in charge here and we've just run out of free stalls."

A.J. snatched the papers back. "Fine, then get out of this trailer and I'll move right along."

The two men stared at her like she was crazy.

"What? You've made it perfectly clear that my horse and I aren't welcome so we're going elsewhere. I'll pay the stable the going rate for use of the trailer and return it in the morning when I come back for my things."

"Now, wait a minute—," her father began.

"Where are you going to go?" Peter asked.

"None of your business."

Besides, A.J. thought, I'm not sure myself.

"Darling, we're a family," Garrett said. "These stables are here for you."

"But you didn't make me an equal participant in their future, did you?"

"Come home and let's talk about this some more," her father begged.

"I'm not going home."

"Don't you think you're being a little rash?"

"Rash? Shouldn't you be talking to your new president? He just tossed me out of my own stables. If you've got a problem with the way things are working out, make an appointment and speak with him."

Peter shook his head. "This is exactly why you could never have made it in business. You're too emotional."

A.J. didn't respond to the dig. She was through arguing and on to planning her next move. She had an animal the size of a bus with no place to put him, it was getting late and she now had nowhere to stay herself. She needed to think of a plan and fast. To do that, she had to get rid of

Peter and her father and find somewhere to gather her thoughts.

She could tell the two of them weren't going to leave the trailer unless she did, so she went over to the door and leapt onto the ground. The men followed close behind. Before they could stop her, she shut the door and jumped into the cab. She was putting the engine into first gear when her father leapt in front.

"Where are you going?" Her father's voice was panicked as he splayed his hands out wide, as if he were prepared to block and tackle the trailer. He looked absurd, wearing his tailored tweed suit and club tie, standing like that.

Peter was shaking his head, trying to drag her father out of the way. "Garrett, let her go. Better that she cool off somewhere else. She'll be back in the morning."

A.J. stuck her head out of the open window. "A change of scenery isn't going to calm me down."

With that, she put her foot on the gas and the mammoth trailer lurched forward. She didn't know what she was going to do if her father didn't move.

Peter yanked Garrett out of the way.

"You'll be back!" her stepbrother yelled after her as she left.

Peter was wrong about that but, after driving around aimlessly for some time, A.J. was growing desperate. Feeling overwhelmed, she downshifted and brought the trailer to a rumbling halt in the parking lot of an all-night diner located at the side of a country road. Most of its customers were local farmers and A.J. was well-known as one of the regulars but she didn't want to go inside, no matter how merry it looked. It would be hard to explain why she was out on her own with the trailer in the dark without letting on about the split with her family.

A.J. sat in the cab, staring into the glow of the dashboard and rubbing her solitaire back and forth. In the back of her mind, she'd been thinking for the past few years that it was time to make a life of her own. She just never figured she'd make a declaration of independence quite so flagrantly, and it was hard not to feel lonely and worried. No matter how constraining she'd found Peter and her father, they offered her protection and security. Now, on her own, the choice she'd made and the responsibility she'd taken on seemed unsupportable.

It was the first time she'd felt that way. She'd always been impulsive and, if things hadn't turned out exactly as she'd intended, she'd usually been able to string something together at the last minute. Now her well of ideas was dry. Nothing was coming to her as she sat in the driver's seat with no place to go. The only thing she knew was that turning back wasn't an option.

A.J. glanced down at the clock again and tried to focus. The other big stables would be closed at this hour but she reviewed the closest ones once more, one by one. It was fruitless. She hadn't found a solution in the mental list before, and she didn't now.

Stretching her neck, which was stiff from tension, she caught sight of her baseball cap. Picking it up, she was struck by a crazy idea. Enticing hazel eyes came to mind.

Did she dare?

A moment later, she was back on the road, heading in the direction she'd come from. Driving past Sutherland Stables and not going in felt all wrong, a disturbing combination of anger, guilt and homesickness. She kept going.

Down the road a few miles, on the left, she saw the diminutive sign she was looking for. Unlike the arching expanse that marked the Sutherland compound, this was a simple clapboard on a post. It read MCCLOUD.

A.J. eased the truck onto a dirt road, its surface wide and even, perfectly suited for horse trailers and farm equipment. Driving up the lane, she went through a wooded expanse that soon opened to a stretch of meadows that was intersected by dark rail fences. Moonlight washed over the landscape, giving it an otherworldly glow, like a dream.

Up ahead, buildings appeared. There were two stables, small compared to Sutherland's, but she guessed they were able to hold at least six horses apiece. A jumping and schooling ring was to the left and there were several dirt paddocks to the right. Beyond, in the distance, she could see a farmhouse with a faint light in one of its windows.

Halting the trailer in front of a stable building, she took

a deep breath and stepped out of the cab. Without stopping to let herself think, she went back and checked on Sabbath. To her relief, he seemed content. His head was down and one of his back feet was turned up, resting on the tip of its hoof. He looked like he was asleep. A.J. checked his water, the fastenings on his halter and the lead that was anchored on the front of his stall. She didn't like the idea of leaving him unattended but she knew she wasn't going to be gone long. She was going to get one of two answers, and knowing Devlin McCloud, he wasn't going to waste time letting her know which one it was.

She was about to step out of the side door when she paused, catching her reflection in the floor-length mirror the riders used to dress in front of at competitions. Her auburn hair was a frazzled mess. Her jeans carried dirt and hay on them, as if they'd never seen the inside of a washing machine, and the flannel shirt she wore was an untucked, floppy wreck. Her barn jacket didn't help, looking like a big tan bag billowing around her.

She looked like a charity case. Something, she supposed, that wasn't far from the truth.

But she didn't want Devlin McCloud to see her like this. In all those fantasies she'd whipped up, she'd always looked halfway decent when they'd accidentally run into each other. In her daydreams, he'd had half a chance to see her as a woman, not just a stable hand, and, in her heart, for whatever asinine reason, she wanted him to find her beautiful. To see her as an object of mystery and desire. For her to be someone he wanted to touch and kiss and dive into with his body.

A.J. struck an alluring pose in the mirror, pouting her lips and leaning on one hip.

As if.

Trying not to feel defeated, she reached up and pulled her hair together, smoothing wayward wisps. Her hands brushed free as much debris as would let go of her pants and then she tucked in the shirt. Scrubbing off a smudge from her cheek, she took one last look at herself, thinking she'd be lucky if the man didn't call the cops to haul her away.

Stepping out of the trailer, she took a deep breath, drawing in a heavenly scent of grass and soil. It was a crisp fall night, not too cold, and majestically clear. As she walked toward the white farmhouse, she looked up and saw the vast stretch of the Milky Way above her, waves of stars shimmering in a dark velvet sea.

When the heels of her leather boots hit a flagstone walkway, she slowed down, trying to approach the house as quietly as she could. It was a two-story antique home with cozy lines and a lot of four-pane windows in the front. The roof was black and pitched at soft angles, with several chimneys breaking through its peaks and valleys. Stretching out from the rear of the house was another wing, behind which there was a garden.

It had to be the original farmstead, A.J. marveled, noting that someone had taken great care to keep the place up. The house, like the rest of the stable grounds, was in meticulous condition, gleaming with fresh paint and the close attention of its owner.

Arriving at the front door, she saw no doorbell or door knocker. Trying not to take it as a sign, she rapped her knuckles on glossy wood. There was a long silence and then she heard an uneven footfall inside.

As the steps got closer, the enormity of everything she'd done broadsided her with terrible clarity. She'd blown her savings on an undisciplined horse, left her stables and her family and was about to throw herself on the mercy of a man who was widely known for having little for himself. And less for others.

When Devlin McCloud opened the door, A.J. felt his presence as a physical blow. The impact of seeing him again was something she wasn't prepared for, daydreams to the contrary, and meeting his eyes was like getting pulled into a whirlpool and wanting to drown. Those hazel eyes alone would have been enough of a shock but then she noticed he was wearing a pair of pajama bottoms and nothing else.

It was impossible not to look.

Moonlight hit his chest and arms with a caress that further defined the muscles under his smooth skin. His body was sculpted and powerful, a perfect example of man in his prime, from his imposing shoulders to his rippled stomach to the hint of his hip bones showing over the waistband of his pajamas. Mouth going dry, A.J. had to wonder what the lower half of him looked like.

She felt his eyes pass over her and, when she looked up, she saw something flicker in their depths, some kind of re-action that he hid quickly. She thought for sure he'd noticed how flushed she was becoming and fought the urge to put her hands up to her cheeks. She decided he was probably annoyed with her ogling his body, and was searching for something intelligent to say, when he spoke first.

"I knew this wasn't someone selling Girl Scout cookies but you are a surprise."

Wait until you see what I have in the trailer, she thought.

Before she lost her nerve, she blurted out, "I need your help."

Instantly, his face grew tight. "I gave you my answer this afternoon. And as much as I appreciate your tenacity, I'm not going to reprise the conversation. Especially standing in this doorway, in the middle of the night, wearing only my pajamas."

She had a passing thought that he really didn't have to remind her he was half-naked. "But I—"

"I'm not going to train you. Now, go back to Sutherland Stables and resume the high life. I need to get some sleep."

He turned to go.

"I can't."

Her soft words stopped him and he looked back at her. "What do you mean, you can't?"

"I'm no longer affiliated with Sutherland Stables."

His brows came down over those hazel eyes. "You re-nounce your birthright or something?"

"Essentially."

"Why would you do that?"

"Let's just say management and I had a falling-out."

"Over Sabbath."

"Looks like he and I are both orphans now."

He let out a frustrated breath. "And where do you think I fit in? I'm not exactly the Mother Superior type. I don't run a safe haven for wayward children and their pets."

"But I need a place to train and board him."

"I'm not a trainer and I don't board."

"I can pay you."

A.J. wasn't sure with what, but now wasn't the time to get bogged down in particulars.

"I don't doubt that," he said wryly.

"Look, at least let him stay the night."

"That animal is still in the trailer?"

"Yes, but—"

"Are you out of your mind?"

"I didn't plan for this to happen."

"That's obvious," he said, turning away. "I'll bet you don't plan for much."

"That's not true!"

At least broadly, A.J. thought, deciding that the night hadn't exactly been a masterpiece of rational thinking.

"Where are you going?" she called out.

"I'm not interested in the little drama between you and your family," he said over his shoulder. "But I'll be damned if I'm going to stand by and have an animal pay the price for human theatrics."

He disappeared into the house, leaving A.J. speechless on the front stoop. Numbly, she noted that the back of him looked as good as the front did.

She wanted to argue with him. However her actions might appear, she would never compromise a horse's safety or security, but she didn't feel as if she could afford the luxury of explaining herself. It appeared as if Sabbath had a stall for the night and she wasn't going to put that in jeopardy just because she'd been misjudged.

Instead of waiting for him, she smothered a yawn and went back to the barn, wondering where she would spend the night. It certainly wasn't going to be at the mansion. Approaching the trailer, she regarded the cab with a jaundiced eye, deciding that the space was probably roomy enough for her to stretch out. It wasn't glamorous but at least she'd be horizontal.

Moving with the practiced coordination of someone who'd done it countless times, A.J. put down the ramp, freed Sabbath's lead and backed him out of the trailer. He seemed perfectly content to have her take his head and she walked him around to stretch his legs as she waited for McCloud. The stallion was lipping at the ground happily when the man emerged from the house.

As he approached, she felt a stir go through her. It was hot and urgent, like a flash of lightning, and it seemed to her as if her body were communicating in some secret language with his. While she pushed the sensation away and focused on the lead line in her hands, she wondered if he felt it, too.

Silently, he went past her and unlocked the double doors of the stable. They slid back soundlessly on well-oiled runners and he reached in and flipped on the lights. Peeking inside, she saw six generous stalls, three on each side, separated by a spacious aisle. To the left, she could see the tack room, and to the right, a small office. The place was immaculate and had everything a horse and rider would need, but the moment she led Sabbath inside, she noticed something was wrong.

The silence of the place was overwhelming. All of the chatty background noise she was used to hearing around horses was absent. There were no stomping of hooves, no welcoming whinnies of curiosity, no sound of brass on brass as halters were shaken. The place was a ghost town.

Her heart ached for him.

"You can put him in here," Devlin said, sliding open the gate to one of the first stalls.

She led the stallion inside and removed his halter, noting that there was fresh dirt on the floor but no water or feed.

"I've got some hay in the trailer," she said, going out into the aisle, "and if you show me where the hose is—"

"I have an automatic watering system," he replied, shutting the bottom half of the door. "But you're going to want to bring in some feed."

She headed outside.

When A.J. returned, she saw Devlin and Sabbath measuring up each other like two boxers in a ring. The stallion's head was out of the stall and he was fiercely meeting the eyes of the man who stood, still as a statue, inches away. She slowed down, waiting to see what was going to happen.

Sabbath snorted against the jacket Devlin was wearing

and stomped a hoof. Concerned he was going to bite, A.J. rushed forward, only to be halted by the sound of Devlin's voice.

"Stay back," he said. "This is between him and me."

Feeling at a loss, she did as she was told.

The stallion breathed in a barrelful of air and threw it at Devlin. The man remained standing, his cane cocked at an angle as he braced himself against the force that hit him. Like his body, his eyes were steady, never wavering, even as Sabbath kicked the side of the stall and threw back his head, letting out a roar.

A.J. dropped the hay and ran ahead, only to stop in surprise. After the fuss was over, the stallion's ears relaxed and he pulled back into the stall on his own.

"Round one is a tie," Devlin said, a smile playing behind the straight lines of his lips. "And that's one hell of a horse."

A.J. found herself returning his grin as she tossed hay into the stall. Satisfied Sabbath was comfortable, she shut the top door and they walked back out into the night air.

"Thank you," she said, pausing in front of the trailer.

He shrugged. "He'll be comfortable for the night."

"I appreciate it."

"When will you be back tomorrow morning to pick him up?"

"Actually, do you mind if the rig takes up some of your driveway space tonight?"

"Of course not. But how are you going to get home?"

"I'm not going home."

With that, A.J. wrenched open the driver's-side door and crawled in, so tired she hurt.

"What are you doing?"

"I'm exhausted and, as you and just about everyone I've run into today has pointed out, not thinking all that clearly. If you don't mind, I'm just going to spend the night here."

"You can't be serious."

She shut the door and rolled onto her side, tucking an arm under her head. Abruptly, she found herself on the verge of tears.

A sharp rap sounded against the window.

A.J. put her other arm over her ear, trying to block out

the noise. The last thing she wanted was to cry in front of him.

The butt of the cane continued knocking.

Bolting upright, she cracked open the window. "What?"

"You can't sleep out here."

"As long as you keep making noise, you're right about that."

"You're not sleeping out here."

"Why? You can't have big plans for this patch of dirt tonight."

"It's cold and I'm not in the habit of letting people freeze solid on my front lawn."

"What are you suggesting?"

"Come inside."

His voice was gentle, as if he knew she'd reached the end of her rope. Unfortunately, his concern just made her more upset.

"I'll do just as well out here." The words were choked and she fumbled with the window. Once it was up again, she lay down and put her arm back over her ear.

The rapping resumed.

"I'm ignoring you," A.J. called out.

"And I'm not stopping until you come inside."

"Your arm will give out before I do."

"Don't be so sure about that," she heard him say.

It turned out Devlin was right.

A few minutes later, A.J. emerged from the cab. Tired and frustrated, she didn't trust herself to say anything so she crossed her arms over her chest and stuck out her chin. Devlin led the way to the farmhouse.

3

THE CHILLY night air and a desire not to appear weak in front of him made her feel more in control by the time they got to his front door. Following him inside, A.J. found herself in a foyer with a staircase ahead and a kitchen beyond. To the left, a modest living room was furnished sparsely but glowed with the warmth of cherry paneling and some embers that were dying in an old stone fireplace. On the opposite side of the entrance hall was a dining room with an exquisite antique table in the center and a set of carved chairs pressed in tight around its flanks.

Throughout the rooms, oriental rugs covered wide oak planks, and the ceilings, lofty and creamy white, provided fair skies. Everywhere she turned, there were banks of windows stretching from the floor to above her head and she knew light would flood into the rooms during the day. With spectacular views and antique details, it was a gorgeous house but there was something sterile about it. She noticed that there were no family pictures, no snapshots of friends, no random trinkets from vacations. And where were all of his trophies and medals?

"You'll have to sleep on the couch," Devlin said, indicating the navy blue slipcovered sofa. "I use the other bedrooms as an office and . . . for storage."

She looked up at the hesitation but his face gave away nothing as he put his cane in an umbrella stand and hung up his coat. She followed his lead, taking off her barn jacket and putting it on a peg on the wall, next to his. Side by side, their coats hung tightly together, the sleeves mingling. She found the sight appealing and, as she got her bearings, she felt an air of tantalizing pleasure just being in his home.

Devlin disappeared down the hall and returned with a freshly laundered men's shirt, still warm from the dryer. "I'll be back with some pillows and blankets."

Holding his shirt in her hands, she watched him tackle the stairs with the caution of someone twice his age. Each time he put up the foot of his injured leg, she couldn't keep herself from wincing. Even though his face remained impassive, she could tell the strain he was under. It was in the flush that covered his face and in the ironfisted grip he had on the railing.

On impulse, A.J. put down the shirt and went after him. At the top of the stairs, she saw several doors and quickly put her head inside one. With only the dim light of the hall for illumination, it was too dark to see anything but odd shapes in the room.

"What are you doing?" His voice cracked like a whip. Reaching past her, he shut the door.

"I wanted to save you the trip back down the—"

"I'm not an invalid and I don't want you poking around. Why don't you go down and sit still so I can wait on you?"

A.J. held her tongue and left him in a hurry, wondering what the fuss was about. The more she thought about it, though, she figured he was sensitive about his limp and she'd probably hurt his pride. Considering she was spending the night on his couch and her horse was in one of his stalls, she figured she owed him a little slack.

Minutes later, he came back down the stairs. This time she looked the other way, wishing there was something on the walls to occupy her. She'd have preferred even a velvet Elvis painting over trying to pretend the wood paneling was fascinating as he approached.

Silently, he held out the bedding to her and then disappeared into the kitchen. As soon as she was alone, she released the breath she was holding and made up the couch quickly. With a glance over her shoulder, she made sure she wasn't going to flash him and changed into his shirt.

As it covered her naked body, she was amazed to find she was wearing Devlin McCloud's shirt. It was a shirt that, given how soft the cotton was, he wore often, and it was tantalizing to think that what was now against her skin had once been against his. She passed another quick check in the direction he'd gone and then lifted the sleeve to her nose and breathed in deeply. The scent of his fabric softener was heavenly, and that was when she decided she'd completely lost it. The instant a person started to think of Downy as a cologne probably meant a rubber room couldn't be far behind.

Feeling off-center himself, Devlin McCloud came back around the corner just as the woman he'd been preoccupied with all afternoon and all evening was bending down and sliding between a set of his sheets. Without meaning to, he caught a long view of her shapely legs and his hand tightened hard against the glass of scotch he was holding. He couldn't help but keep watching as she got in the makeshift bed and pulled up the sheets to her chin.

"Now what have I done?" she asked.

"Nothing. Why?"

"You've got that jungle-cat-measuring-an-antelope look, so I figured I'd ask."

Instead of responding, Devlin turned off the overhead light and took a healthy swig of the brown liquor. He wasn't much of a drinker but he had a feeling that sleep was going to be elusive. And that was before he'd caught a glimpse of the smooth expanse of her calf and thigh. Now there was heat swirling around his gut and he knew it wasn't just the scotch.

"Bath's down the hall. Shower's upstairs if you need it in the morning."

"Thanks again," A.J. murmured, obviously giving herself up to exhaustion.

It was a long time that he stayed in the shadows and watched the woman until, totally disturbed, he went to the stairs. Even then, he found it difficult to leave. He stood, with one foot on the bottom step, and looked at her in the reflected glow of the fire he'd banked hours before. Auburn hair was spread across the pillow he'd given her in a glorious dark wave, and in the dim light the perfectly formed features of her face seemed heaven made, not of the earth at all. In his mind's eye, he saw himself going to her, slipping a hand under the silken weight of her hair and lifting her lips to his. She would taste like honey. All warm golden sweetness.

Shit, he thought. Why couldn't she have turned up looking for nothing more complicated than a date?

Although, when he thought about it, he knew an evening out with her would be anything but simple. The woman had a way of lighting up a room that distracted him like nothing else he'd ever run across.

I may be in trouble here, he thought.

He found the strength of his attraction to her surprising and told himself it must be because he hadn't been with a woman in a long time. Before the accident, he'd never had much time for a personal life. Since then, he hadn't had any interest in one. It had been a long time since he'd felt anything other than pain and he'd forgotten his heart had the capacity for anything else. Now, for the first time since his accident, he was looking at something he found beautiful.

Or someone, as was the case.

A.J. stirred, letting out a soft sigh.

It was like an invitation had been whispered against his ear and he found himself getting hard.

With a fumbling movement, Devlin tossed back the last of the scotch and went upstairs.

The next morning, A.J. was up with the sun, pulling on her jeans and boots and putting the couch back in order as quietly as she could. As she sneaked out the front door to hightail it down to the barn, she glanced up at the windows on the second story. She wondered whether Devlin was sleeping. And what he looked like when he was at rest.

He was probably back in those pajama bottoms again, she thought. Or had he pulled them on quickly to answer the door because he slept in the nude?

Suddenly, the early-morning chill didn't seem all that chilly.

Doing her best to push her wayward thoughts out of her mind, she rushed down to the barn. The first light of dawn was coming across the meadow in all its peach-hued glory but she didn't pause to savor the majesty of the morning. She was in a hurry to see the stallion and was relieved to hear him stomp a hoof and whinny a greeting as she slid aside the big wide door.

Now, that's what a stable should sound like, she thought, as she opened the top half of Sabbath's stall door. He reached out to her, nudging her shoulder and snuffling over her jacket.

"Good morning to you, too," she said, giving him a scratch behind the ears. She was pleased by how happy he was to see her. "You know, I'm beginning to think you might be a real mushball."

Sabbath flicked his ears back and forth and then thrust his muzzle under her arm, lifting her off the ground.

Laughing, she entered the stall, checked his water and then went to the trailer for some oats and hay. When she returned, his head was out in the aisle and he was surveying his new surroundings. Ducking under his neck, she hung a bucket of feed on a brass hook next to the water tub and waited while he lipped the food and began to eat. Figuring he'd like some peace and quiet as he had breakfast, she left the stall.

As soon as she shut the door, Sabbath's head was back out into the aisle and he started nickering. Concerned, she went back over to him, only to watch as he pulled his head inside and tucked into the sweet feed again. With an indulgent smile, she leaned up against the door and talked to him as he ate, using the time to try to figure out a plan for them. By the time he was licking the bottom of the bucket, their future was no clearer but she'd enjoyed the quiet time with him. As she shut his top door, she decided he could be pretty endearing when he wanted to be.

When A.J. went outside, she stood for a moment looking at the farmhouse. In the tender morning light, it was a needlepoint sampler, all that was good and cozy, and autumn made the place seem even more inviting. In a blaze of color, the rich reds and yellows of fall were beginning to manicure the tips of tree branches, emphasizing the house's radiant white exterior.

The image was picture perfect, postcard ready, she thought. Drop it in the mail and remind someone of the fantasy home everyone wished for. Too bad Norman Rockwell's model of farming America was making her stomach feel like she'd swallowed a box of thumbtacks.

A.J. rubbed her belly, thinking maybe her father's thing with stress and antacids might be hereditary.

She was feeling trapped between being thrilled to see Devlin McCloud again and knowing that she had to leave. It was a one-two punch. She doubted she would run into him again and that made her curiously distraught. She was also back where she'd started the night before with no place to put the stallion.

Why couldn't they just stay here?

The facilities were what she wanted. Perfectly kitted out, with no distractions from other horses or riders. And working with someone of Devlin's stature would be a once-in-a-lifetime chance for any rider. The only drawback was the effect he had on her, but even that was exciting. She imagined that working with him would be stimulating on so many levels and, as long as she could stay focused, it would be a wonderful way to see if something could develop between them.

Put like that, it was hard to figure out which was more attractive. The training or the man himself.

So what could she say to change his mind?

Good morning, nice sheets, by the way, are you sure you don't want to spend the next two months with me and my big black stallion?

She didn't think that was going to cut it.

All was quiet as A.J. stepped inside and she wondered if she shouldn't just leave. Probably it was the right thing to do but it wasn't an option as far as she was concerned. She wanted to see him one more time so she padded into the kitchen, wondering where the coffeemaker was. She found it, next to a Crock-Pot full of freshly ground beans. As the aroma of coffee seeped through the room, she took a seat at the battered oak table and stared out a bank of windows at the mountain range behind the house. High in the sky, above the undulating shoulders of the hills, birds were surfing lazily on invisible currents and she coveted their nonchalance. Tossing and turning in the wind, they seemed content to be pulled in unexpected directions.

When the percolator was done, she searched for a mug, poured some steaming brew into it and returned to her waiting. Soon she heard noises overhead. When Devlin appeared a while later, he was walking more slowly than usual.

"Good morning," A.J. said, glancing at him. He'd showered and shaved and she could smell the clean scent of his soap. Something tangy with a hint of cedar.

Yummy, she thought.

"I see you've made yourself at home."

"Just trying to make myself useful."

"Thanks for getting a head start on the coffee."

Covertly, A.J. studied him as he crossed the room to the pot. His hair was glossy from being damp, and the flannel shirt he wore, which accentuated his broad shoulders, had been rolled up to his elbows. He was wearing a pair of well-washed jeans that were faded over the thighs and, she noted with a flush, on the backside. He looked comfortable, casual, and yet totally in control of himself and his surroundings.

He was a man she could get used to seeing in the morning, she thought.

This made her wonder how many women had come down those stairs with him after a night spent in his bed, how many had joined him at the rough oak table she was now sitting at. Whom had he loved with his body? With his heart? Was there someone for him now?

A.J. shook her head, telling herself it was none of her business. It didn't help. With the way she reacted to him, his relationships with women were an inappropriate but undeniable priority to her.

Devlin groaned as he sat down. Catching her look of concern, he muttered, "Nothing to worry over—just takes some time for my leg to get going in the morning."

"Does it bother you a lot?"

"It makes itself known, all right."

"Will you be able to ride again?" she blurted out.

He froze, mug halfway to his lips. Pain tightened his features, drew the blood from his face.

"I'm sorry," she said. "I didn't mean to—"

"No," he said softly, "no, it's all right."

He was silent for so long that she thought he'd forgotten she was even sitting across from him. And then he answered.

"It isn't so much that I can't ride anymore. . . . It's that I can't fall again." He looked into his coffee mug. Took a sip. "This leg of mine is held together with metal screws and plates. One more trauma and it's game over. As it stands now, I'm still working to get the mobility back. I guess I should feel lucky that it wasn't worse. There are some people who don't get to walk again after what happened to me."

"What a horrible accident," A.J. whispered. "It must have been awful to lose . . ."

"Mercy? It was worse than losing my career. Putting her down was the hardest decision I've ever had to make." He stared ahead, lost to his memories. "I can't describe what it was like after we hit the ground. She was flailing around, her foreleg shattered. Absolutely shattered. Irreparable. It was cockeyed at the knee, hoof facing the wrong way."

A.J. reached out to him, needing to soothe his anguish somehow. Her hand settled on his forearm. His skin was warm to the touch and she could feel the fine hair that sprinkled over it.

His eyes shot down to the contact and she saw that she'd shocked him. Hazel eyes narrowed on her. There was a wealth of suspicion in their depths. She imagined that the media and everyone in the business had been after him during the year for some kind of insight into his inner torment. Not wanting to press him, she removed her hand.

"I don't know why I'm talking to you," he said quietly. "But I think it has something to do with your eyes."

She felt herself becoming breathless. "My eyes?"

He nodded. "I'm usually wary of people. But it's hard to be suspicious of the clear blue sky."

A.J. gulped, feeling as if she were on the edge of a cliff. And that leaping off was a really great idea.

Devlin continued. "I stayed with Mercy when the vet gave her the shot. Her head was in my lap as the light went out of her eyes. I told myself that the pain was leaving her, draining away as the beat of her heart got slower and slower. That her agony would soon be over. It didn't really help." His eyes drifted out of the bank of windows. "I feel selfish about that. That I wanted her to stay even though she was suffering."

"She was your partner. Of course you didn't want to lose her."

His gaze shifted back to her and then he moved. She thought he was going to stand up, but instead she felt the touch of his fingers on the top of her hand. She froze. Slowly, he traced the fine blue veins that ran just under her skin. It was the softest of contact, barely more than a brush of air, but it devastated her. She felt as though he had reached in and taken her heart into his palm.

They stayed there at the table, linked by his gentle explorations, until the grandfather clock in the hallway sounded eight o'clock. The chiming broke the mood and they came back from the place where their hearts had been linked.

"Well, I guess I better go," A.J. said. She didn't bother to hide her disappointment.

"Where are you headed?" He sat back and the contact of their hands was broken.

"I don't really know." A.J. stood up. Taking her mug to the sink, she rinsed it out and put it on the counter. "Thanks again for the stall and the couch."

"You're welcome."

She paused on her way out of the room, hoping he'd say something or come and see her off. He just stayed at the table, though, drinking his coffee as the sun poured into the kitchen. She lifted her hand in a wave she wasn't sure he saw, and left.

While she walked down to the barn, she wondered if she'd ever get the chance to see him again. She didn't think it was going to be soon and she knew it wouldn't be in the quiet intimacy of his kitchen. Both were, she thought, losses to mourn over. All it had taken was twenty minutes in the morning glow with him and she felt like she had a sense of what true love could feel like.

Sabbath greeted her with a whinny when she stepped inside the barn.

"Time to get you back in the trailer," she told him, feeling depressed. "No use having you get used to this roomy stall when I'm going to have to vacuum-pack you like peanuts in a jar for the foreseeable future."

She picked up his halter and was slipping it on over his ears when she heard Devlin come into the stable.

"We'll be out of your hair in a moment," A.J. said, without looking up. She led the stallion out of his stall.

"I'll get you and the horse to the Qualifier but that's as far as I'm going."

A.J. stopped short. "What?"

"You can board him here for the going rate and I'll charge you a fair trainer's fee."

She couldn't believe what he was saying.

"Really?"

He nodded.

"That's fantastic!" Her heart pounded with happiness and she wanted to throw her arms around him. "But why the change of heart?"

"I think I'm ready to . . ." He didn't go any further. "We'll start today. Where's your tack?"

A.J.'s mind started spinning. "At the Sutherland compound. And I need to return the trailer."

"Fine. Take it back and be ready to ride in one hour. I'll meet you in the ring."

Devlin left and she looked at Sabbath. The stallion returned her stare quizzically, as if he knew their direction had taken a sharp turn.

"It looks like you have a home after all," she said, grinning. "At least for the next two months."

She put the stallion back in the stall and checked a clock hanging on a side wall. If she rushed it, she could get over to Sutherland Stables, pick up all her things and still not have to deal with Peter. He'd be playing squash at his racquet club and wouldn't show up for work until later in the morning.

When A.J. drove up to the compound, she was relieved that his sleek sedan was indeed nowhere in sight. In a smooth motion, she pulled the eighteen-wheeler into its parking space and hurried into her private tack room. In the course of packing up her gear, other riders stopped by, their curious eyes telling her that many had no idea why she was leaving. She found it difficult to answer their inquiries with anything other than shrugs and wobbly smiles. Her own complicated feelings did not fit easily into simple answers.

When there was a leaning pile of tack and supplies stacked up in the doorway, she brought around her car. The cherry red Mercedes convertible had been a birthday present from her father and, if truth be told, she didn't like it very much. The slick European design and racy engine were all well and good if you were just going out for lunch but they didn't mean squat when you had to move an entire horseload of stuff. What she really needed was a wide-bed truck but she knew it would have broken her father's heart to give his gift back, so she'd kept the car.

Measuring her load of gear and the size of the backseat, A.J. shot an envious look at a pickup parked across the way. She quickly realized the only way everything was going to fit was if she put the top down. When she finished, there were horse blankets, leg wrappers, saddles and bridles sticking out of the backseat and draping over the sides of the car.

It looked like a bizarre rendition of Santa's sleigh, she thought, sliding into the leather bucket seat. And in this case, Rudolph had high beams.

As A.J. headed out between the pillars, she was ready to go straight back to Devlin's but she paused before getting on the main road as one more complication occurred to her.

She was homeless.

Where was she going to sleep? Her bedroom at the mansion wasn't any more of an option than it had been the night before. She just couldn't go back to her father's house. Not yet. Getting sidetracked by a family that was right out of a *Dynasty* rerun wasn't going to help her get through the Qualifier in one piece.

The thought of a hotel filled her with dread. Doing the math in her head, she knew she wouldn't have much cash left over after she made the transfer from her savings account to cover the check for Sabbath. And she wasn't going begging to her father.

Her fingers went to work on the diamond as she pondered the situation. With a tight laugh, she found it ironic to be sitting in a Mercedes and worrying about how to pay for things. Abruptly, she considered selling the convertible but shrugged off the idea. She needed a car and knew it was probably in the Sutherland's name anyway, given Peter's affinity for business deductions.

Devlin McCloud's couch had several selling points. It was cheap, close to the stallion and close to the man. The idea of the two of them holed up in that beautiful old farmhouse was captivating. Cool nights, fires in the fireplace. Some wine . . .

Wait a minute, she told herself. Back up the love bus. Just because the man had offered to train her didn't mean he was going to have her jumping anything other than fences in the ring. No matter what her libido hoped to the contrary.

A.J. glanced down at her jeans in disgust.

One thing was clear, she decided. Whether it was McCloud's Unwitting B and B or a motor lodge, she couldn't spend two months in one set of clothes. The damn things would be walking on their own in a matter of days.

She'd have to go to her father's house.

Grimacing, she threw the car into drive and traveled the short distance to the mansion.

Looming at the top of a private road, it was a grand house with a formal face, the only home she'd ever known. She treasured the place but couldn't say that she liked living there. What she valued were the few memories she had of her mother from Christmases in the gracious library, Fourth of July parties down by the pond, Easter-egg hunts in the terraced gardens. But all that was in the past. The recent day-to-day existence she'd known wasn't easy.

As she turned the car off, she was hoping her luck would hold and Regina would still be getting dressed in the master suite. If everything went smoothly, she'd be able to run in, grab her things and be out before anyone knew.

Her prayers weren't answered.

Just as A.J. reached the last of the marble steps leading to the grand entrance, her stepmother wrenched open the ornate front door. That in and of itself was unusual and A.J. knew she was about to get an earful.

Standing ominously in the doorway, Regina was dressed in one of her perfectly tailored suits, a diamond pin flickering on her collar like a constellation of stars. The subtle peach color of the outfit set off her dramatic coloring, highlighting her coiffed black hair and dark eyes. It also emphasized the woman's angry flush.

"You've done it this time," she said. "Your father is in bed with a stomachache, Peter has had to take the day off to get a massage and my dinner party tonight is going to be ruined because of all the tension in this house. I hope you're happy!"

This was exactly why she couldn't stay at the mansion, A.J. thought.

She tried to get through the door but Regina blocked the way.

"How you can be so selfish is beyond me. Your father has given you everything you've ever wanted and you've consistently repaid him with heartache."

"Look, I'm honestly sorry he's upset," A.J. said, faking left and scooting into the house. Heading quickly through the grand foyer to the winding staircase, she hit the stairs two at a time, leaving her stepmother to shout up at her.

"What time are you coming home tonight? The guests are arriving at seven and we will be sitting down for dinner at eight. I don't want you showing up in your barn clothes in the middle of the soup course like you did last weekend."

The woman was still fuming at the foot of the stairs when A.J. reappeared ten minutes later with her luggage.

"What are you doing with those?" Regina demanded.

"I'm going to be gone for a little while."

"What do you mean gone?"

"As in not here." A.J. walked past her stepmother, who suddenly seemed all too pleased to get out of the way.

"What should I tell your father?"

"Nothing. He already knows. I'll phone him soon. Just tell Papa I'll call him."

"You can believe I will," Regina said, softly. She appeared to be mulling things over and liking what she saw in a future that included less of her stepdaughter.

With a final nod, A.J. disappeared from the grand house. Cramming her bags on top of the equipment pile, she took off down the driveway, deep in thought.

This is my life. I'm choosing this. I'm free.

She felt stronger than she ever had, more sure than ever about her decision to buy the stallion and move away from her family's influence. When she pulled up to Devlin's stable, she leapt from the car, ready to take on the world. With an armload of leather and brass, she hurried inside, bound for the tack room.

And ran smack into Devlin.

He was coming out of the room just as she was rounding the corner, and the two collided, bouncing off each other. Tack exploded everywhere. Sputtering in surprise, A.J. grabbed on to the first thing she could to keep from hitting the ground with the bridles and girths. It was Devlin. As soon as she reached for him, she felt the iron strength of his arms come around her and she was pulled against his body.

A.J. gasped and looked straight into his eyes. They were hooded, full of heat. His chest was a solid wall against hers and one of his thighs was between her legs, their hips fusing. She felt a sensual pull toward him that was undeniable. In that instant, all she could think of was kissing him. She didn't care that there were so many good reasons for her not to do so. She didn't care that they were in broad daylight. She didn't care that he was supposed to be her trainer. She didn't care about anything except the way he made her blood pound and her head spin and her body melt.

Devlin's mouth hovered deliriously over hers, just inches away. She willed it to get closer and slid her hands across his shoulders to the back of his neck. Digging her hands into his hair, she felt its silky texture and then the solid bone of his skull.

"You okay?" he asked, his voice low and thrilling.

All she could do was nod, even though it was a lie. She felt a lot of things but *okay* wasn't one of them.

As he continued to support her weight, she felt his hand move up across her back to support her neck. Goose bumps prickled across her skin. He paused, as if he might pull away, and she held on to him harder. And then very slowly, as if in a dream, his lips closed the gap between them and pressed against her mouth firmly.

It was like getting struck by lightning.

When she didn't stop him, his lips began to move over hers, caressing, cajoling until she had to open her mouth because she couldn't breathe anymore. When she did, his tongue stole inside, sliding into her deeply. She pulled against his neck, urging him closer, and pressed her hips into his.

One of Devlin's hands splayed across her hips and he rubbed his lower body into her. The heat at her core soared and her body began to weep for him. Their kiss took on a heated urgency that bordered on desperation and, just when she thought she couldn't handle any more, his mouth moved down to her neck, nibbling at the delicate skin, nipping at her earlobe. She cried out. Working on nothing but reflex, her fingernails bit through the flannel of his shirt and she thought seriously about giving herself to him right there, on the ground, in front of the tack room. . . .

Sabbath's indignant whinny interrupted them. At the sound, Devlin looked up from A.J.'s neck and shot a glare at the stallion, whose head was out of the top of his stall. When the horse let out another howl, they reluctantly straightened, panting.

"Doesn't like competition for your attentions, apparently." Devlin's voice was deep with a very masculine tension. He still had his arm around her waist and didn't seem in a hurry to break the contact. Which was just fine with her.

A.J. let out a shaky laugh. "I feel like we've been caught by a parent."

Devlin stepped away. As he put his hands in his pockets,

he cleared his throat. "I feel like I should say something apologetic. But I'm not sorry I kissed you."

A.J. wasn't sorry, either, and she was about to tell him when he continued. "I'll do my best not to do it again. You can't very well have your trainer be your lo—be anything other than your trainer."

Even though A.J. knew he was right, it was hard not to feel rebuffed. And as if she were going to pass out from sexual frustration.

"Right. Er—I guess I should get my gear. . . ."

"I'll help."

There was an awkward silence as they went about picking up the mess their impact had created. Tack was fumbled in hands that were usually steady; awkward half sentences were started and left dangling.

The kiss had changed the center of gravity between them, tilting them off-balance. What had been a hypothetical attraction was now very real thanks to the taste of pleasure, and both retreated into their own thoughts as they grappled with the implications.

When they came back out of the tack room, Devlin said, "Tell you what—I'll unload the car. You get the hall monitor ready."

They looked back at the stallion, who was still staring at them with grave censure. A.J. had to laugh.

It was a sound Devlin liked and his eyes lingered on her as she walked toward the horse. Watching her hips sway made him harden again and he shifted his jeans, feeling like a teenager. That thought made him smile grimly and, trying to forget how she smelled like lavender, he gathered up some gear and supplies. As he carried the load into the tack room, and apportioned the equipment onto various empty pegs and saddle posts, he resolved to think about something other than how good she'd felt against him.

Anything else, dammit.

To distract himself, Devlin walked past the rows of dust-covered saddles and bridles to the lone window at the far end of the room. He could see the ring beyond and the mid-level jumps he'd struggled to put together while she'd been gone. The physical labor of moving the long wooden poles and adjusting the cups to change the jump heights hadn't been taxing. The problem was his leg. His limp had meant it took twice the time it should have to set up for their first training session.

It made him think. He was going to need help.

To get her and the horse ready for the Qualifier, he was going to have to work the pair over a variety of jumps and combinations, and that meant there was going to be a lot of shuffling in that ring. Much as he hated to acknowledge his injury, he had to admit he couldn't handle the job efficiently. It would save them a lot of downtime to have someone around who could reset the jumps if the horse faulted, change the combinations and haul feed. It looked as if he was going to have to call Chester.

Never thought I'd need to, Devlin marveled, shaking his head.

He and Chester had been together since Devlin had started out as a stable boy himself. The old man had great horse sense and was a tireless worker, and the two had been a terrific team. Letting his dear friend go after the accident had been one more loss for him to bear but Chester had always said he'd be back. Devlin hadn't believed him.

Now things were different, he thought, hearing A.J. moving around outside.

Leaving the room, Devlin caught sight of her coming out of Sabbath's stall and leading the stallion out to the crossties. She was wearing well-worn jeans that hugged her thighs and hips like a second skin. The sight of her legs flashing underneath his shirttails came to mind and he sucked back a groan of need.

It was going to be a long two months, working with someone he wanted so badly. And there was no doubt that they needed to keep things professional. He knew pursuing a relationship with her would put them both in a difficult, if not impossible, situation. The training they needed to do with the stallion was going to mean a grueling schedule of workouts and long hours. He was going to have to be objective about her riding and her efforts and they were both going to need to keep level heads, something that would be impossible if they became passionately involved.

And passionately was the only way they'd become involved, given the explosion that had happened in front of the tack room.

Keep it down to business with her, he told himself as he went out to get another armload of gear.

Good luck, an inner voice taunted.

After Devlin finished unpacking the car, he picked off a battered clipboard from a hook on the wall next to the tack room. It had been as integral a part of his former training as his saddle and his boots, the place where he scribbled his thoughts and his plans. Cradling it for a moment in his hands, he was struck by how odd the familiar weight felt. He'd never thought he'd be holding it again. Sliding the stub of a pencil free from its top and feeling the rough texture where his teeth had chewed the wood ragged, he felt disconnected with his own past. How much time had he spent with the clipboard on his lap, deep in thought, planning his attack on another course? Laying siege for another victory.

More hours than the night has stars.

Devlin leaned up against the main door of the stable, once again putting lead to a page. He became lost in his thoughts, seeing jumps in his mind and transcribing the pathways of flying hooves. Frowning in concentration, he was carried away, back to a world remembered so well. And had missed so badly.

From under Sabbath's belly, where A.J. had wedged herself to pick out one of his hooves, she glanced at Devlin. Her body was still raging like an engine on overdrive and she felt like she'd been marked indelibly by their kiss. It was unlike anything she'd ever experienced before, as profound as it was frightening.

Even though his words afterward stung, she had to agree that keeping some distance between them was the right thing to do. If they did get involved, it wasn't going to be casual. That kiss had been too electric and she already felt an emotional connection with him because of their conversation in the morning.

She came here to ride and to win, she reminded herself.

Not to get entangled in an affair that could get her seriously hurt.

A.J. moved over to the stallion's other foreleg. He protested when she asked him to lift it and she had to lean into him to get it off the ground. Sabbath, she was learning, had very sensitive feet. He flinched as she dug the pick in to free the impacted dirt but she ignored him as she thought more about Devlin's kiss.

That kiss.

She could still feel his lips against hers and she wondered whether he was as amazed by what flared between them. For her, it was something uniquely powerful. Did he feel the same way? Or was he just a passionate man?

Come on, A.J., she told herself. You smell like a horse, you're wearing the same jeans you had on yesterday and the only makeup on your face is moisturizer. Not exactly the trappings of seduction men respond to. Or do you think all those posters of babes in bikinis are there for the bathing suits?

She looked over at him again.

Devlin was leaning against the doorway, the sunlight tripping across the strong lines of his face and falling down over his arms and onto his hands as he worked. She wondered what they would feel like traveling over her skin.

"What are you staring at?" he asked, without looking up.

"Nothing." She flushed, looking away.

Sabbath yanked his leg away and she let him go. As she stood up, she caught sight of her car, which was now empty except for her luggage. Seeing the duffels, she remembered that she still needed to find a place to stay. And, with a flush, she realized Devlin's couch was now far more than simply a cheap solution to her housing problem.

4

When Sabbath was tacked up, A.J. stood back and looked at him with satisfaction. She was the one who had fed him, groomed him and mucked out his stall. Her fingers had carefully fit the bridle and bit to his head. Her saddle was on his back and soon he would be carrying her weight. He was her horse. Hers alone.

And to top it off, all morning he'd been unbelievably compliant.

A.J. was falling for none of it.

This was why she put a martingale on him. The leather strap, which ran from his head to his barrel chest, and was anchored by the bridle and the girth, would hinder his ability to toss his head or rear. It was a common piece of equipment and likely one he was already familiar with.

So, when he decided to drop the act and start careening around the ring, she had half a chance, A.J. thought. Like wearing a seat belt in the car.

Hell, if they could fit him with an air bag, she'd have done it in a heartbeat.

Before A.J. took him out to the ring, she put on her pair of old leather chaps. When she'd bought them years before, they'd been a fawn-colored suede. Now, after countless hours in the saddle, they'd darkened to a rich brown and the nap was as smooth as cream. Belting them around her slim waist, she began to zip the leather down each leg so that her jeans were completely covered.

Devlin looked up from his musings, instantly losing his train of thought. The first thing he noticed was that her riding gear showed the mellow glow of age. Considering all her father's wealth, he was surprised she hadn't thrown spanking new tack all over the stallion or tied one of those nylon bridles to his head. Instead, the saddle on Sabbath's back bore the marks of heavy use. It had originally been a very expensive piece of equipment, he granted, recognizing the lines of a famous saddler. But it'd been used hard and well and he couldn't help approving of the way someone had cared for it. The leather was in prime condition, as supple as it was strong, and it sure wasn't the saddle of a pampered little rich girl. It was the equipment of a real rider who understood that the utility of fine tack increased over time if carefully tended.

His eyes then went to the chaps. Watching her put them on, he envied the leather as it wrapped itself around her thighs. The heat pooling in his gut made him grit his teeth and he found himself imagining what it would be like to have his hands traveling over her legs on the brass zipper.

Although if it were up to him, that zipper would be going up, not down, and her jeans would be the next thing to hit the floor.

Devlin tried to pull it together.

"You guys ready?" he asked.

"He sure seems ready to go somewhere, all right."

The stallion was twitching with eagerness, knowing full well what the tack meant.

Seeing the horse saddled and pumped for a workout, recognizing the glint of anticipation in A.J.'s eye, Devlin realized he hadn't had a horse readied to go in his barn in almost a year. With an ache in his solar plexus, he felt what he'd lost acutely.

When A.J. looked at him and smiled, he said, "God, what I wouldn't give to be where you are."

Sabbath tossed his head, yanking at the crossties.

"You sure about that?" she blurted. "I'm tying my professional star to a loose cannon here."

He watched her flush as she heard her own words.

"What am I saying?" she muttered, and then looked into

his eyes with compassion. "Of course you want to be riding. God, I'm sorry."

"Don't be," he said, getting to his feet. "Actually, it's almost enough just to see your nervous excitement. All the possibilities of success and failure are dancing in your eyes."

"You know, that's how I feel right now. I don't know what's going to happen so I have the luxury of predicting success." Sabbath stamped a hoof and she regarded him quizzically. "What's the matter? Oh, the martingale strap's turned around here."

Devlin watched as she tended to the stallion, and found himself hoping she appreciated the moment. He hadn't when he'd been in her place. Too busy trying to accomplish his goals, he'd never appreciated that the pursuit of them was just as important as the winning. The toil and grind were so much of what he'd enjoyed about his life, he realized now, and seeing A.J.'s passion reminded him of it all.

How ironic, Devlin thought, that it took the well going dry for him to realize how much he liked pushing water uphill.

When A.J. was finished making the adjustment, she grabbed her helmet and freed Sabbath from the crossties. As she led the stallion out into the cool fall breeze, the horse began to prance, his hooves doing a soft-shoe on the gravel path that led to the ring. Thrashing his head, he flared his nostrils as he breathed in the scents of early October and primed his blood for the work ahead.

"He's a live wire, isn't he?" Devlin said, tucking his clipboard under his arm and picking up his cane.

"With itchy feet."

The three of them walked to the ring.

A.J. halted Sabbath and put on her helmet as Devlin shut the gate behind them. The ring was about half the size of a football field, an oval formed by interlocking rails that was filled with loose dirt and open to the elements. It was spacious, even with the jumps taking up the bulk of the middle. There was plenty of room for her to exercise the stallion around the perimeter and to use the avenues between jumps to work on changing strides and shifting directions.

In the center, some fifteen jumps were set up at regular intervals in combinations and as stand-alones. Constructed mainly of brightly colored rails, every one was in the pristine condition she'd come to expect from Devlin's equipment. They were set in a variety of types and heights, providing excellent opportunity for her to get comfortable riding the stallion over the hurdles they'd confront in competition.

It was a jumper's paradise.

And the stallion's blood was running hot as he looked around at his new playground. The horse knew what he was going to be doing and his eyes held the relish of a warrior facing a worthy opponent. Impatient footwork and fervent whinnies told A.J. he was ready to get started.

Not yet, Flash Gordon, she thought.

First, they'd have to get through some flatwork. Less exciting by far than galloping over fences, it was a critical part of training. Working together in the various gaits, she and the stallion would have a chance to get to know each other better as well as warm up before the more strenuous part of the workout.

Devlin asked, "Need a leg up?"

"Thanks," she said, and took Sabbath's reins over his head, holding them in her left hand. She put her other hand on the back of the saddle and lifted her left leg, waiting for Devlin to boost her up.

He stepped in behind her, bringing his body close to hers. As he bent down and touched her lower leg, he smelled again the subtle lavender scent in the waves of hair tied at her neck. He couldn't help wondering if her skin would smell the same.

The training, he reminded himself as he touched her ankle. You're here for the training.

A.J. was caught off guard by the sensation of his hand on her leg, and then she was plucked from the ground and up on the stallion's back. She felt the saddle come under her and Sabbath shift his weight but it was the way Devlin's hand lingered on her calf that she focused on.

"You settled up there?"

"Yup," she croaked.

A.J.'s stomach lurched as she watched him go to the center of the ring. She was wondering what color his eyes were when he made love and had to bite her lip to keep from cursing aloud in sexual frustration.

The only color she had to worry about was brown—the color of the dirt she was going to eat if she didn't pay attention. She was on an unfamiliar horse who was known for trouble and if she wasn't on top of her game, she was going to get thrown. Just then, Sabbath threw his head up and pawed at the ground, as if to emphasize her point.

Good thing they were going to warm up slowly, she thought, struggling to rein him in. A little easy flatwork was about all she felt up to at the moment.

The stallion had other plans.

Just as she leaned down to check the martingale's fit one last time, still dwelling on Devlin, the horse's keen sense of timing kicked in. He knew that her shifting weight meant she was distracted and he used it to his best advantage. Half rearing on his hind legs, he kicked out for the center of the ring, flashing toward a jump at breakneck speed.

A.J. had to think fast. She regained her balance on instinct alone, narrowly saving herself from being thrown by Sabbath's powerful surge. With lightning speed, the stallion's massive chest and hindquarters were eating up yards of ground and she had to quickly assess where he was so hell-bent on taking them. Looking at the approaching fence, she had no doubt they could handle it but he was fresh out of the stall and she didn't want him to get injured. More important, she had to teach him he couldn't fly out from the bit and take off anytime the mood struck him.

Throwing her body deep into the saddle, A.J. used her weight to push into the stirrups and draw back on the reins like she was trying to uproot an oak stump. The stallion's thundering hooves slowed down some and she seized the opportunity to shift herself to one side. The change in balance derailed his course so he missed the jump and came to a sputtering prance at the far end of the ring.

It all happened so fast that Devlin would have missed the defection except for the sound of pounding hooves.

Glancing up at the noise, he saw the towering black horse lunge forward and he watched for A.J.'s reaction, knowing that it would tell him more about her skills as a rider than he'd learn in a week of structured training. Instead of becoming flustered by the unexpected, she focused and reeled the horse in without being too hard on his mouth or injuring either one of them. It was the measured response of a real pro and Devlin felt relief. When a horse bolts, all the training in the world couldn't help a rider with poor instincts. In the saddle of an out-of-control animal, a rider either had the right impulses or suffered from their lack by hitting the ground.

The woman's instincts were good.

And she was going to need them, he thought, walking over to the pair.

"Good defensive riding," he said.

A.J. heard the approval in his voice and warmed to it. "Well, we know one thing. He's strong and fast."

"Great timing, too."

Sabbath was fidgeting under her, impatient. She held his head firmly with the reins.

"I should have been more prepared."

"You did fine. It was inevitable he'd try something."

Devlin smiled at her and she felt optimistic. The horse was every bit as athletic as she'd hoped and her trainer was showing real promise as an ally. So what if the former just tried to toss her like a football and she was completely attracted to the latter? Even though her half-cocked decision had cost her a lot of money and an argument with her family, she thought things might just work out all right.

Sabbath whinnied and threw his head, hooves pawing at the air.

Or maybe not, she thought, getting him under control again.

"Now that he's made his point about being a rebel," Devlin said, meeting the stallion's eyes evenly, "let's see what happens when he's asked to behave."

A.J. nodded and directed Sabbath to the perimeter of the ring, keeping his stride at a trot. He fought her for his head with every footfall and she began to feel like she was in a tug-of-war. The stallion was testing her strength, assessing her determination. She just hoped he'd get over it before her arms were stretched so far her knuckles dragged on the ground.

Devlin watched as she let the horse work out his initial enthusiasm at being in the ring. Her hands were firm but gentle and she sat up in the saddle with the comfort and poise of a natural. Together, the two looked good, even though it was their first time together and the horse was pulling at the bit like the reins were made of taffy. The stallion's height and obvious strength meant he carried A.J.'s long body with ease and her calm confidence was the right match for his itchy high-stepping.

They just seemed to fit.

He thought of Mercy and, to avoid his feelings, he began calling out gait and directional changes. A.J. and the stallion spent the next hour going through a gradually escalating workout. When he was satisfied with their efforts, Devlin called them to the center of the ring.

A.J.'s smile was as blinding as the afternoon sun. "Isn't he wonderful!"

"He has his good moments but there's a lot of work ahead of us. That horse has his own ideas of how things should go and he's got to learn to be more disciplined."

"On the bright side, he hasn't tried to ditch me for over an hour."

"He puts up quite a fight, doesn't he?"

She nodded.

"How's he feel?"

"Smooth as water," A.J. said, taking her helmet off and brushing some hair from her face. "It's like swimming. As long as he isn't fighting with me."

As he looked at her, Devlin realized he loved watching her move. There was something innately fluid about her strength, something womanly and totally appealing. She might be lean but she was tough and resilient and yet still very feminine.

He smiled. "When he hits his stride, he's quite a looker from ringside."

And the horse wasn't the only appealing thing to look at, he thought.

A.J. grinned down at him as she replaced the velvet helmet. "Maybe he just gets bored easily."

"Then let's give him something to think about."

Devlin held up his clipboard and described a course of jumps. His sequence started with some straightforward uprights of low height and increased in difficulty. The most challenging of the group was an oxer combination. Each single oxer was made up of three upright rail fences that gradually got higher and tested height as well as distance. A combination meant that there were two or more of the same jumps separated by a single stride between them.

"I would have you try the water jump but I didn't have time to fill it," he said. "If Chester comes, he'll get it set up."

"Chester?"

"An old friend," Devlin replied, and changed the subject.

A.J. shrugged off her curiosity and asked for some clarification on distance and strides. He answered her questions and told her what he was looking for. Each jump was a test of a particular skill, either for her or the horse, and she was impressed with his thinking.

Harebrained scheming aside, one thing was clearly in her favor, she thought, turning the horse around. Her trainer sure as hell knew what he was doing.

A.J. set Sabbath into a light canter at the rail and they approached the first fence tensely, both battling over the reins. Sabbath won and took his head, galloping over the simple upright with a huge leap and clearing it with far too much room to spare. They landed like a sack of oranges hitting the floor. Charging around the ring, the round went from bad to worse, and by the time they cleared the final oxer, A.J. felt like she'd been in a paint mixer.

When she directed the stallion over to Devlin, she felt defeated, ready for his criticism. "So much for smooth as water. I think my molars are loose. That was a travesty."

A.J. frowned as she saw his expression. "Why on God's green earth are you smiling?"

"He's a temperamental giant. And he's rough around the edges but he's got a great stride and he's fast as a hot rod. He could be one of the great ones."

"Are you out of your mind?" she said, her arms feeling like noodles from fighting the stallion's mouth. "I might as well have been on the ground doing commands in semaphore for all he listened to me."

"We can teach him to pay attention to you." Devlin's hazel eyes were rapt. "What we can't do is motivate him. This horse is thirsty to feel air under his hooves and he's taking these fences like they're flat as mud puddles."

"I think it's a case of too much air between the ears," she muttered. "He takes his head all the time. I'm just luggage on his back."

"That's what training's for." Devlin nodded to the jumps. "Now do it again."

It was growing dim by the time A.J. put her saddle away in the tack room and paused to watch Sabbath munch on some hay in his stall. Her arms were numb, her hands were throbbing and she felt the beginnings of a headache. It was as though she'd been on a speeding train all afternoon and, even though her feet were now on solid ground, she still thought she was moving.

So much for a strong start, she thought, arching her back and feeling nothing but aches and stiffness.

The rest of the jumping hadn't gone much better than the first round and the afternoon had been a blur of wild leaping and hard landings. As she lamented the session, she decided there was nothing like reality to get in the way of a fantasy. It looked as if a good round in the training ring was what she should be shooting for, to hell with winning a championship.

A.J. sensed Devlin's approach.

"You did good work today," he said, standing in the stable's doorway.

She turned, not bothering to hide her disappointment, and found some relief. Beyond his wide shoulders, the sun was settling over undulating green hills. Its liquid gold light spilled across the grass and drifted into the stable's interior like honey. She could smell the sweet perfume of fresh hay and hear the reassuring grinding of Sabbath's teeth. But more than all that, there was a tenderness in Devlin's eyes that went further to replenish her spirit than any words he could have offered.

As she faced him, Devlin knew he was looking at someone whose energy was spent. There was a pall of fragility hanging from her, as if she were on the verge of shattering. Not that he blamed her. He knew only a handful of riders who would have been up to the task of tackling that black beast's headstrong ways all afternoon.

He was totally impressed. She'd muscled Sabbath around those jumps countless times, reeling the stallion in before each fence, pulling him through the corners, fighting to make sure his strides were right. It'd been exhausting just to watch but she'd kept at it. Every time Devlin had commanded her to run through that course, she'd done it, over and over, without a word of complaint. To say he'd been surprised at her grit was an understatement. Spoiled little rich girls didn't behave like that. Hell, a lot of professional riders wouldn't have put up with the demands he'd laid on her or the bad behavior of that stallion.

But then, she'd really awed him. Without asking for help, even though she looked ready to pass out from exhaustion, she'd carefully tended to the stallion's needs as meticulously as if she'd spent a lazy afternoon puttering around the barn. Her time in the ring had been about determination but her behavior outside of it was character.

"I think it's time to call it a day," he said, hanging the clipboard back on its nail.

"Let me just check on the tack."

"I'll take care of that," he said. "You need to head home."

"It'll just take me a—"

"Go home and get some rest." He watched as she tried to hide a yawn with the back of her hand. "What time can you be here tomorrow?"

A.J. grimaced.

"What?" he said. "Don't tell me you want to sleep in here with him. Haven't you had enough for one day?"

"Actually ..."

"You can be sure he'll be fine here. You want one of those baby monitors?"

"I want your couch." Her words came out in a rush. "Mind if I bed down in your living room again tonight?"

Devlin looked surprised. "Are you that tired?"

"No."

He frowned. "Your father's mansion is big enough to house a small liberal arts college. He suddenly decided to offer classes or is this more fallout from the split with your family?"

"Space is not the problem."

"This isn't just for one night, is it?"

"No."

Devlin's eyes grew remote and she could see his mind working.

"I can pay you," she offered.

He rolled his eyes. "Not that again. Like I said, money's not a big enticement to me."

"I wouldn't want to take advantage of your hospitality. I know it's an imposition."

"It's not you I'm worried about," he said under his breath. He wasn't sure he could share a bathroom with someone who made him feel like she did.

This woman moves in, he thought, and he'd be lucky if he didn't grind his teeth to stumps with sexual frustration. He'd be sucking meals through a straw and mumbling incoherently inside of a week.

Abruptly, Devlin pictured her coming out of his tub, skin flushed from hot water, mist swirling around her like an incantation of ecstasy. He tried to derail the fantasy and failed. With a harsh movement, he stuffed his hands in his pockets to be sure he kept them to himself.

If she stayed here, it would make training easier, an inner voice said. Less commute time for her, more time with the horse.

An argument ensued in his head between his professional responsibilities and his base instincts, a pair of dueling mental banjos that drove him nuts.

Finally, he decided. "If you want to trade in a feather bed for an old couch, it's okay with me."

A.J. sagged with relief. "Thanks. I know you don't have to do this."

"Right now, I'm thinking of it more as a public service. You don't look like you should be operating heavy machinery and that includes flashy red convertibles."

They walked out to the car to get her luggage, both fully aware of the position they were now in. They were two people linked by a powerful attraction they were committed not to give in to. Who were going to cohabitate for two months. Right before one of them faced the most grueling event in the equestrian world.

I can't believe I'm doing this, A.J. thought, feeling like she could begin giggling with hysteria at any moment. She was going to live with Devlin McCloud.

"Good thing you came prepared," he said, picking up one of her bags.

"It was either you or the exotic one-star motor lodge, Nero's Palace." She took out the other one and then put up the roof.

When they got to the farmhouse, Devlin held the door open for her and she brushed against him as she went inside. She felt a shock from the contact.

"I'll take care of dinner," he said, dropping her bag next to the couch. "You know where the shower is."

A.J. thought he seemed in a big hurry to leave the room. After he left, she put down the luggage she was carrying, hung up her coat and wondered whether she should follow him into the kitchen to help. Looking down at her dirty hands and feeling her hair itch from having been under a helmet for the afternoon overrode her desire to be polite so she headed upstairs.

The bathroom wasn't big but it had every modern amenity, including a whirlpool bath, which she eyed with naked lust. Cranking on the water, she watched greedily as the deep tub started to fill and the jets began working their magic. She fished through her bag and found some bath salts, which she sprinkled into the frothing water, releasing a delicate lavender scent.

When was the last time she'd taken a bath? Some dim memory from the previous winter came to mind. She'd been sick, if she recalled, with a nose that looked like a clown's and a honking cough to fill in for her lack of a circus horn. At that time, her submersion had been medicinal.

Now it was going to be pleasurable.

Despite her exhaustion, A.J. shed her clothes with glee and stepped into the undulating, perfumed water. The tub was big enough that she could lie down and be fully immersed while the jets sent pulses of warm water to her aching muscles. When she stepped out much later, pink and glowing, she felt renewed. Toweling off, she slipped into a comfortable pair of khakis and a cream knit sweater. She left her hair to dry in loose waves over her shoulders and headed downstairs feeling more herself.

Things only got better when A.J. hit the ground floor. Some heavenly smell was drifting out of the kitchen and her stomach grumbled with appreciation as she walked into the room. Devlin was at the stove, stirring the contents of a pot. On the table, there were two deep bowls flanked by man-sized spoons on neatly folded dish towels. The only other things on the rugged surface were wooden salt and pepper shakers and a basket of bread.

"Take a seat and I'll dish it up," Devlin said.

"Smells wonderful."

All the obvious attractions and talents *and* he cooks, she thought as she sat down and spread the gingham towel across her lap.

When Devlin reached over to pick up her bowl and returned it filled with a hearty beef and vegetable stew, she smiled. The meal was a far cry from the sparse gourmet food served on delicate china that she got at the mansion. The menu that came out of Regina's kitchen was restricted to skeletal pieces of meat or fish that were accessorized with flamboyant but insubstantial vegetables. For someone whose only exercise was admiring herself, it was a fine diet, A.J. had always thought. It was far from sufficient for an athlete, however, and she'd long before learned to tuck a spare sandwich under her arm on the way to bed.

But this is what I call dinner, she marveled, looking down at the food.

"You can stop staring at it," Devlin said, sitting down

with his own hefty portion. "I know it's not lobster Newburg but it won't poison you, I promise."

"I was just thinking how grateful I am. I'm tired of dinners that are heavy on preparation and light on the plate. If I never see another damned crepe or something with a garnish of endive, it'll be too soon."

"Well, you're safe here." He laughed. "I'm a meat-and-potatoes kind of man."

Devlin watched as she sampled the stew, thinking what a tangle of contradictions she was. A wealthy dilettante who cleaned her own tack and wanted to sleep on his couch instead of in a castle. A driven competitor who was looking too fragile to have fought the stallion all afternoon. A seductress who made his blood pound but seemed totally clueless about how beautiful she was. A woman who was raised on gourmet food who was now eating his stew like it was the best thing she'd ever tasted.

Maybe I'm not attracted to her, he thought. I'm just confused.

When she took another mouthful of the stew and sighed with contentment, her eyes flashed up at him. "And to think I used to believe laundry fresh out of the dryer was the pinnacle of bliss."

"I'm sure you've had better," he said, trying not to drown in the blue he found so captivating.

"Well, I've certainly had smaller. What I usually get could fit on the head of a pin and is more art than edible."

He cocked an eyebrow.

"Regina's cook likes to express himself in three dimensions. He's great at color, texture and presentation. The man's less strong on calories."

"Regina's the wicked stepmother?"

"More like all-pervasive," A.J. replied between mouthfuls. "For a short woman, she has a way of taking up a lot of space."

"Personality can add inches where high heels fail."

"You got that right. My father really loves her, though, and he seems happy, so who am I to judge? I just sneak a sandwich or two on the way upstairs. Like he does."

"Where's your mother?"

There was a subtle hesitation before she responded. "She's been gone a long time now. She died when I was young."

The words were measured, giving away nothing but fact. She'd spoken them for as long as she could remember, as much a part of what she regularly revealed to people as her address or her phone number. Any real sense of loss she kept to herself.

"I'm sorry."

A.J. shrugged off the concern, as she always did. "I was very young and I didn't really know her."

"It's still a tremendous loss."

"I try not to dwell on it."

"You don't miss her?"

"Of course I do but she isn't in the forefront of my mind."

"You don't think about what it would be like if she was around?"

"I've never known any other way. The normal things people do with their mothers are all hypotheticals to me. It's hard to miss something you've never had."

"You're a very strong woman."

She looked up at him, feeling a respect coming across the table that she reveled in. He was touching her deeply with his steady regard.

"I don't know if it is strength. I just don't like getting lost in a period of my life I can never return to and probably don't remember clearly anyway. A resurrected patchwork of childhood fantasies can be a warm quilt to snuggle up to but it's no substitute for real life."

"How can you let go so easily?" There was an edge to his words.

"I don't have a choice, do I?" she said softly. "I guess I've come to peace with the loss. The idea that everyone is going to live forever and nothing will ever change is just an illusion."

His eyes bored into hers. "I'm still working on the coming-to-peace part. I've been finding that illusion is just as hard to bury as the dead."

Devlin looked away, wishing for the days back when he

believed nothing could ever take him down, that he would go on winning forever. Back when all he worried about was when the next challenge was coming.

"It gets better, you know," she told him. "It really does. I've had a lot longer to get used to my loss than you have. My mother's been gone a lot longer than Mercy has."

She watched Devlin's face shut down and wasn't surprised when he changed the subject. For the rest of the meal, they talked easily about Sabbath's training but after they cleaned up the dishes, he got a serious look on his face again. He was standing at the door of the kitchen, fingers on the light switch, when she walked past him. His hand on her arm stopped her.

"I'm glad you're here," he said softly. "I like having you around."

Surprised and thrilled by his admission, her eyes searched his face. "I imagine it must have been lonely here by yourself. I find it's helpful to be around people when I'm hurting."

"It's not just people. It feels good to have *you* here."

With a swift movement, he bent down and put his lips against hers. She gasped in surprise and he swallowed her breath, taking her into him. His mouth moved over hers and her hands found his chest, lingering on the lapels of his shirt. Instantly, she was ready to have him closer. Time slowed, then stopped.

Then, with a hiss of frustration, Devlin pulled back as he realized what he'd done. Looking into her eyes, he wanted to offer an explanation but knew he had to leave quickly before he kissed her again.

As he rounded the corner and started up the stairs, he caught a glance of the couch. Six cushions, two armrests and fifteen yards of blue fabric, but it was so much more than a place to sit now because that was where she was going to sleep.

What had he let into his house? he wondered as his heart thudded in his chest. Something dangerous had come inside with that woman, he realized, something tight on her heels, so at first he hadn't noticed its presence. Now he felt a threat everywhere around him. From her coat hanging next to his to her barn boots tucked beside the door, her shadow seemed to be across every object that, having once been familiar to him, was now foreign.

What had he done, he thought, going upstairs and walking into the bathroom like a zombie. Immediately, he caught the lingering smell of lavender in the air and cursed under his breath. Like crumbs of a feast, it mocked him and sharpened the hunger in his gut. He imagined her body unfurled in scented water with nothing to shield her from his eyes. At the vision, his body responded in a rush of heat as blood thundered in his veins and forced him to reassess what he thought of as unbearable.

Wrenching a hand through his hair, he went to the sink and stared at his reflection. He looked like a man who was out of air, and that was how he felt. His chest was tight and his head was spinning. The only things he knew for certain were the passion in his body and the pain in his heart.

Instead of giving in to either, he tossed some water on his face and gritted his teeth.

Get a grip.

After putting his toothbrush to vigorous use, he went to his bedroom, where he stripped naked and got into bed. Staring at the ceiling in the dim light, he saw only what he imagined her body would look like, laid out to his eyes and his mouth, its textures and contours his to learn.

Turning restlessly, he punched a pillow hard and looked at his bedside table.

That book on baseball legends wasn't going to do the trick tonight, he thought. He was going to need something more along the lines of a ball-peen hammer to put him out. And it was a damn shame the thing was out in the barn.

5

A.J. PASSED the time while waiting to hear Devlin's bed-room door shut by making up the couch and changing into a clean T-shirt. The stiffness in her arms made the simple tasks a study in soreness but her mind was elsewhere. She was going through the motions, moving through the room in a disconnected daze, and it was only after she knocked herself a good one walking into the coffee table that she cradled her shin and sat down.

Keeping their relationship on a business level was abso-lutely the right thing to do. It had been hard to concentrate on her training after she'd been in his arms and felt his tongue against hers. It was worse now that he'd kissed her good night, because she was reminded there was more than passion between them, more than the heat, pounding blood, electric feelings of lust. . . .

A.J. shook her head.

It was worse now because that kiss had also been about their emotions. About him telling her how much he liked her in his house and her feeling as if he was opening up to her, little by little.

She had to remember she was with him to train for the Qualifier, she told herself sternly. Not to fall in love.

A.J. shuddered at the implications of the L-word.

Her heart pounded in fear and she worried she might be reading too much into their conversation over dinner. Even though he'd said something to the contrary, maybe he'd just reached out to her because he was in the mood for confidences.

The question became, did he know himself?

And thinking of the kisses they'd shared only made her more dismayed. Devlin McCloud was a man with powerful urges. Clearly. She thought again that maybe the fire between them wasn't unusual for him, even if it was a revelation to her.

In A.J.'s experience, she wasn't really the kind of woman men would break down a door to get to. Well, maybe if a house was on fire and they were a Good Samaritan with an ax and an air mask. But she'd never found that they'd do it out of romance.

It wasn't that she didn't have male colleagues. Back at Sutherland's, she was always included in think-tank sessions on show strategy, vet consults and team dynamics. But she wasn't someone who got asked to go out to the local watering hole to shoot pool and drink lukewarm beer with the others.

And as for dates? If A.J. thought it'd been a long time since she'd sat in a tub, the last time she'd been out with a man was back in the Stone Age. Sharing the warmth of someone else's body, exchanging furtive kisses, experiencing a mutual longing that would shut out the world, none of that had happened in a long time.

Try, more like never.

It was like she had some missing parts and men knew it. The problem was, until she met Devlin, she'd never felt broken. The horses and the competing had been enough. Her days had always been full, and the nights . . . The nights had been for rest, not romance, but that had been okay with her.

So what was it about Devlin McCloud that made her think clean living was so underrated? With only two kisses, he'd managed to make her think the life of a harlot had some real potential.

Unnerved, A.J.'s mind leapt away from further thoughts about their attraction, only to latch onto feelings she'd had while she talked with him about her past. She couldn't remember the last time she'd spoken of her mother. It was a topic she kept to herself and she was unnerved by how far she'd let Devlin into the deepest part of herself. Sitting at that table with him, in the midst of sharing their pain, her admissions had seemed only natural, but now, as she sat alone, she was torn. Between the kiss and the revelations, she'd allowed herself to become vulnerable physically and emotionally during a time when she needed her strength the most. She wasn't going to make it through the Qualifier unless she could keep control of herself.

Looking up at the ceiling, she wondered how she was to get through to the event in one piece. And waited in silence for an answer that didn't come.

When she heard Devlin's door close, A.J. quietly mounted the stairs and did a quick pass through the bathroom, getting done with her normal routine in half the time. Passing his closed door as she left, she paused as she realized it was far from over between them, business-only vows to the contrary. It was a premonition that tickled down her spine and she had to tell herself that the spooky sensation was because she was exhausted and unsettled, not because she could predict the future.

If she were psychic, she'd have known it by now, she thought as she went downstairs. And she'd have bought a lot more lottery tickets over the years.

It was hours later when A.J. awoke in confusion. Turning over, she looked out of the windows. Cloud cover had taken over the night sky, smothering the light of the stars and the moon. She looked around the room, unsure what had woken her up. Blinking in the dark, she held her breath, trying to pinpoint the disturbance.

Was it a dream or something real?

Listening, she waited to see if the noise came again, while trying to convince herself it was only her subconscious. In the quiet of the night, she heard the autumn wind brushing against the house and the shutters creak on their old-fashioned hinges, but those noises were unremarkable.

After holding herself tense for some time, she was ready to go back to sleep when she heard a muffled groan, the sound of someone in pain. Throwing back the covers, she leapt off the couch. When the low sound came once more, she realized it was drifting down from the second floor. She ran up the stairs.

With visions of CPR running through her head, A.J. wrenched open the door to Devlin's bedroom. On the antique bed, he was moaning in anguish, thrashing like a man in the throes of torture. The covers were wrapped around his naked body like a snake, trapping his limbs and adding to the traction of his nightmare. She rushed to his side.

Lost to his torment, Devlin was mumbling incoherently and she reached for him, calling out his name. As soon as her hands touched his arm, his eyes snapped open as if he'd been struck. Disoriented, he struggled to get up but the bedclothes clung to the sweat covering his skin. She leaned forward to help free him, trying to ignore the way his bare body was revealed to her.

With a flash of movement, he gripped her arms, looking at her urgently while seeing something else.

"I knew there was something wrong with her leg," he said urgently.

His voice held the anguish of regret, and the feeling sounded fresh despite being tied to events nearly a year old.

"It was my fault. I should never have taken her over those fences."

Tentatively, A.J. reached up and stroked his hair but she didn't know what good it was going to do to calm him. He was lost to his memories, stuck in the prison of his mind.

His hazel eyes, usually so sharp, were like dull stones as he shook his head back and forth. "If only I hadn't pushed so hard . . ."

"Shhh," she said in a gentle voice. "Take a couple of deep breaths."

With the abrupt clarity of light slicing through darkness, he focused on her. Under his sudden regard, A.J. felt like she'd been caught eavesdropping on his pain and began to pull away, aware that he was naked in the knotted sheets.

Devlin didn't let her go.

He moved with decisive speed, pulling her to him and claiming her mouth with a vengeance. A.J. was rocked by the sensation of his body against hers and reacted instinctively, opening her mouth to him. But, as his tongue plunged inside, the voice of reason in her head sounded off alarms. He was still disoriented and very naked and she knew coming together in the darkness, in his bed, was like tossing a match into a gas tank. Enticed as she was, she began to move away, trying to do the right thing.

She didn't get far. When his arms tightened against her back in protest, she tried one more time and then gave up her halfhearted battle, getting swept away by their passion.

Letting herself go, A.J. kissed him back wholeheartedly, unleashing her desire and digging her nails into his bare shoulders. As their tongues dueled, her heart pounded and a feverish heat made her dizzy. She felt her legs move of their own accord. They parted and she straddled the hard length of him, the sheets and her boxers flimsy barriers between his throbbing length and her hot core. As her body took over, conscious thought was pushed into a dim corner, nothing more than debris.

She didn't miss sensibility in the slightest.

As his hands went under her T-shirt, A.J. felt his touch over her skin. He lingered on her ribs, squeezing into the bones, and then came forward, sweeping up under her breasts. When she felt the tips of his fingers caress their tender undersides, she moaned against his mouth. Urgently, his hands swept upward and encased her, his thumbs stroking her peaked nipples until she thought she would go insane with hunger.

In a flash, the world tilted and spun as Devlin rolled her over, and then she felt his lips through the thin cotton of her shirt. She looked down and watched as his tongue licked over her breast, seeking a hard nub. As he kissed her, her shirt grew wet above the nipple, clinging to her skin, magnifying the sensation. Her body arched against him and she threw her head back with a moan. Taking advantage of the soaring movement, he wrenched the shirt up to her neck. As she felt his breath on her bare skin, she cried out and drew up her knees. His hips pushed into her, seeking her heat. When his mouth covered her nipple, she felt a warm, moist tug that was her undoing.

"Devlin!" she called out.

The sound of his name stopped him.

He froze and lifted his head and she became aware of their heavy breathing filling the room. She waited, praying he would continue.

But, with the same staccato change that marked his abrupt embrace, he separated them, leaving her to feel the cold of his withdrawal and her embarrassment. His retreat was like having the gates of paradise shut against her with most of her body jammed in the door. Shame flooded A.J.'s face as she left the bed and it only got worse when Devlin started to apologize. The regret in his voice stung as badly as her own mortification.

"I'm sorry," he said while pulling bedsheets over to cover himself. "I didn't mean—"

"Don't worry about it. It's best to just forget this happened."

He swore softly. "But—"

"Please, don't say anything."

Face burning, she left without another word.

In the quiet night, she could hear the muted sound of his curses as she fled down the stairs.

As the light of dawn pierced a thin veil of early-morning fog, Devlin got out of bed. Not that he'd been sleeping. And not that he had anything to do at that ungodly hour, either. All he had was hope that shifting to the vertical would mean gravity could take a shot at clearing his head. God knew, he'd failed at the effort while lying on his back.

Dressing quickly, he crept down the stairs and stood in the living room doorway. A.J. was asleep, an arm cast over her eyes to block out the light. The makeshift bed was a hodgepodge of sheets and blankets, a sign she'd tossed and turned during the night, too.

At least she was sleeping now, he thought, remembering how he'd spent the night propped up against his headboard, staring off into space. Thinking about them.

Still baffled by his own murky motivations, he couldn't explain why he'd reached for her. Well, he knew why on one level and that level was rising again as he recalled how she'd felt against him. What he didn't understand, and couldn't really forgive, was why he'd given in to his desire after they'd both agreed their relationship would be only a professional one. Blaming his lapse on coming out of the familiar nightmare didn't really hold water. He hadn't been thinking about the past when he'd pulled her to him. He'd been very much in the present.

And look what his impulse had gotten him. Another regret, something else he wished he could undo. It wasn't that he mourned for one instant the feel of her under him. Hell, he'd keep that with him until the day they put him in the ground.

What bothered him was the look on her face as she'd turned to go. It was too full of embarrassment and shame for him to stomach. He was the one who should have to bear that burden, not she. He was the one who'd put their working relationship on a level it shouldn't be on. He'd kissed her first. He was the one who'd pushed the boundaries. Several times.

A.J. stirred and he retreated to the kitchen, going straight to the phone. He felt the need to do something reasonable, to make a difference that made some sense. Even though it was just past five o'clock, he dialed a familiar number.

"Yup," came the voice on the other end.

"Chester, it's me."

"Yup."

"You want to come back?"

"Yup."

"Half hour?"

"Yup."

Devlin hung up.

Now, that was what he called a good working relationship. Clear, concise communication. No complications.

He frowned.

But then, maybe it was easy because he had no desire to see Chester Raymond coming out of his bathtub.

Moving around the kitchen stiffly as his leg loosened up, Devlin made the coffee, got out three mugs and was cutting thick slices of whole-grain bread for toasting when Chester came through the front door. There was no need for a knock. They'd lost that formality years before.

Devlin watched as his friend halted and looked over the sleeping figure on the couch.

Chester Raymond was almost seventy, as gnarled and lean as an ancient birch tree, and tough as a northland winter. He was also a man who took surprises in his stride.

"Mornin'," he said, after he marched into the kitchen. He took off his battered baseball cap, revealing tufts of white hair over a face that had years of hard labor etched in it. When he cracked a smile, which was often, he looked like his skin was too big for his head.

"Mornin'," Devlin replied as he filled up a mug and put it down in front of the chair the man always sat in. "Thanks for coming."

"Glad to. What's on your couch?"

"I'll introduce you when she wakes up."

"She?"

Devlin nodded.

"Does this she have something to do with what's down in your barn? I heard some whinnies when I pulled up, so I took a look."

"Uh-huh. You want breakfast?"

"Sure do." Chester knew not to push. The story would come out eventually and he was a man who bided his time.

Immediately, they fell back into their old pattern. The groom took his seat at the table and stirred three heaping spoons of sugar into his mug while Devlin got out a bowl and filled it with two measured cups of cereal, one tablespoon of peanut butter and just enough milk to cover it all. Chester had been eating the same breakfast for fifty years. Maintained it gave him a youthful glow.

Devlin put the bowl in front of the man and sat down with his own mug. "Why do I think I'm the only one who's surprised we're back having breakfast together?"

Chester shrugged, digging in. "A'cause y're the only one."

A ghost of a smile played across Devlin's face. "You always were unflappable."

"No, just more easygoin' than you. You been wound tight since the day I met'cha. Always a fighter, even when things are going your way."

"It's been a while since things have gone my way."

"Not true. Ya just can't see where y're going next right now."

There was a long silence as the phantoms of the previous year danced on the table between them.

"So, it's been a while," Chester said between mouthfuls. "How're ya doin'?"

"I'm getting by."

"Saw the jumps set up in the ring."

"They're not for me."

"Didn't think so."

"I'm finished competing and, even if I could ride, I don't know. . . . Losing Mercy was just too awful."

"Don't I know it. Missin' her myself. But things, they come into a life an' they go out an' that's the way it works. You can't hold yourself back because it hurts. What ya need to be doin' now is looking for what's come to take her place."

With that, A.J. walked into the kitchen. And Devlin thought he was going to choke on the symbolism.

"Good morning," she said, skirting her eyes over him before looking at Chester. Her flush told Devlin she was remembering what had happened up in his bedroom and he thought the color in her cheeks made her look radiant. She was wearing blue jeans and a work shirt and had yet to pin back her hair, so its amber weight was a glorious stole around her shoulders. With her smile of greeting for the older man, she lit up the room like a bonfire.

Chester blinked twice, as if he'd seen an angel.

"I'm A.J.," she said, offering her hand.

"An' I'm glad to have somethin' better to look at over breakfast than McCloud's face," the man replied, shaking her hand awkwardly. "Chester Raymond."

She laughed. Chester looked away and looked back.

Devlin frowned and went to get A.J. some coffee, muttering, "Better watch out. For a confirmed bachelor, he's a real lady-killer."

"That your stallion in the stall?" Chester asked.

"He's my ball and chain, yes."

"Good composition, smart eyes, lot a' trouble. What'll save you is his heart. He'll perform well for the right person."

A.J. accepted the mug from Devlin. "You know him?"

"Don't need to. Took a peek into the stall when I got here." Chester polished off the last bit of his cereal. "One look at an animal an' I know what's in there. Just like catchin' the headlines of a newspaper."

"That's amazing." A.J. sat down.

"He's a speed reader, all right," Devlin interjected.

"Well, when a body's seen as many horses as I have, a person goes on instinct."

A.J. leaned across the table. "You know, I'm so relieved to hear you say that about Sabbath. It's what I thought from the moment I laid eyes on him, but after our first time in the ring yesterday, I've been doubting myself. Going over fences wasn't a good experience for either of us."

"Don't be doubtin' the instinct. A body's more likely to go wrong ignoring it than listenin' to it."

"You are so right," she said.

Devlin began to feel left out.

"You two want to keep going down this personal empowerment road or should we get to work?" he asked, crossing his arms over his chest.

They looked at him like he was being a grouch and he felt ridiculous. Imagine him, jealous of a seventy-year-old man. Who looked like a basset hound.

Obviously, insomnia could drive a person mad, he decided.

A.J. stood up.

"I'll meet you all down by the barn," she said, grabbing a piece of toast and gulping down the rest of her coffee. She gave the old man a radiant look before leaving Devlin without a glance.

Devlin watched her go into the front hall, shrug on her coat with the toast in her mouth and then hurry out the door.

"So when ya gonna marry her?"

Chester's calm question fell on his head like a bucket of fish bait.

Devlin sputtered on the rim of his mug. "Excuse me?"

"Myself, I've always liked the spring weddin's."

"Are you channeling Martha Stewart or something?"

"Go ahead, fight this one like ya do everything else you

can't control. Don't know why ya bother, though. It's obvious what's hangin' in the air between you two."

"No, wait—you're doing Ann Landers."

The older man shook his head as he took his bowl to the sink.

"Say what ya will, but y're a goner."

"I hate to break the news but you're way off base. She's sleeping on the couch, not in my bed, and it's only until the Qualifier." Devlin shot to his feet. Took his own mug and plate over.

"Whatever ya say."

"I'm not *saying* anything. That's what's happening."

"Like I said, whatever ya say."

The two bickered their way to the door, just like old times.

"There's nothing going on."

"Yup."

"I'm serious."

"An' so is what's not goin' on."

Devlin let out a curse, halting in front of the coats. "Since when did you turn into a romantic?"

"At least I'm improving with age."

"Delusions aren't improvement. They're evidence of squash rot."

"Better than goin' blind from sheer bullishness."

"Listen, old man," Devlin said with a grin, "you want to help me set up the ring, or what?"

"I'm ready to go. Y're the one dragging your feet."

Devlin pulled on his barn jacket. "For God's sake, will you stop it?"

"I'm not the one with the problem."

"Well, I don't have one, either!"

"I can tell."

Devlin had just swung open the front door when Chester put a hand on his shoulder. The older man's eyes were grave.

"I know this ain't easy, boy. I'm glad you're back."

"I'm not back," he said gruffly. "It's not me up on that stallion."

"Ya don't have to be on the horse to be back in the game."

Devlin found that he couldn't reply.

Before they stepped outside, he looked at his wooden cane, which was leaning against the doorjamb. The handle was worn from his grip and its sturdy length showed the nicks and chips of having been knocked against a variety of things. It had been with him since he'd gotten out of the hospital.

Today he left it behind as he and Chester went down to the stable.

When the two men came through the sliding double doors, Sabbath was on the crossties and A.J. was grooming him.

"I'll be groomin' for ya now," Chester said, stepping forward.

She smiled. "Thanks, but I'd like to do some of it. Gives this lunkhead and me a chance to get to know each other. I'd welcome some help, though. There's plenty of surface area for two."

"I'll say." The man picked up a currycomb and approached the stallion, who flattened his ears back.

"Oh, get over yourself, ya big baby," Chester said sharply.

Shocked, Sabbath pricked his ears forward and seemed hurt at being dismissed so easily. He settled down with a sheepish look as the groom went to work.

Shaking off a feeling of nostalgia, Devlin retrieved his clipboard and reviewed his notes from the day before. Instead of throwing in a new complement of jumps, he decided to keep working the stallion over the course he'd laid out yesterday. He was hoping the continuity would help focus the horse.

After Sabbath was saddled, Chester went out to check the fences.

"Want me to bring the hose out there an' get busy fillin' the pool?" he asked Devlin.

"Not today, Ches, thanks. Think we'll stick with what we did yesterday."

Heaven knows the day before washed up in a tangled mess, Devlin thought. Why add more water to the equation?

Watching the groom amble out to the ring, he chewed on

his pencil, finding familiar grooves. He was wondering how the stallion would handle water jumps. It wasn't uncommon for high-strung horses to have difficulty with them. The shimmering surface looked threatening and some jumpers had problems with visual stimuli. He'd seen fierce creatures like Sabbath throw their riders just to avoid mud puddles. The key was knowing whether your horse was a "spook" or not. It was important information to have but, as he contemplated the day's work, he decided they had enough to worry about. The water jump would have to wait.

With a final review of her equipment, A.J. led the stallion into the ring. The day was bright and sunny and the clear fall sky stretching overhead was a vast blanket of blue. As she and Sabbath approached Chester, who was waiting to shut the gate, A.J. thought ahead and asked the man to give her a leg up. Devlin wasn't an option. The memory of his body stretched over hers was still vivid and she didn't want him too close. She got light-headed just from recollections of the night before and had no intention of getting more distracted.

Once up in the saddle, she threw a smile at Chester while securing the chin strap on her helmet. Coaching Sabbath into a jog at the rail, she felt him bounce under her, his feet light over the earth, his ears flicking front and back. Devlin took up his position in the center of the ring and began calling out gaits. Surprisingly, the flatwork went well and she tried not to get her hopes up though it was hard not to get excited. Even as she urged herself to keep her enthusiasm in check, she was thrilled to get to know the stallion's rhythms, to recognize how he felt as he changed gaits and directions. She decided that, when he wasn't acting up, he was responsive and a damn good ride.

Soon enough, Devlin called them over and reviewed the course again.

"You ready to do this?" he prompted, noting how she was stretching out her arms. It seemed as if she was uncomfortable.

"Of course we are."

"Your arms look sore."

"They're fine."

He approached the stallion and put a hand on her leg. He imagined he could feel the warmth of her skin even through the chaps, and when she jerked her leg away, his eyes turned grim.

"A.J., talk to me. Don't be tough. Are you strong enough to do this?"

"Absolutely. I don't stop just because it hurts."

"Perseverance is a good quality. So is knowing when you need a break."

He watched as she looked around at the jumps, flexed her arms and settled back into the saddle. Sabbath stamped a hoof and tossed his head, impatient.

She said, "We don't have time—"

"There's always time. Trust me on this. It's better to be clear about any weakness you or your mount might have than pretend you don't have one."

"I'm fine. Why won't you believe me?"

A.J. wheeled the stallion around and he watched her go, taken by her command of the horse. And herself. She would no sooner give in to physical exhaustion than back away from a challenge. She was, he realized, so very much like himself.

Which meant he was going to have to watch her very carefully. When a competitor's hunger was as strong as hers, good judgment could easily be a casualty. It was a lesson he'd learned the hard way. He found himself hoping he could spare her the pain of his own insight into what someone loses when they focus on a goal to the exclusion of everything else.

At ringside, A.J. stared down the course, jaw set in preparation for the battle ahead. She was so sore from the day before that brushing her teeth in the morning had been a challenge. The warm-up hadn't been too bad but she knew what was coming. Could she hold out long enough?

The discomfort in her body wasn't the only thing she found upsetting. Devlin's concern for her was both touching and frustrating. Didn't he understand the pressure they were all under? They were going to need every day they had to train the stallion. Taking time off just because of some muscle soreness wasn't going to get them where they needed to go.

With resolve, she tightened her grip on the reins and gave the stallion some leg. He surged forward, approaching the first fence faster than she would have liked. The jump went startlingly well. Some of the smoothness she associated with his flatwork showed up unexpectedly, but then, as if he remembered he had to be a badass, he fought her at the turn, throwing his head up and sidestepping. She had to pitch her weight in the opposite direction in hopes of controlling him.

A.J. succeeded in muscling him into the next jump, a low-slung wall that he cleared as if it were big as a barn. He fought her through another turn and, when he was confronted by the oxer combination, he took the bit and plowed through the jumps like a wrecking ball.

"Halt," Devlin called out. Normally, he would never have interrupted a rider's concentration in the middle of a course but he didn't want them going any farther. The horse was out of control and they'd only be letting him get entrenched in bad behavior if the round continued.

A.J. curbed the stallion with a mighty pull while Devlin approached on foot. She was panting as if she'd run a mile.

"You want to rest?" he asked.

"No."

He hesitated. "All right, let me know when you do."

She nodded but he knew the idea had been tossed out.

Devlin said, "I think we need to school him over some singles. The course is too much right now. He's just going to keep fighting you, first because he's testing you and then because he's used to doing it."

Devlin pointed to the left.

"Let's start with that first upright. Just run him over it once and bring him to a halt. We're going to get this animal so bored, he'll be too numb to fight."

The rest of the training session was spent leaping over the jump and coming to a full stop until A.J. thought she was going to go mad. It worked, though. By the end of the morning, the stallion was clearing the one fence and coming to a halt without turning it into a battle.

"I think that's enough for today," Devlin called out.

A.J. didn't bother to hide her relief. She was always willing to work hard but the two extremes of constant vigilance and mindless tedium had begun to wear on her. The stallion seemed likewise exhausted.

"Hypnosis takes over where the battle leaves off," Devlin said with satisfaction as they walked toward him. Both were glassy-eyed.

"Is it me or has there been some improvement?" A.J. asked.

"By the end, he seemed to be coming around."

"Thank God."

Even though Devlin wanted to, he didn't ask about how she was feeling. Besides, with the way she was looking, he knew. Her features were pinched and her eyes dragged down at the corners. Neither was a good sign.

"Let's cool him down and have a strategy session over lunch," he said.

"Good idea."

While she coaxed the stallion into a slow walk at the rail, Devlin went over to Chester. "What do you think?"

"Stallion's a natural but a pain in the neck." The man scratched his chin. "Girl's a gem. Rides like a lady but's tough as old shoe leather. She'll win 'im over in the end but it's gonna take the starch outta both of 'em."

"That's what I thought."

Sabbath and A.J. walked by slowly, looking like a couple of worn-out boxers.

"Shootin' for the Qualifier, are ya?"

Devlin nodded.

"It's two months away."

"Don't I know it."

"Ya gonna test 'em out in competition aforehand?"

"We'll have to. There's an event coming up in two weeks. Some good competitors will be in the ring but it won't be covered heavily by the press because the purse is small. We can let them cut their teeth in relative peace. I just hope there's enough time to get some kinks worked out. I don't want her getting discouraged by a bad showing early on."

"They're gonna make it," Chester pronounced.

Devlin cracked a grin. "I love it when you agree with me."

"Two weeks!" A.J.'s turkey sandwich hit the plate and bounced apart. "Are you out of your mind?"

"We need to get the two of you into competition as soon as we can." Devlin's eyes were steady across the table.

"I agree, but in case you haven't noticed, that horse and I can barely make it over one upright without turning it into armed combat. How are we going to get up to speed over a whole course in two weeks? Much less go into a competition?"

"I'm not saying you two will be polished or that I expect you to win."

"That's a relief. Because I'd hate to let you down when he ditches me and tries to herd the crowd again."

"Not much chance a' that," Chester piped up as he came into the kitchen. He went straight to the luncheon meats on the counter. "The animal likes you too much. And y're too good a rider to let 'im get away with it, anyway."

A.J. shot the man a grateful smile and Devlin felt like he'd been pricked by a needle. There was something about seeing her look at Chester with such affection that irked him.

He said, "We're going to use the next two weeks to get you as buffed up as we can."

A.J. groaned and Devlin got lost looking at her. Sitting with her back to the sun, there was a halo around her that made her hair glow with the deep red of coal embers. Its warmth gave her flawless skin the luminescence of pearls and, when she flashed her eyes back to him, Devlin caught his breath.

"Is there anything we can do to fast-track the training? Assuming you don't have a time machine hidden somewhere around here?"

There was a long pause as she waited for Devlin to answer, and Chester smiled. While putting together his sandwich, he'd been looking at them and chuckling to himself. He'd been with Devlin McCloud a lot of years and there wasn't much about the man he didn't know. Working in intense situations brought out the good and bad in people and Chester had seen his friend in a lot of different moods. Nothing compared to the effect the woman had on him. The guy looked like someone had come up the back side of his head with a broad board.

Ever since the accident, Chester had watched as Devlin retreated into himself and closed off from everything. Now, though, that angel with the dark red hair had come down and there was light in his friend's eyes again. Of course, Devlin was too obstinate to realize his salvation had arrived and he'd fight the redemption tooth and nail all the way. But that was his nature. After all, you can't be surprised when a hardwood tree sprouts up from a chestnut.

Chester pitched a pickle onto his plate and poured himself an iced tea before taking the seat next to A.J. She was still waiting for a response and he figured he'd better answer, because the man on the other side of the table was too addled to do it. Although it wasn't the first time he'd rescued his friend in some way, having a woman put Devlin McCloud out of his wits was a new one.

"Ya can't rush the trainin'," Chester said to her. "But ya don't need to."

A.J. looked at him, doubts hovering in her eyes.

"Ya can do this. Ya just need to work with 'im. That stallion'll come around," he affirmed before wrapping his jaws around the sandwich and chewing.

"But all we did today was—"

"Y've got to let go a' the disbelief in your head."

"I can't."

"Then y're focusing on the wrong place. The strength's in your heart, not your head."

"Right now, all I can see is failure." A.J. pushed her plate away.

"Them thoughts are only as strong as ya let them be."

Devlin came out of the spell and saw A.J. was looking at Chester as if the man were the source of all knowledge.

"You done, Swami," he said dryly, "or do you want to hop up on the table and do a few yoga postures?"

"Just sayin' what I think. I have faith in her."

Devlin let out a snort as A.J. smiled at his friend. Feeling like someone left out of the loop, he got to his feet. "I hate to miss more of the glowing admiration between you two but I'm going to get some work done."

Chester rolled his eyes with a good-natured grin. "I guess this table's not big enough for both of us, Pilgrim."

He got a grunt in return.

Devlin knew he was behaving like a five-year-old but he couldn't pretend any differently. Putting his dishes in the sink, he left the house, only to realize he didn't have a clue what he was going to do with himself. His study was always ripe for attention but there was no way he was going to march past the two of them again. Not after he'd left in such a huff.

Hoping to trip over some kind of purpose, he headed down to the barn, where he found Sabbath napping. One black hoof was resting on its tip and the horse's ears were lolling lazily. They pricked up as Devlin leaned on the front of the stall.

The stallion, for once not taking a combative stance, ambled over. His eyes flicked over the discontented man at his door and he seemed to offer his condolences.

"I look at that woman and all my neurons start firing at once," Devlin said. "My head shuts down and that's not the worst of it."

But he wasn't about to describe the effect she had on his body. Even if the stallion was looking particularly supportive. The memory of A.J. in his arms was potent enough without adding to it the power of words.

"What the hell am I going to do?"

If the stallion had an answer, he wasn't sharing, and Devlin pulled away from the stall with a frustrated groan.

"To top it off, she's got me turning to a horse for advice."

6

THE TWO weeks before her first competition on Sabbath passed in a blur of early mornings, hard labor and relentless training. As A.J. brushed her teeth the night before the event, she felt ambivalent. They'd made some progress with the stallion but it didn't seem like enough. Although she and Sabbath had graduated from the crushing repetition of doing single fences to tackling courses, the battle of wills continued in the ring.

She sighed and took out her hairbrush.

At least everything wasn't acrimonious between them. Miraculously, the disobedient jumper had turned out to be a real charmer when he wasn't going over fences. Every time A.J. came into the stable, his head popped out of the stall and he nickered a greeting. He was always ready for a rub behind the ears from her and he repaid the effort with a muzzle nudged under her arm or a snuffle across her shoulders.

Gradually, the stallion had learned to tolerate Chester and Devlin but he was A.J.'s horse. Or, more accurately, he'd decided she was his person. This meant, when it came to his many idiosyncrasies, A.J. had to be the one on deck or things went bad fast. The stallion was especially finicky about his feet and only A.J. was allowed to pick out his hooves. Chester had tried once and Sabbath revolted so violently, he yanked one of the crossties out of the wall. And when it came to getting shod, if A.J. wasn't standing by his head, the blacksmith refused to get within two yards of the stallion with a horseshoe. No one blamed the man. Left to his own devices, Sabbath had tried to make lunch out of the man's overalls, starting with the back pockets.

When it came to real feed, the kind he was supposed to nibble on, the stallion had a funny quirk. He hated being alone when he ate. If A.J. wasn't around, the oats or hay went untouched. Only when she was leaning against the stall door, looking over him and talking quietly, would Sabbath dip his muzzle down and start chewing.

Between his phobias, bizarre habits and the way he behaved in the ring, it was easy to see why Sabbath had been passed from owner to owner. If it weren't for his obvious and overwhelming affection for her, A.J. thought they all would have lost patience with him by the end of the first week.

She finished untangling her hair and put the brush back in her toiletries bag. Then she slipped on a pair of thick socks to keep her toes warm and picked up her small bag. She was on the way downstairs, running through the checklist of things to do in the morning before they left for the show, when she heard cursing. Curious, she followed the expletives into Devlin's study. He was crouching in the corner of the room, frustrated.

He looked up as he heard her approach. Their eyes met in the dim light, and the flash of attraction, which always flared whenever they were together, made her feel warm inside.

"Sorry for the colorful language." His voice was deep and low.

"Highly descriptive as well as educational." She tried to smile nonchalantly. "I didn't know you could do that to a filing cabinet."

She leaned against the doorjamb, keeping her distance. They hadn't been alone since the night of the kiss up in his bedroom, by silent agreement. He'd taken to conveniently disappearing whenever she had to use the bath and she pretended to be asleep every morning when he came downstairs to start breakfast. Chester was with them the rest of the time.

She hadn't found the forced distance helpful. Since reality wasn't offering a release to her sexual tension, her fantasies were picking up the slack. Instead of growing more dim, the memory of their kisses haunted her, taking on mythic proportions.

Which is what happens, she thought, when you spend so much time staring at the wall at night. Perspective is the first thing to go. Followed closely by good humor.

"Anything I can help with?" she asked.

"My filing system's failed me."

A.J. glanced around the room. Papers were everywhere. Covering the floor, stacked on top of filing cabinets, crowded in piles. It was a jungle.

"I don't know that I'd call it filing. More like stationery landscaping."

"I find things easier if it's all laid out," he said, crouching down over another stack. "Usually."

"What are you after?"

"Receipts from a feed company. You ready for tomorrow?"

"I wouldn't say ready. More like resigned. Reminds me of when I got my wisdom teeth removed. One way or another, it'll be over tomorrow night."

Feeling restless, because of the event in the morning and because she was finally alone with him, she fingered the bottom of her T-shirt, pulling apart the frayed hem and creating a hole. The shirt was at least ten years old and she was wearing it for good luck. On the front, there was the name of the local high school football team as well as a big lion's head. On the back it read, DON'T MESS WITH THE CATS.

Coming up empty from another excavation, Devlin got to his feet, shaking out his stiff leg. "You two have come a long way since that first day. You've got longer to go but it's not like you're standing still."

"What are we going to do if there's water in the ring tomorrow?"

They'd been so busy working on the basics, the water jump had remained unfilled. It was one more source of anxiety. Neither of them wanted her to take the stallion over one in competition for the first time.

"If there's water, you're going to take your best shot and

hope he holds, but I'm betting you won't have to worry about it. This is a regional competition. There'll be some good riders there but it's not a huge event. They're not going to get too fancy."

"I know you're right but my mind just keeps spinning." Her hands sped up their work.

"Stop picking at that shirt before there's nothing left of it," he said darkly. Not that shredding the damn thing isn't totally appealing, Devlin added to himself.

Her hands stilled. "I'm a little keyed up."

Looking at the hole she'd created, Devlin felt the power of his lust for her. Staying away from A.J. for two weeks had been hell and the virtues of self-restraint were losing their ability to fortify his willpower. The last thing he needed was to be talking to her and imagining what she'd look like with her breasts bare to his eyes.

The mere thought was enough to make him get hard. Every night, in his dreams, she came to him, drifting up the stairs, through his door, into his bed. He would feel her skin against his, get lost in her mouth, smell the lavender in her hair. And then he would wake up and wonder why the hell she was sleeping anywhere else but beside him.

His jaw tightened.

"You look fierce," she said softly.

"Sorry. I guess I'm keyed up myself."

Liar, he thought. He wasn't anxious about the event. He wasn't even thinking about it. It was A.J. that was on his mind. The fact that they were alone in his house. That with two steps forward she would be close enough for him to kiss her. On the lips. On the neck. On the—

"I want you to know, I won't let us down. I'm going to give it my very best tomorrow."

"Of course you will," he said, trying to focus. "You've been giving it your very best every day in that ring. You've been amazing to watch. You're so much more than I ever expected."

"I can't tell you how much that means to me." Her blue eyes were downcast and her face flushed, as if she was embarrassed by his praise as well as pleased with it.

He cleared his throat, feeling like he should offer her

more support. "Your entire future doesn't rest on tomorrow. Not your riding career, not your chances at turning Sabbath into a champion. It's one competition in what hopefully will be a long list of shows with you on his back. You're just starting down the road, and if you stumble in the first few feet, it doesn't mean you can't go the distance."

A.J. smiled at him and he felt as if she'd stolen the breath from his lungs. Standing in the doorway, wearing that pair of flannel boxers and the old T-shirt, she was the most enticing woman he'd ever seen. Her hair was around her shoulders in thick waves and her skin glowed in the dim light. As his body throbbed, he realized it wouldn't matter what she was wearing; he'd always be attracted to her. To him, she could turn a burlap sack into a negligee.

Devlin cleared his throat. "Listen, I know Chester is more your go-to guy for pep talks, but if you need an affirmation for tonight, I think I could scare one up."

She laughed huskily in a way that made him itch to get his hands on her.

"What would you suggest?" she asked. "Something like 'Believe in yourself and all things are possible'?"

"I think mine would involve more scotch."

"I'm not much for liquor. It makes me feel loopy."

"Then, as your guru for the evening, I'd advise you to stick with the believing in yourself part."

"Good advice," she said as she turned to go. "See you at first light?"

Devlin nodded.

And all through my dreams, he thought.

As she was leaving, he raked his hand through his hair and took a steadying breath. He decided it was just as well she was going downstairs. He'd learned his needs got stronger in the nighttime, so they were both better off if she was on a different floor. Hell, on that logic, he should be sleeping in the barn with Sabbath.

Devlin looked around his study, trying to remember what he'd been hunting for. All that came to mind were images of A.J., so he gave up his search. As he turned off the light, he thought it was a pity he'd have to go past her to get to the scotch.

*   *   *

It was a little after seven o'clock in the morning when the
McCloud Stables trailer pulled into the fairgrounds where
the competition was being held. The rig wasn't as big as the
one A.J. was used to, but then, she'd seen double-wides
smaller than the Sutherland behemoth. Funny thing was,
she preferred Devlin's to the one she used to go around in.
It was easier to maneuver and far less ostentatious.

Devlin had been behind the wheel for the hour-long trip
through the Virginia countryside while A.J. and Chester sat
comfortably in the cab beside him. The three had been up
since the crack of dawn, falling into a precontest routine of
checks and balances designed to ensure that no piece of
equipment was forgotten and no contingency left unantici-
pated.

As Devlin piloted them to the competitors' area, which
was down a dirt road past lines of cars that had been parked
on the grass, A.J. surveyed the scene. Teenagers, looking
bored and embarrassed in their orange bibs and matching
baseball caps, were directing traffic on either side of the
road. Beyond them, the fairground was a vast open area,
marked by white fences and a few modest buildings. The
field had been used for growing corn and wheat for genera-
tions until it became a casualty of big-business farming.
Now it was owned by the county, a big draw for rodeos,
jumping shows and the odd traveling circus or two.

And that drive-in retrospective on Godzilla hadn't been
bad, A.J. reflected. There was nothing like seeing Mothra up
on the big screen.

As Devlin scouted around for an open spot to park in,
she found herself bracing to see the Sutherland logo plastered on the side of a trailer or on the back of a T-shirt worn
by one of the grooms. A team from Sutherland's would be
at the competition; she was sure of it. Knowing she was going to have to compete against people she used to see every
day, but now had no stable affiliation with, made her feel
the gravity of her dislocation. As long as she was seques-
tered at Devlin's, it was as if the compound didn't exist. Her
days were so full, and her mind so preoccupied with training, she hadn't had time to think of much else.

Now, amidst the surging energy of an event, she was reminded of everything she'd left, including her father. The
only contact with him had been a message she'd left on his
business line, informing him where she was in case of emergency. It was a cold way to leave things and she regretted
the distance as much as she felt relieved by it. She didn't
want to cut herself off from him permanently but she
needed time to get over the hurt, and his decision to put
Peter in charge without consulting her still burned.

Devlin pointed out a spot at the far end of the grounds
and, when they all agreed on the choice, drove them over to
the quiet corner. Shaded by trees and set away from most
of the activity, it was perfect for them.

As A.J. stepped from the cab, she stretched and looked
around. Beyond their secluded site, there was a practice
ring with warm-up jumps, a bank of concession stands and
merchant tents overflowing with riding equipment and
clothing. Set apart from the retail activity was the show
ring. With a set of bleachers and plenty of space around it
for the crowd to sit on the grass, the arena was twice the size
of the one she'd been training in at Devlin's.

All over the fairgrounds, people were about, ambling
around with cups of steaming coffee and programs tucked
under their arms, if they were part of the crowd, or moving
quickly, if they were involved with putting on the show or
competing in it. There were groomsmen and trainers, judges
with their badges, fresh-faced volunteers who would grow
up to be the next generation of champions. For a moment,
it was easy for A.J. to forget her worries and get lost in the
sheer wonder of the human parade. And, in the midst of it
all, she felt a thrill go through her. There was no place she'd
rather have been.

"I'll go check the start board and make sure you're all
set," Devlin said to her. Chester had already gone back to
check on Sabbath.

"The first round doesn't go off until nine, right?" she
asked.

"Plenty of time."

It was a lie. They both knew the two hours would go like
brushfire.

The jumping competition was being staged first and would be followed by dressage and novice events in the afternoon. She didn't think they'd be staying for the full day, not with Sabbath in tow. Getting through the morning was going to be exhausting and the sooner they got him away from the crowds, the better.

A.J. came around the trailer just as Chester was backing the stallion out of it. The horse was antsy as he hit the ground, wrenching his neck back and forth with eyes that were a little wild. It wasn't a good sign.

"This is a competition," Chester was scolding him. "Not a time to be worryin' about the ladies."

A.J. laughed nervously, going to Sabbath's head to try to soothe him. "I'm not ready for him to start dating."

"Neither is he."

Sabbath was prancing this way and that, his glossy black coat flashing like obsidian in the bright morning sun. Chester, on the other hand, was standing firmly in place, with an iron grip on the lead.

A.J. could feel the looks of the crowd as they walked by, their eyes measuring the horse with undisguised curiosity and then looking her over with a similar expression. She wanted to believe they were arrested by the sight of him and wishing her well, but she knew better and did her best to meet the stares calmly. She might be anxious about what was going to happen in the ring but she was going to do her damnedest not to show it.

When she was satisfied that the stallion was under some control, she decided to take a look at the ring. "I'm going to walk the course. Want anything?"

"I don't think they're sellin' what I need," Chester said as the stallion threw his head again. "An anchor to hang off this one's forehead would be great. Last longer than m' arm, too."

"I think we're out of luck on marine supplies but maybe I can scare up some other kind of deadweight."

Would give me a use for Peter, if I run into him, she thought with humor.

Heading to the show ring, she wanted to find Devlin, get close to the billboard to check the order of riders, and study the jump course. Already, competitors and trainers were crowded around the board so she had to stand on the tips of her toes to see over all the heads. She was arching forward when she felt someone put an arm around her waist.

"And so you are back with the bronco."

The French accent cut through her nerves like a chain saw. She turned to face Philippe Marceau and took a step away at the same time.

"Ah, but how the morning light suits you." His wide, placating smile showed a lot of dental work.

She acknowledged him with a reserved nod and found it amazing how something so melodious as that accent could be so grating coming out of his mouth. Was it all the caps on his teeth?

"I see you come after me in order," he was saying while striking a pose. His riding clothes were conventional and top quality but he was wearing a pair of extreme wraparound sunglasses. "You are a woman of great courage to bring that beast into the ring. But then, I hear you have help, *non*?"

"I have a trainer," she confirmed while searching for an escape route.

Standing close to this man is like being stuck in an elevator, she decided. You'd bargain with God to get free.

"But not just any trainer. Not only does this woman tackle a stallion no one else can seem to tame but she resurrects the dead, *n'est-ce pas*? You have done wonders to stir McCloud's blood again, or so I have heard."

A.J.'s mouth dropped open at the insinuation. "What are you talking about?"

"Surely you jest. The news is all around." He gesticulated with a limp wrist. "Although I must say, you are faithless to leave your family in favor of a man who is not your husband. No matter how good you find his *services.*"

Her vision narrowed on the man's jugular. "Why, you little—"

Devlin appeared at her side. "A.J.! Time to go pace off the course."

"Ah," Philippe said grandly. "And here is your good teacher, the man you gave up so much for. Myself, I could not imagine leaving my family for someone else's stable, but I am French and we are known for our loyalty. Then again, I also don't need the particular kind of *instruction* this McCloud offers."

A.J. could sense her face turning brick red and felt like a boxer winding up for a punch.

"Come on," Devlin said.

"Yes, run along, you two. I imagine there is much you must do to each other."

That did it. She lost it.

"Why, you tar-mouthed gossip hound—"

She was itching to go further but Devlin put a firm hand on her arm and began to lead her away.

"And speaking of gossip," the Frenchman called out as they left, "you would do well to keep your ear to the floor. I myself am going to make an announcement soon."

"That's 'ear to the ground,' you—"

"Enough," Devlin hissed, dragging her off.

When they were out of range from the crowd, A.J. whirled on him, eyes flashing turquoise.

"How could you let him go on like that? You didn't give me the chance to defend us!"

Devlin said nothing, which infuriated her further. He just stood there, staring at her calmly. Didn't he have any pride?

"I mean, come on! Marceau made insinuations that were insane and you hauled me off before I could respond."

When that didn't get any reaction, she frowned.

"Hello?"

"You finished?" he asked. "Or do you want to give him more of what he's after?"

A.J. looked confused.

He said, "Tell me what you're thinking about right now."

"How I'd like to crown him with a bag of feed."

"Anything else?"

"How wrong he is about us. How ridiculous it is for that man to talk about loyalty after he's dated so many women simultaneously, his bed needs a waiting room."

"Good. Now tell me why we're here."

She looked at him like he'd gone daft. "To compete."

"Right. And you're blowing all your energy and concentration on Philippe Marceau about thirty minutes before you have to go into the ring."

"But the things he said—"

"Were exactly what he knew would get you rattled."

She shook her head. "But why would he bother?"

"Because he sees you're becoming a threat."

"I doubt that. Sabbath is worse than an unknown and I'm not the seasoned competitor Marceau is. He doesn't have anything to worry about."

"You're closing in on him faster than you think. As rough as he is, Sabbath could eat up the ground under any of Marceau's mounts and you have more natural talent than he could ever hope to train for."

"I can't believe he's threatened by me. That performance is just his personality, not strategy."

"Don't bet on it. He's got great instincts when it comes to human nature and he uses them to his advantage. Always."

A.J. opened her mouth but he cut her off.

"You've been in some competitions but you obviously haven't had enough experience with the kind of head games people like Marceau play. As you rise up through the ranks, you better get ready for it. Competition has a way of souring people and, in Marceau's case, he was pretty damn close to rotten before he started."

A.J. thought about it and began to see Devlin's point. She saw how she'd played into Marceau's hands and started to feel like a fool.

Watching her deflate, Devlin couldn't stop himself from reaching up and tucking a stray lock of hair behind her ear. It was the first time he'd touched her since the night they'd kissed. His hand lingered on her cheek.

"The best technical rider doesn't always win," he said gently. "And Marceau's star has risen a lot higher because of it. He's great at unsettling competitors. I've seen him do it before."

She heaved a sigh. "How could I be so gullible?"

"Look, you should take it as a compliment. The man never wastes time on riders he's sure he can beat."

A.J. stayed silent for a moment and then he watched as

she pulled herself together, those arresting eyes of hers re-lighting with purpose.

"Well," she said sharply, "the man's getting no more from me. Let's walk that course."

"Hey," he said.

She looked at him.

"I'm proud of you."

She flushed and a slow smile spread over her features. It was like watching the sunrise over his mountains at home, he thought. Beautiful, glowing, magical.

"Thanks," she said, and then started back for the crowd around the billboard.

"Don't worry about going into the fray," he said, stopping her. "I've already sketched out the course and you're going second to last in a field of fifteen."

"That's great."

Together, they bent over his clipboard and analyzed the course order. There were eleven fences, with two combinations. Mercifully, Devlin's prediction that there wouldn't be a water obstacle was correct. After A.J. was familiar with the layout, they went inside the ring and walked the course, pacing off the distances between the jumps. Taking three-foot steps, they counted four as one of Sabbath's strides. Other competitors and trainers were doing the same and the lot of them looked like a platoon of confused soldiers, high-stepping in different directions.

After they'd walked the course once, Devlin coached her on how to handle the turns.

"The first three jumps are straightforward. Going into the turn that follows, get him into a lead change as soon as you can before heading over to the first combination of uprights. Six is going to be the first real test. It's a tight crank and he's going to fight you for his head. Seven and eight are relatively easy but then comes the cruncher. He's going to get barreling fast during that straight shot before the turn into nine and ten. You're going to have to hold him as best you can so you don't go cockeyed into the corner and miss that last combination of oxers. Get through them and you're home free with the wall at eleven."

A.J. nodded and asked him some specific questions

about where she needed to take jumps at an angle in order to get the stallion into the best position to handle the turns. She knew that her late start position was going to be an advantage. She could watch the first couple of jumpers and see where they were having problems. Typically, courses had one or two fences that the competitors tended to fault on, and discovering where those were was important information. Sometimes, it was surprising where the problems came up.

The goal in competition was a "clean round," which meant the horse and rider made it over all of the fences without knocking down a rail. A point system, made up of "faults," measured any deviation from a clean round. If a rail was knocked down, it would mean four faults for the rider, and there were other transgressions such as a horse refusing a jump or failing to cross the start or finish line. There was also a time limit on the course, and if a rider's time came in above it, they would be disqualified.

After all the competitors finished the first round, if there was only one clean round or only one rider with the lowest number of faults, that competitor would win and the others would place accordingly. If there were multiple clean rounds or lowest number of faults, there would be a jump off, a timed round over a half dozen fences. The rider with the fastest timed clean round would then win or, failing any clean round, the rider with the lowest number of faults would take first place.

A.J. and the competitors all knew the rules by heart. They also knew the standards were the only predictable thing in an event. There was no way of knowing what would happen when someone went into the ring. During the two minutes it took for a rider and horse to go through a course, anything and everything could happen. It was this kind of triumph and tragedy that kept them all, competitors and spectators alike, coming back for more.

As she ran the course order through her head again, A.J. was thinking she had no idea how the stallion was going to behave. Well, she knew what the downside could be. Putting Sabbath into a foreign ring and surrounding him with people, some of whom would be moving around while he was jumping, was asking a lot. It would be visually arresting, a feast for the roving eye, and she knew how easily he lost concentration.

After walking the course one more time, she and Devlin headed back to the competitors' paddock. By the time they returned to the trailer, Chester had wrapped each of the stallion's lower legs to prevent injury if he knocked a rail, and had already put A.J.'s saddle on his back.

"We've got a good position," Devlin said as they approached. "How's he been behaving?"

"I think he's engaged to that mare over there but I can't be sure."

Devlin laughed. "Maybe you'll get that spring wedding after all."

"I'm hopin' for one."

A.J. shot them both a curious look but the subject was dropped.

Going inside the trailer, she retrieved the bag that held her show clothes. In one of the empty stalls, she tossed aside her barn boots and undressed, feeling chilled by the early-morning air. In a hurry to get warm, she quickly put on a crisp white shirt with a priest's collar and tucked it into a pair of tan jodhpurs. Fishing around in her bag, she found her good-luck socks. Bright pink, they had pigs with angels' wings flying in formation and she covered them up by stepping into a pair of highly polished black boots that came up to her knees.

Out of her purse, A.J. retrieved a gold pin, which she affixed at her throat in the front, and then she plaited her hair into a long braid that she twisted tightly into a bun at her neck. Looking around for a mirror, she didn't find one so she tried to get a sense of what she looked like by using a compact.

Frustrated because she couldn't see herself, and feeling conflicted because she was wondering what Devlin would think of her outfit when she should have been focusing on the event, A.J. took her blazer from its wooden hanger and put it on with a smooth motion. The tailored black jacket was lined with red silk and had two brass buttons on the front engraved with the Sutherland logo. She tried not to dwell on the insignia as her fingers did up the blazer. With a crisp tug at the double vents in the back, she was armored in genteel battle gear and she emerged, velvet helmet dangling from one hand, ready to go into the ring.

Devlin's eyes went dark as he looked up from adjusting Sabbath's martingale. With all the preparations and chaos of an event day, he hadn't been thinking about what he was missing but it all came back to him as she stood in the early sunlight, dressed in her show clothes. He knew how she felt, wearing that jacket. The marbles in her stomach, the course order she'd be memorizing like a treasure map, the delicious agony of waiting for her time in the ring. Those were things a competitor never forgot. And even though he was happy for her, he ached for what he'd lost.

"You all set?" he asked as she approached.

A.J. reached out and put a hand on his forearm. "Hey, are you okay?"

Devlin was surprised at her concern, having assumed he'd kept his emotions to himself.

"Of course. Why do you ask?"

"You look like you're hurting."

He debated whether or not to brush off her concern. The last thing she needed to be burdened with as she headed into the ring was his problems, but he found it hard to keep things from her. With those piercing blue eyes staring up at him, seeing through him, into his pain, he couldn't help but respond.

His eyes drifted toward the show ring. "I miss it. I really miss . . . all of this. I haven't been to a show since . . ."

"You don't have to stay," she said. "If it's too hard—"

"I would never leave. I'm here for you."

Their eyes met and held. Abruptly, the crowd evaporated, the teeming noise around them stilled, the competition ceased to exist. For the span of a heartbeat, they were the only two people in the world.

And then Sabbath stamped a hoof and Chester called out a question about the tack and someone behind them let out a curse as a bucket of water was knocked over.

As he fought the urge to take her into his arms, Devlin

nodded toward the stallion. "So what do you say—shall we find out if we can work and play well with others?"

The two looked at Sabbath, whose eyes were darting around his head like Ping-Pong balls, and then toward the practice ring. Already, there were riders scaling jumps and trotting at the rail. All competitors shared the one ring and the same three or four fences for warm-up. At the same time.

"Any chance we can put a bag over his head for this?" she quipped as they went over to the horse. After taking the reins in her hands, Devlin gave her a leg up.

"I'll tell you what," he said. "If he misbehaves, he's grounded. No phone privileges, no TV. We're taking a hard line."

She laughed.

"A.J.," he said softly.

She was still smiling as she looked down at him. "What?"

"Thanks for knowing me so well. For understanding me."

His hand squeezed her leg.

"I . . . care about you," she said softly.

"That makes me a very lucky man."

They started out for the practice ring, A.J.'s heart swelling with joy.

Even though it was difficult to concentrate on anything other than Devlin, Sabbath demanded, and got, her full attention as soon as he entered the ring. Rearing up and letting out a royal holler, he announced his arrival to the other horses who were warming up. As A.J. struggled to get him under control, she thought again how getting romantically involved with her trainer was dangerous.

"Let's get him loosened up at the rail first," Devlin told her.

With some difficulty, A.J. coached the stallion into a trot. Head cocked like a gun hammer, he was eager to start something and everyone else in the ring knew trouble when they saw it coming. They all gave Sabbath a wide berth.

While she was trying to keep the stallion as calm as possible, the first competitor was ready to go into the big ring.

A.J. kept one eye ahead of her and one eye on the event course, anxious to see what was going to happen. When the buzzer sounded, the rider was off, the woman's mount eating up the distances between jumps and sailing over the fences with great bursts of strength. It was a strong round but not a clean one. The horse had faulted over the second combination, the trouble spot Devlin had predicted.

Even though she would have liked to watch more of the event, A.J. knew she had to focus on Sabbath, and by the time the first eight competitors had gone through the course, she'd managed to muscle him over a few practice fences. The results weren't promising. The stallion was skidding out from under her commands, fighting her at every turn, running free from under the bit. They looked like amateurs, as if she didn't know what she was doing and the stallion didn't know any better.

Bringing him to a halt at Devlin's command, she wrung out her arms and tried to keep the string of curses in her head to herself. She was feeling like she'd made the worst mistake of her life and was showing it off to a peanut gallery that wasn't inclined to be charitable even on a good day.

"Let's get away from here," Devlin said.

"But my turn's coming up fast."

"I know, but trust me on this. Your eyes are glassy and you look as if you've already lost. You need to focus."

A.J. let him take the reins and lead the stallion out of the ring to a shaded area. Hidden by the side of a barn, they had some privacy.

"Look at me," he said.

She turned slowly, like she was coming out of a dream.

"At this point, you've already lost and not because of the horse. If you don't pull yourself out of this funk, you're going to have more to be sorry for than the fact you took a chance and right now are feeling rocky about it."

"I'm so embar—"

"Stop it. Going into the ring as you are now, this horse is going to plant you in the ground like a marigold. He's going to hit those jumps and go hell-bent for trouble and you're going to wish you were back here, in this moment, making the choice to pull it together instead of pity yourself."

A.J. shook her head, visions of failure swirling in her mind.

"What have I done?"

"It's too late to rehash a decision you made weeks ago. Quit with him after this event if you have to but don't throw in the towel ten minutes before you're supposed to be in the ring. It smacks of cowardice and you know it."

It took her a moment to absorb the advice. He was right. Turning away wasn't the answer because she'd only end up with more regrets later. In her mind, she pictured returning to the stables without having gone into the ring, knowing she'd backed down.

Whatever happened, A.J. decided it couldn't be worse than how she'd feel if she walked away.

With a nod, she began to wheel Sabbath around.

"It's going to be okay," he told her.

As she looked at him, Devlin was facing her with such conviction, she felt herself buoyed by his confidence in her. She wondered how she could possibly go into the ring without his support. In the midst of her chaos and self-doubt, he was as steady as bedrock. She didn't think for a moment he wouldn't be there to encourage her, coach her, pick her up if she was to fall.

"With you here," she said, "I believe that to be true."

Her mind wandered as they went over to the show ring. There was a feeling in the middle of her chest that defied easy description. It made her wonder whether true love wasn't a combination of the calming warmth of security backed up by the intense heat of passion. It was a hell of a mix, she thought.

Together, they paused in front of the show ring's main gate and got updated on the competition. There hadn't been a clean round yet and there were two riders left ahead of her with one of them about to start the course. When she heard Philippe Marceau's name, A.J. didn't bother hiding her disgust.

The Frenchman was astride a tall roan mare, one of his

frequent mounts. A good jumper, the horse was at the top of her form and, from the moment the buzzer sounded, she took the jumps with ease and power. Up on her back, Marceau was in total control, angling the mare well and driving her over each fence with confidence. As he led them into the final sharp turn, and barreled around to confront the oxer combination, A.J. held her breath with the rest of the crowd. If the two made it through, they'd end with a clear round; she was sure of it.

The mare took the combination and the last jumps perfectly and, as the two galloped over the finish line to a smattering of applause from the crowd, A.J. looked over to Devlin. "For a miserable human being, he sure can ride."

"No, that's a good horse. You could have put a bag of doughnuts on her back and she'd have done just as well."

She grinned.

There was one more rider before her and A.J. waited impatiently for her turn. Sabbath began to feed off her tension, so she tried to hold herself as still as possible, regulating her breathing. The last thing they needed was any more juice in his blood.

When her number was called, she swallowed her fears and jogged the stallion into the ring, bringing him to a skittish pause in front of the judges. As she looked around, she noticed that all activity on the fairgrounds had come to a halt. It seemed as if every pair of eyes in the whole place were trained on her and the towering black stallion.

So this was what fifteen minutes of infamy was like, she thought, removing her hat and bowing her head to the judges.

What A.J. didn't know was that people might have glanced up once to see what all the gossip was about but they stared because of how spectacular she and the stallion looked together. Sabbath's imposing power and height as well as his midnight coat and flashing eyes would have been noticed anyway. But teamed with A.J.'s long-limbed grace and classic beauty, the two were a knockout.

Putting her hat back on, A.J. guided the stallion out to the rail. When she heard the buzzer, she coached him into a canter and approached the first fence. He fought hard for his head but she didn't let him get away with much and they cleared the jump well enough. Going into the second, he tried to skid out of bounds but she held him firmly and they went on to take the next several fences with no faults.

Underneath her saddle, A.J. could feel Sabbath surging over the ground, his great barrel chest drawing in gallons of air to feed the enormous muscles of his haunches. Pounding over the ground and then leaping off for moments that lasted an eternity, she could feel a rhythm growing between them. His power became her own as they leapt free of gravity and then crashed back down. It was a thrilling, pumping, harrowing journey.

And for a moment, she was grateful.

Unfortunately, her joy was short-lived. Heading into the straightaway before the final tight turn, A.J. defensively tried to slow their velocity but the stallion had no intention of giving in. No matter how far back she threw her weight, he charged ahead as if he were getting ready to jump out of the ring itself. They came into the turn out of control despite her efforts, and he fought her as she tried to bring him around, throwing his head and skipping out from under his hindquarters.

There was no way they were going to make the oxers, A.J. thought desperately as she tried to rein him around. The angle was all wrong.

She tried once more to shift her weight back and to the side. Sabbath's breath was coming in great steamy explosions and she felt his body heaving under the tremendous pistons of his legs. She knew if they didn't slow down, they were going to get hurt. Missing the turn at that kind of speed meant they would have to jump the ring's fence or crumple into the corner in a heap.

That thought must have dawned on the stallion because, in the nick of time, he came about and shifted direction like a gale-force wind. It was too much, too late. They took the first oxer wide and scaled its mammoth girth at a thick angle. This meant they had to cover more horizontal distance than they would have if they'd approached the jump head-on.

A.J. heard his back hoof strike a rail hard but didn't have

time to dwell on whether it hit the ground. They were so far off course, she'd have to steer them hard right so they didn't make the second jump harder than it was, or worse, miss it altogether. Even more alarming, she had only one stride to correct their direction. She knew if she leaned too far or pulled his head too much, they'd take the jump off-balance, and that wouldn't just be bad form; it was dangerous. They could both end up sprawling over the towering fence and, between their speed and its height, that could mean serious injury.

In a split second, it occurred to her the only way they were going to get over the oxer without getting hurt was if she let go and gave him his head. If Sabbath wanted to take the jump, he would. If he shot around the side of the oxer, it was better than her face-planting in the dirt, bouncing off the oxer or him injuring himself.

As soon as she loosened her hold on his head, Sabbath responded with a quick jab to the right. They sailed over the jump but lacked the good approach that would have let them clear it cleanly. As they landed, she heard the unmistakable sound of a rail hitting the ground.

Crossing the finish line, A.J. felt a measure of relief. The round hadn't gone well but it wasn't a complete disaster, either. Considering that Sabbath was prone to be more trouble than just being genetically disobedient, she figured she'd gotten off pretty easily.

But they hadn't won. Not even close.

The announcer proclaimed their time and their eight faults. With Philippe's clean round and the other riders who had only four-faulted, she knew they weren't going to place.

Devlin was the only person she saw in the crowd.

"How do you feel?" he asked, walking up to them. He took the reins to give her a break.

"Okay, I guess."

He thought she looked discouraged and he sympathized. It had been an exhausting round for him to watch. He'd tracked every movement of the pair, willing them to clear each of the fences cleanly, his hands clenching and unclenching each time they left the earth and returned to it.

He'd been caught up in the drama with the rest of the crowd but the stress had been compounded by a very special concern for her.

"You did a good job."

A.J. tugged her helmet off. "Considering the potential for complete chaos, I suppose so."

Devlin knew just what she was feeling. She'd been born with a competitor's need to win and, like the color of her eyes, it was immutable. Even though she and the stallion weren't ready to take an event trophy yet, he could feel her disappointment at not winning as if it were his own.

A.J. dismounted and they were walking Sabbath away from the ring when the final competitor finished and his results were read over the loudspeaker. As they headed back to the practice ring to walk the stallion out, the silence between them was filled by the noise of the crowd and then, shortly thereafter, the proclamation that Philippe Marceau had won.

After Sabbath had been cooled down, and Chester went to work grooming him, A.J. took a break and went over to the various booths where tack and riding apparel were being sold. As she meandered through the velvet hats and leather boots, breathing in the smell of fresh leather spiced with a whiff of the barbecue being started for lunch, she ran the round over and over in her head. The stallion's actions and her responses. The way he'd felt over one jump and another. The battle into that final turn. The stallion's abrupt choice to take that oxer after she'd given him his head.

A.J. knew Sabbath wanted to jump. That was what she'd learned again when she'd loosened the reins and left the choosing up to him. His abrupt correction, which she couldn't have pried out of him by fighting in that short amount of space, told her he wanted to feel the clean air over those fences as badly as she did.

The revelation troubled her. It meant he was fighting her for the sake of fighting and that was a bad sign. Locked in a battle for control, he seemed to value the warring over his instincts to fly. And that would put an end to her ambitions for them as sure as more of those rails bouncing off the dirt.

A.J. was about to return to the trailer when she overheard two competitors talking.

"No wonder they call that holy terror Sabbath," one was saying. "That horse'll put the fear of God right in you."

"He fought her tooth and nail," the man's companion agreed. "Every single jump. That woman's got to have arms of steel."

"At least he didn't fly off into the crowd. You hear what happened at Oak Bluffs?" Both men laughed.

"I sure did," the one said. "Even took a few steps back when they came around that last corner. I thought they were bound for the parking lot."

"Can you believe she left Sutherland's for that kind of trouble?"

"I don't think the horse is the only reason." The voice dropped to a conspiratorial whisper. "McCloud's no dummy. He may be out of the horse business but he knows a good-looking filly when he sees one. That leg of his is rusty but I'll bet the rest of him is in working order, if you know what I mean."

A.J. paled.

"Well, at least she's out of commission. The woman's no threat on the circuit as long as she's on the back of that bad-tempered show-off."

"Bulls for her. She'd shown some promise."

As the two left the tent, A.J. stood in stunned disbelief, feeling like she'd had cold water poured over her. She'd felt capable of standing up to curious looks and handling the vague idea that people were talking about her. She'd even resolved to ignore Marceau's nasty commentary on the basis of his unpleasant disposition. But hearing firsthand such insinuations, from run-of-the-mill competitors, was different.

Walking through the crowd back to the trailer, she couldn't imagine being in a worse state of mind. She'd set an impossible goal, on a ridiculous timeline, and any progress she'd made could have been measured in inches, not feet. Her name was the favorite bone of the gossip hounds and her own horse was treating her like the enemy in the ring.

To top it all off, she thought she might be falling in love with her trainer.

How could things be worse?

Then she saw Peter and her father standing nose to nose with Devlin. She looked up at the sky in exasperation.

"That was a rhetorical question," she said out loud. "I wasn't really looking for a demonstration."

7

THE THREE men were a tight knot of tension. Devlin, standing head and shoulders above the other two, was grim. Garrett wore the expression of someone in gastric distress. Peter looked offended and irate.

And people think a coven of witches is a sign of trouble, A.J. thought.

As she passed Chester and the stallion, who were standing at the back of the trailer, she raised an eyebrow in inquiry.

"Don't look at us," Chester said. "For once, Sabbath's been behaving in public and I was born in Switzerland."

She rolled her eyes.

"You're clearly taking advantage of her," Peter said in a loud voice.

"You don't know what the hell you're talking about," Devlin retorted. "I'm her trainer, not her lover."

"Just how stupid do you think I am?"

A.J. interjected, "If you're wasting time speculating on that, you're not too bright."

Her stepbrother wheeled around and she got a full view of the outfit. It was a tailored black suit with a yellow tie and shirt. He looked like a cartoon character, drawn in colors too bold for real life.

"You and McCloud are ruining our reputation," Peter pronounced. "I won't stand for it."

"And how exactly are we doing that?"

"A newspaper reporter just came up to your father and me and demanded to know how long you two have been together."

"So? He's been my trainer for almost three weeks."

"We're not talking about jumping horses, A.J. He says he has an intimate picture of you two."

"What!"

"You heard me."

"Wait a minute." A.J. was shaking her head. "I don't understand—"

Garrett asked, "Are you really living with him?"

She turned and met her father's distressed eyes. "Yes, and sleeping on his couch. It's easier for me to train that way and Devlin has been more than accommodating."

"I bet he has," Peter said.

"Don't be so insulting," she bit out.

"I think you should come home immediately," her father said. "It's better for everyone that way."

"Somehow I doubt that."

Peter snorted. "And you think staying with this guy is a better option? It's hardly becoming to be *involved* with your trainer."

"We are not involved! And I don't know anything about a picture."

"Well, then I guess all of us can be surprised at what's going to be in the paper tomorrow morning."

Her father cut through their heated volley. "*Please* keep your voices down."

"But he doesn't know what he's talking about!"

"And you don't know what you're doing," Peter countered.

Garrett's eyes implored her. "Darling, I want you to come home."

"And what am I going to do with my stallion?"

"If you come back, Sabbath will be welcome at the stables."

"No, he won't," Peter cut in. "When I said I'd never allow that beast on Sutherland soil, I meant it. If she insists on keeping that animal, the least she can do is behave respectfully and stop shacking up with this limping has-been."

A.J. gasped and watched as Devlin, who had been silent, closed the distance between himself and Peter. Her stepbrother's response was priceless. He looked like someone who'd stepped into the path of an avalanche.

"I'm going to do you a favor," Devlin growled, "and forget you ever said that." Turning to A.J. and her father, he continued with a disarming softness. "I think this argument is best left between family members. However astounding it is to witness the collective wisdom of the Sutherlands, I'd rather do something more constructive. Like watch paint dry."

He turned and began walking away.

A.J. immediately went after him, reaching out and taking his arm. "I'm sorry he's such a—"

Devlin carefully removed her hand. "I think you better settle this with your family first. Then we can deal with what's going on between you and me."

After he'd dissolved into the crowd, A.J. wheeled on her stepbrother.

"If I didn't think he'd give you a shiner that would clash with your Day-Glo tie, I'd demand you go and apologize."

"After the trouble he's caused, I wouldn't spare the breath."

"Trouble? That man has done everything to help me after my own family pushed me out the door, and you just had the good graces to insult his character as well as his physical condition."

Peter's hand slashed through the air with anger. "Spare me the Scarlett O'Hara, kindness-of-strangers drivel. Thanks to your antics, the Sutherland name is on everyone's lips and not in a good way. You're an embarrassment to the family, and if it weren't for the fact that your lunacy is making me look like a hero for kicking you out, I'd really be upset."

"First of all, it was Blanche DuBois who said that. And exactly what kind of trouble are we causing the stables?"

A.J.'s father jumped in. "Peter is just concerned that all the speculation could hurt business. People don't want to be associated with a farm that's considered controversial."

"I am *not* affiliated with Sutherland's anymore."

"But you're going to want to come back," Peter interjected, glancing over at Chester and Sabbath, who were still standing by the McCloud trailer. "How long are you going to be satisfied being with a boutique stable? How long until you want a new piece of equipment that costs more than most people's houses? What's going to happen when that trainer of yours can't cut the checks to keep you interested?"

"You bastard."

Garrett stepped between them. "Peter, why don't you head back to the car? I'll be there in a minute."

"Fine," he spat. "Just don't expect her to be reasonable. I don't have the patience to wait that long."

After Peter marched off, Garrett took her hands in his.

"Arlington, I know this is difficult for you and I'm sorry. But Peter has a good point."

"Peter's had a lot of good points lately, hasn't he?"

"I know he can go too far but so can you sometimes. I just want us together as a family. I want you to come home."

"I can't do that. Not now. Maybe not ever." Her father looked like his heart was breaking so A.J. squeezed his hands with as much reassurance as she could muster. "I can't go on living with my daddy forever. This break with the stables . . . I think it happened for a good reason and at the right time."

"I worry about you."

"I know. But I'm happy right now. I really am. I love that horse and I think I can make a difference with him. I'm anxious, scared and thrilled all at the same time. I'm alive. Even though I miss you, it feels good to be out on my own."

"Believe me, I'm grateful that you're fulfilled," he said carefully. "Still, I have to ask. Are the rumors true? About you and . . ."

A.J. shook her head, meeting him square in the eye.

He released his breath. "I didn't think so."

But he was lying. She could tell because the relief in his voice was fresh.

"Even if we were," she asked, "why would that be so wrong?"

"He's your trainer."

"So?"

"Well, he's not . . ."

"One of us? Are those the words you're looking for?"

"No, not at all. It's just that his background is very different from yours."

As much as she loved him, A.J. lost her patience.

"Look, I've got to get the stallion back to the stable. I need to get him ready for the trip."

"Arlington, please don't turn your back on your family."

"I don't feel like I'm the one doing that."

As she turned to go, he halted her with a request.

"I want you to come to my birthday celebration. It's in two weeks. It wouldn't be the same without you," he insisted.

She swallowed a wave of frustration. It was the last thing she wanted to do but how could she say no?

"All right."

"Thank you."

She went back to him and they hugged stiffly.

"I love you," he said to her. "Please remember that."

"It's hard sometimes. I feel like you don't understand me."

"But I will always try. You know that, don't you?"

A.J. looked deeply into his eyes. "Yes. Yes, I think I do."

With an awkward wave, she walked over to Chester.

"Where is he?"

The man shrugged. "Just disappeared into the crowd."

Unsettled, A.J. changed back into her barn clothes and helped Chester pack up. The two worked in silence until there was nothing left to hang, fold or tie down. When everything was arranged, she was stuck with nothing to occupy her while they waited for Devlin's return. She filled the free time composing an explanation and apology for the family dynamic he'd witnessed but it was far from a relaxing distraction. She'd have much preferred cleaning something but had the feeling Chester was going to scream if she reorganized the brushes in the grooming kit one more time.

A while later, Chester's stomach began to growl and she volunteered to stay behind while he went in search of food. After he wandered off, she sat down on the back lip of the trailer bumper, the metal cold through the seat of her jeans. Sabbath, still moored at the side of the ramp, came over to her, his muzzle soft against her skin as he breathed on her neck.

"You're an unreliable ally but I appreciate the concern." Slipping her arm under his neck, she gave him a stout pat. "And you're surprisingly sympathetic."

They huddled together, the sunlight of fall battling an early gust of winter wind and winning. Above, a wide, clear sky went on forever, the seamless expanse of space tinted a safe, reassuring blue.

She was worried what Devlin was thinking. About her family. About herself. Most of all, about the two of them.

And then there was that nonsense about a reporter. She groaned as she tried to imagine the kinds of lies the story might contain. The last thing she wanted was more attention on her work with the stallion and she knew Devlin hated publicity, particularly of the personal variety. And, being confronted with it for the first time herself, she couldn't say she cared for it, either.

Why was everything hitting at once? It seemed like events were conspiring to pull Devlin and her apart when all she wanted was for them to be closer. In fact, she realized with clarity, what she really wanted was for them to be lovers. And to hell with everything and everyone else.

When there was a shuffle of leaves created by footsteps instead of wind, she looked up to find Devlin standing in front of her.

"Hi," she said.

"Hello." He ran a hand down Sabbath's neck.

"So how was the paint?"

His look was confused.

"You know, the whole paint drying thing." She was shooting for levity and missed.

"Sorry about that crack."

"Well, considering how far out of line Peter was, I don't blame you."

He made a noncommittal reply.

"Devlin, I don't know anything about a picture. Do you?"

He shook his head. "Maybe the reporter was just fishing."

"Maybe."

There was a pause.

"We need to talk." His voice was low, serious.

Fear, cold and damp, settled between her shoulder blades at his tone. "About what?"

"Us. Our relationship."

"What about us?"

"I don't know if you should stay at the farmhouse."

"But why?"

"Your stepbrother's right. It's not professional."

"Don't tell me you take him seriously?"

"You can be a jackass and still have a good point."

Chester rounded the corner, munching on a chili dog the size of his head.

"Hey, ya guys need food? They got good dogs over there."

"That so?" Devlin replied easily while he started fishing around in his pockets.

For all the tension he showed, she thought, they could have just been talking about the weather. The look he gave her, however, said they'd finish the conversation later.

"Sure 'nuff." With a stretch of his jaws, Chester polished off the rest of his lunch. "But ya need two of 'em to really curb the hunger."

"I'd be careful," Devlin said, taking his keys out. "We're going to have to airlift you to a trauma center if you keep eating like this. One day you're going to explode from the extremes. Too regimented during the morning, a wild man after noon."

"Stomach a' steel an' the will to match," the man said, patting himself. "Could live on nails an' rubber bands if I had to."

"You may be already," Devlin muttered. "God only knows what they make those things out of."

After an awful ride home during which A.J. and Devlin sat in silence and Chester snored, the three worked together to unload the stallion and return the tack and supplies to their proper places. It was still midafternoon by the time Chester left the stables, and A.J. regarded the remaining daylight with dismay. She was anxious to talk to Devlin and get the conversation over with but scared he was going to make her leave.

Devlin had already returned to the farmhouse when A.J. started to clean her tack, and after she was done, she went in search of him. She was dreading the thought of having to stay somewhere else. The idea that she wouldn't have a ready excuse to sit down and have dinner across the table from him every night or see him in the morning over coffee made her ache. Even if she couldn't be with him, she needed to be around him.

As soon as A.J. put her hand on the front doorknob, he opened the door. His hair was still wet from the shower and he'd changed into a pair of black slacks and a black shirt. He looked dangerously handsome as he shrugged into a leather jacket.

"I'm going out," he told her.

"Will you be back for dinner?"

"I don't think so."

"I wanted to finish our conversation."

She watched him stiffen and knew he was feeling as conflicted as she was. It was obvious in his preoccupied expression and the way he wouldn't look her in the eye.

"A.J., I need some time to think. I want to do the right thing by you. I really do."

"And what's the right thing?"

"To stay away from you. To be your teacher and your trainer and your friend. To support you unconditionally as you reach for your goal."

"But you want me to go."

His eyes became fierce. "Having you leave is the last thing I want. All I want is you."

He closed the distance between them and pulled her against him. She could feel his body, hot and throbbing, and his eyes roamed over her with a hunger she found thrilling.

"I can't get you out of my thoughts," he said. "I'm consumed by the need to be with you. I *feel* you in my dreams

and wake up aching when you're not there. I don't want you
to go. I want you in my bed. I want to be in you."

"So take me."

Their lips met in a blaze of passion and she welcomed
the invasion of his tongue, matching his urgency with her
own. His mouth moved hungrily over hers, demanding what
she was all too ready to give him, and in response, she
pressed her body against his, her breasts straining for his
touch, her hips welcoming the rigid length of his need.
Underneath her hands, his chest was a solid wall that
housed a pounding heart and she thrilled at the knowledge
she was the object of his passion. As they kept kissing, she
was aching, aching at her very core, to have the ultimate
union with him. He was a fever in her blood, the sole cause
and only relief for her longing.

"I want you more than I've ever wanted a woman before," he moaned against her mouth. "More than I've
wanted anything."

His kisses rained down on the skin of her neck and she
gripped his shoulders, scratching into the leather of his
jacket. She wanted him to go further, to rip off her clothes
and press her down onto the couch. She wanted him naked
against her skin, thrusting deep inside her and making her
feel the burning pleasure until she screamed his name.

But then he slowed down and soon he was pulling away.
With a tender motion, he stroked her cheek. His hand was
shaking.

"This is dangerous," he said softly. "This heat between
us . . . I can't be rational when I'm so attracted to you."

"I don't want you to be rational."

"You're going to need me to be. Sometime, in the course
of getting to the Qualifier or when you're in the throes of it,
you're going to need me to be there for you in a way that's
strictly professional. The problem is, I can't think clearly
because I'm consumed by the need to have you."

"We can make it work."

"No, we can't."

"Are you saying it's either you or the Qualifier? Either
we live apart or you won't train me?"

To Devlin, her eyes were pools of need and her body an

aching torment for him, everything he wanted but was determined to deny himself. He could feel her breasts pressing against his chest, her hips as they fit into his, the passion that swirled in the air between them. His will, slipping away again, told him to put his mouth down on hers. He wanted more of her honey, more of that intoxication that was for him better than any drink.

Deliberately, painfully, he stepped back from her.

"I don't think I can hold back anymore. I can't have you in this house and walk into the bathroom after you've bathed and smell that lavender in the mist. I can't toss and turn in my bed alone, wanting you. I can't keep going like this and I hate myself for it." He zipped up his jacket with a sharp, frustrated movement. "What I'm saying is that I can be your lover or your trainer. And I need you to choose."

Devlin looked at her for a moment, tracing over the lines of her face with eyes that were conflicted and sad. Then he stepped out of the house and went down to his truck. She watched him get in and drive down the dirt lane until he disappeared into the curve of the woods.

It was a long time before A.J. could shut the door. She was willing him to come back and take her into his arms and tell her she didn't have to pick between her passion for him and her drive to compete. But she knew he wouldn't.

With a heavy heart, she put her jacket on its lonely peg and was careful not to look at the empty space where Devlin's usually hung. Wandering around in a daze, unable to confront the decision she was being forced to consider, she eventually went into the kitchen to lose herself in cooking. It was the only thing she could think of doing in a house that had no TV, no magazines, and books only on carpentry and baseball.

She decided to make lasagna, figuring it would be straightforward. With no cookbooks to consult, she knew it was best to keep it simple. After all, how hard could it be to layer noodles and sauce in a pan and throw it in the oven?

It was a prophetic thought. Between her lack of know-how and a preoccupied mind, she turned the kitchen into a combat zone in less than an hour. She burned the canned

sauce while heating it up and the noodles congealed into
something close to Spackle when she forgot to take them
out on time. After she started cramming the mess into a
pan, she discovered there was no mozzarella. With dubious
genius, she substituted sour cream, clumping it on the top
in big scoops.

Looking at the finished product, she almost threw it out
but she'd come too far to back down and had hopes that
something magical would happen in the oven. Heat didn't
improve the situation. When smoke came pouring out, on
account of her having turned the knob to *broil* instead of
bake, she took out the monster and recognized it for the
nightmare it was.

She was Dr. Frankenstein, maker of horrors, A.J. thought,
looking at the pan. But at least it had killed an hour.

After laying the hideous creation to rest in the compost
heap out back, she returned to the kitchen and surveyed
the tornado path of her efforts. Cleanup was going to be an
involved project. While A.J. was wiping off sauce from the
refrigerator, and wondering how she had managed to get it
on its far side, she realized how much she was used to having Devlin around. The house seemed more than empty
without him.

How could she be so attracted to the one person in her
life who was off-limits?

He was an intoxicating man physically but there was
more to it than that. During the past two weeks, she'd felt
supported in a way she'd never been before. Always fiercely
independent, she was someone who didn't share her inner
fears easily, and yet, confronted with Devlin's strength,
she'd found a way to be vulnerable. And he offered her a
wealth of comfort. There seemed to be no end to what he
would do for her.

With their common goal of getting her to the Qualifier
on the stallion and the passion they had for each other, they
connected in every way possible: professionally, physically,
emotionally. It made sense.

Unlike her attempts at Italian cooking.

Getting down on her knees, A.J. began to corral the basil
she'd spilled under the table onto a piece of scrap paper.

Except now she had to pick.

As a trainer, Devlin was superlative. Patient, exacting when he had to be, constantly supportive, an expert. As a lover? Well, she hadn't had the full experience but she imagined he'd be unlike any man on the planet. His touch over her skin, the way he moved against her, those strong arms . . . Everything pointed at pure, unadulterated bliss.

She went to get off the floor and smacked her head into the table.

Rubbing the sore spot as she gingerly got to her feet, she was grateful for the pain in a ridiculous way. It gave her something else to think about for a moment.

By the time A.J. finished cleaning up, the kitchen was sparkling and the smell of burned tomatoes and sour cream had been aired out of the house. Satisfied, she sat down at the table and rested her chin on her hands. Even if she was still a mess, at least something had been cleaned up.

After sitting for a while, she realized she was hungry but uninspired so she ended up having canned soup for dinner. Remembering what she'd done to the tomato sauce, she put on the stove timer while heating it up. Having already been through one olfactory nightmare, she didn't want to know what toasted chicken and rice smelled like.

While she was eating, every sound, every murmur from the house, had her looking to the door, wondering if it was Devlin getting home. Hope and anxiety would spike in a rush and then abate, only to send her flying again when she heard another noise. It was an exhausting ride because the farmstead, like an old man with rickets, had a lot of creaks, and pretty soon she decided she knew why dogs slept all the time. Sentry duty was tougher than it looked.

As things got dark outside, A.J. settled on the couch, curling her legs up under her and pulling a throw blanket across her knees. She was looking out over the moon-drenched landscape, tracing the rails of the paddocks and the ring with restless eyes, when she made up her mind.

She couldn't choose. More to the point, she decided she wouldn't choose between the lover she wanted and the trainer she needed. They would make it work and that was that. And as for Devlin's concerns, she would just explain to him how important he was on all the different levels he touched her life. She would make him understand. She just had to. And surely he'd appreciate her reasoning. After all, if she was picking anything, she was picking him. All of him.

Relieved, she fell asleep, and when she woke up, he was standing over her.

"What time is it?" she asked, glad he was home.

"Late."

A.J. sat up, pushing her hair back from her face.

Against Devlin's better judgment, he sat on the couch next to her. He wanted to know what she'd decided before he got too close. If she picked him as a trainer, he'd have to leave the room quickly before he did something they'd both regret.

Before he could ask for her answer, she said sleepily, "I've made up my mind. I want you. I need you. That's all I know."

His eyes darkened with need.

"Kiss me," she said.

8

"I'VE WANTED this so badly," he said, just before they kissed.

Devlin swallowed her sigh as their mouths came together. When he became breathless, he broke the commandment of her lips and buried his face in her neck as he sought to recover.

He needed more, so much more. Licking the outline of her lips, because he couldn't get enough of the taste of her, he pulled back and shed his coat, flinging it to the ground. As it flew away, the jacket took with it the wall of self-control he'd built and tried to sustain over the past weeks. Crumbling like sand, its absence left him naked and at the mercy of his passions and, as he felt her pull him down on the couch against her, he shuddered with a need so great he thought he was going to be lost.

A.J. was also overwhelmed with anticipation. Running her hands over his shoulders and to the front of his shirt, she sought the buttons that were keeping his skin from her touch. She knew there was no turning back and didn't care about anything except the stiff anticipation of his body and the way his hands felt traveling over her skin. Her world receded until her only reality was the weight of him over her, the delicious slide of his lips across her collarbone, his teeth as he nipped at her earlobe. Urgently, her hands fumbled with his shirt, ripping cloth as she struggled to get to the skin of his back. Her voice called his name hoarsely.

She watched as Devlin tore the shirt from his body and

then wrenched up her own. She felt cool air tickling her skin and helped him free it, letting it fall into the heap that was growing as more of their clothes were tossed aside. She felt wanton and liberated, revealed not exposed, and all she wanted was to feel him seeking the heat at her core with the shaft that throbbed at his hips.

When her breasts were bare to his eyes, Devlin sucked in his breath. She was resplendent with her hair spilling over her satin skin, her lips full and bloodred from his kisses, the salmon pink tips of her nipples peaked with invitation. With delicious anticipation, he brought his mouth to her breast, tugging at the hard marble nub until she writhed under him. Slowly, he moved his hands down her taut stomach and began to unzip her jeans. Fevered though he was, he didn't want to rush her, but when she lifted her hips and made it easier for him to free her, he clenched his jaw. With hands that trembled, he slid the pants down over her creamy thighs and then he was stroking her delicate ankles, learning the strength of her calves and finding the sensitive area behind her knees.

A.J. sought him out, bringing his lips up to hers and feeling his tight length over her. She struggled with the waistband of his slacks and he pulled back, swiftly peeling them off before returning to her in a rush.

"Devlin," A.J. moaned. "Devlin?"

He made a noise that was an aching groan punctuated by a question mark. It was the best he could do.

"Devlin." She was struggling to make her mouth work. "You should know I . . ."

Her voice trailed off as he slid his hands across the top of her panties.

"It's been . . ." A.J. bit her lip as she felt him stroke over the flimsy cotton.

"Are you okay?" He saw passion and torment in her eyes. "Do you want to stop?"

Devlin prayed she wouldn't say yes.

"I don't know how to tell you this," she murmured awkwardly.

His body throbbing and aching, vision blinded by passion, he asked in a hoarse voice, "What is it?"

"I haven't done . . . this"—she hiccuped over the noun like a broken record—"in a long time."

The very malest part of him was thrilled. "We don't have to do anything that makes you feel uncomfortable."

"I want you," she said, putting her lips to his. "I want to do this."

As Devlin absorbed her response, A.J. felt tremors pound through his body. It gave her a sense of power, and with it, she went about learning the hard contours of his chest and belly, using her hands and her mouth. He thrashed under her, calling out in a desperation that made her go even further. She tormented him and teased him, bringing him to the brink but no further, until he let out a growl and rolled over onto her.

He ripped her thin panties in haste and settled himself over her. Their eyes met and he slowly slid into her body. It was paradise. In that first instant, as their hearts beat together and their bodies and breath mingled, they both knew they would never be the same again.

Starting slowly, and growing with urgency, he moved within her. They held each other tightly against the impending release, which built and built until they thought they could stand it no longer. Finally, with rough cries, and heaving breaths, their bodies climaxed in a burst of ecstasy.

Much later, after he noticed the chill in the air and covered them with the throw blanket to keep her warm, Devlin found himself in awe. Now that they'd been together once, he couldn't wait to be inside of her again. She was the kind of lover he'd been looking for without knowing he was on a quest. Gifting herself with honesty and abandonment, she had taken pleasure from him and given it back to him without any artifice. With her, he'd known true intimacy for the first time.

A.J. stirred in his arms and his breath caught as her eyes opened. Her expression was that of a cat in sunshine. Satisfied, glowing, content. He'd do anything to keep her looking like that.

Devlin kissed her softly.

"How do you feel?" he asked.

"Wonderful." She ran a hand across his chest as he laughed huskily, thrilled.

"Devlin?"

"Yeah?"

"I didn't know it could be like that."

"Neither did I."

"And I'm glad I'm not leaving this house. Leaving you."

"Me, too. I never wanted you to go."

She sighed, relieved that everything was going to be fine and nothing would change. Except for the nights. And they were only going to get better.

Devlin felt her relax against him and was likewise glad the decision had been made. Now they could move forward and see where all the passion and emotion would take them. First thing in the morning, he'd start looking for another trainer. Someone close by so she wouldn't have to drive far. Someone who was good and would take care of her in the ring.

In the tight cradle of the couch, they fell asleep against each other with just the blanket to keep them warm. When dawn tripped over the mountain ridge, taking a tumble and spilling its light across the hills and sky, Devlin woke up and reached for A.J.'s mouth. Wordlessly, she rolled under him and he entered her body with a powerful surge. When they climaxed together, her name was a moan that came from the deepest part of him.

As they floated back down to earth, Devlin knew they had to get off the couch and put some clothes on before Chester came through the front door. Turning to look into A.J.'s face, he was struck again by her loveliness. Never had morning light been quite so tender, or the quiet of dawn seem so gentle, than as his eyes caressed her. As she looked back at him, there was shy inquiry in her expression that was spiked with remembered ecstasy. He felt light-headed.

"I feel so damn lucky that I met you. And that this happened," he said. Her smile was full of happiness and he felt his heart grow light as he told himself everything was going to be okay. "I guess I should head upstairs before Chester comes through the door."

"You get the first shower."

"I'd rather share it with you."

"You know what they say: Save water. Shower with a friend."

"You're a hell of a lot more than a friend," he replied, taking her mouth. His kiss was fevered, despite the fact that they had just made love. When they took a break so they could breathe, he said, "I better go."

Quickly, before they became lost in each other again, he got up off the couch. Before he left, he was careful to tuck the blanket around her so she wouldn't be cold.

A.J. watched him move around and pick up his clothes, delighted with the chance to see his body in the light. With all that they had shared of themselves, physical beauty seemed trivial and yet she was thrilled by his strong arms and flat, muscled belly. It was only when she saw the scars on his bad leg that she felt bad. The crisscrossing disfigurements, a map of where the limb had been rebuilt, still looked fresh and angry. She wanted to reach out and smooth the knotted lines with her fingers, to bear some of his loss for him.

After blowing her a kiss, Devlin went up the stairs. When she rolled over onto her back, she was smiling.

Nothin' like a little lovin' to perk a girl up, she thought, feeling a bulge under her back and pulling out her T-shirt. She shrugged it over her head and looked down at the wrinkles, a road map pressed into the cotton by the weight of their bodies.

By the time Devlin came back downstairs, A.J. had gotten up and was folding their blanket. He leaned against the wall.

"What are you looking at?" she asked playfully.

"I'm trying to imagine you in a little French maid's outfit. It's quite a picture, let me tell you." His eyes were soft and warm.

"I hate to ruin the fantasy, but I'm not the frilly type. Petticoats make me itchy."

He walked over to her, took her into his arms. "Just as well. I think you're more beautiful like this."

"With my hair a mess, wearing a wrinkled shirt?"

"You're right. I'd prefer you totally naked."

His hands gripped her hips and pulled them into him. She could feel him harden the instant their bodies came into contact.

The footsteps coming up the flagstone told them Chester had arrived, and they parted just as he burst through the door. He had the newspaper under his arm and his hangdog face was cheery.

"I won twenty-seven fifty last night at the bingo parlor!"

"That's quite a haul, old man," Devlin said smoothly.

His eyes were on A.J. as she bent down and picked up her toiletry bag. He couldn't wait until the day was over and they could be alone again. He was also feeling good about the prospects for his replacement. Up in the shower, he'd reviewed the trainers and stables he respected and there were at least two viable candidates he wanted to invite over to meet with A.J. He was certain they could find her another trainer soon and that her work with the stallion wouldn't be interrupted significantly.

"So's breakfast ready yet?" Chester asked.

"It will be when we make it."

As the two headed into the kitchen, Devlin sent her a wink over his shoulder and A.J. blushed. By the time she came back down, they were at the table. Chester, between spoonfuls of cereal, was leafing through the paper.

"Well, will ya get a load a' this."

With a ruffle and a snap, he folded the newspaper in half and pushed it across to Devlin. A.J. glanced over at it.

Taking up almost the full page was a picture of the two of them together, taken just before she went into the ring the day before. Devlin's hand was on her cheek and their eyes were locked. She remembered the moment vividly, and, looking at the photograph, she saw the bond between them was as powerful as it was obvious.

"Oh, God," she groaned.

The headline read SUTHERLAND BEAUTY TAKES UP WITH FALLEN CHAMPION. The article that followed was a combination of speculation, rumor and innuendo. Quotes from various competitors were used to inflame her purchase of the stallion, her split with her family and their relationship.

"What are we going to do?" she wondered aloud.

Devlin got to his feet, his chair scraping across the floor.

"I wouldn't worry too much about it," he said darkly. "As soon as you and the stallion leave here, it'll all die down and the reporter will look ridiculous for making a big deal out of nothing. We'll just put up with it until the end of the week."

"End of the week?"

"I think I can have a couple of trainers come by tomorrow. We can pick the one who works best and transport the stallion to his new stable ASAP."

A.J.'s voice cut through the kitchen. "I already have a trainer."

Devlin frowned.

Chester said, "I better get on down to the barn."

Neither of them noticed as the man left and took his breakfast bowl with him.

"A.J., I thought we agreed on this."

"I told you last night. I want you. I need you."

"And you agreed to choose."

"I did. I need all of you."

He started shaking his head. "Wait a minute. I was very clear about what I wanted."

"So was I."

"I assumed we made love last night because you were going to go with another trainer."

"And I told you I wasn't."

"No, you didn't."

"Yes, I did."

They squared off across the table.

"I don't recall hearing those precise words come out of your mouth."

Her eyes implored him. "Look, we can make it work. We can do both."

Devlin cursed, wrenched his hands through his hair in frustration. "I never would have been with you if I'd known this was what you were thinking."

His words and the regret in his voice brought tears to her eyes.

"A.J., for God's sake, please don't cry. I'm sorry it came

out like that." He went to her and tried to hug her but she pushed him away.

"So am I. I'm sorry you have so little faith in us."

"This isn't just about us." He picked up the paper, only to toss it aside with contempt. "Everyone's going to read this crap."

"Why do you care so much about what some idiot prints in the newspaper?"

"You've got no idea what it's like to be the topic of conversation. I've spent the past year being whispered about and stared at. Any room I walk into, the murmuring starts up. And my notoriety isn't even prurient. I fell off a goddamn horse. They'll have you in bed with any man you talk to or look at for the rest of your career."

"Well, thanks for the heads-up," she said, wiping away angry tears, "but I'm not rearranging my life just because someone else doesn't like the way it looks from the outside."

"You want to be like Philippe Marceau? He's the laughingstock of the circuit because he's been with so many people. As a woman, it's going to be worse. They'll rip you up and use the pieces as fertilizer."

"Marceau is a topic of conversation because he's a conceited blowhard."

"And you've got your own liabilities."

"What? People know I can't do long division in my head? My closet life as a comic-book addict suddenly comes out?"

"There may be a lot of money in the horse business but not a lot of folks have their *daddy* build them a stable compound. Your stepbrother looks like he belongs on the cover of *GQ* and his attitude stinks. You tool around in a convertible that costs more than most people's mortgages and—"

"So I can't be with the man I want and the trainer I need because Peter's into fashion and my father went over the top for my birthday? That's ludicrous."

"I'm just telling you what people will say."

"And I refuse to buy into the talk."

"But that's my point. They're already saying you're trying to buy your way to the top. You want them to add you're sleeping your way up, too?"

His frank challenge slapped the fight right out of her.

"Listen," Devlin said more quietly, "I've got to tell you like it is. The higher the profile you have, the more you serve as target practice. Who your family is and buying that stallion aren't exactly making you blend in with the crowd. Sleeping with your trainer isn't going to help."

He approached her again, and this time she let him put an arm around her.

"A.J., competing at the highest level is tough. Don't add to the burdens."

"Are you sure that's the only reason you want me to go?" she asked.

"I don't want you to go. That's the whole point of getting someone else to train you. Someone who can be objective."

"But I don't want someone else!" She pulled away. "And I don't need you to be objective. I want you to be passionate about what we're trying to accomplish with Sabbath and I think you are. I can see it in your eyes when we work together. We're a terrific team. You know that."

"A.J., you need to take the stallion somewhere else."

"I can't believe you're throwing us out."

"I'm not throwing you out."

She didn't hear him as she paced around the room. "First Peter, now you. I expected it from him. Coming from you, it's a surprise. I thought I meant more to you."

"Do you remember what it felt like when I was inside you?"

The low words brought her to a halt as a flush bloomed in her body. She didn't have to answer him. As she turned around, her expression told him all he needed to know.

"Do you honestly think we're going to be able to deny ourselves now that we know what it's like? I don't know about you, but I doubt I'm that strong."

A.J. refused to answer him because she knew he was right. There was no way they could go back.

But because of their predicament, she glared at him. "Right now, McCloud, I'm not sure I can be with you at all. I'm pretty damn close to hating you."

"Hatred is the flip side of love."

"Then I must be falling hard because all I want to do is scream at you right now."

"You've got to understand, I'm only doing this because I want to give us a chance. We have something really rare here. I just don't want to lose it."

A frustrated breath escaped her. "Why can't we at least try?"

"A.J., be reasonable—"

"You sound like my father. *Be sensible. Be serious.* Well, I think I am. You've spent almost a month with Sabbath and me and look at how far we've come. You know my riding style. You know the stallion's faults and strengths. You're sure as hell the best damn trainer I've ever had. That horse and I have a shot at the big time but we can't go it alone. And we can't go it without you."

He looked away.

"Devlin, admit it. You want to train us as much as I want you to. You know you're making a difference and you like being back in competition. After a year on the sidelines, you're feeling that excitement again. I've seen it on your face. Can you really walk away from that? What are you going to feel like at the rail while someone else is in the ring with Sabbath and me?"

She watched his face closely. On the surface he seemed composed but she'd learned to read him well.

"Not a great position to be in, is it?" she prompted. "Having to choose between us and the work?"

A.J. fell silent as he mulled their situation over.

Devlin was caught and he knew it. He'd focused only on getting another trainer to work with the stallion. Taking himself out of the picture hadn't seemed like a big deal, but then, he'd never really considered what it would be like watching someone else put A.J. and Sabbath through their workouts. Would someone else recognize when they needed a break? When they needed to be pushed? Would they understand how A.J. needed to talk through a course sometimes three or four times until she was completely comfortable with where she needed to be?

Would someone else care as much as he did?

And, even assuming he wouldn't be at his most objective, was there anyone else who could do as good a job with them as he could?

When his eyes shifted back to hers, he realized there wasn't anyone else he could trust to take care of them.

Devlin swore out loud. When it didn't make him feel much better, he tried it again.

"I'd say that just about sums it up," A.J. said, feeling a little better. Given his sour expression and raunchy vocabulary, she could tell he was coming around. Now was the time to push.

"I'll tell you what," she said softly. "We'll try it for a week or so. See how we both feel. If we think it's not working, we can do it your way."

She sidled up to him, relieved when he let her put her arms around his waist.

Devlin snorted. "Are you trying to charm me with your feminine wiles?"

"If it'll get me what I want, absolutely."

He wrapped his arms around her. "This isn't a good idea."

"How do you know? There've been plenty of people who have mixed business and pleasure and had it work out."

"Yeah, like who?"

"George Burns and Gracie Allen. The Captain and Tennille."

"How about a pair from this century?"

"Bill and Hillary."

"I don't know that I'd count them necessarily."

She reached up and touched his face tenderly. "This is going to work out. You'll see."

"I just don't want to lose you," he told her.

Despite the stress of the argument, they were able to go down to the stables with a united front. Devlin wasn't completely comfortable with their decision but he wasn't going to back out. If it became apparent he couldn't train them, he had to have faith he'd be able to let them go to someone else and that she'd have the sense to move on to another coach.

The day's work went predictably, with small steps toward improvement. Sabbath was feeling energetic, so the session went longer than usual and both A.J. and Devlin were pretty pleased with the results. Afterward, she and Chester went through their ritual of putting Sabbath down and feeding him while Devlin reviewed his notes and planned the next day's jump course. It was a day like any other except the turmoil over breakfast lingered.

A.J. was leaning against Sabbath's stall, and watching his muzzle search out the last of the sweet feed in his bucket, when she felt exhaustion come over her. She decided the last twenty-four hours had been like drinking from a glass you expected to be full of water but turned out to be holding vodka. A big ol' burning surprise.

Although she was encouraged by Devlin's agreement to continue training her, she'd experienced firsthand one of his concerns. In the ring, she felt the heat between them flare every time he looked at her. Every glance between them was a history book of images to relish. A promise of what lay ahead as soon as they were alone together. Questions asked and answered without words. And the powerful undercurrents made the unremarkable seem sublime, took simple nods and turned them into vows, elevated a conversation about striding counts to a plane it had never been on before.

It was heady. And dangerously distracting.

She heard Devlin approaching as if she'd called him.

"I'm going to go start dinner," he said, coming in close.

"I'll be up after I finish with the tack."

They fell silent and she thought he was going to touch her, but then he gave her a smile that knocked her socks off.

It was almost as good as a kiss, she decided, as he walked away.

Going into the cramped confines of the tack room, A.J. took out a chamois rag that had seen good use and a bottle of Murphy's Oil Soap. As soon as she wet the cloth, the familiar lemon smell rose to greet her like a good host and she took a deep breath. Rubbing her saddle in the circular motions she'd used since she was nine, her mind wandered off into hazardous territory.

What did their future hold? Was this just an affair? Or the beginning of something that meant so much more?

Head bent and eyes too rapt for the simple task, she didn't know Chester had paused in the doorway until he cleared his throat. She looked up and was struck by his appearance. With a pitchfork in one hand and his overalls hanging like curtains on his whip-thin frame, he was right out of *American Gothic*. In that moment, standing in the late-afternoon sun, he was one pinpoint along a long chronology of farmers and laborers, a tradition worthy of pride.

He was timeless, she thought, just like the smell of lemon and leather in the room.

"Ya want to get the blacksmith here this week?" he asked.

A.J. wiped a lock of hair away with the back of her sponge hand. Water and soap ran down into her sleeve and she smothered a curse.

"I think we better. That right front shoe just won't stay tight."

"With it comin' loose all the time, a body's gotta wonder. I don't know what goes on here after dark, but I think that horse has designs on bein' the next Fred Astaire. At night, he's gotta be tap dancin' in the aisles, or something worse."

"Jazz?" A.J. grinned.

"Vegas kick line."

She laughed. "More likely his hooves are soft."

"Believe what ya have to, but afore ya know it, he could be jumpin' in high heels an' a thong."

A.J. smiled at the image, wiped off the last of the soap from her saddle and stood up.

"Let's see if that poor man can get here the beginning of next week," she said, referring to the blacksmith. "I'm hoping if we give him some notice, he'll like us more. Probably use time to gird himself for the experience."

"Good call. I imagine he'll need to order appropriate equipment."

"Better nails?"

"Hockey pads," Chester said as he turned to go.

A.J.'s laughter rang out. "Hey, how long have I got before dinner?"

He checked his watch.

" 'Bout twenty minutes. An' speaking of time," he said,

"I'm glad you an' Devlin finally got off your duffs. You two've been draggin' your feet like a couple a' wallflowers waitin' for the right song."

The rag hit the floor along with her composure. "What?"

"Life's too short to not be where you should. You two are both missin' a piece without the other."

Oh, my God, she thought, I've got a scarlet *A* on my forehead.

Without realizing it, she rubbed the place over her eyebrows.

"I don't know what you—"

"There's nothing wrong with it. Devlin's a good man and you're good for him. Now, about that blacksmith—ya think Tuesday's okay?"

After Chester left, A.J. plopped down on a box of leg wraps. Was it that obvious? She thought they'd been discreet all day long.

Damn these horse-sense types, she thought. You can't have a steamy affair around them in peace.

Stomach clenched in a knot, she felt like her life was spiraling out of control. Between buying the horse, the split with her family, facing the Qualifier and falling for Devlin, it seemed as if she'd thrown herself into a paint mixer. Even worse, she had the notion that eyes were watching, everywhere.

She stood up, feeling trapped, and raised her voice. "Are you finished with me or is there anything else I need to worry about right now?"

Then she knocked the bottle of saddle soap over and it spilled into her barn boots.

Ah, yes, she thought. Now I need dry socks.

"Ask, and ye shall receive," she muttered as she wiped up the mess.

When A.J. went back to the house, a soggy protest sounded out every time she put her right foot down. It was like being trailed by a whoopee cushion. As soon as she came in from the gathering cold, she shrugged off her coat and leaned against the door, removing the offending shoe and sock. When she glanced up, Devlin was standing in the doorway of the kitchen.

And looking at her like she was his favorite entree.

Warming under the glow in his eyes, she decided she could get used to the expression.

Devlin took a step forward just as Chester leaned in from the kitchen and started a conversation. "We're having the behemoth shod on Tuesday. . . ."

The man continued talking even though his audience was far from captivated. With the reluctance of two people getting up from a good meal before it's done, Devlin and A.J. stoked the fire between them for later.

"We'll finish this soon," he whispered before going into the kitchen.

With a blinding smile of anticipation, A.J. went upstairs to change.

As she stood in front of the bathroom mirror, brushing out her hair, she couldn't help noticing the change in her reflection. There was a sparkle of excitement in her eyes, like she had a delicious secret, and a glow on her cheeks that wasn't just windburn. Even to her jaundiced eye, she looked radiant.

Who needed to waste time with facials and makeovers when you could toss a little passion and chaos into your life and get the same effect?

After she washed up and changed her clothes, A.J. hit the stairs with far more enthusiasm than the mild hunger in her stomach justified. Following the down-home smell of meat loaf into the kitchen, she grinned as she saw Devlin bending over the stove and pumping a masher over a pot of potatoes like a jackhammer.

He looked up the instant she came through the door. "Almost ready. You want to ride shotgun on Chester's salad?"

"Sure," she said, pushing aside unexpected shyness.

Hearing Chester grunt in frustration, she went over to the other man, who wasn't having a lot of luck with a pile of fresh greens and vegetables. Wielding a knife with all the finesse of a backhoe trying to put pansies into the ground, he'd made a mess. Huge chunks of red peppers had fallen victim to his hacking and a misbegotten cucumber looked like it'd been mauled by a dog.

"How you doing there, chef?"

"Damn vegetables," he said while almost slicing off his finger. "Who the hell needs roughage anyway? Do I look like a damn rabbit?"

"No, you look like a madman. And I think the last thing we need in your hand is a knife," she said, nudging him aside.

"Ah, c'mon, now," Chester grumbled good-naturedly. "I'm a pussycat."

"Tell that to this pepper," A.J. said, picking up the gnarled carcass. "It looks like it's been in an accident."

Before long, they were all sitting down at the table. The food was good but A.J. didn't really taste it. She was too preoccupied with what awaited on the other side of the meal and Devlin's eyes flashing across the table egged on her impatience, making her wish dinner was over before it started.

Seemingly oblivious of the undercurrents around him, Chester prattled along, keeping up the conversation by himself. When he wasn't talking, he was lingering over each mouthful, pausing to savor his meal in a way his two companions had never seen him do before.

By the time the man cleared his plate, after his third helping, he thought the other two were so itchy they looked like a pair of kids in church. A.J. was pushing a bit of meat loaf around her plate like it was a soccer ball, and Devlin was stacking and unstacking the salt and pepper shakers with an urgency Chester found highly amusing.

The groom smiled broadly, an expression they both missed.

"That was a good meal," he said, leaning back in his chair and rubbing his meager stomach, satisfied with the angst he was stirring up.

"Yes, it was," Devlin blurted, getting to his feet like there was something on fire in the oven. A.J. leapt out of her chair, picking up plates from the table in a frenzy.

"What, no dessert?" Chester asked.

"Here," Devlin said, wheeling around and opening the freezer door. He tossed an ice-cream sandwich across the room with an air of desperation.

"Maybe I'll just help with the cleanup," the groom drawled while he unwrapped the paper carefully.

"Wouldn't hear of it," Devlin told him.

"You're a guest," A.J. said, picking up Chester's plate.

"So are you," the man quipped. After he polished off the dessert, he began folding his napkin with the precision of an engineer. "I should probably pitch in somehow—"

"No!" they both said, freezing over the sink.

Before the chorus of denials continued into another refrain, Chester laughed out loud. When his jacket materialized in front of him and he was bid a sturdy good night, he felt like he'd been bootlicked through a doggie door, but didn't mind. He'd had enough fun at their expense for one night.

As the man stepped out into the cold air, he paused to zip up his jacket. When he turned around and glanced back at the house, he saw through the window that Devlin and A.J. were entwined in an embrace, oblivious of the world.

His smile as he turned away was one of approval. Devlin was looking more and more like his old self. And that girl, well, she was pretty as a picture and had the stuffing to take him on. It was a good match, he decided.

Betcha those dishes won't be done till the morrow, he thought.

9

It was a week later that A.J. rolled over in Devlin's bed and realized she was in love with him. Coming out of a wistful dream, something about riding Sabbath through Virginia's best hunt country, she felt very male arms wrapped around her and the cushion of a sturdy chest against her back. She turned over slowly, careful not to wake him.

In the gray light of the early-morning hour, his face was a study in strong shadows, from the hollows in his cheeks and the deep sockets of his eyes to the arching iron of his jaw. He was beautiful, a sublime model of masculine form, a living, breathing dream.

And with the deepest, most feminine part of herself, she knew he was hers. Just as she was his. Their hearts and minds had come together. They'd become so close, she wasn't sure where he left off and she took over and she didn't care about her lost individuality. She was half of herself without him, more than her whole with him.

A.J. put her lips against his throat, over the thick vein that pounded with the beat of his heart. Against his surging blood, she whispered, "I love you."

It was the first time she'd ever said the words to a man.

This realization made the statement seem even more powerful.

When it came to men, she'd never given herself easily. There had been a few boyfriends in college, but she'd been so focused on riding, the relationships had been brief and casual. The trend had continued as she'd turned professional. Before Devlin, men had always seemed an unnecessary complication in a life long on challenges and squat on time. But he was different. Her heart told her so.

Given her lack of experience with romance, she found the confidence with which she could say, "I love you," surprising. In previous relationships, she'd never been able to return the sentiment. She hadn't been sure what love was, only that she didn't feel it. Now it was clear. What else was so thrilling, so frightening, so intoxicating, so precious, so overwhelming, as love?

Part of her wanted to nudge Devlin awake and break the news but she held back. She was assuming he felt the same way but she wasn't sure. She was ready to make a commitment to him, to their future together as life partners and professional allies, but her newfound love for him made her vulnerable. She wanted him to make the declaration out loud first.

A.J. stretched, feeling her legs slide against Devlin's. He groaned in his sleep and gathered her even closer to him, tucking her into his side. As his breathing returned to the soft, regular rhythm of deep sleep, she found herself smiling, despite her heavy thoughts. There were so many benefits to being with him. Aside from their sensual exploits in the night, sleeping in a real bed again was another bonus. She hadn't quite lost the appreciation of having some space to move around in at night, even though Devlin tended to take up more than his fair share of the bed. The couch had been good enough for a short stay but there was real luxury in being able to stretch out without running the risk of rolling onto the carpet and winding up under a coffee table.

Her smile didn't linger. With a painful lurch, her thoughts drifted to her father. His birthday was the following weekend. She was dreading the idea of going and wished she could bring Devlin with her.

He began kissing her neck. "What are you stewing about?"

"How did you know?"

"I'm psychic."

"Really?"

"Don't tell anyone, but I moonlight as a fortune-teller."

"So where's your crystal ball?"

"Don't need one. They've been replaced by a Web site with links to the other side."

She laughed. "I guess the Internet's everywhere."

"Well, it was fine until Gates came in. Now there's only one server you can channel Elvis on and a single search engine to find people's past lives and dead relatives."

When her giggles subsided, he asked again what was on her mind.

"What if I said I was just relishing the morning light?"

"You'd be lying."

"What would you say if I asked you to go to my father's birthday party next weekend? I know it's going to be torture but I'd really like you to come with me. I need your support."

He tilted his head down. "Then I can't say no, can I?"

His smile was slow and tinted with passion, but when he went to kiss her, she stopped him with a hand on his chest.

"Devlin, I need to know. Are you okay with this?"

"Sure. If it's important to you for us to go, then of course we will."

"No . . . I meant us."

So much for waiting, she thought.

Devlin moved his hips against her pelvis. "I'm a little more than just okay with you. Fantastic. Delirious. Desperate. I think those are a little more apt."

"I mean about continuing with our training."

He took a deep breath. "I think we're working together well. We're making progress. What do you think?"

"I wasn't the one who had a problem with it."

His words became slow, deliberate. "From an objective point of view, I still believe it's just not smart. But I can't give you up and I don't want anyone else training you, so I think we're stuck with each other."

A.J. smiled and kissed his lips. "I just knew you'd come around to my way."

As his tongue slipped inside her mouth, she decided they could talk more about their relationship later. Now was a time for making love. And then there was breakfast and training and another meal or two. And then they could go back to bed together.

"I think we're ready to try the water today," Devlin said later as Sabbath was being tacked up on the crossties.

When A.J. nodded in agreement, Chester headed out to the ring to fill up the jump.

A little later, after she'd led the stallion out of the stables and gotten a leg up, A.J. noticed Sabbath was particularly antsy and sensed it was going to be a long training session. Unlike the horse, she was feeling sluggish. After she and Devlin had made love, she'd fallen back asleep, snoozing all the way through breakfast until she'd been woken up by her name being shouted up the stairs. It was obvious why she'd crashed. There was such relief in knowing Devlin was now committed to both her and their training. She felt as though they could now move ahead freely and that some of her bigger worries were behind her. Unfortunately, the consequence of her napping was that her reflexes were slow and she wasn't riding as well as she usually did. The stallion sensed it. Unlike the last few sessions, when he'd settled down and begun to focus, now he acted up, resenting her lack of concentration.

When the flatwork was finished and A.J. brought the stallion toward him, Devlin toyed with the idea of calling it a day. Things hadn't gone well in the warm-up and the rest of the session probably wasn't going to be much better. He was thinking it might be wise to hold off trying the water jump but A.J.'s face held a wealth of determination.

"You still ready to do the water?" he asked.

"You better believe it."

Bringing up the clipboard, he detailed the jump order. "Just take it slow and easy. See how he handles it."

She nodded, reining the stallion around.

Sabbath tossed his head, impatient to get jumping. He always perked up when they started going over fences but today his exuberance had an edge to it. When she urged him into a canter, she found herself having to hold him back.

They took the first two uprights in the rough form characteristic of their early training, and coming into the corner the stallion was shaking his head, fighting the lead change. They took the next series of oxers badly and rails hit the ground in their wake, a drumroll of failure. A.J. tightened her lips and the reins, feeling frustrated as she brought Sabbath around to face the water jump that was set up in the dead center of the ring.

It was an unassuming low rail fence followed by a square pool. The purpose was to test the horse's ability to cover distance as well as his reaction to visual stimuli. Depending on the weather, the water could look relatively benign or very intimidating, as it did at the moment. In the gray morning, wind licked across the surface of the water, agitating the reflection of a dingy, cold sky.

As soon as Sabbath caught sight of what they were heading toward, A.J. could feel him tense. During the flatwork, they hadn't used the middle of the ring, so it was the first time he'd noticed the jump. She gave him some encouragement with her leg and held steady, prepared for trouble. Surprisingly, he settled down and seemed to concentrate while continuing forward. For a split second, A.J. was lulled into relief, but then the stallion shied to the left so violently, she lost her seat and was thrown from him like a doll. It happened faster than a breath.

This one's going to hurt, she thought in midair.

The ground rushed up to meet her with an eagerness she could have done without. Landing in a heap, she tasted dirt in her mouth and felt a shooting pain in her upper body. With a groan, she rolled over to free the arm that had taken the lion's share of the impact, cradling it against her chest as she squinted up at the disinterested sky. She felt as if someone were needling her shoulder and elbow with a hot poker.

Devlin ran to her while shouting for Chester's help in corralling the stallion, who was galloping frantically around the ring.

As Devlin's face pierced her tunnel vision, A.J. noticed he was white as a sheet.

"I'm gonna feel this one in the morning," she said through clenched teeth.

"Can you sit up?"

"You got a crane handy?"

With his help, she managed to lift her upper body off the ground and she found, after blinking a few times, that the stars dancing in front of her eyes disappeared.

"I don't think he likes water," she said, struggling to get to her feet. Leaning on Devlin, she took a few tentative steps, trying to inventory any other contusions. Luckily, it seemed like only her arm was hurt. When she felt a bit more steady, she shrugged Devlin away and walked on her own over to Sabbath. Chester had managed to catch him. The stallion's eyes were wide with fear, his body twitching in spasms.

"He lame?" she asked tightly.

Chester shook his head. "Ya seem to be carryin' that load."

"Give me a leg up."

Behind her, Devlin felt nauseated.

"I think we should break for now," he said, trying to remain calm.

He didn't like the wild panic in the horse or the pain carved in his woman's face.

In fact, there were so many things he didn't like about what had just happened, it was hard to pick the worst of it all. The moment he'd seen A.J. was going to take a fall, his life had come to a halt as he confronted losing her. In the eternal second it'd taken for her to become airborne and then hit the ground, his heart had stopped beating and cracked in half with terror.

And now she wanted to get back on the godforsaken horse.

He watched as she took the reins from Chester.

"A.J., don't be ridiculous," Devlin said sharply. "That stallion is a live wire and you may have a broken arm."

"Get me up on this damned animal," she bit out at Chester, lifting her left leg impatiently.

For a man who thought he knew all about suffering, Devlin found a new kind of hell as she settled into the saddle.

"You can't be serious!" His voice was surging with emotion.

When A.J. headed back out to the jumps, he felt Chester's hand on his shoulder.

"Ya fall off, ya get back on. Ya know the way."

Devlin had done it countless times himself. Except that last time.

"Well, it's a damned stupid idea! What the hell is she thinking?"

"You'd have done the right same."

"And look where the hell I ended up," he said, limping over to the rail. He wanted to leave the ring but couldn't.

Up on Sabbath's back, A.J. was blinded by pain. The stallion was skipping under her but it wasn't playfully. The horse was nervous and that made him more unpredictable than usual. The fact that she had the use of only one arm made the situation especially dangerous.

Every time a hoof hit the ground, she felt a white-hot sensation shoot from her elbow to her shoulder. Worse, she lacked the strength to hold her arm tightly against her body and the injured extremity was flopping around, making the pain unbearable. With resolve, she tucked her hand into the waistband of her pants to reduce the jarring and noticed in the process that her fingers were becoming numb. She wasn't sure how much longer she could go without passing out, but she was determined that they go over one jump.

As she struggled with her agony, A.J. told herself she wasn't going to die from the pain. All she had to do was get over a jump and then she could baby herself. It wasn't going to take long.

The pep talk didn't really help so she gritted her teeth, pulled Sabbath together as best she could and took him over two uprights, avoiding the water hazard altogether. By the time she was finished, the horse had calmed down but she'd broken out in a sweat from the suffering.

She steered the stallion over to the two men and fell to the ground as she dismounted.

Devlin helped her to her feet, his face a tight mask.

"I'll take care of the spook," Chester said to no one in particular and left with the horse.

"We need to take you to the doctor." Devlin's voice was flat.

"I'm going to take a bath."

"Get in the truck."

A.J. ignored him, preoccupied with her aching arm as she left the ring. She'd carefully taken the hand out of her waistband and was trying to keep the arm from being jostled. Her stomach felt queasy and she was light-headed but she felt better than she had in the saddle. Her one goal was to get into some hot water and the idea of not moving was really attractive.

Devlin followed close behind. "You need an X-ray."

As she walked by the truck without stopping, he swore a blue streak.

"A.J.!" he barked, and, reluctantly, she turned around.

She was shocked. He was shaking with rage.

"It's not broken," she told him.

"How the hell would you know?"

Struggling not to have a meltdown, she said quietly, "If you'd just relax and let me get to the house, I'd really appreciate it."

"Did hitting the ground knock the sense out of you? Be reasonable for once in your life and get in that damned truck."

"No."

"You need a doctor! You look like you're ready to fall over."

"And this argument is *really* helping me."

"Then grow up and stop behaving like a child."

The words ricocheted around in her head, piercing the fog of pain. Blue eyes clashed with hazel.

She said, "In case you don't remember, I just fell off a horse in that ring. I need a break. What I don't need is you playing mightier-than-thou with the orders, okay? And I'm not being childish."

"When you're hurt, you go to the doctor. It's really that simple for most people."

As the sounds of the argument drifted through the air, Chester came out of the stable. One look at A.J.'s pale green face and he grew alarmed. "Go easy on her, McCloud. She's in shock."

"Stay out of this," came the thorny reply.

"McCloud!" Chester's voice cracked like a whip. "Back off before ya say anything else you'll regret."

Devlin wheeled on the man, full of fury. "What the hell's your problem?"

"Stand down!" Chester ordered, meeting him square in the eye. "Y're just takin' your worry out on her hide."

"I don't need your half-baked psychology," he growled.

"An' she doesn't need this kind of air show."

"Then to hell with you both."

Stalking over to the truck, Devlin wrenched open the door, gunned the engine and peeled down the driveway, out of sight.

A.J. felt her knees buckle and Chester was the only thing that kept her standing. Unnoticed, tears began streaming down her cheeks and she started to shake all over.

"He didn't mean any a' that," Chester said. "It's just the fear talkin."

She tried to nod but emotion was boiling up and overflowing, her shoulders quaking as sobs left her. As if he were handling an unbalanced load, Chester carefully led her to the door of the farmstead.

"Ya go in now an' take that bath. I'll make sure Sabbath's put up right an' then we'll see about that doctor."

Lacking the will to argue, A.J. did as she was told, walking up the stairs like an old woman. After she'd undressed in the bathroom, she looked at the arm in the mirror, seeing that it was swelling up already and had a big purple bruise forming at the elbow. Tentatively, she stretched it out to its full length and then back again, relieved that she had some range of motion. Focusing with difficulty, she went to the tub and cranked on the faucets, watching the water fill up while feeling as empty and lonely as she ever had.

When she slipped into the water, she grimaced as she tried to position her arm in a way that didn't hurt. It was impossible. There was no comfort to be found, no precise combination of crook or bend that would ease her pain. She thought it was probably because so much of her suffering wasn't physical.

Looking around the bathroom, she remembered moments with Devlin that had been warm and intimate and the images went through her with a rusty knife's imprecision, cutting deep and jaggedly. She leaned her head back against the porcelain, tears sliding down her cheeks, falling into the water surrounding her body.

She needed his tenderness now and he was gone. She felt very cold inside, despite the bath's warmth.

When Chester came back to the house a half hour later, A.J. was waiting on the couch downstairs. Beside her was a piece of luggage.

"I'm going to go to the doctor," she said, looking down at her hands. The fingers on her injured arm were still numb and it felt funny to rub them against the ones that were working properly.

"Ya want a ride to an' from?" he asked out of hope, knowing full well what her answer would be.

She shook her head. "I'm not coming back here. I'm going to take a few days off."

"Probably wise," he said slowly. "Ya need some time to heal."

Wasn't that the truth, she thought as she stood up.

A.J. bent over to pick up her bag but he got there first.

"Ya goin' to your family's?" Chester asked.

"I think so." All A.J. knew was that she had to get away. The destination didn't seem important.

Before she got into her car, she went to Sabbath's stall. He was snoozing in the far corner but as soon as he caught her scent, he looked up and came ambling over.

"You walked him out really well?" she asked Chester, who'd followed her inside. She was running her good hand down the stallion's nose.

"Real good."

"Any lameness?"

"He'll be stiff tomorrow but I'll lunge him an' he'll be right as rain in a day."

She nodded, relieved Sabbath hadn't hurt himself, glad he was under Chester's watchful eye. With a soft kiss on the stallion's forehead, she left the barn.

"Ya want me to tell Devlin anythin'? He's goin' to feel awful about this."

She hesitated and finally said, "Tell him I'll be in touch. I need some time to myself."

"All right."

Chester put her luggage in the trunk and stepped back from the flashy red car.

"Bye," she said.

"Come back soon."

A.J. simply waved in response and drove away.

Out on the main road, she found it hard to drive and shift with only one arm but she didn't take the fastest route to the doctor's. Instead, she went along winding roads she'd learned long ago, following twists and turns she knew well. A soft rain began to fall and its delicate touch soon turned the bark on the passing oaks and maples black, making the yellows and oranges of autumn stand out like splashes of paint.

When she finally pulled into the parking lot of her doctor's office, she was feeling more calm but no better. Even though she didn't have an appointment, the doctor fit her in promptly. Dr. Ridley, who was by now in his sixties, had treated her family for years and always made time to squeeze in any of the Sutherlands. It was a courtesy he'd extended to her often, considering she'd been crashing into jumps since she was a teenager.

The doctor was a small, birdlike man, with a sweet, high voice and the cheeriness of a chickadee. Flitting into the examining room, he didn't bother to sit down but hovered while he examined her arm and had X-rays taken. After eyeing the films and doing some careful prodding with his hands, he pronounced that the limb was badly sprained and had a stress fracture that would heal well enough if she behaved herself. With a flurry of activity, he wrapped her up in an Ace bandage, which started at her forearm, went over her elbow and ended in the middle of her biceps.

As she was shrugging back into her shirt, he wrote out a prescription and gave it to her with a sprightly smile.

"Ice it as soon as you get home, take this for the pain and you should be good as new in a couple of weeks."

A.J. groaned. "Weeks?"

"You heard me."

At her bleak expression, he said, "I'll tell you what. You come back in a week or so and I'll take another look at it.

Maybe we can negotiate your sentence." Dr. Ridley tried to give her a stern look but it was hard for him to pull it off because of his sunny nature. "Just remember, the more you sit still and let it heal, the faster you'll be *back in the saddle again*."

He laughed as he sang the last few words.

"Don't look so down," he told her. "It could have been much worse."

"I could have fallen on my head?"

"I could have sung you something I knew more words to."

She smiled a little.

"That's better. You're too old for lollipops but at least I can have you leave with some cheer on your face."

The modest improvement in her mood lasted as far as the parking lot. She didn't want to go to the mansion but, in the gathering dusk, she didn't have the energy to get creative with her options. Flipping on her headlights, she drove to her father's in a listless daze. As she pulled around the circle drive and saw the house in all its glory, she thought the glowing light pouring out of so many leaded windows was a false prophet of serenity. Between the estrangement with her father, Regina's rigid formality and Peter's contentiousness, the place wasn't a refuge for her no matter how bucolic it looked from the outside.

She drove around back and pulled the convertible into its garage slip. Shouldering her bag on her good side, she entered the house through the rear entrance, which led into the industrial-sized kitchen. Dinner was in the process of being realized from its base ingredients and the cook, a European with no patience for interruptions, shot her a look of condemnation.

A.J. ignored him and headed through to the dining room, where she paused, looking over the vast mahogany table. There were three place settings clustered at one end, with linen napkins folded stiffly and silverware metastasizing out from stacks of china that bore the Sutherland family crest. In front of each elegant mound, there were three glasses, one for water and two for wine, and all over the table, like a swarm, were little silver bowls holding salt, pepper and butter squares.

It looked like a china store, A.J. thought, already missing the simplicity and ease of living at the farmhouse.

Devlin's was a place where people propped themselves against the kitchen counter to gobble down lunch. It was a house where a towel could be hung on a doorknob and a barn coat tossed over a chair back. She'd walked around in her socks and let her hair dry on her shoulders, had even pranced around naked just because she felt like it.

That kind of freedom wasn't to be had at the mansion. Not even close. Hell, she could face criminal indictment just for showing up at dinner wearing blue jeans.

Heart aching, she checked her watch. Whatever faults Regina had, a clock could be set by her schedule and it was one of the few things about the woman A.J. appreciated. Dinner would be served in one hour, which meant Peter would still be at his club's bar having a libation of some fruity variety and Regina would be in her room donning her evening finery. Six o'clock also meant her father would be alone in his study, a stout glass of scotch next to his elbow, reviewing papers.

Moving quickly, she left the dining room and crossed the vast foyer space. With a quick trip through the library, she found herself at her father's study, the hefty oak door partially closed.

Garrett looked up as she walked in.

Pleasure and concern mixed as he saw her face and then the sling.

"What happened?" He came around the desk.

"Hi, Daddy," A.J. said into his shoulder as they embraced.

Taking a deep breath, she smiled sadly. Her father smelled as he always did, a lovely combination of the obscure English cologne he imported and the pipe tobacco he loved so much. The scent brought her back to childhood, when safety and comfort were easily found in his arms.

It was a shame, she thought, that the complications of an adult life couldn't be as readily soothed as the stubbed toes and scraped knees of youth.

"Now, will you tell me what happened?"

"It's nothing."

"If it's nothing, why is it in a sling?"

"At least it's not in a cast."

"True."

He led her over to the old chesterfield sofa.

Her father's study had always been one of her favorite rooms in the mansion. It was decorated in maroon and gold and was dark in a reassuring way. With its mahogany paneling and shelves filled with books on subjects like engineering and business management, it was a lush cave, suitable for thought and industry.

It was also home to a portrait of A.J.'s mother, the only one Regina had been unable to persuade her new husband to remove. The painting, which showed a woman who looked just like A.J. staring out from a sea of burgundy satin, was resplendent. Lights from overhead flooded the work of art, making it glow with life.

"Are you staying for dinner?" he asked.

"And for a few days."

"Regina will be so pleased."

"No, she won't." A.J. shot him a knowing smile.

"*I* am so pleased."

"That I believe."

Silence stretched between them.

"Why are you really here?" he asked.

"I just need a few days to heal."

"From what injury?"

"I can't ride like this."

"The last time you took a day off was because you had a concussion from hitting some jump and landing on your head. It was only because we threatened to put you in a hospital bed that you agreed to stay in your room. Having your arm in a sling may prevent you from being up on that horse but it wouldn't cause you to take time off."

She looked away.

"The rumors are true, then," Garrett said. "You are having an affair with him."

A.J. was tempted to lie. A plausible denial was all she needed, but she didn't have one she felt like offering.

In the silence, she could feel his disappointment. Her father had always hoped she'd marry a businessman like him and settle down into the cloistered life of a society wife. It would have been an existence he could understand, a vocabulary he was familiar with. She knew he imagined such a marriage would be easy, that it would be one endless, pretty stream of parties and dresses fronted by a man who cared for her, provided for her. Watched over her.

She knew he'd never understand it but, for her, a passionless marriage carpeted with jewels was no luxury, just a very pretty mausoleum where women rotted while walking around in Manolo Blahniks. When it became clear she was headed for a different future from the one he'd planned for her, they'd stopped talking about her life's direction. Her father's convictions were as tightly held as her own so they didn't argue. Instead, they were both waiting for some future time when the other would finally see the light.

Her father was looking pained and she knew what he was thinking. Her affair with a riding champion turned tragic recluse was just one more part of a life he couldn't relate to. The love for her was in his eyes but so was his sadness.

"I'll be fine."

She was trying to reassure them both.

"Is there anything you need?" he asked.

She shook her head.

What she needed, he couldn't provide.

10

A WEEK later, Devlin stood at the rail of his ring, one boot resting on the lower rung to give his leg relief. His face was grim. It'd been a long, hard afternoon of doing nothing but cleaning up messes. Preceded by several days of the same.

Holding the line against chaos isn't progress, he thought. Just self-preservation.

From the day A.J. left, things hadn't gone well. First, there'd been a water main break in the stable. That calamity caused a flood in the storage room where the feed was kept, turning eight bags of oats into mush. Then, in a freak windstorm, a tree limb had broken off, landed on his truck and turned its bed into an arboristic Barcalounger.

But the worst had undoubtedly been the Blacksmith Disaster.

The blacksmith who had been by once before backed out without explanation the morning he was scheduled to come. Fortunately, a new man was located. He arrived with the tools of his trade and in a good mood, only to leave an hour later with a Band-Aid on his forehead and a vow never to return. Sabbath had been impossible, no matter what Devlin and Chester did. Even with two grown men dangling off his head like earrings, the stallion still managed to nail the blacksmith a good one with his hind leg.

And, once the loose shoe was secure, the man flat-out refused to get within a stone's throw of the stallion's other hooves, saying that the horse's combination of tender feet and good aim was an occupational hazard he could do without. The Garfield Band-Aid plastered on his forehead didn't help. The only one to be found, it was the insult part of the injury.

Devlin was still amazed that they'd been fired as clients by someone who was used to high-strung animals. It was like getting kicked out of a family restaurant because your kids set a new standard for food throwing.

He shifted his weight, heard a crack of protest and felt his foot hit the ground.

Now I know what it feels like to be cursed, he thought, looking down at the fallen rail.

Devlin put it back in its place and made a mental note to fix it. As his eyes returned to the ring, he went back to watching Chester lunge the stallion. Standing in the middle of the arena, the man was holding on to the end of a long lead attached to Sabbath's halter. In theory, the horse was supposed to get some exercise by moving through various gaits while traveling around in a circle.

The stallion had different ideas and was highly resistant to changing them. The first time they'd tried lunging him, he'd hauled Chester after him, turning the lead line into a towrope and the man into a drag anchor. Days later, Sabbath still hadn't warmed up much to the idea of concentric circles. He was cantering around in an uneven and disagreeable path, thwarting the discipline and throwing up his hooves in protest.

The cause of the stallion's bad behavior was no mystery. He was antsy to get back to jumping, and the display of theatrics in the ring was only one of the ways he was making his frustration known. Aside from the fiasco with the blacksmith's forehead, the horse had torn two blankets off his back, shredded them to ribbons and chewed the front of his stall until it looked like a beaver had gone at it.

Sabbath was angry and they were losing ground with him but there wasn't much anyone could do. Chester certainly wasn't up to the task of schooling him over fences and, with his bum leg, Devlin wouldn't have been much better. All three of them, stallion included, were in a holding pattern until A.J. returned.

It was time for her to come back, Devlin thought for the umpteenth time. And not just for the damn horse.

Like his rotten luck, the need to apologize to her had also been dogging him all week. As soon as he'd calmed down that day, he'd gone rushing back to the stable. He wanted to tell her how much he regretted being so pushy and leaving her when she needed help. He wasn't sure what the precise words to use were, although ones like *coward* and *bastard* certainly came to mind.

But by the time he'd returned, she'd already left. And when Chester had given him her message, Devlin had been caught in an awful limbo. He wanted to track her down and make her hear him out but he had to respect the distance she'd put between them.

He knew she came to visit the stallion every day. She always showed up at lunch, confirmation, as if he needed any, that she was avoiding him. From the kitchen, he'd hear the throaty purr of the convertible as she drove up and he'd drop whatever he was doing to go over to the window and watch her walk into the barn. Each time, he hoped she'd look up at the house and come inside and he found himself assuming a daily vigil, eating his sandwiches standing at the window. He was waiting for her to give the slightest indication that she was ready to talk. Inevitably, he was disappointed. Every time, when she was finished with the stallion, A.J. would emerge from the barn with her head down, slide into the powerful car and leave.

In the days since she'd been gone, he'd thought a lot about her accident. Seeing her fall had been terrifying for him. When he'd thought about training A.J., it had always been in terms of what they needed to accomplish. The focus was on the work and the winning. Never once had he considered what watching her go down in the ring would be like. In that awful instant, when he saw her shake loose of the saddle and hit the ground, he'd been flooded with agony, and the depth of his emotion had scared the hell out of him. He'd assumed losing his horse and his career was the worst thing life could throw at him. He'd been wrong. Having something happen to A.J. was so much more terrible, and confronting that vulnerability and pain was what had made him lash out.

At night, as he lay in bed, he saw images of her face and remembered how much he'd hurt her with his careless words. It was eating him up inside. Every night, as he slept alone, missing her, he hoped on the next day she would come to him.

And then, at last, he'd had a glimmer of hope.

Today, at noontime, A.J. had emerged from the car without her arm in the sling. Waiting at the window while she was inside the barn, his turkey on rye hanging in midair with his hopes, Devlin tensed as soon as she stepped back out into the daylight and walked to her car. With her hand on the door, she paused. And finally looked up at him.

Their eyes met for a moment and he willed her to come inside. He was desperate to smell her, hear her voice, see her up close. At the slightest indication from her, he was ready to rush outside, to try to put things right between them, ready to speak. . . . But she'd looked away and then driven away. And his mood had gone from foul to something darker.

It was a change in attitude that had not been met with enthusiasm by his lunch partner. He knew Chester had just about had it with him skulking around. And who could blame the man? Devlin was getting tired of being around himself, too.

That was the trouble, he thought. Everywhere you go, there you are.

Coming back to the present, he focused on Sabbath's pathetic workout.

"I think that's enough, Ches," he called out.

Chester reeled the stallion in like a sailfish and approached Devlin with an annoyed look. The man and the horse were both out of joint.

"Just in time," Chester said, dryly. "He's gettin' tired a' the lunge an' I'm gettin' tired a' him."

"I know, Ches."

The expectant look in the groom's eyes was a demand.

"What?" Devlin asked.

"You know what."

Devlin looked past the ring, to the mountains beyond. Was the eye contact they'd shared enough of a signal that A.J. was ready to hear him out?

He had to try.

"I'll go talk to her."

"About time," Chester grumbled, leading the stallion back into the barn and leaving Devlin with a dilemma.

Having decided to take a chance and reach out, he found himself too impatient to wait for A.J. to show up the following day. And what he had to say was too important to do over the phone. He wanted to do it in person.

Then it dawned on him. It was Saturday. Her father's birthday.

He thought for a moment. Then made up his mind. It looked like he was liberating his tuxedo from the mothballs.

Later that evening, while standing in her underwear, A.J. put the last pin in her hair and surveyed her new look in the bathroom mirror. Her thick auburn waves were twisted off her neck and piled on her head in a remarkably adept shot at a chignon. She'd been mostly interested in getting it all out of the way but the fact that the style emphasized her high cheekbones and heart-shaped face didn't hurt.

She turned to the side, staring over her shoulder. With some eye shadow and a little lipstick, she looked like a different person. Granted, she wasn't in jeans and muck boots, and lacy lingerie did add an allure.

A.J. heaved a sigh, and let her shoulders collapse. She didn't feel like putting on a face and pretending to be happy. She didn't want to interact with the kind of socialite crowd who were about to show up. She wanted to sit in her room, stare off into space, and try not to go crazy while her arm healed.

But duty called.

Resigning herself to the evening's festivities, she went over to the dress hanging on the door. It was a filmy black creation, made of layers of paper-thin chiffon that fell from a tight, strapless bodice. She'd bought the dress for the coming holiday season, the only good outcome of an afternoon with her stepmother.

The two rarely spent any time alone and they never shopped together. Garrett, however, wanted some measure of connection between the women in his life and had a quiet way of getting his way. By playing to A.J.'s better nature and buying Regina off with the promise of a week at Canyon Ranch, stepdaughter and stepmother had gritted their teeth through a strained lunch followed by a trip to a high-profile boutique.

The gown had been heaven the moment A.J. slipped it on and now, standing in her bathroom, she felt its delicate waves go over her head again like a sigh. As she zipped up the back, she could feel the bodice clinging to her breasts and the floor-length skirt brushing against her legs. She took a twirl in front of the mirror, thinking the discomfort of shopping with her stepmother might have been worth it.

It wasn't like anything she normally wore, even to formal parties. If she had to dress up, she usually put on silk pants and bolero jackets or tailored floor-length skirts with simple, classic tops. With her hair done up and wearing makeup, she imagined people were going to be surprised. Staring at her reflection, she decided the look was part damsel and part seductress. It made a very feminine and powerful statement.

She wondered what Devlin would think of her.

The thought was like hitting a speed bump.

Devlin was never far from her mind and she missed him so badly it stung. Every day, when she went to visit the stallion, she knew he watched her from the kitchen window and there was a big part of her that wanted to follow the blue stone walkway up to the farmhouse, knock on the door and fall into his arms.

But she was still angry at him for lashing out at her. And she was scared. Scared by how much it had hurt to have him walk away from her. Frightened by the strength of her love for him. Terrified that he was right and they couldn't have it all.

If she'd been just any other rider, he probably would have let her go after suggesting she see a doctor. That devastating argument would never have occurred. Instead, they'd had a blowout, she'd run away and now they were estranged. It was exactly the kind of situation he'd warned her about.

During her incessant introspections, A.J. often wondered

if he was hurting as badly as she was. The need to know what he was feeling was why she'd finally looked up at him today. Across the distance that separated them, she'd seen the regret in his face and a yearning that went a long way toward making her feel better.

As she'd returned to the mansion, she'd decided it was time for them to talk. After almost a week of being away from him, she was ready. Tomorrow, she would go up to the farmhouse after she visited with Sabbath. She would tell him how much he'd hurt her and hear what he had to say.

And she prayed that whatever it was went far enough.

The idea of seeing him up close made her heart pound with a heady combination of emotions that was hard to separate. So much of her was just desperate to be with him and put the argument behind them but the rest was a jumble of unhappy contradictions.

A.J. sighed, refocusing on the full-length mirror. The woman staring back at her looked beautiful and confident.

What a lie, she thought. But let's hear it for some damn good window dressing.

Turning away from the image, she left the bathroom and walked into her bedroom. It was an elegant space she knew well but she didn't feel like it was hers anymore. Her childhood furniture, which she'd liked, had been thrown out when Regina arrived and redecorated everything. The baroque antiques and heavy satins that had been installed weren't to A.J.'s taste but she'd learned to live with them. They'd been a concession so she could keep her trophies and ribbons displayed on the walls.

The only thing she still liked about the room was its bank of French doors that let in an abundance of light. Both sets opened up to a patio for her private use. Sitting there, she could look out over the magnificent sculptured gardens of the estate, four square acres of flower beds set off by blooming apple, cherry and pear trees as well as majestic maples, oaks and willows. In the distance, rising above the wooded tree line at the far end of the gardens, there was a mountain range that framed the lush flora beautifully.

Surveying her bedroom, A.J. found herself questioning its luxury for the first time. With her equestrian trophies sitting on antique mahogany and her show ribbons hanging off silk walls, it dawned on her how much she had taken for granted.

A knock interrupted her thoughts and she padded to the door in her stocking feet. When she opened it, Garrett was standing in the hall. He was looking dapper in his tuxedo and happy as he took in her appearance.

"You'll be the most beautiful one there."

"You never know," A.J. said, accepting his kiss on the cheek. "I haven't put on my shoes yet and barn boots are still a possibility. Far more functional than the pinpointed high-risers I got to go with the dress."

"I'm so glad you're back home."

"Papa, I told you not to get used to this. I'm only staying here until I can find a place of my own."

"I know, but I keep hoping . . ." At her warning glance, Garrett cleared his throat. "I'll let you finish dressing but I wanted to give you a little something."

He pressed a leather-bound box into his daughter's hands and interrupted her string of protests.

"It's my birthday. You can't turn me down."

"You shouldn't have."

"I know. Now, when this is all through, you and I will get together at the end of the night, won't we? Just like we always do."

Holding his gift in her hand, A.J.'s eyes misted over with tears as she recalled their yearly ritual. "Yes. Yes, we will."

Garrett reached out and stroked her cheek. "Your mother would have been so proud of you. Of your strength and your independence. All that fire inside of you comes from her."

She grasped his hand. "I love you."

"Thank you for saying that. I really need to hear it, some nights even more than others," he said softly. Then he disappeared down the hall, the familiar smell of that spiced cologne drifting after him.

A.J. closed the door and went over to her bed, the dress draping in a cascade around her as she sat down. Unlatching a golden clasp, she opened the box and gasped. A pair of ruby and diamond earrings were nestled in a bed of satin.

Even to her jaundiced eye, they were glorious. She plucked one out and held it up to the light, watching the sparkle and flash of the stones. She put them on to please Garrett and to shore up her confidence a little more.

After she stepped into her shoes, she smoothed the dress over her waist, did a recheck on the backs of the earrings and straightened her spine. Leaving the safe haven of her room, she took the winding staircase cautiously in her heels, telling herself not to feel nervous. She'd been through similar evenings countless times and, though they were unpleasant, nothing was going to happen that she hadn't seen before.

Reality turned out to be quite the opposite.

When she walked into the formal living room, which was filled to capacity with a glittering crowd, she wasn't prepared for the reaction. Tolerant smiles turned to surprise and astonishment as people saw her and stopped talking.

She felt like Elvis, back from the dead.

Then the whispering started. She wasn't sure whether they were commenting on her return to the family fold or her stallion or her trainer or her gown. She felt like she'd been hit with a spotlight on a stage and the glare was overwhelming.

Faced with all the stares and murmurs, she forced herself not to turn around and run back to her room. Stiffening her resolve, she dived into the crowd and started to weave her way through the throng of people, with no particular destination in mind.

One step into the room and she was accosted by a stuffed shirt and his trophy wife. The manufacturer of toothpicks and a renowned womanizer, the man ran his greedy gaze over A.J. like she was a piece of art up for sale. The woman beside him, his third wife if memory served, looked fierce.

"If you aren't full of surprises," he was saying before he came even closer and whispered in A.J.'s ear, "Why you've hidden such talent under those riding clothes is a mystery."

With men like him, she thought it was self-explanatory. As gracefully as she could, she tried to peel his arms off of her.

To A.J.'s relief, Garrett materialized out of the crowd to

rescue her. The lech immediately assumed the guise of propriety though it didn't reach his eyes, and it was a relief when, after some conventional talk, she and her father headed over to the bar. By the time she had a glass of chardonnay in her hand, she was getting a sense of what Devlin had been talking about. At every turn, she heard her name floating in the air, part of the swell of conversation that swirled in the room like acrid smoke. Catching the quick eyes and faster tongues of the crowd, she felt like public property. She didn't like it.

And she liked it even less as the evening wore on. After the elaborate buffet was unveiled in the dining room and picked away at, the crowd returned to the grand living room for an evening of dancing and dessert. If she'd thought her big entrance was bad, she found the ball intolerable. Men who'd spent the evening looking at her finally had a socially acceptable excuse to touch her. Once on the dance floor, their intentions were obvious, earning her more vicious looks from their wives. After an hour, she had a headache coming on from the clash of a dozen different colognes and she was exhausted from fighting off cloying arms.

The life of a siren was overrated, A.J. decided, scratching her nose.

Not able to stand another dance, she tried to take refuge in conversation, only to get trapped by a former English professor who'd retired from his day job at a prestigious university but hadn't given up his avocation for being a verbose blowhard. He was a curmudgeonly old man, with white hair growing out of everywhere. There were little tufts at his ears, twin hedges over his eyes, a section of beard under his chin, which he'd been missing for quite some time.

As he droned on, A.J. put herself on autopilot and found she was more than ready for the speeches to start, the white chestnut cake to be cut and the evening to come to an end. The fact that her toes were numb and she was tired of feeling like she was walking on top of a fence didn't make time pass any faster.

"So that, my dear, is the difference between crass innovation and an enduring classic," Professor Rogaine's voice crescendoed as another couple of people joined them.

Though they did dilute the elderly man's dull conversation, A.J. found herself squirming under the eyes of one guy who seemed all too interested in what she might have been hiding in her bodice. She felt like asking him whether he thought he'd lost his wallet down there.

Breaking free from the group, she pivoted, only to find herself caught in another tight knot of people. Her escape foiled, she tried to take a deep breath but all the air had suddenly been sucked out of the room. Her chest grew tight.

All this and now she was coming face-to-face with claustrophobia. She eyed the doorway with desperation and ambition. She was about to bolt, had committed to making a bid for freedom, even if it meant missing her father's birthday toast, when she saw a guard there was no sneaking past. Between her and the salvation of the stairway stood Regina, holding court.

Her stepmother was addressing a crowd flamboyantly. She was flanked by Peter and Garrett, two human topiaries she watered with adoring looks but clipped into place with a fast remark if they got more attention than she did. The courtiers around her clung to her every word like it was a toehold on greatness, which explained the happiness radiating from her face.

Or maybe that was just reflected light bouncing off all the jewels, A.J. thought, taking in the choker of diamonds and pearls around Regina's neck and the pair of matching earrings that dangled from her lobes.

Peter caught A.J. eyeing the group and gave her a stiff nod. By unspoken agreement, the two had studiously ignored each other over the past week. Seeing him across the room, she became even more determined to leave.

As she turned toward the doors that led out to the rear terrace, she halted, feeling odd. She looked down at her flute of champagne. It hadn't been touched and she hadn't finished her one glass of wine.

It couldn't be the alcohol, she thought.

Maybe all the insomnia she'd been suffering from was catching up to her?

Even though she tried to shake it off, the sensation persisted. A quick look behind didn't yield an explanation, just more of the same people she was determined to get away from. Craning her neck, she peeked over more carefully coiffed heads, wondering what the eerie feeling was all about.

Then she saw Devlin.

Gasping in shock, she watched as he scanned the room. As soon as he saw her, he started moving through the congestion. There was single-minded purpose to his expression but something far warmer in his eyes as he looked at her.

A.J.'s heart began to pound and she felt dizzy, as a feeling of dislocation took over. The sounds of people's voices and the clinking of glasses, the music and the dancing, everything disappeared except for the image of him striding through the crowd.

Confusing emotions blocked out reason. She was thrilled to see him but still hurt and angry. Ready to hear what he had to say but certain the conversation needed to be private. Pleased that he'd made the effort.

And overwhelmed by how beautiful he was.

In his tuxedo, Devlin was devastatingly handsome. His wide shoulders filled out the midnight jacket like an I beam and the startling white of the shirt brought out the tan in his skin. He moved with the same grace and power he always had, as if the formal clothes were nothing special and the glittering guests were of no more note than stable boys and grooms.

He was who he was, no matter what the surroundings.

She really liked that about him.

Her body flushed with heat and her hand tightened on her champagne flute until she thought it might snap. A powerful impulse to go to him struck her, as though he were her magnetic north. And the pull got stronger the closer he came to her.

"What are you doing here?" she asked when he stopped a few feet away. She sounded breathless to her own ears.

"You said it was important for me to come. I didn't want to let you down. Again."

The sound of his voice was like the stroke of his hand over her skin. Enticing and yet tender. She felt his eyes travel across her shoulders, over the swell of her breasts, down into the dip of her waist. She watched his pupils dilate with a yearning he didn't hide. When their eyes met again, there was a fierce heat in his. She couldn't help but be moved even though she remained wary.

"You are very beautiful," he said roughly.

Before she could respond, a man inserted himself between them. She watched Devlin's expression darken.

"I'm Cosgood Rhett the Fourth," he said in an imperious voice as he slipped his arm around A.J.'s waist. "Your father does business with mine, remember? Anyway, I believe it's my turn. I've been waiting all night."

Devlin stepped in the way, laying a hand on the guy's shoulder. It wasn't a friendly gesture.

"And you're going to wait a little longer. Like until hell freezes over."

The intruder's face registered a glare until he looked into the icy pair of eyes trained on him. A.J. suppressed an inappropriate giggle as the hand fell quickly from her waist and a variety of apologies were offered.

"Thanks," she said after the man left. "It's been a long night."

"I bet," Devlin growled as he watched the other guy disappear.

When he looked back at her, his expression softened.

"That dress is . . ." His voice trailed off. And his eyes finished the sentence.

"It's all a lie, if you want to know the truth. My feet hurt, the zipper itches and I think I lost an olive down the bodice."

"I have to say it again. You're so beautiful."

Her expression reflected pleasure and caution.

"How's the arm?" he asked.

"Better every day."

"Sabbath really misses you."

"I've been trying to keep in his good graces by bringing carrots. I don't know if the bribe's working but he's getting plenty of beta-carotene. I'm guessing Chester's been trying to lunge him?"

"That's right."

"The poor man must be going out of his mind."

"They're both getting tired of each other. And they're not too fond of me, either." At her curious look, he explained, "I haven't been so easy to be around lately."

"Oh?"

In a low voice, he said, "I miss you. So much it hurts."

Her eyes flickered from his, trained on the champagne glass.

"A.J., I've tried to stay away, just like you asked. But I can't do it any longer. Is there somewhere we can go and talk?"

"You must be Devlin McCloud," Regina said with a strident voice.

A.J. turned and saw her stepmother look Devlin over like he was a pork chop up for inspection. He must have passed as Grade A meat because a moment later the woman extended a bejeweled hand to him.

"Welcome. I'm Regina Sutherland," she said, giving him her best social smile. Broad and calculated, it was a cheerful facade that did nothing to hide her hard edges. "I didn't know you were coming."

The woman shot A.J. a look and, like tractor beams, her dark eyes narrowed on the ruby earrings.

My father's going to pay for these twice, A.J. thought.

"I'm a gate crasher," Devlin was replying.

"Well, I'm glad our gate was crashed," Regina cooed.

Peter came up behind his mother.

"I didn't know you had a date," he said to A.J. dryly.

"Of course, you've met my son," Regina offered. "Being in the horse business, I'm sure you've heard about him."

"Most people have," Devlin replied.

She beamed, missing the point.

"Now, if you'll excuse me, I'd like to dance with A.J.," Devlin said.

"There's time for that later," Regina dismissed. "You really must come and meet—"

"A.J.?" He held out his arm.

Regina blinked as if she'd been addressed in a foreign tongue. "But surely—"

Devlin smiled and began to lead A.J. away.

As they left, Peter grabbed her arm. "You should make sure you're here for the speeches. You might hear some news of interest."

A.J. shrugged him off. With Devlin at her side, she had more important things to think about.

As soon as she and Devlin were on the dance floor, she felt familiar arms come around her and pull her close. Despite their clothes, her body responded as if they were skin to skin and she felt him harden. Heart in her throat, she allowed herself the dangerous pleasure of leaning into him and smelling his cedar soap.

"God, I've missed you," he groaned against her ear.

She opened her mouth to speak but nothing came out. She was too caught up in the moment, in him. She told herself they needed to talk first but the sensible voice was drowned out. Just for one dance, she thought. And then we'll find someplace to go.

Too soon, the song came to an end, and he said, "Where?"

But before A.J. could answer, Regina stepped up in front of the musicians, spreading her arms wide and smiling like she was a featured act in Las Vegas. Devlin and A.J. got trapped by the crowd as it came forward.

"Thank you all for joining us here on this very special evening," Regina said, beckoning to Garrett with a glittering hand. He joined her reluctantly.

"Garrett and I are so appreciative that you have graced us with your presence." She said this even though no one in the room would have dared turn down the invitation and she knew it. A-list parties were A-list parties. You went or were never asked again.

The crowd began shifting and A.J. spied Peter working his way toward his mother. Someone was following close on his heels but she couldn't see who it was. When they came into view up front, she saw that it was Philippe Marceau. Behind the Frenchman was an impossibly tall, leggy blonde with more highlights in her hair than her eyes. With Peter, the two joined Regina and Garrett in front of the audience.

"The Sutherland name has been tied to a great number of successes," Regina was proclaiming. "And I'm proud that the next generation is following suit. My son, Peter, who has built up Sutherland Stables as a force to be reckoned with in the horse world, is about to announce an important new relationship."

A.J. stopped breathing.

Peter took center stage. "I'm thrilled to introduce to all of you the new star of Sutherland Stables, the man who is going to take us to victory at the Qualifier, Philippe Marceau!"

There was a smattering of applause. Most of the people in the room were businessmen and, though there were some people from the horse set, they were owners, not riders. Only competitors would really care about the new addition to the Sutherland team and A.J. had to wonder why Peter was using her father's birthday party to put out the message.

Unless it was to get at her.

And then it made perfect sense.

11

As PETER's eyes sought out A.J. in the crowd, she thought the happiness on his face was misplaced and wondered how long it was going to take for him to find out his new bread-winner was a booby prize.

"Sutherland Stables is more than a loose affiliation of riders and owners," he was saying. "We are a family business in every sense of the word, because champions are all related in spirit. The bond between those of us who seek excellence is stronger than blood—which can be far less reliable."

A.J. shook her head, surprised at his remarks. Marceau wasn't known for being faithful. The man's professional loyalties were no more constant than those he offered the women he bedded and discarded with the morning paper. He'd bounced from one stable to another since the day he'd turned professional, always because he felt his unique talents were being underappreciated. In fact, people on the circuit ran a betting pool whenever he started somewhere new. The winners typically put their money on dates within the calendar year. She could have sworn Peter knew all this.

But even if it was a bad idea for the stables, seeing Philippe Marceau standing under those lights with her step-brother made her blood boil. To have been summarily thrown out with Sabbath only to be replaced by the notorious Frenchman was insulting. Subconsciously, she flexed her arm. It was still acutely painful and she'd intended to go back to the doctor's in a few days, but now she felt an urgent need to get back to training. Courtesy of her stepbrother's pronouncements, she was more determined than ever to win and she wasn't going to sit on the sidelines any longer.

Turning to Devlin, A.J. looked at him for a long moment. In spite of his intense expression, the eyes that met hers were steady and warmhearted. She wasn't sure what the future held for their relationship but she knew she needed to go back to work. And she needed him at her side.

She told him, "I'm back tomorrow. And make sure there's water in that ring."

He nodded and she saw relief in the rugged lines of his face.

Peter droned on until he was upstaged when Regina stepped forward into the lights. Elbowing her son aside, she launched into an affected stream of adulation for Garrett that was something between a Barbara Cartland narrative and a car commercial. A.J. found it nauseating.

As his mother performed her monologue, Peter entered the crowd. Marceau and the blond appendage were right behind him and they all were heading straight for A.J.

"Aren't you going to congratulate us on our new partnership?" Peter said as soon as he was in earshot.

"Of course," A.J. replied. "I don't think you two are necessarily destined for greatness but I wish you well."

"Marceau is going to get the Sutherland name in lights."

"Maybe. Or perhaps he'll just move on to some other stable."

Peter's haughty air bloomed. "When Philippe starts winning every major event on the circuit, and the Sutherland name is on everyone's lips in a good way, you're going to rue the day you picked that horse over your family."

"Are you forgetting who put me in the position to choose?"

"You were the one who bought him. Now you're going to see what it cost you."

A.J.'s anger swelled, masking how much it still hurt that her father had given Peter the stables. Her voice became sharp. "That stallion cost me thirty grand and the dubious pleasure of seeing you every night over dinner. All things considered, he'd have been a bargain at half a million."

Her stepbrother's face flushed an ugly red. "You didn't exactly leave us heartbroken, either."

Time to go, A.J. told herself, noting the argument was taking on more of an edge than usual. The last thing she wanted was to stage a fight with Peter out in the open at her father's birthday gala.

"Much as I'd like to continue this," she said, "I'm going to say good night and good luck."

"Winning teams don't need luck," he said heatedly.

"When you find one, let me know."

"You're looking at the partnership that is going to revolutionize this sport. And you're getting left behind with that crazy load of dog meat. Your career is over."

Emotions running high, A.J. lashed out. "Just because you recruited the only other Froot Loop in the business with taste in clothes as bad as your own doesn't mean you're a lock for success. You need more than a stunning lack of fashion sense and a blind tailor to win in the ring."

Peter lunged at her, catching everyone by surprise.

In the nick of time, Devlin stepped forward to protect her, blocking the way.

"Back off, Conrad," he said darkly.

All around them, people were turning curious eyes toward the scuffle, eager for more drama to unfold.

A.J. was shocked by Peter's outburst. They'd always argued but he'd never lost control like that before. Hearing his labored breaths, feeling her own heart pounding in her chest, she found herself truly regretting their relationship. Why did things always end up badly between them?

Tangled in her own thoughts, she watched mutely as Peter stepped away from Devlin. Her stepbrother tugged his tuxedo jacket in place with hands that shook.

With the situation defused, Marceau took the opportunity to insert himself gallantly in front of his new partner. "Do not arch to her level."

"That's *stoop* to my level," A.J. corrected absently.

Devlin took her elbow. "I think we should go."

"Yes, do remove her," Philippe said. "With your leg, I imagine babysitting is all that you are good for now."

Emotion surged again and a stinging retort came to the tip of A.J.'s tongue. But, instead of going with her instinct, she cleared her throat and straightened her shoulders. "Good night, Philippe. Peter."

Her stepbrother's voice was bitter. "You're going to regret this."

"You know something, I think you're right," she replied. "In fact, I think I'm beginning to feel sorry for us."

Peter looked at her with utter confusion before she and Devlin left for the foyer.

When they got to the front door, they paused.

"I'm sorry you had to see that," she said. "Again."

"There's a lot of anger between the two of you."

"Yes. But it's high time to change that. I just wish I knew how."

As much as Peter could be a source of intense frustration, she didn't hate him and knew he wasn't truly evil. She also was beginning to see her own role in their dysfunction. If she took a moment to think about it, what she was really upset about were the unresolved issues between her and Devlin and the amount of time her injury had cost her training. The announcement about Marceau, and Peter's jabs, had given her something to react to and had unleashed her anxieties. Add to all that the fact Peter knew how to play her well, and ka-*boom*.

"I don't like arguing with him. I really don't," she said softly.

Aware she'd been silent for a long time, she looked up into Devlin's eyes and forgot about Peter and her family and her concern over the lost training. Everything else drifted away.

"Is this good night?" she asked him.

"Only if that's what you want. I came here to talk with you."

A couple walked by and peered over curiously.

"Why don't I walk you to your car?" she asked.

He smiled. "Isn't that a man's job?"

"In this neighborhood, you never know what'll happen

after dark. You might get accosted by a bond trader or some rabid media mogul."

"Better than some twenty-year-old Internet guru who's hit the skids," he said, opening the front door.

As they stepped free of the house, they were greeted by the crisp night air. The noise of the party faded away, and her ears rang in the silence.

Before anything could be said, they were approached by one of the uniformed parking attendants who'd been hired for the night. The boy must have been in his late teens and he was wearing a black blazer that was too big for him and a pair of running shoes. Shrugging, Devlin handed over his ticket and the kid went sprinting off down the driveway, out of sight.

"As far as privacy goes, I guess this didn't make a lot of sense," A.J. whispered. "I forgot about the valets."

She glanced over her shoulder at the lineup of young men loitering around.

"We can drive around the block and park," he suggested.

"Like two kids hiding from their parents?" A.J. giggled, partially because she found the idea funny, mostly because she felt anxious about what he would say when they were alone.

"You have no idea how much I've missed hearing your laugh."

Her breath caught. She saw his hand rise up and nearly touch her elbow, but then he hesitated.

"I came tonight to ask for forgiveness," he told her quietly. "To apologize. And to ask you to come home."

A.J. flushed with happiness and was sorely tempted to throw her arms around him and tell him that was exactly what she'd hoped he'd say. But she needed more from him. She was far too in love to be able to risk going back to the farmhouse without a clear understanding of where things stood between them.

The fleet-footed attendant returned without a vehicle. The kid looked worried. "Excuse me, sir. I can't find your car."

"Maybe because it's a truck," Devlin said dryly.

"You mean that thing? With the bed all bent out of shape?"

"I know she's not pretty but she's sound under the hood."

"It's the back end I was worried about." Abruptly, the boy blushed and shut his mouth.

"What happened to the truck?" A.J. asked.

Devlin clapped a hand on the kid's shoulder, slipping him a couple of dollars. "Not to worry. I'll go get her myself."

"Hey, thanks," the boy said, looking at the cash. "But I didn't earn this."

"With that crowd in there"—Devlin nodded over his shoulders—"you most certainly will have by the end of the night.

The teenager looked happy as he rejoined his friends.

"What happened to the truck?" A.J. asked again.

"Nothing good." Devlin shrugged and noted her shivering. "Should you go in? It'll kill me but I can wait until tomorrow if it means you don't get the flu."

She shook her head, thinking she didn't care if it was snowing and she was barefoot. She was determined to hear him out.

"Come on," she said, and started down the driveway, heading in the general direction she'd seen the attendant go. Devlin caught up with her, slipped his jacket over her shoulders and fell into step at her side.

"It's to the left," he said as they approached the end of the driveway.

She turned blindly.

"No, your other left."

She went the other way.

Down at the end of a long line of cars, standing out among the Mercedes and Jaguars, the truck was a workhorse in a field of Thoroughbreds. As Providence would have it, the thing had been parked right under a streetlamp and the added light wasn't kind to its fading paint job or the recent damage.

Which was extensive, A.J. noted.

"Good Lord! What happened?" she exclaimed, going in for a closer look. Crushed and mangled as it was, she wondered why the bed was still attached to the cab. "You back into something? Like maybe a wrecking ball?"

"Run-in with a tree limb."

"That fell out of the sky like a meteor!"

"Yeah, something like that," Devlin muttered.

A.J. inspected the truck briefly.

"Those are beautiful earrings," he remarked when she came back and stood in front of him.

"Thank you. They were a gift from my father."

"They're a magnificent color." She watched as his hand reached out and caressed one of the stones. "Although I prefer the red in your hair."

She warmed under the husky desire behind his words but remembered she should be wary. "Devlin, I—"

"I'm so sorry," he said. "I'm so damned sorry. I can't believe I yelled at you when you were injured and hurting. And then left, for chrissakes. I don't blame you for being mad. I've thought about nothing except you for the last week, trying to come up with a rational explanation for my behavior, some way of explaining why I became so un-glued. When I saw you go down, I was terrified, absolutely terrified. I had images of you in a hospital bed, never to get up again. In retrospect, that was highly unlikely but I wasn't thinking clearly. When you were able to get to your feet, I thought, Okay, she's all right. But then you got up on that stallion, who was halfway to insane and looking like he was going to jump out of his skin, and I felt like I was in a nightmare. It was awful, watching you hold your-self up by will alone, driving that panic-stricken animal over those jumps."

He shook his head with regret. "When you wouldn't go to the doctor, I lost it. I wanted to throttle you for not tak-ing care of yourself, for making me feel so afraid. There was the woman I loved, nearly fainting from—"

"Wait a minute. What did you say?"

"I felt like I was in a nightmare—"

"No, no. After that."

"I was feeling out of control."

"A little further."

"The woman I love—" Devlin halted, cocking his head to one side.

A.J. felt a glow all over her body.

"The woman I love." He spoke the words slowly. "I said that. I really said that."

"You seem surprised." Her smile grew more radiant.

He laughed. "Only because it feels so natural. Considering how long it's been since I said it, I would've assumed I'd be more rusty. Well, that and the fact that the last time I was talking to a horse."

When he reached for her, she went into his arms.

"I really do love you," he said urgently. "You're every thing to me. Whenever I look into your eyes, I can't explain what happens. I just feel *new*."

They were the words she'd wanted to hear from him, grounding and earth-shattering at the same time. And she knew that she loved him back. Fiercely.

Dropping his head down to hers, he murmured, "Can you forgive me?"

"Yes," she said against his lips. "I think I can."

Their mouths fused with a special softness, as if they were kissing for the first time, and she felt his fingers brush against the side of her neck tenderly. In that moment, she couldn't remember the pain she'd been feeling or the separation that had torn them apart.

When they pulled back, she was smiling.

"If I thought it was going to get me this far, I would have fallen off that stallion on day one."

The wind brushed against them.

"We need to get you out of the cold," he said.

"And out of this dress."

"Now, that's a fine idea. Come home with me."

"I want to." She arched her breasts against his chest. "You have no idea how much I want to."

"So get into my chariot, sweet princess."

"I can't." She sighed. "After my father's birthday parties, he and I go into his study and light a candle for my mother. It's their anniversary. They were married thirty-four years ago tonight."

Devlin swallowed his frustration. "You can't miss that."

"I'll come tomorrow morning."

"For breakfast."

"Maybe a little earlier."

"Promise?"

His tongue slid into her mouth and she grabbed on to his shoulders. As his hands traveled down from her waist to cup her buttocks, he drew her against his lower body. When they finally parted, his eyes glittered in the moonlight.

"I better go," he drawled, "before I can't leave."

"I wish I were going with you."

"If you were, I'd cancel my date tonight."

"You have a date?"

"With a cold shower. As soon as I walk in the door." He nodded to the truck. "You want a ride back to the house?"

"No, I think I'll walk." A.J. wanted a moment alone to savor what had happened before rejoining the noise and crush of the party.

Opening the door, he got into the cab, a gentleman in a farmer's truck. She liked the image.

"I'll see you tomorrow, then." She started to take off his jacket.

"No, keep it. It's a long walk back." From out of the open window, Devlin was smiling at her with a wistfulness she didn't normally associate with him. "Come here."

She stepped in close. Gently, he took her face into his hands.

"Good night, my love." The words were soft against her lips. And then he was gone.

The next morning dawned cold, just a degree or two above frost. Before anyone else was even stirring, A.J. got out of bed, showered and packed. In a rush, her bag slapping against the corners of antique sideboards, tables and chairs as she hustled through the rooms of the mansion, she was halfway to the back door when she remembered Devlin's tuxedo jacket. Dropping her things, she doubled back, retrieved the coat and ran free of the house without getting caught.

Behind the wheel of the Mercedes, speeding to the farmhouse, she was wide-awake, despite having had little sleep the night before. After Devlin had left, she'd drifted up to the mansion on a cloud of bliss, entering the party with a secret smile only her father recognized as evidence of the reconciliation. When the celebration finally let up, she and Garrett went into his study and lit a single white candle, which they placed on the mantelpiece, below the portrait of A.J.'s mother.

"You're leaving tomorrow, aren't you?" he said softly as they stared into the glow.

There was a pause and A.J. replied, "It's time for me to start training again. My arm's almost healed. But how did you know?"

"You're radiant and I know you disappeared for a while with . . . Are you going back to him?"

She didn't want to reveal too much but she wasn't going to lie. "We did get a chance to talk."

"And he's righted a wrong, hasn't he?"

"Yes, he has."

"Please be careful."

"Are you warning me because you don't like him?"

"No. Because I love you."

"I'll be fine."

"When will you be back?"

"I don't know. Sometime, I'll call." She turned to go.

"Arlington?"

"Yes?" She faced him again.

"Your mother would have liked him. He's a strong man and I can see in his eyes the love he has for you."

Her father wasn't looking at her. Instead, he was staring up at the portrait. When at last he pivoted around, A.J. saw him framed against the image of her mother. Tears came to her eyes.

"Thank you for saying that," she whispered.

As they embraced, A.J.'s eyes drifted up to meet her mother's.

Yes, she thought. Mummy *would* have liked him.

Pulling into Devlin's driveway, she couldn't wait to go up to the farmhouse but, as soon as she stepped out of the car, she heard Sabbath whinny for her. Hastily scooting into the stable, she opened the top of his stall door. The horse's head came out like it was sprung from a toaster and he snuffled over her.

"I'm back," she reassured him as she slipped him a sugar cube.

After a few more moments with the stallion, during which she checked his water and ran her hands over his legs to reassure herself, for the umpteenth time, that he wasn't lame from their debacle, she took a deep breath. He was good to go. And so was she.

A.J. shut the stall door, and with an erotic anticipation that had her burning, she rushed back to her car, picked up the tuxedo jacket and her bag and ran to the farmhouse. She found Devlin in the kitchen, filling the coffeepot with water. As soon as she came into the room, he dropped what he was doing and captured her in an embrace that bent her almost in half. Lips clamoring together, hands searching out zippers and buttons, they undressed their way up to his bedroom and collapsed in a mad tumble onto his bed. When he entered her with a deep, hard drive, his name left her lips in an explosion as their bodies came together, thrusting and pounding. With a shattering of sensation, they gripped each other fiercely as they were overcome by white heat.

After they came back down to earth, it was a while before Devlin lifted his head and spoke.

"Sorry about that. Usually I have a little more self-control."

A.J. licked his lower lip, making him groan. "Discipline is overrated, in my book," she said.

"God, I want you all over again."

In the silence of the morning, they heard noises drift up from the barn.

"Chester's here," he muttered, wishing for once his old friend would have had the courtesy of being late to work.

In a tornado of shirts and blue jeans, the two scrambled into their clothes, just making it to the kitchen as the groom burst through the front door. He was wearing a happy grin.

"Well, it's just fine to have the family back together again," he said, looking over at A.J.

"Sure is," Devlin said, going back to the coffeepot. He'd left the water on and the sink was close to overflowing.

Chester noted the near-accident with a knowing smirk before asking A.J., "Are ya rough-ridin' ready?"

She smiled as she sat down. "And rarin' to go."

"Well, so's that stallion, let me tell ya. Almost pulled m' arm out a' the socket yesterday on the lead line." The groom settled down at the table as Devlin pushed his breakfast in front of him. "Speakin' of arms, how's yours feelin'?"

"Perfect. Just perfect." She flexed for him, hiding a wince with laughter. "Sabbath was so happy to see me this morning, he was on the verge of speech."

"He's missed you, all right," Devlin said as he put a couple of English muffins under the broiler.

"And wasn't the only one," Chester interjected. "This one with the nooks an' crannies was miserable to be around."

"I wasn't that bad."

"Compared to someone with their foot in a bear trap, maybe."

After the muffins were done, Devlin threw them onto a plate and offered them to A.J. Taking a few for himself, he settled down into his chair, stretched his long legs under the table and rubbed his foot against her ankle. She smiled at him.

"Better eat up, girl," Chester said. "That stallion a' yours is goin' to be a lot to handle today an' breakfast is the most important meal a' the day."

"Hey, I've got to ask," she said. "How many years have you been eating that same breakfast?"

"Since fifty-nine."

"What'd you have before that?"

"Bananas."

"Just bananas?"

"Yup."

"Nothing else?"

"Nope."

"You are what you eat," Devlin offered.

"Have you always had such odd eating habits?" A.J. inquired.

"Like to start m' days off simply," Chester explained. "Life gets complicated real quick on its own. No need to anticipate chaos with a breakfast a' confusion."

"But you eat spicy things in the afternoon. Those chili dogs I saw you wolfing down at the fairgrounds could melt paint off a car door."

"Look, you're talkin' to a man who ate white food for m' first twenty-three years. The tan color a' peanut butter's about as far as I like to go in the mornin' but I've got a lot of eatin' to make up for."

"You only ate white food? How's that possible?"

"White bread, rice, potatoes, the insid'a apples, spaghetti, chicken, turkey. Although not the dark meat, a' course. There's really a lot to choose from."

Devlin laughed. "Now, I've always thought of poultry as more of a bisque color."

"I was willin' to grant certain leniencies."

"Generous of you."

"No sense in bein' rigid."

"Of course not."

"You're amazing," A.J. said.

"Don't I know it. Almost seventy an' in great shape. Ya find something good, ya stick to it."

"That's for damn sure," Devlin said, nodding at Chester's bowl. "You've been eating out of the same dish here for the past five years."

"And a damn fine piece a' pottery she is."

They all laughed.

When they were finished eating, Devlin disappeared upstairs briefly and Chester leaned across the table toward A.J.

"You know," the man said softly, "it really wasn't the same around here without you."

"You don't have to say that, but thanks."

"It's true. He missed ya somethin' fierce. Was a god-awful terror. You two belong together."

A.J. smiled. "You know, I'm inclined to agree with you."

Down at the barn, Sabbath was beside himself with excitement, unable to stand still as A.J. groomed him on the crossties. While Devlin and Chester were out in the ring, dealing with the jumps, she talked to the stallion and was struck by how much she'd missed him.

When Chester came back inside, he said, "All set for ya out there."

"Thanks." A.J. returned the hoof pick to the groom box. "Say, I notice that loose shoe's looking really good."

"Can't say the same for the blacksmith. But then, no man's at his best with a picture of Garfield over one eye."

"Come again?"

"It was on the Band-Aid we gave 'im."

"And he needed the first aid because . . ."

"Twinkle toes over there decided to reach out an' touch the guy."

"You're kidding me." A.J. shot the stallion a glare.

Sabbath stared back at her, the picture of innocence.

"Don't give me that look," she said to the horse. "When he comes back, you better behave yourself."

"He won't."

"Of course he will. I'll be here to hold his head."

"Not the animal—the blacksmith."

"Huh?"

"Man's not gonna come back."

"Ever?"

"I don't want to use his exact language, you bein' a lady an' all. Let's just say it'll be a long time an' a different horse before he'll set foot back in this stable."

"You're kidding me."

"Wish I was."

Devlin came into the barn. "Are we ready to go yet?"

"Just about," Chester said as A.J. went to get her saddle and bridle.

She was muttering something under her breath about meatheaded Thoroughbreds as she went into the tack room. And walked right into a stack of grain bags as tall as she was. She poked her head out into the aisle.

"What's all the feed doing in here?"

"I'll get your stuff," Devlin said, marching past her and meeting her inquiring look with one of nonchalance. While he banged and crashed around in the little room, she glanced over to Chester, who rolled his eyes.

"Let's just say, things didn't run so good when you weren't around."

"I guess so," she murmured, trying not to laugh as Devlin took a header into a pile of blankets.

"Did you see the truck?" Chester whispered.

A.J. nodded, covering her smile with a hand as Devlin emerged with his hair messed up and hay hanging off his sweater. He looked like he'd been through a war.

"You okay there, champ?" Chester asked. "Those there grain bags can be tough when they come atchya in a pack like that."

Devlin shot the man a look as he handed the tack over to A.J. "Say what you will. At least the stuff is dry. Now, when you two are finished giggling, you can join me in the ring. I'll be waiting out there to get started."

"He gets so huffy when he's embarrassed," Chester remarked after Devlin left. "Always has."

"You really shouldn't tease him."

"It's the only exercise he's been gettin' lately."

Once the stallion was saddled, A.J. tugged on a pair of gloves to keep her hands warm and accepted a leg up from Chester. Before they even entered the ring, Sabbath started tossing his head and prancing.

"Let's get him working on the flat," Devlin called out as Chester closed the gate behind them. "Before he jumps out of his skin."

A.J. nodded. It felt good to have a pair of reins in her hands again but immediately she recognized the pain in her arm. The stallion was strongheaded under the bit and every time he arched his neck forward, she felt like she was getting stabbed in her shoulder. Telling herself the limb only needed to warm up, she set her teeth and struggled not to show the difficulty she was having.

As A.J. and the stallion approached the center of the ring for a gait change, Sabbath caught sight of the water jump. Rearing in protest, he stopped short. It took all of her patience and control to get him to trot past and he did so reluctantly, all the while looking as if something were going to pop out and get him. Up on his back, she realized they had a big problem.

Devlin called out, "For now, let's steer clear of the water. We'll all feel better after he calms down a little."

A.J. nodded and continued to work the stallion on the flat, staying at the rail. When Devlin and she decided it was time, she took Sabbath over some smaller fences. He was energetic and strong but not as interested in a good battle as he usually was. Even when they tried a combination of jumps, the stallion responded well, biting into the corners and accelerating like a slingshot into the straightaways when she asked him to.

It would have been one hell of a training session, if it hadn't been for all the pain she was in.

After an hour, Devlin called them over.

"Now, that's what I call jumping!" he said. And then sensed there was a problem. "A.J., what's wrong?"

"Nothing," she answered with a forced smile. Her arm was throbbing to the beat of her heart and she felt queasy. "Should we go through the round again?"

"No," he said slowly. His eyes were measuring her intensely. "You sure everything's okay?"

"Absolutely. I think we should do it again."

He shook his head. "That's enough for his first day back."

Nodding, A.J. tried to keep her relief to herself as she took Sabbath out to the rail and cooled him down. When the stallion was ready to go in, she walked him over to Devlin, who was waiting by the gate. Aware she was being watched closely, she dismounted as smoothly as she could and led the stallion back to the barn, careful to put her good hand on the reins.

12

As soon as A.J. had Sabbath secured on the crossties, she told Chester and Devlin she needed to run up to the house for a minute. Devlin was tempted to follow but didn't want to seem overbearing. Settling himself against the barn door, he began to write out his notes but he couldn't get far because his mind was on A.J. About twenty minutes later, she came back looking more like herself.

"I think I know how to get him over it," she said as she went over to the stallion. Chester had finished grooming him and his coat shone like black ink.

Devlin looked at her blankly. His mind was still dwelling on how pale and shaky she'd looked coming off the course.

"The water jump," she prompted.

"Oh, yeah. What's the plan?"

"Y're gonna teach 'im to swim?" Chester quipped, throwing a blanket across Sabbath's back.

"Just about. It's the same way we got my cousin to go on airplanes. Well, almost got her on planes."

"Drugs?" Devlin asked.

"Exposure over time. We shipped her off to a boot camp for people with a fear of flying. They actually managed to get her on a plane."

"So she flies now?"

"Well, not exactly. But she did sit in one for twenty minutes before they had to give her a paper bag to breathe into." A.J. frowned. "Maybe this isn't the best example."

"I think we should give it a go," Devlin said. "Desensitization works with humans and animals. It's a good idea."

Pleased, A.J. took Sabbath off the crossties. "Then it looks like we're going back into the ring, champ."

She led him out of the barn, carrying her injured arm close to her body so the stallion wouldn't knock it as he craned his head around. The pills Dr. Ridley had prescribed for her, which she'd taken back at the farmhouse, had gone to work and given her some relief from the pain. Unfortunately, they also made her feel a little spacey, so she decided to stick to over-the-counters in the future.

Anyway, it'll feel better tomorrow, she told herself. She probably wouldn't need to take anything else.

Devlin opened the gate for them and she led the stallion into the center of the ring, halting some distance from the jump. Sabbath eyed the water nervously. After she gave him a moment to adjust, she walked him closer while speaking in soft tones, but he balked. Craning his neck away, his eyes began rolling wildly and his hindquarters seized with power. Digging into the loose dirt, he refused to get less than a couple yards away from the water.

With two thousand pounds working against her, A.J. had to relent and she led him away, only to circle back and approach the jump again. They did this a number of times, getting closer to the water at each pass. All the while, she was calm and focused on the horse, trying to manage his fear, working with him patiently. When Sabbath would get really antsy, she'd give him a break and walk him over to Devlin, who'd offer them encouragement. By the end of the session, the stallion was looking to A.J. when he would get scared, drawing strength from her calm, soothing voice.

Later, after they'd returned to the stable, A.J. found herself deep in thought. She felt a little better knowing they had a plan for getting Sabbath acclimated to water. It was another issue whether or not it worked but at least they had a direction.

What was really on her mind was Devlin.

While they'd been in the ring jumping, he'd obviously picked up on her discomfort and been worried by it. His concern for her had been in his face, in his words, in the intense scrutiny he gave every movement she made. When he'd asked, she should have told him how she was really feeling. Instead, she'd flat-out lied to him.

But what could she do? If his expression was anything to go by, his first concern was for her and not the Qualifier. And she loved him for that. The trouble was, they needed to train. Considering how he'd reacted to her accident, she figured if he knew how much pain she was in, he'd probably demand she take more time off. They'd already lost a week. The stallion came unglued at the mere sight of water. And time was running out.

The last thing she wanted was to pull out of the Qualifier, especially after announcing to everyone she was entering Sabbath in the event. With all the attention paid to her buying him and leaving her family's stables, walking away from the competition would be a public pronouncement that she couldn't handle the horse. That everyone had been right and she'd been wrong. That she couldn't go the distance and meet her goals.

But there was more to her determination than just a fear of being embarrassed. Now that she was on her own for the first time, she was eager to prove she could make it independently. She wanted people to know that she wasn't just a figment of her father's money, that she was talented and could compete at the highest levels. She was convinced that turning around the stallion no one else could handle, and taking him into the ring at the Qualifier, would establish her as a serious competitor in the sport she loved. It would put her career on the track she wanted it to be on. Hell, if they did well, she could be on her way to a spot on the Olympic team.

One thing was clear. If they missed any more days of training because of her arm, she'd be forced to give up. Given the stallion's reaction to water, and the fact that he still needed a lot of work over fences, they had to press on. Every second in the ring was critical and she was determined not to let up just because her body hurt. Besides, it would probably feel fine in the morning.

Going over to Sabbath, who'd been resting in his stall,

she stroked his muzzle. She told herself that she was just being an alarmist about her arm. She was coming back from an injury and she should have expected to be sore the first day. It didn't mean that she was going to have continuing problems with it.

With a hiss and a boil, the automatic water system kicked in and sent a stream into Sabbath's trough. The stallion flicked his ears nervously and edged his body away from it.

"I wonder why you're so afraid," A.J. said aloud.

Chester, who'd started moving grain bags out of the tack room, answered for the horse. "Probably saw *Jaws* as a young colt an' never got over it."

A.J. smiled softly. "I think it's more than that."

"Well, that movie sure made a big impression on me," the man said, coming out with another bag of grain. He dumped it in the wheelbarrow he'd parked in the aisle and rolled the heavy load into a vacant stall, talking as he went. "Haven't been swimming since. Even in fresh water."

With a light laugh, A.J. scratched the special spot under the stallion's chin that made him go limp with pleasure.

There was something lurking behind his phobia; she was sure of it. He was a bad boy, prone to fits of showing off and random acts of playful mischief, but his expression when confronting that water jump was different. She knew naked fear when she saw it, in humans and animals.

"Any chance you're daydreaming about me?" Devlin whispered into her ear.

She gasped. For a big man, he could move as quietly as a breeze.

"Didn't mean to startle you." He wrapped his arms around her and she relaxed against his body.

"You can come up behind me anytime," she murmured, rubbing her hips against his. His groan of need was satisfying.

Suddenly, there was a crash in the adjoining stall. Sabbath let out a shriek as A.J. and Devlin rushed toward the sound.

They found Chester facedown next to the wheelbarrow.

"Chester!" A.J. gasped.

She and Devlin crouched over the man, who was mumbling incoherently and clutching his chest.

"I'll call the ambulance," Devlin said, and ran out.

A.J. took the stricken man's hand, feeling for his pulse. It was erratic and fast.

"M' chest feels on fire," he gasped.

"Breathe slowly with me," she instructed, watching for signs that he was losing consciousness.

"Help's on the way," Devlin said as he came back in. "Just hang on."

The wait for the medics was interminable. A.J. and Devlin communicated through long, desperate looks, traded over Chester's suffering. Marked by murmurs of support and the man's rasping breath, the minutes drifted by far too slowly considering the urgency of the situation. When sirens were finally heard, Devlin got up and ran outside, directing the paramedics inside the barn.

The two women entered briskly and cracked open their orange-and-white tackle boxes to reveal medical instruments that made A.J. shudder. As the medics went to work, she and Devlin stepped back, holding on to each other while they watched. Moving quickly, the women spoke in a foreign language of medical terms while trading plastic tubing and needles and, as soon as Chester was stabilized, they loaded him into the back of the ambulance. Devlin rode along and A.J. followed in her car.

Once she got to the hospital, she parked and ran into the emergency room, finding Devlin right away. He took her into his arms.

"How's he doing?" she asked against his shoulder.

"They'll know more in a little while. All we can do is wait."

"Did you call his family?"

"I left a message with his closest relative but she lives in another state. I'm all he has." Devlin's features were pale and tight with worry but his eyes were clear.

"I can't imagine going through this without you," he told her.

"I'm glad I can be here," she said softly.

He led her into a sparse waiting room and they took up a vigil on plastic thrones of worry. Besides a fleet of ugly orange chairs, the only other furniture around were a couple of exhausted-looking tables. Their chipped, laminated tops, done in a repeating fake wood grain, were covered by dog-eared copies of popular magazines. In the far corner, there was a vending machine and hanging from the ceiling was an old TV that had a black-and-white picture but no sound. On it, soap-opera characters were emoting to one another with mute intensity.

"I don't want to lose him," Devlin muttered. "Mercy was bad enough but him as well?"

A.J. stroked his shoulder as he leaned forward.

"He's the closest thing to a father I've got," he said.

She sensed that, in the midst of the nightmare, he wanted to talk. "How long have you known him?"

"Years and years and years. He was my first boss. The first adult I ever listened to. He taught me how to be a man." Devlin pushed a hand through his hair. "God knows, there was no one else around willing or able to. I never knew my own father."

"Your mother raised you?"

"No. I had a series of foster parents, was bounced around every couple of years. No one wanted to adopt an older kid, particularly after I got in some trouble."

"How did you get orphan—" She flushed, not wanting to add any pressure. "I'm sorry. I don't mean to pry."

"That's okay." He flexed his arms and brought his hands together in a bridge. Resting his chin on them, he mused, "My past is as good a distraction as any."

After a long moment, he said, "According to my file, my mother was seventeen, unmarried and alone when she died giving birth. No one came forward to claim me. My father had deserted her in the middle of the pregnancy and I guess her parents were horrified at their daughter's indiscretions. Didn't want evidence of a moral lapse kicking around their house."

"Your grandparents just let you go?"

Devlin nodded.

"Once, when I was sixteen, I looked them up. An old man with eyes like mine shut the door in my face after telling me never to come back." He leaned back in the plastic chair. "Growing up, I acted out a lot. Got arrested a few times for stealing. Never graduated from high school, and college wasn't even on the radar screen. When I left the system, I had nothing to do, nowhere to go and was mad as hell with everyone and everything. At the age of eighteen, I was wandering around aimlessly, trying to make enough money to feed myself, when I showed up at a stable, looking to groom. I don't know why I thought they'd take me in. I'd never been around horses before."

Devlin's smile was sad. "That's when I met Ches and he saved my life. After I walked up a long, dusty drive to the stable, he was the first person I met. I don't know what he saw in me but he took one look at me and said, 'Boy, I'm gonna take care of you.' And he did. He always has."

A.J. was enthralled by what he was revealing. It was all the intimate details she'd wanted to know, all the things that articles on him hinted about but never quite got right. She felt an overwhelming compassion for him, for everything he'd been through, as she imagined how hard his early life had been. How alone he must have felt as he went from home to home, always as an outsider. How much Chester's love must have meant to him. How incredible his journey to the top echelons of the sport was.

"When did you start riding?"

"About two weeks after I arrived. One of the Thoroughbreds, a champion jumper, was being led into the barn after a workout. I looked up from the manure I was shoveling and told the rider the horse was lame. The guy brushed me off like dirt but Chester came forward, checked the leg and backed me up. Turned out the mare had a hairline fracture in her foreleg.

"Later, Chester asked how I knew and I said I just did. Then he wanted to know if I'd ever been up on a horse. I said no but I'd like to give it a try. An hour later, I was in the ring." He looked at her. "Everything I've done coaching you comes from him. He's the master at it and could have been famous but he never was inclined to tip his hand to the talent. He's always been a free spirit, never wanted to be tied down. I was the only one he ever trained."

"Then he certainly was a success, wasn't he?"

Devlin shrugged. "He taught me to channel my anger into winning. That and my natural knack for riding did the trick."

She smiled gently. "I know it took a lot more work than that."

"But it isn't work to do something you love."

"No, you're right. It isn't."

They shared a moment of understanding.

"After my accident, after Mercy was put down, Ches understood that I needed to be alone. He always said he'd be back. I never believed him. That's one of the reasons you're so special to me," he said, reaching out and taking her hand. "You came into my life and opened everything up. And you're the only one other than Chester that I've felt I could trust."

She leaned forward and kissed him on the lips. It was a bare whisper of contact, a soft sliding of their mouths, a vow full of love.

A.J. felt him squeeze her hand and then watched as he leaned his head back and shut his eyes as if he were exhausted. She stared at him for a long time, rerunning parts of the conversation back in her head. She was deeply affected by what he'd said and had the sense that a lot of it had never been revealed to anyone before.

Eventually, she glanced up at the TV and noted the soap opera was still droning on. She tried to remember the name of the series. *Wings of Faith*?

No, that wasn't it.

She watched the characters parade around in glamorous clothes, gesticulate wildly, occasionally kiss or slap one another, and found she was able to keep up with the stories even without the sound. Every now and again, she'd come back to reality as someone in a doctor's coat or nurse's uniform would cut through the room. Most of the time, the medical staff just walked over to the vending machine. The sound of metal clinks as change was dropped in the slot and the whirling noise as food was kicked off the reserve bench became all too familiar.

She turned back to the soap. Damned if she could recall the name.

Wings of Fortune?

After a time, Devlin stretched, got up and went to the nurses' station like a man on an expedition into the wilderness. He returned minutes later, empty-handed. A.J. looked away so he wouldn't see her disappointment.

Up above, the soap came to a finale, with some woman putting white powder into a man's cocktail. The closing credits read, *Wings of Fate*.

Over the next several hours, she and Devlin were joined and deserted by the families of other patients. People came and went, the cast of characters in the room changing and yet remaining the same. Everyone was going through a similar loss of control, desperately waiting for an answer, some news, some kind of hope. And none of them knew who was going to get their life back and who was never going to be the same again.

Finally, after she'd decided her butt was so numb it would never regain feeling, one of the white coats called out Chester's name. She and Devlin leapt to their feet, the room dissolving away as they searched the doctor's face for clues.

He was too young to be making life-and-death decisions, A.J. thought at first. Then she saw that his eyes were very old behind delicate, gold-wire glasses.

"Are you the family?" the physician asked with a heavy Southern accent.

"Is he all right? What's going on?" Devlin demanded.

"You're Devlin and A.J.?"

They nodded.

"We think we know what the problem is. Come with me.

Following their white coat redeemer from the hell of the waiting room, they went through *Star Trek* doors into the real hustle and bustle of the emergency department. Rushing around, everyone seemed to know where they were going and, compared with the stillness of where Devlin and A.J. had been, the urgency was overwhelming but reassuring.

The physician led them over to one of the treatment bays, which was sectioned off by thick white curtains to provide privacy. They braced themselves for what was on the other side.

When the drapery was pushed aside, they stopped dead.

Chester was sitting up and smiling, as chipper and alert as a daisy.

"For chrissake," he said, "don't just stand there. One a' them nurses might see me in this getup an' be overcome by m' physical attractions."

As they went to his bedside, A.J. didn't know whether to laugh or cry. In spite of the tubes coming out of his body and all the machines whirling around him, the man looked fine. His color was back and his eyes were free of the terrifying opaqueness of pain. She promptly burst into tears, having prepared herself for everything but the man's being all right.

Chester and the doctor looked at her awkwardly. Devlin put an arm around her, holding her tight.

"What the hell happened?" he asked.

The doctor began to explain, using medical terms that didn't register.

"Cajun gumbo got me a good one," Chester interrupted, grinning.

"What?" Devlin pegged the doctor with a stare.

"In plain English, gastric distress."

"Indigestion? As in the plop, plop, fizz, fizz variety?"

"In a manner of speaking, yes. He suffers from acid reflux that—"

"M' crawfish backed up on me." Chester shot them all a cheeky grin as Devlin laughed out loud with relief.

"Actually, it is a real concern," the doctor said. "He's got to change his eating habits or this will happen again. His cholesterol is too high and he's not as young as he thinks he is. He needs to cut back on his physical labor and eat better."

"I told you this was going to happen." Devlin was shaking his head. "All that hot, spicy food finally caught up with you. Just because you stick with the bland stuff for breakfast doesn't mean you can go hog wild in the afternoon."

"Bland food?" the doctor said.

"Long story," Chester mumbled.

Devlin took the time to fill in the details. When he was finished, the physician was dumbfounded and the patient was looking sheepish.

"Mr. Raymond, why didn't you tell me all this?"

"Didn't think it really mattered."

"You need to see a nutritionist." The man scribbled on a piece of paper. "Here is a prescription-strength antacid and the name of someone who can work with you on that diet of yours."

"Why do I need a nutritionist?"

"Sir, I've heard a lot of stories but your eating habits are right up there with the best of them. Call me if you need anything."

With a nod to A.J. and Devlin, the doctor left.

"Don't see why I need to go see someone about what I choose to put in my face," Chester grumbled.

"You catch the *MD* after the guy's name?" Devlin said. "It doesn't stand for *Me Dummy*. If it did, you'd have the initials after yours."

A.J. reached for Chester's rough, worn hand. It felt like shoe leather and gripped hers back tightly. "I'm so glad you're all right."

"I didn't mean to worry the two a' you."

"Well, you sure as hell did," Devlin told him gruffly. "We've been out of our wits."

"Listen, I ain't leavin' you yet, boy," Chester said emotionally.

"Thank God for that. I'm not ready to let you go."

Wiping his eyes in the crook of his elbow, Chester cleared his throat. "So, can we unplug me and get me outta here? I'd justa soon have this all behind me and forget about it."

"There's going to be no forgetting about this. Things are going to change," Devlin warned.

"Now, wait a minute. I don't need no keeper."

"Do what the doctor said and you won't have one."

"What the hell does he know? He looks like a paperboy."

"Who's the one who ended up in the ambulance?"

"Just checkin' out the interior. Always wanted to know what the inside a' one looked like."

Just then, a nurse swept aside the curtain.

"You ready to go home?" she asked with a reassuring smile.

"We'll go wait outside," Devlin said, his arm going around A.J.'s shoulders.

"I'll tell ya one thing," Chester said as the nurse went to work. "I'm never mixin' shellfish an' pineapple upside-down cake again."

It was a serious undertaking to wedge everyone into the convertible with the top up. A.J. had to move her seat forward as far as it could go to give Devlin any legroom as he squeezed into the back. Hunched over the steering wheel, she found driving difficult but at least Chester was comfortable up front. He liked it so much, he announced that he was going to invest in a chauffeur with his bingo money.

By the time they pulled up to the man's small home, which was buried in the woods not far from the farmhouse, night had fallen. Devlin tried his best to con Chester into staying with them for a while but the man refused.

"Can we at least bring you dinner?" A.J. asked.

Chester shook his head. "I've got some chicken soup and saltines. Think I'm goin' to take it easy tonight."

"Wise idea. You may want to stick with white food for a week or so."

"I was thinking the right same thing." Chester got out of the car and Devlin walked him to the door. An argument ensued.

"Don't bother showing up to work tomorrow."

"Don't be tellin' me what to do. I don't curry no favor over bossy types."

"If that were true, you and I would have parted ways years ago."

"I only make an exception for you a'cause ya need me so badly."

"I'll grant you that, but don't change the subject. You're taking a few days off."

"One."

"Several."

"One."

Devlin cursed.

"You ain't winnin' this round, boy. Now go take your woman home."

A.J., who could hear them through the open car door, smiled at the words as she waved good night to Chester. When Devlin came back and sat down in the passenger seat, he gave her a long, appreciative look.

"What are you smiling about?" he asked as they headed home.

"I like the idea of being your woman."

She felt his hand caress her thigh. "So do I."

They were pulling up in front of the barn when she asked, "Does Chester do anything other than play bingo once a week?"

"I don't think so. Why?"

"He seems lonely. I hate leaving him there by himself after all he went through today."

"He's a loner by nature. Always has been. I think he likes the peace and quiet."

"Well, maybe he needs to expand his horizons."

Over dinner, they traded riding stories and reminisced about horses they'd known. After cleaning up, they sat down on the couch in front of a crackling fire. It was as enjoyable an evening as A.J. had ever had, one that was free from worry and marked by loving touches and glances full of meaning. For several hours, she didn't think of the Qualifier or her arm or Sabbath, just reveled in their love for each other.

Her concerns returned the next morning. With the dawn's arrival, she felt the heavy weight of her goal settle on her shoulders once again. Lying next to Devlin, she began to fidget, feeling trapped between wanting to spend all day in bed with him and being uneasy and anxious to get to work.

"You're like a live wire this morning," he said.

"Sorry. I'm just thinking about Sabbath."

"What about him?"

"Well, he's terrified of water, right? It makes me think about all his other quirks and things he doesn't like."

"Like eating alone."

"Loud noises."

"The blacksmith," they said together.

A.J. propped her head up on her hand. "I'll bet if we knew more about his history, we might be able to understand him better. I'm going to do a little digging. Find out where he came from, try to figure out where this all started. He can act badly but he's not a bad horse. I just hope he wasn't . . ."

"You're worried he was abused?"

"I'm trying to think of some other explanation for all of his problems. I'm hoping there's another reason."

After a quick breakfast, they left the farmhouse. Devlin headed out into the ring to adjust the jumps and A.J. started grooming the stallion. Without Chester's help, it took longer than usual to get Sabbath tacked up and ready, especially with her arm hurting as it did. Despite taking several Motrin, which she'd swallowed as soon as Devlin had gone downstairs to make breakfast, she found lifting a saddle onto the stallion's back difficult.

Riding him proved more arduous. Even though they had a good session, A.J. was in agony. With every leap into the air, and through the dozens of hard landings, she had to bite her lip to keep from yelping. To hide her distress, she took to avoiding Devlin's eyes for fear he'd read her discomfort.

As they led Sabbath back to the stable, she tried to discuss the day's work but by then her arm was throbbing. When Devlin offered to help groom the stallion, she saw the simple courtesy as a lifesaver. With him preoccupied with a curry brush, she had time to rush into the tack room and swallow two more pills. When she came back, he was putting a blanket on the horse.

"You ready to try some more work around the water?" he asked.

A.J. nodded, stripping off her chaps and then freeing Sabbath from the crossties. As she was leading the stallion out of the barn, Devlin stopped her.

"You look tired."

"I'm fine."

He put his hands on her shoulders. "You don't need a rest?"

"We don't have time for breaks," she said brusquely, then tempered the words with a smile. "At least not until later tonight."

His eyes grew sensuous. "Say, I don't know if you're aware of this but there happens to be some loose hay up in the loft."

"Really?"

"Uh-huh. Bet it'd be good to roll around in. Just in case we can't wait to get up to the farmhouse."

A.J.'s body flooded with heat. She glanced out at the jumps. "Let's get going. The sooner we start—"

"The sooner we're done," he finished, dropping a lingering kiss on her lips.

In a hurry, A.J. led the stallion into the ring and then over toward the water. Immediately, he began to buck in fear and protest. Over and over, they approached and retreated, getting a little closer every time. Stroking his neck when she could and keeping her movements slow and reassuring, she put aside her physical pain and tried to calm him.

After more than an hour, A.J. led the stallion out of the ring, feeling discouraged and exhausted. She put Sabbath into his stall and removed his halter and then Devlin came over with an armload of grass and dropped it over the door. They both stared ahead as the horse ate, the soft rustling of a muzzle against grass the only sound in the barn.

A.J. was rolling her mother's solitaire back and forth between her fingers when Devlin finally spoke.

"You've got to slow down."

She looked up at him in surprise. "What do you mean?"

"I'm worried about you."

"Why?"

"Because you're exhausted."

"We worked hard today."

"You're coming off a fall. You need to ease back into all of this."

"I don't have that luxury," she said softly. "I don't have the time to take it easy."

"A.J., I know you're focused on the Qualifier but you run the risk of burning out if you keep up this pace. I know you don't want to hear this but I think you need to consider the bigger picture."

Her breath left in a rush. "That's what I'm doing. There's always a water jump at the Qualifier, along with a whole host of other things. The crowds, the noise, the other horses. Sabbath's going to be beside himself. We need to prepare him—"

"You're not going to fix him in two months. No one could."

"But—"

"And nobody wants you to hurt yourself trying. Especially me." Devlin tucked a strand of hair behind her ears. "Working yourself to the bone is not the answer."

"There's just not enough time," she said to herself.

13

LATER THAT afternoon, A.J. went up to Devlin's study. Smiling at his organized but daunting stacks of paper, she took a seat in his creaky old wooden chair and settled in for some sleuthing by unfolding Sabbath's bill of sale and pedigree. The prior owner's name was one she recognized and she recalled him owning a stable located in Lexington, Kentucky. After some footwork with a phone operator, A.J. got the number and dialed. The gruff voice that answered didn't inspire confidence.

"Yeah?"

"Mr. Tarlow?" she asked. In the background, she could hear stable sounds like hooves clapping on concrete and whinnies echoing through a barn.

"Hold on." The phone was dropped, landing hard on something metal. The racket was still ringing in her ear when someone else got on the line.

"Albert Tarlow here."

"This is A. J. Sutherland. I bought a Thoroughbred, Sabbath—"

"The sale is final!"

"I know, I know. I just wanted to ask you a couple of questions about him."

"What kind of questions?" He sounded suspicious, like a man being offered a package that was ticking.

"About his background."

"I don't know how much I can help you. I didn't own him

for all that long, although I must say he made a vivid impression."

"He tends to," A.J. said wryly. "Were you aware of any problems he had with water?"

"What didn't he have problems with? He kicked up a fuss about the stall he was in, the riders, the trainers, his hooves—do you know he hates blacksmiths?"

"Yes, but it was the water I wanted to—"

"That horse went through three blacksmiths. He thought they were punching bags, I'm quite sure. Never seen anything like it and I've seen a lot of things."

"About the water—"

The man interrupted her again, his voice wistful. "But that animal had so much potential. When he decided to jump, which wasn't often, he was incredible. Are you having much luck with him?"

"Some."

"You must have the patience of Job."

It was more Noah's territory she was interested in, A.J. thought.

"Mr. Tarlow, I specifically want to know if you tried to take him over any water jumps."

"Only once." The man laughed grimly. "Planted one of my riders in the dirt so hard I thought we were going to have to dig the poor guy out. After that, I decided to sell the horse. Even if we could get him over the uprights and the oxers, which was a big *if* in my mind, I knew no one had a chance on his back over water. That horse put up such a stink over a six-inch-deep puddle, you'd swear it was out to get him."

"Did he have any trouble with hoses or wet ground?"

"I do recall a groom turning the hose on him after a workout to help cool him down. That horse went crazy, and I mean really crazy. Trampled two of my men, tore out a pair of crossties like they were dental floss and ran around, dragging chains behind him, until he wore himself out. Nobody could catch him."

"How long did you own him?"

"Only six months or so. It seemed like years."

"Who did you buy him from?"

"My cousin picked him up for his own use and dumped him here when it became obvious the stallion was a handful. Always told Billy, you get what you pay for. He figured he'd gotten a deal but really he'd done the previous owner a favor by taking that animal off the man's hands."

Just like you did for me, his tone said.

"Any idea where your cousin got him?"

"Don't know that, although I think he'd been passed around a lot before Billy got him."

"Thanks so much," A.J. said.

"Good luck," the man replied, hanging up.

Looking over Sabbath's pedigree, she found the name of his broodmare and her stable and was able to track the place down. Unfortunately, the manager couldn't recall anything in particular about the stallion's time as a colt. He'd been sold as a yearling to another stable, the name of which escaped the woman.

Frustrated, A.J. leaned back in the chair, tapping a pen on the edge of the desk and trying to decide what she should do next. Offhandedly, she noticed a stack of bills in front of her and glanced at the top one. It was for the vet who'd come to check Sabbath's leg after her fall. She picked it up and looked at the next one, which was from the feed store, and the next, which was from one of the blacksmiths they'd used. Then there was another from an insurance company, one from a tack shop and then a hardware store's statement.

She frowned as she added up the amounts. The total was staggering. Devlin had incurred thousands of dollars of debt in her behalf. Why hadn't he told her?

Then it dawned on her. She'd never paid him a cent. They'd agreed from day one she'd pay him a reasonable trainer and board fee but it had been well over a month and she hadn't given him a thing. She resolved to write him a check.

A.J. froze.

And cover it with what? she wondered. All two hundred dollars in her bank account? Groaning, she thought about how poor she was.

Buying Sabbath with her own money was the first independent thing she'd done in her life. She wouldn't go back on the decision but it occurred to her that being headstrong wasn't the same thing as being self-sufficient. Cutting that $30,000 check and walking away from Sutherland's, letting go of her safety net and taking a long-overdue step toward adulthood, it had all been necessary. She just hadn't thought out the financial particulars and now she was paying for it.

Or not paying, as the case may be.

As she confronted a stiff bill with a sagging wallet, she was determined to carry her own weight and not ask Devlin to suck up her expenses. He wasn't earning any income now that he wasn't competing and she had no idea what his net worth was. Anyway, even if he had deep pockets, he didn't owe her a living. She would have to find a way to pay her own way.

And A.J. was determined not to throw herself on her father's financial mercy. She wasn't going to compromise her newfound independence from him simply because of money.

With a flash of insight, she realized how easy she'd had it while under her father's wing. Even though she'd never been paid anything for her work at the stables, there had always been plenty of money. Her father was generous with cash and had covered all her expenses, in school and out. All her clothes, her tack, the horses she rode, the cars she drove, the meals she ate and the vacations she went on ... Garrett took care of it all. She had no credit cards in her own name, had never paid a phone bill, couldn't remember the last time she'd written out a check to some kind of vendor.

Sure sounded like the life of a princess, she thought, struck by what a bizarre existence she'd had. Between Peter running the business of Sutherland Stables, and her father taking care of her so well, she'd become completely divorced from her own finances. Why hadn't she noticed before now?

Because she'd never actually paid for anything until now, A.J. thought, her fingers seeking out the solitaire and rolling it around.

So how was she going to cover her debt?

Maybe she could just sell something.

The trouble was, she didn't really own anything. Which she guessed made sense considering she'd never really bought anything with her own money. Well, except for wildly unpredictable Thoroughbred stallions with water phobias and the predilection for torturing blacksmiths.

Why couldn't she have started out with something a little less ambitious? Like a goldfish?

She mentally thumbed through the things she used on a daily basis. The convertible was in Sutherland Stables' name for the write-off; her furniture back home was more the mansion's than hers; her clothes had been bought on credit that her father covered. Besides, she didn't imagine there was a huge market for used barn boots.

What was she going to do?

Her fingers stilled, the solution painfully clear.

God, growing up hurts, she thought, dropping her hand to her lap.

Chester showed up for breakfast the next morning with a saucy grin. Devlin and A.J. were just sitting down when the man walked in.

"Good mornin'! Good to see ya set m' place at the table. Didya miss me?"

"Welcome back," A.J. said, smiling up at the man.

"How're you feeling?" Devlin asked suspiciously.

"Right as rain. Fit as a fiddle. All the usual." Chester slid into his chair and picked up his spoon. "I'm ready to get back to work. Couldn't stand kicking around the house yesterday. Hey, listen. After the trainin', I was thinkin' I could retrofit those water pipes that busted. The plumber said he fixed the line but—"

"You're doing nothing but the bare minimum today and I'm going to be watching you," Devlin said. "If you're not on good behavior, you're back on the bench."

Chester opened his mouth to argue but obviously thought better of it.

"Fine," he grumbled. "If the two a' you want to play nursemaid, that's your business."

"Glad you see the light," Devlin said with a grin.

Down at the barn, they fell into their regular rhythm of work but it was strained under the surface. A.J. had to perform many of her tasks with one hand, which meant she was slow and dropped things. The worst for her was picking out Sabbath's hooves. She had to use her arm to do the job, and, by the time she was finished, beads of sweat were dotting her forehead from the pain. She was forced to sit down and recover, cradling her arm in her lap while pretending to make small talk with Chester. After a while, the pain passed but it took longer than the day before.

Devlin had his own concerns. He was worried Chester would overdo it and unsure how much lifting and pulling was safe for the man to do. The groom behaved himself for the most part, but when he came down from the loft with a heavy load of hay, Devlin had to step in.

"You sure you should be carrying all that?"

"Humpin' bales a' hay is what they make men for."

"It's what they make wheelbarrows for."

"Aww, come on. I've been toting this kinda load for years."

"And maybe it's time you eased up." Before the man could argue, Devlin pointed a finger to the back of the barn. "You know where it is."

Moments later, Chester showed up grumbling but pushing the wheelbarrow.

"Much better."

"Hate this thing," Chester grumbled. "Wheel's bent cockeyed an' the barrel's too shallow."

"So buy a new one. You're going to spend a lot more time using the thing, so you better like it."

Chester looked as if he was going to squabble.

"Tell you what," A.J. offered. "I've got some errands to run today. We'll hijack the truck and pick up a new one together."

"You askin' me on a date?" Chester asked wolfishly.

"I suppose I am."

"You buyin' or am I?"

"If you're talking about the wheelbarrow, I am," Devlin interjected.

"But what about food? If it's a date, ya need food."

"Probably not a lot of that at the local hardware store," A.J. said with a grin. "Considering your days of eating nails are over with."

"Well, I'll pay for lunch if we go to the Pick a' the Chicken."

"Okay, but you should know, I don't kiss on the first date."

"Neither do I."

They all laughed.

Before heading to the ring, A.J. ducked into the tack room and dug out the pills she'd put in a plastic bag and shoved deep into the pocket of her jeans. She'd taken two as soon as she'd gotten out of bed and she'd intended not to take any more until after the session but she knew she wasn't going to make it through the workout without more.

Devlin walked into the room just as she tilted her head back to swallow.

"Hey, do you want to—?"

Caught by surprise, she choked and began coughing.

"Sorry," she gasped, knocking herself in the chest.

Devlin gave her a strange look. "You okay there?"

As soon as she could breathe again, she said, "Fine. I'm fine. You caught me on the thin edge of a sneeze."

"Well, if you need mouth-to-mouth, I'm the right man for the job."

She went over to him, slipping her arms around his waist. "That so?"

"You better believe it," he said before dipping her and catching her lips in a searing kiss.

"What I was about to say before you turned blue," he murmured against her lips, "was how'd you like to go on a date tonight?"

"A date?"

"Dinner and a movie. Just the two of us. We could eat pizza and nuzzle in the back of a dark theater." His tongue stroked her bottom lip. "I've heard the smell of popcorn is an aphrodisiac. Not that we need the help, of course."

"I'd love to go on a date with you."

"Good." He kissed her again and left.

Alone in the room, A.J.'s shoulders sagged. She hated

lying to him. Hated her injury. Prayed that she would hea
fast.

Going to the windows, she saw the ring beyond, its mul
ticolored jumps bright in the sunlight. She reached out a
hand, putting the tips of her fingers against the cold, leaded
glass that wrinkled the landscape. It was just until the
Qualifier, she told herself. Then she would take a break and
let the arm rest. Only a matter of weeks.

The thought didn't reassure her much. Turning her back
to the window, she straightened her shoulders. And pre
pared to soldier on.

After the training session, A.J. and Chester piled into the
truck and rambled to the outskirts of town. First stop was
the hardware store, where they found a shiny red wheelbar
row that fit Chester's precise specifications. They loaded it
into the back, tied it down with some rope and then headed
downtown.

Although hardly a metropolitan standout, the city
proper wasn't without sophistication. There was a small but
bustling financial district, two four-star hotels, a convention
center and a tidy row of shops on the main street. All along
the sidewalks, people were walking with gracious purpose
more friendly than those found in bigger cities but without
the meandering gait of folks who lived in truly small towns

Cruising down the street, A.J. pulled into a parking space
in front of one of the antique shops. Chester shot her a
quizzical look.

"I know I'm old and priceless but ya don't have to get rid
of me just yet," he said.

A.J. smiled stiffly. "I'll be right out."

He watched her go inside with interest. Through the
wide windows in the front of the store, he saw a well-dressed
man come forward to greet her warmly and then observed
the two disappearing into a back room. Sometime later,
when they returned to view, A.J. shook hands with the man
It seemed like she was trying to reassure him of something.
When she came back out of the store, a slip of paper in her
hand, her face was grim.

"Everythin' okay?"

She nodded but as she pulled out of the parking space, she almost sideswiped a car, and they were saved only by the horn of the other driver. As she recovered, Chester noticed her hands were shaking on the steering wheel.

"Sorry about that," she murmured, shooting him an apologetic look.

Concerned, Chester found it difficult to respect her privacy as they pulled up to the local bank.

"This won't take a moment," she told him.

When she returned, she was tucking something into her back pocket. She didn't offer explanations and he didn't ask for any. This time, she was much more cautious as she pulled out into traffic. Silence reigned as they left town, unbroken until she turned into the parking lot of the auction house.

"We biddin' on something?" Chester asked.

A.J. took a deep breath.

"No, we're doing a little detective work," she said, parking the truck.

"Concernin' what?"

"Sabbath's background."

"I don't know that y're gonna like his rap sheet."

A.J. tried to smile as she opened her door. Chester disembarked with her.

"You know, I can really see you as the Nancy Drew type," he said. "Determined, fearless. Only no matching hat an' handbag kinda thing. Can't see you botherin' with all that girlie stuff."

This time she was able to offer a better grin as they crossed over the blacktop and headed toward the business office.

Chester kept up the conversation. "I'd even guess you'd be related to that Drew girl, what with the reddish hair an' all. I could see the two a' ya huntin' around scary old houses, findin' secret passages, diggin' up things."

"Actually, the one with the shovel's my cousin, C.C."

"Clamdigger?"

"Archaeologist."

"Same thing." Chester opened the door for her. "Say, do they give you girls anythin' more than initials in your family?"

"Actually, she goes by Carter, now. I just keep forgetting that we've all grown up."

As they approached the counter, Margaret Mead, A.J.'s old friend, came out from the back room. As soon as she saw A.J., she broke into a wide smile.

"Ah, now, there's a sight for sore eyes!" The Irish lilt was a welcoming sound. "And who'd you be bringin' with you this day?"

A.J. glanced over at Chester, who'd removed his tattered baseball cap and was the color of a beefsteak tomato. She raised her eyebrows, struck by a thought.

"This is a very dear friend, Chester Raymond," she replied, nudging the man forward. He hung back, barely touching Margaret's hand as the woman reached over the counter.

"Pleased to meet you," Margaret said with a twinkle.

Chester mumbled something that could have been "Hello." Maybe in some foreign language.

"And what brings the two of you here?" the woman asked.

"Do you have any records on that stallion I bought? His name is—"

"I remember the animal," Margaret said. "Don't tell me you're giving up on him?"

"Not in the slightest."

"Ah, I knew you'd have the stuff." She looked over to Chester. "A right talented lass, she is, don't you think?"

Chester shuffled his feet but managed a "Yes, ma'am."

"What kind of information are you lookin' for?"

"Former owners. I know where he was bred and the last stable he was boarded at but it's a blank slate between the two."

"Hmmm. I do believe we sold him a couple of times but I'd have to go through the files. Let me see what I can come up with."

"I'd appreciate it. I'm at the McCloud Stables. You can find me there."

"Will do." Margaret settled her eyes on Chester. "And how do you know such a lovely thing as the Miss Sutherland?"

"I groom over at McCloud's."

"He's one of my coaches," A.J. corrected.

Chester looked up, surprised. "I suddenly get a promotion?"

"Devlin helps me over the fences," A.J. said to Margaret. "Chester helps me get over myself. He's full of wisdom, insight—"

Chester cleared his throat.

A.J. fell silent.

Margaret's eyes positively sparkled.

The two women looked at each other, a common purpose forged like iron.

"Thanks again, Margaret," A.J. said.

"I'll be in touch," the woman replied.

They both looked at Chester, who appeared to be on the verge of another seizure.

"Ma'am," he said, nodding to Margaret.

"It was very nice to meet you, Mr. Raymond."

A.J. turned to go and Chester followed but not before he glanced back one last time at the Irish woman.

Outside, as he and A.J. walked to the truck, he said, "I'm not a used car, you know. Ya don't have to sell me like I'm some jalopy lookin' for a garage to park in."

"Was I doing that? I thought I was just being accurate. You are an incredibly important part—"

"That fine woman in there has no need for a man to be pressed on her."

"So you noticed."

"Noticed what?"

"What a nice person she is."

"'Course I did," he grumbled. "But she could be married, for all I know."

His question dangled like a hiker off a cliff, ready for rescue.

"Margaret's a widow," A.J. said, tossing down a lifeline. She got in the driver's side and put the key in the ignition.

"Really," Chester murmured as he slid into the passenger seat. "I mean, that's a shame. How long's it been?"

"A couple of years. And she isn't seeing anyone now."

The engine came to life.

"Not that it's any a' m' business," Chester said firmly.

"Of course not," A.J. agreed, putting them into reverse.
He shot her a look. "Ya settin' me up, girl?"

"Now, why would I do something like that? You can
clearly take care of yourself."

"That's right. I don't need any help with the ladies."

She turned the truck around, trying not to smile too
much.

"Ya think she liked me?" he asked.

A.J. and Devlin were on their way out to dinner when she
took the slip of paper she'd gotten from the bank and
handed it to him.

"What's this?"

"The money I owe you."

He frowned.

"When I started here," she said, "you and I agreed I'd
pay for training and board. That should cover it. At least
according to what we charge at Sutherland's."

Without looking at the check, he tried to push it back at
her. "I don't want your money."

"Devlin, I saw the bills."

"What bills?"

"The ones upstairs on your desk."

"So?"

"There's a couple thousand dollars' worth of debt up
there. You need this money. You're not competing anymore."

"Thanks for the reminder," he said darkly.

"I didn't mean it like that."

"So you think I'm going to go broke feeding your stallion?"

"I didn't say that."

"In any event, let me put your mind at ease. I may not be
in your father's league but I'm not strapped for cash, either."

"Devlin—"

"Too bad you didn't get into my investment files while
you were nosing around up there. Then your mind would be
at ease."

"I wasn't nosing around."

"So the bills just fell into your hands while you were on the phone."

"Look, I'm just trying to live up to my obligations."

"And I'm telling you not to worry about it."

A.J.'s eyes implored him. "I've spent too much time letting other people take care of me. You and I should be partners. Will you let me do this, please?"

She watched him cross his arms over his chest, the check getting buried in the crook of his elbow. While she waited for him to speak, she reached to her throat out of habit but there was nothing to rub between her fingers. She dropped her hand.

Devlin frowned, unsure exactly what was missing in the movement.

Finally, he said, "Is this money yours or your father's?"

"Mine."

If it were her father's, it would have been easy to tear up the check. He had no intention of taking Garrett Sutherland's cash. Ever. As for it being A.J.'s, he wondered whether it would change things if she knew he had several million dollars in various stocks, bank accounts and real-estate investments. Would she find it easier to let him bear some of the burden for her?

"Devlin, I may have brought this up because I'm worried what the stallion and I are costing you but there's more to it. It's about me being independent. For the first time in my life, I want to support myself." She paused. "I need to be self-sufficient."

"I don't like this."

"I can tell. But you know it's the right thing for me to do, don't you?"

He raked a hand through his hair. "I don't want you to think I can't take care of you."

A.J. went to him, putting her hands on the rigid muscles of his upper arms. "I know you can take care of me. I've never doubted that."

He looked down at her for a long time.

"I didn't know I was such a traditional guy," he muttered, putting an arm around her shoulders. "Taking care of my woman and all that caveman, chest-thumping stuff."

"You're very sweet when you're being protective and overbearing."

Reluctantly, he slipped the check into his back pocket.

"Was this our second argument?" he asked as he opened the door for her.

"I think so," A.J. said, slipping her arm through his. "And I think we did just fine."

"Does this mean we get to make up later?"

"You better believe it."

They were getting into the truck when she said, "By the way, I've asked Margaret Mead to look into Sabbath's records. She might be calling for me sometime in the next few days."

"You get anywhere with his last owner?"

A.J. shook her head. "Came up empty on his first one, too."

Devlin drove them to the next town over and they ate at a restaurant that was known for its lasagna. After her failed attempt at cooking, A.J. seized the opportunity to pick up tips from the pros. The waiter humored her through her interrogation and eventually the chef himself came over to their table. She took notes on cocktail napkins and whenever she looked up at Devlin he was watching her with eyes full of amusement and warmth.

The movie they saw had more special effects than story line but it didn't matter. As they pulled up in front of the barn again, they both agreed the evening had been perfect. After checking on Sabbath, they went to the farmhouse, hung up their jackets and headed upstairs, one after the other. Together, they took their clothes off, mingling their laundry in the hamper, and brushed their teeth, side by side. When they were lying together in bed, A.J. closed her eyes, feeling a profound peace.

Devlin, on the other hand, was wide-awake and staring at the ceiling. Before pitching his khakis in with the rest of the dirty clothes, he'd cleaned out the pockets and found the check. He'd been surprised at how large an amount she'd written it for.

What did he expect, he mused. She probably had a trust fund that made Fort Knox look like a piggy bank.

The next morning, though, something was still nagging at him. When Chester and he had a moment alone, he asked the man, "Where did you two go yesterday?"

"The hardware store, an antiques dealer an' the auction house."

"Antiques dealer?"

"Yup. An' the bank."

"Which one?"

"National Savings an' Trust."

"No, which dealer?"

Chester thought for a moment. "The real fancy one on State Street. Got all kinds of silver an' jewelry in the front window. Looks like you'd have to pass a credit check just to get through the door. Needless to say, I stayed in the truck."

Devlin frowned.

"What's the problem, boy? You look like you got a bee-hive between the ears."

"It's nothing. Forget I asked."

14

A WEEK later, Devlin was calling out commands as A.J. and Sabbath warmed up. Watching from the rail, Chester was impressed.

From train wreck to poetry in motion, he thought. 'Course, ya coulda raised a barn with bare hands for all the work it took.

Moving lithely, the pair was working as one as they went from a bouncing trot into a loping canter. Even to Chester's expert eye, he couldn't tell when A.J. was giving direction to the stallion. It was like they were communicating telepathically, and when they started jumping, he was awestruck. All pounding hooves and leaping arches, they charged through the course, making quick work of the mammoth fences. And they did it with an elegant confidence, as if it was no more than a whim.

A new champion's just entered the sport, Chester thought, and everybody's gonna know it at the Qualifier.

In the center of the ring, Devlin was thinking the same thing. When they came jogging into the center, he started clapping.

"Congratulations. That was great."

But A.J. barely responded. Her features were tight, her cheeks pale, and he saw that her hands shook as they held the reins. She was in the same state after every session and he couldn't understand it. When prompted, her response was always, "I'm fine. It's just stress. It takes a lot of concentration to keep Sabbath in line." Always a plausible denial. Except he wasn't buying it anymore.

"Chester," he called out. "Walk out the beast, would you?"

A.J. looked at him in surprise.

"You and I need to talk," he told her.

"About what?"

"Why you look like you're going to fall out of the saddle."

"I'm perfectly fine."

"Bullshit. You look like hell."

"Just an off day."

"It's like this every time we finish up in the ring."

"It's hard work."

"Not that hard."

She frowned at him, the pain in her arm and his insight making her defensive. Her voice grew sharp.

"I appreciate the concern but I feel fine. And I don't need help cooling down my horse." She called out to Chester, who was coming across the dirt, "It's okay, I'll take care of him."

As the groom shrugged and turned around, Devlin shot her a dark look. "Suit yourself but I'll see you back at the house. This conversation isn't over."

A.J. watched him stalk out of the ring and groaned. The last thing she needed was an in-depth discussion about her stamina. As the stallion fell into a walk at the rail, she let down some of her guard, wincing as she settled her arm across her lap. The pain hadn't gotten any better and she wasn't surprised Devlin had noticed her fatigue. Being in constant agony was exhausting.

And the excuses were getting harder to tell every time.

When she finally dismounted, she found herself swallowing another pair of Motrin before she could lead the stallion back to the barn. Feeling wretched, she was closing the ring's gate and girding herself for the rigors of grooming, when an unfamiliar car came up the drive. Margaret Mead disembarked from the compact, waved to A.J. and smiled when she saw Chester hovering in the background.

Walking over with the stallion, A.J. did her best to cheerfully greet their visitor while waiting desperately for the painkillers to kick in.

"Good mornin'," Margaret said.

"You didn't have to come all the way out here," A.J. replied, glancing back at Chester, who was standing just inside the stable door. "But I'm glad you did."

The two women shared a meaningful look.

"Why don't you come inside and get out of the wind," A.J. said in a voice loud enough to be overheard. She was hoping to give Chester a moment to collect himself.

In the shadows, the man took advantage of it. He tore off his baseball cap and smoothed down the thin hair on his head. As Margaret approached, he was shifting his weight from one foot to the other, a nervous metronome.

"Did you find out anything?" A.J. asked as they halted the stallion at the crossties. He craned his head forward, snuffling over Margaret.

"Aye, I did," the woman said, eyes growing sad as she stroked his muzzle.

A.J. felt her insides grow cold.

"Seems to be he was sold as a yearling to a stable not known for the humane treatment of its horses. I can't say I could tell you exactly what happened to him there but, if what I know about the place is true, it's likely he had some very tough times."

"Oh, no . . ."

"The stables were closed down by the state two years ago. We've sold a lot of horses that had been trained there over the years and they've all had behavioral problems of one sort or another. After some kind treatment, most of them come round, though they're never completely the same again. The abuse stays with them."

"And no wonder," A.J. said, putting a hand on the stallion's neck. He turned his head to her, giving her an affectionate nudge.

It all made such awful sense. The way he got so aggressive with handlers and in the show ring, his finicky behavior about his feet that became violent if he was pressed, his suspicion of people he didn't know. His fear of water. She'd heard of horses who were treated badly, knew some stories

of abuse, but usually owners and stables took good care of
their stock, if for no other reason than the vast sums of
money that got pumped into show horses. Unfortunately,
there were tragic exceptions.

"I think I remember hearin' about that place," Chester
spoke up. "The guy who ran it was a real sick bast—er, man.
He used to have his grooms turn hoses on the horses. Said
it was a way of exhaustin' the animals out a' misbehavin'. If
the grooms didn't do it, they'd get fired. An' that was early
on. By the time they got closed down, the man'd gone mad.
Starvin' an' floggin' the stock. It was a mess."

"I'm sorry I don't have better news," Margaret said.

"Me, too," A.J. said sadly.

It was incomprehensible to her how anyone could hurt
something as magnificent as the stallion who was nibbling
at the edge of her jacket collar. His breath was warm on
her face and his butter-soft muzzle was ever so gently
brushing up against her neck. Her heart bled for the cruelty he'd suffered and for the other animals that had been
brutalized. The fact the stable had been closed down
would never make up for what had happened to any of
them.

"Ah, lass," Margaret said, slipping an arm around A.J.'s
shoulders. "Your heart's in the right place. This stallion was
lucky to find you and you him. It's a fine pairin'."

Chester nodded. "Very fine."

"I need to go talk to Devlin," A.J. said. "Will you excuse me?"

Margaret smiled. "Of course."

"I'll groom him real good," Chester said before the question was posed. "Go on, now."

Margaret and Chester watched the young woman leave.

"That's a fine girl," Margaret said.

"Yup. An' you should see her on that horse. She's brought
'im around like ya wouldn't believe it."

"Amazing what a little love will do."

They were silent for a little.

"Say," Chester said, looking down at his feet. "You like
to play bingo?"

*   *   *

"Devlin?" A.J. called out as she came in the door.

"I'm in here."

She followed the sound of his voice to the kitchen. He was eating a sandwich and offered to make her one. She shook her head.

"Margaret Mead just stopped by," she said.

The distress in her voice made Devlin's eyes sharpen.

"What did she say?"

As A.J. related the news, his face grew grim.

He let out a curse after she finished speaking.

"I knew some riders at that place. The stable had a high turnover rate and for good reason. There were rumors but a lot of people assumed it was just talk from grooms who'd gotten the pink slip or riders who didn't agree with the management. Took the state too damn long to shut them down."

Devlin reached his hand across the table to her and she took it, holding on tight. They talked for a while about the stallion's misfortune.

"But he's getting better with the water," A.J. said, getting to her feet. "I think it's because he really trusts me. I'm going back out with him now and try to—"

"I think you better take the afternoon off."

"Why?"

Frustration crossed his face. "You're upset. You're tired."

"Devlin—"

"You need a break."

"No, I don't. The Qualifier is only three weeks away." She reached her good hand back and began unraveling the braid in her hair. When she was finished, she braided it up again, securing it in a tie.

"You're working too hard."

"I'm f—"

Devlin exploded, crashing his fist onto the table. "If I hear you say you're fine one more time, I'm going to put my head through the wall!"

A.J. jerked back, surprised at the depth of his emotion. His eyes glittered with anger as he looked at her.

"You're not eating. You look like hell. You spend all

night tossing and turning." She opened her mouth. "And don't deny it. I'm in that bed with you."

He held up his hand before she could defend herself.

"A.J., you're not going to make it if you don't relax a little. You're working yourself too hard and if this continues, you're going to be no good to anyone the day of the Qualifier. You have to trust me on this."

She looked away from him, crossing her arms over her chest.

In a much softer tone, he asked, "Why is this so important to you?"

Devlin could hear the thread of desperation in his voice. It was a cadence he didn't recognize as his own and he might have even been ashamed of it at other junctures in his life. The weakness was of no consequence to him now. All that mattered was the woman he loved and the purple scars of exhaustion under her dull blue eyes.

When she didn't answer him, he thought she was going to shut him out. Then, in a somber voice, she began talking.

"When I was younger, people used to tell me I looked like my mother. That I was her little shadow. As I got older, I became my father's daughter, the rich girl who rode horses. Now I'm known for being trained by you and buying that horse." She looked him in the eye. "When the hell am I going to be described by my own adjectives?

"Ever since I left home, I've been looking back and thinking that my life has been one long freight train of other people's definitions. And part of it is my fault because I lived on the fringes of my father's life for too long. But I don't want to do that anymore. *I* picked Sabbath. *I* picked the Qualifier. *I'm* doing the work." She took a deep breath. "I don't want to be Garrett Sutherland's society princess. I don't want to be just another marginal rider. And I'm willing to sacrifice to get what I want."

Devlin got up from the table with a sharp motion.

"Are you walking out on me?" she asked.

He shook his head and offered her his hand.

When she wound her fingers through his, he took her up the stairs to the top landing and paused in front of the door that had been shut the entire time she'd been at the farm-house. When he opened it, the hinges creaked from lack of use.

A.J. let out a gasp as she looked past him.

The room was filled with competition trophies, ribbons, photographs. There were large silver plates and event cups, two Olympic gold medals, honorary jackets and horse blankets, pictures of Devlin and Mercy on countless magazine covers. She stepped inside, struggling to take it all in.

Most of the objects had been mounted on the walls, hung lovingly and in order. But not all of them. There was a saddle in one corner that seemed to have been discarded. It lay dying on the floor, distorting under its own weight as it splayed out. Across the pummel was a tangled bridle, and in front of the ruined tack, there were pairs of riding boots that fell across one another haphazardly, like a platoon of wounded soldiers.

All over this anarchy, and covering even those things that had been carefully tended to, there was a sheen of dust.

She turned to Devlin with wide eyes.

"I didn't mean for this to become a shrine," he said, glancing around. "I had to put all this stuff somewhere as it accumulated, and my need for order turned it into one. Now it's more a mausoleum than anything else."

"All these pictures," A.J. marveled, focusing on one. It was of Devlin and Mercy at one of the Qualifiers. She remembered having watched them from the stands. "I was there for this one."

He joined her. "That was a lot of years ago. A lifetime ago for me."

"And I saw you win this," she said, going over to one of the framed medals. It was like seeing part of her own history. "I was enthralled watching you and . . ."

A.J. stopped talking but kept looking.

When she'd surveyed the contents of the room, she said, "Thank you for showing me this. I'd always wondered where it had all gone."

"This is the first time I've been in here in . . . God, it seems like forever. For a long time, I could barely stand walking by the door." Devlin went over to the splayed saddle and picked it up off the floor. "I can't tell you how much time I spent in this."

He dusted it off and repositioned it carefully.

"This was my whole life," he told her. "From daybreak until well into the night, the riding and competing was everything. Nothing else mattered."

When he looked at her, his voice took on a strident tone. "Which is why I'm telling you to back off."

A.J.'s brows crashed down over her eyes. "You didn't get all these trophies and ribbons because you gave up. You worked hard. You made sacrifices."

His laugh was harsh. "I sure as hell did. I sacrificed my goddamn partner."

"Don't say that."

"It's the truth. That morning when the accident happened, I took Mercy out for a warm-up I knew damn well she wasn't fit for. She'd cracked a rail the day before and landed funny but I told myself she was fine." His voice thinned. "I made the choice to press her because all I wanted was to win that goddamn cup again. I killed her for a goddamn silver cup."

Devlin's eyes shot over to the four sterling-silver Qualifier trophies that were mounted on the wall. A cold emotion, something close to hatred, settled into the lines of his face as self-blame washed over him in a wave.

A.J. went to him, stroking his arm.

He told her, "I can tell you it wasn't worth it but I know you won't believe me."

"Of course I do!"

"Then you're lying to yourself. Every day, when you get in that ring with Sabbath on the verge of exhaustion, you're taking a dangerous sport and making it worse."

She took his hands and brought them to her lips. "I don't want you to worry. I can handle it."

"I'm not just worried. I'm frustrated and I'm angry because I'm trying to save you from yourself." He expelled a breath harshly. "Which is pointless. If someone had tried to put the brakes on me, I wouldn't have listened, either."

"Devlin, I'm strong and determined but I'm not reckless with that stallion. I'm scrupulous about keeping after his legs. I'm so careful—"

He was shaking his head. "You just don't get it, do you? It's not just about Sabbath. It's about you."

"And *I* need to do this."

"If you don't make it to the Qualifier, what do you think is going to happen? There won't be any more trophies to win? No more events? Don't get so fixated on three weeks from now that you forget there's a whole damn calendar year full of rings to compete in. It doesn't have to happen all at once."

"But you're the one who told me not to pull back at the fairgrounds. You were the one who refocused me after Marceau jumped all over us. Why are you telling me to turn back now?"

"Because you don't look well."

"Thanks," she said gruffly, and pulled away. "Just because I'm not in show clothes, you don't think I can take it."

"That's a cheap shot and you know it. Besides, what I'm telling you is to slow down, not walk away."

Their eyes met and he hoped he'd reached her but when A.J. turned toward the windows, he knew she wasn't going to change her course.

"What will you do if I keep going?" she asked finally.

"I love you," he said to her back. "And I made a promise to you. I'm not going anywhere."

He watched as her shoulders relaxed.

"I can't get through this without you, Devlin."

"Then don't ask me to sit back and watch you self-destruct."

"I'm a lot stronger than you think."

She came over to him and he felt her arms come around his waist. He accepted her body against his, tucking her into him, wishing he could shelter her.

In Devlin's heart, he prayed that getting her to the Qualifier wasn't going to tear them apart.

Devlin and A.J. returned to the barn in a tense silence they tried to camouflage with banal conversation. Chester had just finished grooming the stallion and was putting the brushes away.

"It's back to the pool for you," A.J. informed Sabbath. "And this time, you're getting your feet wet."

"You're going to try and get him into the water?" Devlin asked.

"That's what I've been shooting for. The more exposure he gets, the better. What could be closer than getting four hooves in the jump?"

"But it's cold out there." Devlin was silent for a moment. "Wait. If you're going swimming, I think I've got what you need."

"Oh, no," Chester said. "Not the Swamp Thangs."

A.J. shot the man a curious look. "What's a Swamp Thang?"

"They're pretty indescribable."

Devlin returned with the ugliest, most misbegotten set of rubber waist-waders A.J. had ever seen. They were big, they were motley green and they smelled awful.

"You're kidding me."

"These are no laughing matter."

"You got that right."

"They happen to be specially made."

"Out of old trash bags?"

"You'll thank me later," he said, holding them out.

"Only if you make me."

A.J. put them up against her and then went to step into one side. It was like volunteering to go into a mudhole.

"Hold up. You're going to have to lose the shoes," Devlin told her. "They're meant to be worn with only a pair of socks."

"An' a blindfold, if ya happen to be around any mirrors," Chester said.

With a curse, she stripped off her barn boots. "Offloading some self-esteem no doubt helps as well."

When she pulled the waders up, the waistband came to her chest and she had to readjust the suspenders to their limit. Excess rubber flapped around her as she walked around, sounding like fish on the bottom of a boat.

"They smell like old sneakers," she said, wrinkling her nose.

Chester laughed. "When they made 'em, had to make sure all the senses were offended. Seemed only fair."

"I feel like I'm wearing the Jolly Green Giant's Depends."

"Enough with the wisecracks," Devlin cut in. "They'll keep you dry and that's what matters."

"All right, then, let's get down to it. These things aren't going to look better with time."

She took Sabbath off the crossties and saw he was giving her outfit the once-over. His look seemed to say, *You can't be serious.*

"Don't start," she told him. "In a few minutes, you're going to be so busy being nervous you're not even going to notice what I'm wearing."

Once A.J. and Devlin got the stallion into the ring, they turned him loose for a few minutes. After Sabbath had settled down, A.J. hooked a lead line to him and took him over toward the water, being careful to keep her injured arm out of the way. As a result of their hard work, she was able to get him standing at the edge of the pool but he balked as soon as she asked him to step into the water with her.

Turning around, they approached again. And again. In time, the stallion eventually gave in, tentatively reaching a foreleg out and pawing at the water as A.J. stood in the pool. Another hoof followed but the rest of him refused the baptism by fire. With his front legs splayed out widely, most of his weight was on his hindquarters and his massive muscles were quivering, ready to contract and propel him backward the instant his fear overwhelmed him.

As it soon did.

With a frantic whinny and a maneuver so abrupt it surprised even A.J., he bolted. Things didn't go well after that. In his panic to leap away from the water, Sabbath accomplished the opposite as he lost his footing and ended up with every hoof he had, and a little more, in the pool. The commotion stirred up a fury of spray, which only scared him more and drenched A.J. as she struggled to hold on.

"I think that's enough," Devlin called out from his position at the rail.

"I don't want to end this way."

"You're soaked."

"Thanks for the news flash." She smiled to take any sting from the words. "But we need one more try."

One more try turned into several. At first, the stallion refused to go anywhere near the jump. Having had his fears confirmed thanks to his own flailing, he was more determined than ever to keep dry and distant. But A.J.'s sweet talking and patience paid off. He was getting ready to put a foot in again when she noticed Devlin walking toward them. Pulling Sabbath around to give him another break, she was annoyed at the interruption.

"What?" she asked, trying to hide the shiver that racked her.

"Time to go in."

"Just one more—"

"Nothing. You're wetter than the bottom of a lake."

"We're making p-progress," she forced out between teeth which chattered like castanets.

"Your lips are blue."

"They mmm-match my eyes."

His look held frank challenge. Now was an opportunity to prove she could be sensible, it said.

"Fine," she muttered, and led the horse from the ring.

Back at the farmhouse and standing in front of the bathroom mirror naked, A.J. raised her arm over her head. It was something she did regularly, a test she took whenever she had a moment to herself. Each time, she measured in vain for some improvement, some lessening in the stiffness and pain.

She grimaced and turned away from the mirror. Devlin was making dinner downstairs and she could catch a whiff of stir-fry vegetables drifting up from the kitchen. As she went into the bedroom, she looked at the bed they shared, remembering all the times they had made love in it.

Their conversation in that trophy room came back to her and her heart ached. With each day that passed, she was relying more and more on her ability to keep going physically by will alone. And as time went on, her lies to Devlin accumulated, raising the stakes. With a cold trickle of fear, she realized how much she was wagering. As long as she was able to tough it out, she was convinced her injury wouldn't be exposed and he'd never have to know what she was really going through. He wouldn't have to worry. And they wouldn't have to argue about her training.

But what if she couldn't make it? What if the pain got to the point where she could no longer go on?

A.J. pulled her hair back and started to get dressed.

She had enough juice to make it to the Qualifier, she told herself once again. She just had to have enough.

"You about ready?" Devlin called up the stairs.

"I'm almost dressed."

"Pity."

A.J. grinned.

And then took two more painkillers.

15

A WEEK later, Sabbath was lobbying for a reprieve like a flounder in a shark tank.

"I mean it," A.J. was saying. "Come on. You've done this before."

Standing in the six inches of ice-cold water she'd learned to hate, A.J. tugged on the lead line again. Her nose was running, she couldn't feel the tips of her fingers even though she was wearing gloves, and her feet were wet. Which was always a mystery. No matter how often she checked for holes in the waders, she couldn't find any. They were supposed to be watertight but her soggy socks told a different story.

Talk about your bad combos, she thought, looking down at the suit. Butt ugly and nonfunctional.

The stallion put out a front hoof as if he stood to lose the entire leg and submersed it with an expression of distaste. The other followed and then Sabbath paused, checking to see if she was serious. When she took a step farther into the pool, he heaved a great sigh and then his hind legs came along. Standing in the water together, with A.J. stroking his neck along with his ego, the magnificent stallion looked miserable. But he wasn't running scared.

It was the breakthrough they'd been working so hard for, A.J. thought. Although more to the point if she was teaching him to swim.

It was hard not to feel frustrated in spite of their progress. Considering they had yet to try him over the jump again, they weren't where they needed to be.

A.J. sneezed.

She was, however, a hell of a lot closer to catching pneumonia.

As she walked Sabbath out of the pool, she gave in to his hopeful look and decided to take him back to the barn. She was leading him out of the ring when Devlin drove up in the truck, back from getting its bed fixed. He waved to her and went to open the gate. As she approached him, she thought the sound of the sloppy waders and her sneezes were like a bad marching band accompanying her. Even so, his eyes were warm as she looked up into them.

"How'd it go today?" he asked.

"'Bout the same as usual. Plenty of time in the jump, no time in the air above it. On the brighter side, he's going to try out for the Olympic Swim Team. With the kind of water he can displace, he's a shoo-in for the hundred-meter butterfly."

They walked to the stable together.

"I have this vision of us at the Qualifier," A.J. was saying. "In the middle of the round, Sabbath comes to a full stop and wades into the pool because that's what we've trained him to do."

Chester popped his head out of the tack room.

"If it ain't Esther Williams and Fernando Lamas," he said.

"Try the Marx Brothers," she muttered, while putting the stallion into his stall. She began unfastening his soaking wet blanket.

"I think it's time to take him over the jump," she said to Devlin.

"I agree. The panic's down enough so he can probably keep his wits about him."

"Then tomorrow it is."

Devlin handed her a dry blanket that she threw over the stallion's back and secured under his belly. With Sabbath taken care of, she went out into the aisle and released the dreaded suspenders, relieved to be free of them. Feeling the waders rush to the floor, she thought they seemed equally anxious to see the last of her. She couldn't resist shooting them a glare.

Devlin helped her step free and looked down at her wet socks.

"They never seem to leak when I wear them."

"Maybe they like you better." She went to hang the waders up in the tack room, hoping she'd worn them for the last time.

When she came back, Devlin and Chester were talking about the condition of the rails around the ring, some of which needed to be repainted.

"I'll be takin' care a' that in the next week," Chester said. "'Afore it gets too cold."

"Good idea." Devlin checked his watch. "So's everyone ready for some dinner?"

"Not me," came a happy reply.

Devlin shot the groom a suspicious eye.

"Why ya lookin' at me like that, boy?"

"You're far too cheerful for someone who just turned down dinner."

"Goin' to bingo tonight."

"You've been going to bingo for close to ten years now and you've always eaten at my place."

"So?"

"You've also never looked so jolly before you went."

"Don't know what ya mean. Can't a man look forward to a little gamblin' in peace?"

Devlin turned to A.J. "Can you believe he's turning down dinner and being so happy about it?"

Her eyes turned fond and indulgent as they focused on the groom.

"Wait a minute," Devlin said. "What the hell's going on here? Have you got a date or something?"

"An' what if I do?"

"You're actually going out somewhere? With someone else?"

"Ya don't have to make it sound like such a miracle. It's not so ridiculous that a lady could find m' unique charm an' fashion sense appealin'."

Devlin laughed and clapped his friend on the shoulder. "Congratulations! Who's the lucky gal?"

"Only the most beautiful girl in the world."

"You two-timing me?" Devlin tossed at A.J.

"Well, he does have a certain flair for living. His food is color-coordinated and he's handy with a wheelbarrow."

"M' girl's name is Margaret Mead," Chester pronounced, savoring the sound of the words.

"Margaret from the auction house?"

"Yup."

"So when's she coming over here for dinner?"

"Ya want to screen her like she's on the block or something?"

"Got to check her teeth."

A.J. sneezed again. "While you two talk this over, I'm heading for the hot water. I hope you have a terrific evening, Chester."

"I'm plannin' on it."

"So how'd you meet her?" Devlin was asking as she left.

As soon as A.J. was back at the farmhouse, she went upstairs to the bathroom. Before she did anything else, she stripped off her socks because she couldn't stand the way they felt a moment longer. Then she cranked up the heat, turned on the water and started to strip. With her teeth knocking together and the beds of her fingernails an alarming gray color, she wondered if she'd ever be warm again.

When she started to peel her turtleneck off, she winced as she brought her arm up, and it took several tries until she was finally able to wrench it from her head. Groaning, she tried to loosen the arm up while assessing its range of motion. After all the time that had passed since she'd fallen, it was still no better. Maybe even a little worse, if she was brutally honest.

Going into her toiletries bag, she took out a bottle of the pills she'd come to rely on with disheartening regularity. The phial was light in her hands and, after she popped off the lid, she was surprised to find it nearly empty. She poured the remaining white capsules into her palm, swallowed them and then threw it in the trash. It was the second bottle she'd

gone through in the past week and she made a mental note
to buy two or three when she went to the store.

As A.J. waited for the bath to fill up, she went to the
window and looked out to the ring.

We better get over that water tomorrow, she thought.

The next day, after a thorough workout over fences, A.J.
wheeled Sabbath around and squared him off against the
water jump. Her arm was throbbing and she questioned her
wisdom of saving the attempt for last. He was always more
calm toward the end of the workouts but her pain was always more intense.

She turned the reins over to her good hand and
stretched the arm surreptitiously, trying to loosen it up.
Under her, the stallion jogged in place, his hooves shuffling
in the dirt. He threw his head up and blew out a burst of
air. Gritting her teeth, she settled into position and gave
him some leg.

Sabbath lunged forward, toward the water. Under her,
she could feel his tension spike but he didn't turn away and
his stride was full and purposeful. They approached with
good speed and, whether it was from internal fortitude or
sheer momentum, he took the jump. Not attractively, not
confidently, not with style.

But they got over it in one piece.

A.J. had been prepared for him to refuse and for her to
pull a floater in the pool. Instead, she'd been pleasantly surprised to see water passing under them while in midair.

"Way to go!" Devlin called out, as she cantered Sabbath
around the ring. Chester, standing at the rail, was clapping.

A couple more tries and the stallion, uncomfortable but
still not refusing, was clearing the water with enough confidence that they began to land a little more smoothly. As she
reined him in, A.J. was thinking she should feel a trium-
phant surge of accomplishment. Or tremendous relief, at
least.

Instead, she felt numb. Sure, they'd gotten over the water, she thought, but on his home turf with only Devlin and
Chester as the audience. What was going to happen in all
the chaos of the Qualifier?

She directed the stallion over to Devlin, her eyes dark with conflict.

"They won't be judging you on form," he reminded her. "Just whether you get over it in one piece."

"We've got six days left. We need more training."

"That's true of every competitor in the ring."

"I know." A.J. dismounted, removing her helmet. "It just seems especially true of us."

"Look at me."

Her eyes rose to his.

"You should be proud of yourself. You've done a terrific job."

She felt his hand caress her cheek. She turned into the palm, seeking his skin with her lips.

"You know, you're pretty good at this supportive stuff," A.J. said softly.

"Just trying to keep my woman happy."

His thumb brushed against and then lingered on her lower lip. As they went on to discuss plans for the Qualifier, her mind drifted to when they'd been alone together last. The afternoon before, Devlin had joined her in the tub, teasing and tempting her until he'd lost control and they'd made love amid the bubbles and the fragrance of lavender. It hadn't ended there. The hours before dinner had been lost to a haze of pleasure until the hunger in their bellies had forced them downstairs to forage for food. Too impatient to cook, they'd eaten cold meat loaf and raw carrots and felt, as they stared across a single candle, that the meal was a feast beyond measure.

Just goes to show passion is the best condiment, she thought. Puts A.1. in the shade any day.

"A.J.?"

"Sorry?"

"Penny for your thoughts."

She smiled.

"They're yours for free if you make them come true again." Her look was full of sensual promise.

Devlin moved closer, his body throwing off unmistakable signals. "Tell me. I want to hear the words coming out of that sweet mouth of yours."

Sabbath tossed his head, stamping a foot.

Looking at his expression of disapproval, they laughed.

"He hates when your attention wanders," Devlin said as they left the ring.

"He does seem to want my eyes on him all the time."

"I know the feeling."

Two days before the Qualifier, A.J. went to the mansion to get some things she'd wear at the event. She'd left most of her show clothes back in her old bedroom and had a specific pair of boots she was looking for.

In the intervening days since Sabbath and she had taken the water jump successfully, they'd made some more progress. The two of them had gotten to the point where they could tackle the water in the middle of a course but there were still problems. Whatever rhythm they had would be broken as soon as they faced the jump, and their pace would slow. Although it wouldn't hinder them in the first round, if they got as far as a timed jump-off, it could be a liability.

And then there was her arm. She had real concerns about it lasting through the rigors of competition. From a stamina point of view, how effective she could be in the saddle would depend on how much Sabbath fought her and how much pain she could handle. It was an equation she wished she had more influence over. The ibuprofen went only so far and she knew better than to hope for a miraculous recovery or for Sabbath to behave like a perfect gentleman.

As she opened the door to her bedroom, she was thinking she should probably soak in a hot bath later on in the evening.

A.J. stopped dead as soon as she walked into the room.

For a split second, she wondered if she was lost. Or had really lost it.

Boxes choked the floor and were filled haphazardly with the trophies and ribbons that had been on the walls. The mouths of her dresser drawers were yawning open, showing loose teeth made up of her shirts and slacks. Even her canopy bed had been savaged, the drapery peeled from its perch and the pencil posts unscrewed and lying on the floor.

In a daze, A.J. stepped over a pile of books and made her way into the bathroom. It was in a similar condition.

Stunned, she went into her walk-in closet, grateful that at least her show clothes were still hanging up and unwrinkled. She took out two blazers and a couple of her starched shirts and reached into a darkened corner to pick up the boots she wanted. Carefully laying the clothes inside a garment bag, she zipped them in securely, feeling as though they needed the protection.

In a stupor, she sat on the bed, wondering what she should do.

Which, in itself, was a change.

Until recently, her first instinct would have been to race down the corridor, take two lefts and a right and pound on Peter's door until it was answered or she peeled it off the hinges with her bare hands. Only he could have created the chaos. No one else would have had the gall to move her out of her own bedroom.

But, sitting amid the ruins of her personal space, she didn't want to find him. She just wanted to walk away.

Then Peter showed up in the doorway.

"I didn't expect to see you," he said, stepping over the threshold. He was wearing his casual uniform, tinted brown. "Sorry about the mess but my painters are coming tomorrow."

He didn't sound very sorry.

"Where are you taking all of my things?" she asked. "And when were you going to tell me you're moving in?"

"The groundsmen are putting everything in the attic. And there's nothing to tell. You left on your own accord."

"Why are you doing this?" She was more curious than hurt.

"It's really a matter of aesthetics. The view from here is better than mine so I'm taking the room."

He stared at her, waiting for a response. She thought he looked eager.

"Well, I hope you enjoy the panorama," A.J. said, getting off the bed and picking up the garment bag and boots. "I know I always did."

When she tried to get past him, he blocked her way.

"That's it?"

"What do you mean?"

"You're just leaving?"

"It's more appealing than arguing with you."

"It never has been before."

"Is that the real reason you did this? Were you looking for a fight?"

"No. But I expected one."

There was a long pause.

"So?" he prompted. "You have anything to say to me?"

"No. I really don't."

His eyes narrowed. "What's wrong with you?"

"You think there's something wrong with me because I don't want to argue?"

"It's hardly the A.J. I've known and loved," he said sarcastically.

"So things have changed."

"Oh, I get it. Your horizons are opening up. You're a new woman. I guess McCloud's been teaching you there's something more than the missionary position, right?"

A.J. winced. "When you say things like that, it really hurts my feelings. In fact, a lot of our arguments have hurt. Both of us."

Peter fell silent and she thought she saw a flicker of something other than anger and frustration in his face. That reflected pain was something she recognized in her own heart. She decided to take a chance and reach out to him.

"Peter, when was the last time you did something you really loved?"

"Excuse me?"

"You're not happy at the stables," she said, putting her bag and boots down. "You never have been."

"Just because I don't think horse manure is a perfume doesn't mean I'm not good at my job. Or have you forgotten the little promotion your father gave me?"

"I didn't say you weren't good at what you do. I just think it's a hell of a way to spend your life, trapped in a job you hate."

"What does this have to do with your bedroom? And I'm not trapped!"

"I think it has everything to do with this. You seem so unhappy." A.J. shook her head. "Do you know how much I love getting up in the morning? I can't wait to get down to the stables, to smell the hay and hear the sounds of hooves in the stalls. I wake up every morning thankful I'm getting a chance to live my dream and I go to bed every night, even if I've failed in the daylight hours, looking forward to doing it again. I can't imagine what it would be like to trudge through the day, hating every minute."

Peter snorted, and she watched his frustration boil up and escape through his fingertips as he began agitating coins in his pocket and drumming on the doorjamb.

"This isn't going to work," he muttered. "You're not going to sweet-talk some revelation out of me that you can use later. I've been running a tight ship down at the stables. I've turned those giant hamsters into profit for your father. He may have you up on a pedestal but he's got me in the driver's seat and I intend to keep it that way."

"I don't want to run Sutherland's. I'm a rider, not a businessman. Besides, you're fantastic at what you do."

Her stepbrother stopped fidgeting.

"What the hell's turned you into Glinda the Good Witch?"

"Let's just say it's a change in priorities. Not that I haven't enjoyed bickering with you all these years on some level. Painful as it's been, we've gotten off some real good ones."

He managed a short laugh. "We sure have."

"Peter, I don't know if we'll ever be friends but I know this: I'm ready to stop being enemies."

He stared at her for a long time and she knew he was measuring her, weighing her new words against their long past.

"Talk to me," she urged. "For once in our lives, let's just talk."

Peter looked around her room, dwelling on the boxes with her trophies and ribbons. "You were supposed to be gone when I moved in here."

"You're right. I should have taken my things out. I don't live here anymore—"

"No, after their wedding."

A.J. frowned.

"Before my mother remarried, she asked me what I thought of Garrett. I liked him a lot and I told her I wanted him, so when she walked down the aisle, I assumed she was doing it to bring him to me. I figured you'd go away so I could have what was mine. Imagine my surprise when I took up residence and you were still around. God, I hated living in the same house with you. You were the perfect student, the perfect daughter, the perfect everything. You rode well, sang well, wrote well. Not only didn't I get the undivided attention I figured was part of the bargain, but I had to compete with a damn superhero."

"But you did well in school," she said, amazed.

"Not like you did. I've never done anything as well as you did."

"That's not true. You've run the stables—"

"I do the ledger but you're the leader." He laughed harshly. "You've always been the leader. I can remember, in the early days, I'd go down to the stables and see everyone looking at you with respect. You were half the age of those champions and yet they *knew* you were special. Everyone's always known you were special. Even my mother."

"Your mother despises me."

"Only because Garrett loves a dead woman more than her. My mother's never been her husband's true love and never will be."

"But they've been together a long time. I know he loves her."

"Your father has one room in this house that's his. Whose portrait is on the wall?" Peter shoved his hands into his pockets. "And as for you, you're the spitting image of a rival she can never beat. But that hasn't kept her from using you against me. Sometimes I think she likes you more than me."

"Peter, your mother adores you. She's always singing your praises."

"In public, yes. Privately, she's more likely to be nailing me to the wall and you've been her favorite hammer. All those trophies"—he pointed to the boxes—"every last one of them has been pounded into me. I know every score, every triumph over the odds, every facile maneuver you've ever made. I used to pray you'd fail just so I could stop hearing about it all. That woman has held me up to your gold standard since the day I first met you and I've hated you for it."

"But the success of the stables—"

"Every quarter, I have to go to her and review the Sutherland accounts like I'm facing a board of directors. She's always feared your little hobby was too much of a cost center. You know how she is about money. If it doesn't benefit her, she's highly suspicious. Every time you've found another thing to buy, some new piece of equipment or new facility, she's badgered me about it. I've had to be accountable for every cent you've spent and I've loathed it. I can't stand defending you."

"I had no idea that was going on."

"I know. You're completely clueless about so many things and always have been. You bounce through life, running after one goal and another, not noticing how much other people have to do to accommodate you. And now that you're gone, you have no idea how hard it is to go to that damn stable. People miss you and they blame me. They know I'm the reason you left." He paused. "Every day, it's like walking into an armed camp and all the guns are trained on me."

"I didn't think anyone cared that I left."

"Of course, they do. Half the damn place is in love with you and the other half wants to be you."

"You can't be serious."

"I assure you, I've spent a hell of a lot more time examining your life than you have."

A.J. stared at him with wide eyes. She was shocked at his introspections and by what his words revealed about him. He was far more self-aware than she'd assumed him to be or would ever have thought him capable of being.

She said, "I never imagined you to be so . . . smart."

"I think you mean that as a compliment."

"I do."

"Well, thanks." There was a long pause. "People really do miss you down at the stables."

"That surprises me. I mean, I try to be good to everyone but I didn't think I made any special effort for them to like me."

"People have always been drawn to you." Peter shifted his weight and leaned against the doorjamb. "You know all those men at the compound? The ones you've spent so much time training with? They used to come to me, wanting to know how to get you to go out with them."

"But none of them ever asked," A.J. said, remembering the Saturday nights she'd spent alone. "What did you tell them?"

"Simple," he replied. "I said you were a lesbian."

There was a moment of silence and then the two began to laugh.

"That explains it," she said.

"There's something else you should know. I was the one who talked Garrett into making me head of the stables. It's something I've learned to regret. After you left, your father was miserable. My mother blamed me for making him unhappy and for driving away one of Sutherland's stars. I'm sorry I pressed your father like I did. I really am. And I'm sorry I threw you out."

"Thank you," she said softly. "I wish we'd talked like this a long time ago."

"You know, so do I." He glanced around the room. "Look, about your things—"

"Don't worry about it. I should have put them in storage myself when I left." A.J. picked up her gear. "I'll come back for them someday."

He took a step back, out into the hall.

"If I don't see you before the competition, good luck. I mean it."

"Thanks."

After an awkward moment, A.J. left. As she drove away from the mansion, she was feeling optimistic about their conversation. It had been totally unexpected. Long overdue. A harbinger, she hoped, of good things to come for them both.

"So your stepbrother isn't as awful as you thought he was?"

Devlin was pulling on flannel pajama bottoms as A.J. settled into bed.

"No, he really isn't," she replied, looking up at him with a smirk.

"Why are you smiling like that?"

"Those are the same pajamas you were wearing the night I first came here."

He pulled the drawstring tight and tied it at his taut stomach. "Are they?"

"I thought you were incredibly sexy when you opened the door. I couldn't believe what your body looked like in the moonlight. I just melted."

His eyes flared with heat.

"Did you?" he drawled, sauntering over to her.

She nodded, responding to the electricity that sparked between them. "And I think you're sexy right now."

"You know what I'm going to do?" Devlin reached out a hand, one fingertip coming to rest on her lower lip. With aching slowness, he traced a path down her neck to her collarbone.

"What?" she asked, breathlessly.

He pulled his hand away smartly. "I'm going to go into the bathroom and brush my teeth. There was a lot of garlic in that clam sauce."

She started laughing.

"And then I'm going to come back and I'm going to start at your feet and kiss my way up every inch of your body."

In a voice husky with desire, she told him to hurry back.

Devlin's body was humming with anticipation as he went across the hall and into the other room. Reaching over the sink, he whipped open the medicine cabinet and grabbed a nearly spent tube of toothpaste. When nothing came out, he knew he had no one to blame but himself. He'd been squeezing from the middle for the past few weeks and now the thing was mangled and deformed, refusing to give up its last dregs with any alacrity. Cursing, he smoothed it out, rolled it up from the bottom and, by putting it on the edge of the sink and leaning on it with his palm, finally managed to cover his bristles with an anemic showing of fluoride.

He leaned over to throw the thing away and froze as he

noticed something disturbing. Bending over, he fished out an empty bottle of Motrin from the dental floss and wads of Kleenex. He'd seen a number of them showing up in the trash lately. Stringing together the seemingly unrelated discoveries, he grew alarmed.

A.J. was impatiently leafing through the pages of the most recent issue of *Horse Illustrated* when Devlin came in with the empty bottle.

"What's this?" he demanded.

She looked up.

"Why are you going through the trash?"

"Why are you taking so many pills?"

There was a pause.

"You find one empty bottle—"

"This isn't the only one. What's going on?"

"Nothing. And don't give me that look. Last time I checked, that stuff wasn't a controlled substance." She looked back down at the magazine, turning a page sharply. "It's perfectly safe."

"Why are you taking it so much?"

"I get sore after training sometimes. It's no big deal."

"I think you're lying to me."

A.J. threw the magazine aside. "It's nothing to worry about."

There was a long silence between them.

"Okay," he said finally. "Whatever you say."

He turned and left. As A.J. heard him go downstairs, she lost her composure and buried her head in her hands.

I can do this, she told herself as guilt and frustration swelled. I can do this. I can do this.

They were so close to the Qualifier. Less than forty-eight hours. And then she could say she took the stallion no one else could control and got him to that event. She told herself that feat, in and of itself, was an accomplishment she could be proud of. Something she could call her own. And that the feeling of achievement she would have would make all the stress worth it.

Really, it would.

By the time Devlin came back upstairs, she'd turned off the light and was lying on her side, looking out at the moon-drenched meadow behind the farmhouse. She felt the bed dip as he slid between the sheets and was relieved when he reached for her. Her hands linked with his.

"I love you," he whispered.

"I love you, too," she replied, wishing the Qualifier was already past them.

16

BOREALIS HUNT AND POLO CLUB, read the discreet sign. The letters were black on a black-green background, barely readable. Underneath, the caption MEMBERS ONLY was in white, very readable. The entrance to the club matched the sign. A pair of stone pillars and a few precisely clipped bushes were understated. The guardhouse was not.

"Back in the land a' the frozen chosen," Chester said, making reference to the patrician membership.

As the trailer stopped in front of the security detail, a dour-looking man dressed in a green-on-black uniform stepped into the road. Leaning out of the cab, Devlin flashed the proper credentials and they were meticulously reviewed. When the guard passed them back, he caught sight of A.J. His face burst into a happy smile.

"Well, hello!"

"Good morning," she said. "How're you doing?"

"Just fine, just fine. Go on through, and good luck," he told them with a wave.

"Amazing what a pretty girl can getcha," Chester said. "Been passin' through this gate every year feelin' like a criminal. Didn't think that man had the front teeth to smile with."

"Membership has its privileges," Devlin said under his breath.

Chester turned and looked at A.J. "Ya belong here?"

"I do, but I only ride here now and then."

"It's an impressive place."

"Well, only because of the sticky buns. The food is over-cooked in the English style, but boy, they can bake well."

"Must move a lot a' white bread at lunch."

A.J. forced a laugh and glanced under her lashes at Devlin. His profile was etched in stone, the handsome features drawn tight. Her chest ached as she realized that, even though they were sitting side by side, she missed him as if he'd been gone for days. Things hadn't been right since he'd found that empty pill bottle. She had yet to find a way to talk to him about the distance between them and tell him how scared she was by his withdrawal.

She looked away from him, back out the window. The winding drive they were on was a half-mile ascent marked by an alley of oak trees. It was a portentous approach, and when the clubhouse was revealed at the top, the building did not disappoint. An imposing structure, it had a formality and majesty of design that spoke volumes about its early-American roots and wealth of its patrons. Built in the late eighteenth century, the historic landmark had a prominent entrance marked with Corinthian columns and a portico. The center portion rose up a towering three stories and flanking wings emerged from this anchor in two L-shaped expanses. There were long paned windows on every side, portals that were marked by black shutters that stood out against white clapboard siding. All around the building, there were vast, rolling lawns.

Behind the clubhouse were the stables, training rings and paddocks as well as the polo field, which was used every year for the Qualifier. This field was a vast, flat plane of perfectly shorn grass that now had jumps cutting into its smooth surface. To one side, a set of green and black bleachers rose. These would soon seat members, who were used to the hard wood and liked it, and spectators, who weren't and didn't.

The inhospitable bleachers were just one way the club let it be known that the comfort of four-legged animals was more important than that of bipeds, regardless of what the evolutionary scale hierarchy might suggest. Whereas the mares and stallions had heated stalls and warm running water for their baths in the stables, outside of the clubhouse, people were forced to use drafty bathrooms with no mirrors, and faucets that might as well have been spitting ice cubes.

This disparity between the creature comforts of creatures and those of humans was part of the tradition of the place and the Qualifier. The Borealis had been playing host to the spectacle since the very first one had been held in the late 1800s but it was an odd choice for the notoriously closed club to sponsor. The open roster of the competition, which provided any professional rider could compete assuming they had the temerity to take on its infamous courses, was peculiarly egalitarian considering that becoming a member of Borealis was close to impossible.

Another disconnect between the club's closed-door policy and the Qualifier was the attention the event drew and the resulting invasion of nonmembers. For one day every year, intruders rushed over hallowed Borealis land. This caused no small amount of consternation among the membership, most of whom would have been content to have the competition staged for their edification and no one else's. They exercised their malcontent by ensuring that the foreigners were treated as inhospitably as possible. No matter how wealthy or important an outsider was, the no-guest policy barred him or her from the clubhouse. This meant there were a lot of well-dressed people using the bathrooms down at the stables, another source of grumbling among people whose butts were already sore, courtesy of the bleachers. These folks had a feeling, unconfirmed but strident, that the bathrooms were better where they weren't allowed. They were right, of course, and nothing was more amusing to members than some woman in a Chanel suit tottering across the grass to a loo she wouldn't have let her gardener use as a toolshed.

In the early-morning light, A.J. saw that the crowd had yet to arrive although the press had taken up residence in droves. Already on the job, they were photographing the competitors, who were still in their barn clothes and not yet frazzled, and the club members, many of whom were wearing Borealis jackets, and looks of disdain if they were approached. The membership tolerated this yearly influx of reporters with even more contempt than they did the crowd's arrival. If there'd been a way to freeze the press out of going to the bathroom at all, it would have been done.

Out of this scorn was born the strict caste system of the event. Members were at the top of the heap because it was their turf, and even if it wasn't, their demeanor tended to create insecurity in Nobel laureates and proletariats alike. The horses were the next rung on the ladder, a status that the crowd was reminded of every time they traipsed through the stables and saw the luxury the animals enjoyed. Riders were behind the horses and far, far above any of the others. There'd even been an exception made to the no-guest policy after one particularly muddy event. Competitors had actually been allowed to use the showers in the clubhouse.

Rumor had it, this was how the nonmembers came to know how much better the other bathrooms were.

Somewhere behind the riders, way behind them, were the nonmember owners of the horses. Lumped in with them were their flashy wives or boy toys and the miscellaneous social hangers-on who thought that by walking on Borealis turf, they would somehow get their foot in the door to exalted status. Last stop on the road to inferiority was the press, but everyone, except the membership, only pretended not to like them. The competitors generally wanted to be interviewed, especially if they won, and the social mavens wanted to be photographed. That was why they wore outrageous hats.

Courtesy of having had her picture in the newspaper recently, and dealing with the aftermath, A.J. was feeling more aligned with her fellow members when it came to the press and she grimaced as photographers and reporters started running after the McCloud Stables trailer. When Devlin parked, the knot of harpies caught up with them and flashbulbs started going off like firecrackers.

"Better brace yourself," Chester said while opening the door.

"Sabbath is going to like these guys about as much as blacksmiths," she muttered.

In a rush, reporters started throwing questions at her, sharp-tongued footballs she let fall to the ground as she went back and checked on the stallion. She was wondering how she was going to get Sabbath out without him getting spooked by all the commotion, when she got a reprieve as the Sutherland truck drove by. Running headlong like a pack of hyenas, the throng went barking off after the semi. She knew they'd be back so she got to work fast.

Sabbath had handled the journey well and he was excited as she started to unload him, his ears flicking back and forth as his hooves clomped down the ramp. As soon as his coat flashed in the sun, a photographer let out a holler that triggered another avalanche of attention in their direction. Gripping the lead line with two hands, A.J. braced herself, ready to have the horse rear up and lash out at them all.

Instead, he calmly looked over his shoulder and practically batted his eyelashes. While she got over her shock, he flirted with the cameras and she could have sworn he was positioning himself so his best side got the most coverage.

"For heaven's sake, you're not Barbra Streisand," she whispered to him.

But what the hell was she complaining about? A.J. thought, as Chester started to strip the stallion of his travel gear. If Sabbath wanted to play Hollywood royalty, it was better than paying for a bunch of broken camera equipment.

After the press finally dispersed, she turned around to look for Devlin.

"He went to get you registered," Chester said without her asking.

She smiled and tried to concentrate on the horse but couldn't. Now, when her focus should have been on the Qualifier and her horse and her riding, concern about their relationship was paramount in her mind. She was terrified about the distance between them, worried about how he felt to be back at the event. Wondering how long it would take them to get back to normal.

She felt trapped. Part of her just wanted to get through the event and then resolve the issues they were facing. But there was also a sense, and a tremendous fear, that there might not be anything left of their relationship if she waited even that short a time. Devlin had been acting strangely around her since he'd confronted her two nights before. His words when he addressed her were deliberate ones, carefully chosen to approximate normal conversation, but lifeless. Even worse, he hadn't touched her or held her at night or taken her hand when they walked down to the barn. The few kisses he'd given her were brief and perfunctory, just pecks on the cheek.

A.J. felt as though he'd left her even though he was still around. The loneliness was unbearable and the one time she'd come close to bringing it all up, he'd quickly left the room, retreated into his study and not come out again until very late in the night. It was as if he didn't want to get her upset right before the event, and to her that meant something was very wrong. Maybe the permanent kind of wrong.

The very idea made her sick to her stomach.

As she went through the motions of getting Sabbath ready, A.J. was feeling a cold fear she'd never known before.

In the growing crowd, Devlin walked around the grounds in a daze, going through the motions of checking A.J. and Sabbath in and getting an overview of the course. It was difficult for him to believe he was back, and he wasn't the only one who was surprised. As he passed the other competitors, he could feel their shocked eyes and double takes. He ignored them. When reporters approached him, anxious for a sound bite on how it felt to be back, he pushed them away.

With painful irony, he realized that no one had any idea how he was really feeling. They had it all wrong. He wasn't in mourning and he wasn't thinking about the past.

A.J. was an ache in his heart that wouldn't go away. He loved her more than anything in his life, but inside he felt frozen. An awful premonition told him she was on a collision course with disaster and he didn't know how to stop her. He found himself in the grips of a terrible paralysis.

As a result, he'd pulled away and knew his retreat had hurt and confused her. He saw the sadness in her eyes and it pained him but he didn't know what else to do. He was at the breaking point of frustration and the last thing she needed was another argument. The distance between them was the only way he knew how to keep from venting his emotions and putting even more burdens on her as she went into the event.

He paused by the polo field, A.J.'s registration papers gripped tightly in his hand. A few competitors were already surveying the course from the outside with their trainers. When one group walked past him, he could hear their voices drop to a hush. Disregarding them, he tried to concentrate instead on the way the morning's pale sunlight felt as it beat down on his back.

Warming though it was, it did nothing to relieve the cold vise around his emotions.

Devlin was grateful for the numbness. He had a feeling it was the only way he'd be able to get through the day. He was torn between wanting to be her trainer and being her lover, between having a job to do and wanting to pack her and the stallion back up and drive them all home.

Forcing himself to focus on the jump course, he stared ahead. At first, he could see nothing but rails and grass. Slowly, though, he could recognize jumps and then find the pathways the competitors would be traveling. The course was laid out in a predictably grueling way, with towering fences set close together. Its compact design meant tight corners and no chance of recovery if a competitor hit a stride wrong or was shaken off-balance.

He thought of A.J. and Sabbath and went back to the trailer.

"Stallion all right?" he asked Chester, who was running a brush over the horse's coat.

"Seems fine, calmer than the last time we took 'im out in public."

A.J. came around the corner. Anxious for a read on Devlin's emotions, she scanned his face. "Do I have a good number?"

"Sixteen."

"The course ready for walking?"

"In ten minutes. We should head over now."

"Okay."

As he turned to go, she saw that his face was closed, his mouth set. Together, they walked to the ring, attracting attention they ignored as best they could.

"Sabbath seems fairly calm," she said.

He nodded.

"Shoes are solid. That loose one is tight as a tick."

There was no response.

"Devlin, are you okay?" When he didn't respond, she put her hand on his arm. "Please, talk to me."

He halted reluctantly. "I don't think you want me to talk right now."

"I've been in agony for the last two days. It's like you've left me. What's going on?"

"A.J., now is not the time to go into this." He looked around, meeting curious stares. "And this is certainly not the place."

He resumed walking.

Catching up with his long stride, she said, "This has got to be hard for you, being back after what happened. . . ."

Devlin wheeled around and gripped her arms fiercely.

"Nothing matters but you, okay? I don't care about what happened to me last year. All that I'm thinking about is you."

"If I'm the only thing on your mind, why do I feel like you're so far away?"

"A.J., just drop it. Let's go and look at the course."

"No!" she hissed, struggling to keep her voice down. "Dammit, will you just tell me what's going on?"

Devlin's expression grew harsh. "What do you want from me? Do you really need to hear how exhausted and strained you look? I sure as hell don't want to bring up all the pills you've been taking and the sleep you haven't been getting again. We've argued about all of it before and we're still standing here, at the Qualifier. None of it has changed your mind, and courtesy of your discipline, I'm going half mad, imagining that the worst is going to happen when you get in that ring."

He swore as he saw the looks they were attracting. Dropping his hands to his sides, he looked uncharacteristically defeated.

"A.J., you don't need this crap right now. Your focus has to be on the course and the stallion and yourself."

"But I don't want you to be upset."

"Then do something for me. Forget about anything but the event. Put all distractions out of your mind. You're going to need to focus if you're going to get through this in one piece and at least I'll have some peace of mind if I think you're concentrating on the job." He pushed a hand through his hair. "Hell, what I should be telling you right now is that I admire your strength of character and your hard work and your determination. That's what your damn trainer should be doing. But I think I'd rather have you safe than successful."

"Devlin, I—"

Over the loudspeaker came an announcement that the course was open for walking.

"Come on," he said. "Let's go."

"Wait. I—"

"You want to be a champion, don't you?" He looked past her, at the competitors and trainers who were heading toward the jumps. "If you do, we've got to get moving."

But A.J. held them in place, standing still. She was searching for words of reconciliation and reassurance, desperate for some magical combination of syllables that would put his fears to rest, and reunite them.

There were none, she realized. As long as she was going into that ring. She flexed her arm, unconsciously.

"Will you be there after this is over?" she asked. "After the round?"

He sounded exhausted. "Of course."

"I mean, will you really be there," she said, meeting his eyes pointedly. "Will you be with me, not just around me?"

In the long silence that followed, her heart thumped wildly in her chest.

"Yes, I will."

Only then did she take a step forward. Devlin followed.

As soon as they got inside the ring, her feet slowed of their own volition. She'd seen the kind of courses that were set up at the Qualifier, just never from the perspective of an entrant.

"The view is a lot more attractive from above," she said, nodding at the stands.

Devlin waited for her to get her bearings, remembering when he'd first looked at a Qualifier course from the ground. It took a little getting used to and she wasn't the only one who was wearing a shell-shocked expression. Only two out of four entrants actually competed. In spite of a hefty registration fee, every year there was a high dropout rate after the jumps were opened for inspection.

A.J. tried to breathe. She'd seen fences of the same height and turns as tight, just not so many packed into one course. There were fourteen jumps in all, including one with water, and they were menacing-looking, done in the club's black and green colors.

The course started tough with three oxers in a row, a brutal combination that would shake up the field from the get-go. A hard turn to the left would be needed to make the next jump, a long, low wall, which was followed by a towering upright and two more oxers. A wrenching turn to the right would have the field coming into a combination of uprights, a vast wall of bushes and then the water jump. Directly thereafter, the competitors would have to double back in order to confront a mound obstacle that the horse and rider would have to leap up onto, then launch off of, to clear a rail fence at its far edge. The last two jumps were separated by a hairpin turn.

The course lived up to the event's reputation.

Maybe even pushed the damn envelope, A.J. thought, staring ahead.

She and Devlin walked the course twice, discussing the strides and the angles, where the dangerous spots were. The water jump wasn't her biggest concern, oddly enough. By dumb luck, it was configured in a way they'd been practicing recently. Sabbath would be familiar with the straight-on approach and the tight turn that immediately followed it. What she was worried about was how the stallion would handle the demands of the course's turns in the midst of the spectators.

By the time she and Devlin returned to the trailer, the crowd had grown to its full size and A.J. saw the first of the socialites. The sight of haute couture made her think about her stepmother and she wondered where her family was. Scanning the grounds, she located the Sutherland trailer easily. She could see people milling around its exterior, unloading horses she knew well. Out of a field of some thirty registered competitors, three, including Philippe Marceau, were from the Sutherland Stables, a good showing by anyone's estimation. Squinting against the direct sunlight, she could see Marceau's roan mare being groomed by one of the staff.

Shifting her gaze to Sabbath, she was thinking their time had finally come. Chester was winding wraps around the stallion's legs and she assessed the horse's mood. He seemed upbeat and not particularly aggressive. She hoped it would last.

Going over to the trailer's cab, A.J. grabbed her bag and her show clothes and went to the back, changing in the unused stall as she'd done before. When she emerged, Devlin was leaning against the back door.

"You all set?" he asked tightly, watching as her hand went to her throat and then fell back down to her side.

"I am."

"How're the nerves?"

"Calmer now that I'm in my show clothes."

"Anything you need?"

She asked him a few questions about course strategy and then they reflected on the field of competitors and Sabbath's good behavior thus far. As he spoke with her, Devlin thought once more that she would always be the most beautiful woman he'd ever seen, and likely the only one he would ever truly love. As they stood in the sunshine, beneath a crystal blue sky that once again reminded him of the color of her eyes, he wished things were different between them. That the distance wasn't there.

When they heard over the loudspeaker that the practice ring was open for competitors, A.J. gathered up her hat and crop. "Let's see if his mood holds."

"Wait," Devlin said. "I have something for you, for luck."

He buried a hand into the pocket of his coat and took out a small velvet bag. "Close your eyes."

When she did, he emptied the satchel and then reached
behind her neck.

"You shouldn't have to open them to know what it is," he
said, next to her ear.

When her fingertips went exploring, they found home.

Her eyes flew open and she looked down at her mother's
diamond.

"How did you—"

"I have ways."

"But this was to pay off my debt."

"I thought you'd want it today. We can argue about the
finances later."

A.J. stared down at the stone, seeing light sparkle in the
familiar facets. "This was my mother's."

"I knew it must have been significant. You don't wear
jewelry, not even a watch, and this you never took off. I
can't imagine why you sold it to pay the debt."

"It was the only thing I had that was really mine."

"Well, it's yours again now. And I understand how important it is for you to cover your own expenses. We'll work
something out."

"Thank you," A.J. said, tucking the stone inside her shirt.
The words didn't go far enough. She hoped the love shining
in her eyes went the rest of the way.

"You're welcome." He hesitated and then stroked her
cheek with the back of his hand. In a voice that was rough
with emotion, he said, "Take it easy over those fences, will
you?"

A.J. grabbed on to his palm. "I promise."

Chester interrupted. "What number are we in the field?"

"Sixteen out of seventeen," Devlin responded, reluctantly looking away. "Course will be chewed up but at least
we'll be clear on where the bomb zones are."

"Saddle him up?"

He nodded to Chester.

Just then, Garrett and Regina approached through the
crowd. A.J. noted that her father looked at home around
the horses. He was dressed in his club pullover and a pair of
dark wool slacks and had a pipe gripped between his teeth.
Fragrant smoke billowed behind him in cloudy puffs. Her

stepmother, on the other hand, was wearing a frown and a tangerine Ungaro ensemble. Her silk shoes, dyed to match, were already dirty. She looked like someone who'd gotten lost and didn't like where the misdirection had taken her.

A.J. went forward to greet them, forcing a smile for their benefit.

"Good morning, all," Garrett said, looking only at A.J.

She went into his arms and kissed his cheek. "Hi, Papa."

"Are you ready for this?" he whispered in her ear.

"I think so."

"Is he?" He nodded over at Sabbath.

"The stallion's in great physical shape and his heart belongs to me. We're going to do the best we can."

"I'll love you no matter what."

"I know."

Behind him, Regina said, "Darling, we really should get to our seats." She looked ready to drag her husband off but then she caught sight of something that interested her. "Oh, look! There's Winnie and Curt Thorndyke—she's chair of the Borealis Christmas Ball for the second year in a row. Winnie!"

She tore off into the crowd as fast as her high heels could cover the ground. Her target, assuming an expression of abject terror, bolted into a tack room.

Garrett shook his head. "She wishes you the very best, as well."

"Thanks."

"Arlington, I know you have to start warming up. I just wanted to make sure you knew I'd be rooting for you in the stands. I hope you win this, if it's what you want."

He embraced her again and she was struck by how much he loved her. As her father went over and shook Devlin's hand, she felt grateful. It was a sensation that continued as Sabbath was presented to her, tacked and ready to go. She felt lucky to have made it as far as they had. After all, they were at the Qualifier. She was going into the ring on the stallion.

As for the outcome? That was up to the fates. But she was going to do her level best to be lucky by trying to ride better than she ever had.

While Chester held the reins, Devlin gave her a leg up. Their eyes met and held.

As she settled into the saddle, the groom lectured the stallion.

"Now, listen here, ya big troublemaker. I'll strike ya a deal. Be nice, mind your manners an' there'll be a bucket a' sweet feed waiting for ya. Misbehave an' I'm feedin' ya nothing but dry grass for the rest a' the month."

Sabbath blinked and offered a snicker, as if he'd consented to the marching orders.

The first rider out on the course was disqualified after his horse refused the wall. The inauspicious start proved providential. By the time eight competitors had gone into the ring, two more had been disqualified for refusals, one had taken a fall and three had twelve-faulted.

It was the kind of competitive carnage that was expected.

In the warm-up ring, Sabbath was agreeable, jumping with sound mastery and becoming only a little rambunctious with the other horses. He seemed to accept the work A.J. was asking of him and this was a huge relief because she wanted to spare her injury as long as she could. She'd taken some Motrin just before she'd mounted, and her arm was feeling fairly strong, but the more energy she could save before their turn over the course, the better.

While practicing, she noticed Philippe Marceau cantering around on the roan mare. He was going tenth, she'd learned. Typically, he was paying more attention to the other competitors than to his own warm-up and he sent several pitying glances at A.J., none of which hid his calculation. Concentrating on Sabbath, she ignored the man and didn't even watch his round or check his results after he finished.

Before she knew it, Devlin was leading her and Sabbath to the ring.

"Watch the mound," he said. "That's where they're falling."

A.J. nodded. "Don't leave me."

"I won't."

Her name was called out through the loudspeakers and

Sabbath took his cue from her heels. With a flash of his black tail, they pranced forward into the ring. Overhead, the announcer went on to describe some of her recent accomplishments, the man's aristocratic vowels and Rs rolling like croquet balls.

A.J. and Sabbath made a pass by the president of the club so she could doff her hat to him and the officials of the event. A minute later, she heard the all-clear sound and set the stallion into a canter. They took one last circle before facing off at the first jump and then crossing the start line.

The stallion took the opening oxers with such grace even A.J. heard the crowd's swell of approval through her concentration. Cutting into the first turn, he didn't fight her; rather he seemed to understand her thinking, and they ended up in perfect position for the next jump. With a stunning combination of poise and power, they soared over the wall and continued onward.

In the crowd, momentum for them grew with every fence they cleared, spurred by the strength of the stallion and A.J.'s firm control of him. Watching from the rail, Devlin heard the rapt sighs and gasps as each jump was mastered and knew he was seeing history being made. A.J. and the stallion were jumping faster and cleaner than any of the other competitors, than anyone would have dared expect.

As the two approached the water jump, A.J. reined in Sabbath, slowing them down, giving him a little time to collect himself. She could feel the stallion's hesitancy, a faint stiffening in his legs, but he didn't shy away and, when he leapt with surprising confidence into the air, they cleared the obstacle with room to spare.

It was, people would agree afterward, the round of a lifetime.

Right up until the unthinkable happened.

Going cleanly into the last three jumps, Sabbath and A.J. approached the mound with its raised platform and rail fence. They had speed and a good angle in their favor. In the saddle, A.J. was feeling solid. With his hooves pounding over the ground, the stallion was bearing down on the jump steadily. They were going to make it.

Suddenly a brilliant explosion of light went off in

Sabbath's face. A photographer, determined to get a picture of them, had forgotten to turn off his flash.

Blinded, the stallion lost his stride and leapt to one side. A.J. tried to correct their course by throwing her weight in the opposite direction and pulling back on the reins. Their velocity was too great, however, and the platform rushed up to them. Sabbath was forced to jump at an angle and they scrambled onto the grass, wildly off-balance.

To keep him from awkwardly leaping over the upright and plummeting to ground level with a landing that would hurt his legs, A.J. yanked back on the reins, trying to redirect them down the side of the platform. It was too much stress on her arm. A stinging pain shot through to her shoulder and she was crippled with agony. Sabbath jerked one way, to clear the rail, and she lurched the other, loosing the traction of the stirrups.

With a sickening dread, she felt herself losing her seat in the saddle and then watched, in the disorienting slow motion of impending injury, as the stallion cleared the jump without her. Her final thought, before she hit the ground, was how beautiful he looked as he sailed through the air.

A.J. landed hard and blacked out.

As medics ran to her, the crowd went silent with shock. Then a heavy, rhythmic pounding began to overwhelm the field. Starting with the feet of the club members, and spreading on a wave of sympathy and regret, the whole crowd beat the bleachers, announcing the awful news. The noise rose louder and higher, until everyone on the grounds halted whatever they were doing, their blood running cold. There was only one reason for the sound, a kind of static death march.

Someone had fallen. And could not remount.

17

DEVLIN WATCHED in horror as she fell from the stallion. With a leap, he cleared the rail and ran into the ring, just behind the medics. Raw fear was raging through him as they did a preliminary examination and ran an IV line into A.J.'s arm. As she was loaded onto a stretcher, her eyes flipped open. He rushed forward and took her hand.

"Sabbath?"

Devlin had forgotten all about the horse. He glanced over his shoulder, seeing that Chester already had hold of the stallion and was walking him around slowly.

"He's with Chester."

"S'okay?"

He nodded to reduce her agitation. It wasn't enough.

"His legs?" She began to rise.

Devlin put a hand on her shoulder, pressing her gently back down. He didn't even look at the stallion. "He'll be fine."

"You'll make sure Chester wraps him tight?"

"I promise."

"Liniment. The foul-smelling one . . ."

"The one they both hate. I know."

"Arlington!" Garrett Sutherland's voice cut through the chaos as he ran to his daughter.

A.J. was muttering incomprehensible syllables.

"Are you her husband?" a medic asked Devlin while they slid her into the back of an ambulance.

"I'm her father," Garrett interjected. "I'm going with her."

Devlin opened his mouth to argue but the man was already climbing inside. As they shut the doors, A.J. lifted up off the stretcher, calling Devlin's name.

Before the doors shut, he shouted out to her, "I'll meet you there."

When the ambulance left, he felt as if his world had ended. Again.

As he was standing there, a flashbulb went off in his face. It was a galvanizing event. He went from frozen shock to raging anger in the split second it took for the brilliant light to fade. Lunging in fury, he grabbed the camera out of the man's hands and threw it to the ground.

"Hey, you broke my—" the man said.

Devlin gripped the photographer's shirt in his fists and hauled him up close. "When I find out which one of you bastards let that goddamn flash go off, I'm going to crack more than a lens."

"Easy there, boy." Chester's calm voice reached him in the nick of time. "Let 'im go. C'mon, now."

Devlin pushed the man away. "Get out of my sight."

The photographer didn't protest any further, just gathered up the pieces of the camera and disappeared in a hurry. The rest of the press backed off.

Devlin turned and looked at Chester, who was standing with the stallion. He was finding it hard to string sentences together. "How're his legs?"

"He's lame. Right front. But it'll heal."

"Good, I'm glad I didn't lie to her."

When Devlin didn't move, Chester gripped his shoulder. "Boy, look at me."

Devlin tried to.

"She needs you."

"I know."

"So go on now."

"How will you get back with the stallion?"

"I'll give them a ride." Devlin and Chester turned in surprise at Peter Conrad's voice. "And you can use our faciliies to rehab the horse if you need to. Anything you want, we've got. It's all yours."

"That's right kind," Chester replied.

Devlin said, "The stallion should go there right after the vet looks at him. He's going to need hydrotherapy first thing tomorrow morning."

"I'll call ahead and have a stall waiting. You know they've taken her to County, right?" Peter asked him. "You get on the highway heading south—"

"I know how to get there," Devlin said.

Peter flushed. "Of course you do."

In a fog, Devlin went to the trailer and drove ten miles to the hospital where he'd been taken the year before. Coming back to the scene of his operations and difficult recovery was too surreal for him to comprehend. He decided it had to be a nightmare. Life's parallels just couldn't be so cruel.

By the time he located A.J. in the Emergency Department, an orthopedist had taken X-rays and was making his report to her and her father. When Devlin walked into the room, the white coat stopped talking.

"Devlin!" A.J. exclaimed, holding out her hand. She was propped up on a bed, one arm lying on a pillow in her lap. He went to her.

The doctor continued. "What you had was a fracture that hadn't healed properly. The pulling motion reactivated the break, which caused the pain you felt before you fell. Then you compounded the injury by landing on it. We're going to put you in a cast but you should be good as new in about six weeks."

A.J. groaned.

"I see you're one of those horse types," the doctor said casually as he scribbled notes in her medical record. "Don't know how you rode with that arm at all. You must have been in some kind of pain. When did you first break it?"

A.J. looked up at Devlin and watched his face tighten. "I fell a couple of weeks ago."

The doctor looked up in surprise. "You've been using that arm for how long?"

A.J. mumbled something, hoping to get him off the subject.

"You're one tough lady." He flipped the metal cover of her chart closed. The clapping noise was loud in the tension of the room. "I'll be back with the plaster."

"Arlington," her father started as soon as the curtain closed, "how could you be so reckless?"

One look from her and he stopped talking. He'd been dismissed and he knew it.

Clearing his throat, he said, "Devlin, will you be able to give her a ride home?"

"Of course."

The good-bye with her father was awkward and rushed because A.J. was anxious to be alone with Devlin. When she finally was, she reached out to him. The arms he put around her were stiff and she felt afraid.

"Sabbath is going to be fine," he told her with a detached voice. "Chester was going to wrap him well and your stepbrother offered the use of the Sutherland facilities to rehab him. I told them to take him there."

"Devlin?"

He didn't meet her eyes. Terror settled cold and hard in her chest.

"Devlin, about my arm—"

The doctor and a nurse came back into the room.

An hour later, she left the hospital with a cast and a broken heart.

During the trip home, Devlin didn't say a word to her. When they pulled up to the farmhouse, he led the way inside. It was dark and he turned on the lights one by one, moving around the rooms of his home like a ghost. She waited for him to stop moving, her heart pounding like she'd run a marathon.

"Devlin, I know you're angry," she said when he came out of the dining room.

"I'm not angry," he said.

She searched his face for any sign of warmth. There was none.

"Devlin, I'm sorry I kept the injury from you."

"I believe that."

"My arm's going to be fine. I'm okay. Sabbath's going to heal. We can resume training here—"

"Not here."

With the bald words, A.J. felt like she'd hit the ground again.

"What are you saying?"

"I agreed to get you to the Qualifier. I did. Now you need to go."

Through a dry throat, she said, "Is it just Sabbath who needs to leave?"

It was a lifetime before she heard his answer.

"No."

Tears, hot and wet, started to fall from her eyes.

"You can't mean this. You just can't. This can't be the end."

She was waiting for a denial, for a sign of weakening from the hard line. She found none.

"You lied to me," he said. "You lied to me deliberately about your physical condition and you did it again and again. Every time you went into the ring on that horse."

"I didn't want you to worry about me."

"When we made love, and you were naked against me, I thought that there was nothing that could come between us. When I held you in my arms, and you told me you loved me, I believed you. When I asked how you were doing, I assumed you were being truthful."

"Devlin, I—"

"I knew something was wrong but I was so in love with you . . . I wanted to believe your words more than I wanted to see the truth."

With shock, she realized he'd spoken in the past tense.

"Don't you love me anymore?"

"I don't trust you. You can't have love without trust. What's worse, I don't trust myself anymore. This is the second time I've ignored my instincts. You'd think after Mercy, I'd have learned the lesson."

"Oh, God," she moaned. "Don't do this. There must be something I can do. Something I can say—"

"I'm going out," he told her. "When I get back, I'll help bring your things over to the mansion. I know that arm's got to be hurting you."

He stepped around her to get to the door. Didn't look back as he left.

Great wrenching sobs of grief and self-blame racked A.J. and she fell to her knees in the foyer. As she gave herself up to the emotions, she knew a pain so deep, she felt as if she would come apart.

18

A MONTH later, Devlin walked out of the farmhouse to get the morning paper, which had landed on the frost-laden grass. It left a green imprint when he picked it up. As he turned to go back into the house, he looked up at the sky. Gray clouds shut out the sun and, against the stark sky, leafless trees moved stiffly in the cold wind.

He didn't look up because he was interested in the heavens. He was studiously ignoring the stables. And the ring. And the paddocks and the trails.

But he felt trapped by their vicinity anyway.

All that was going to change, however, with the phone call he'd made the day before. He was putting the property on the market. The agent had been thrilled with the listing and he'd been assured it was going to go fast despite a hefty price tag. Quick was what he wanted, even though he wasn't sure where he was going to move. He was contemplating somewhere far away, in distance and spirit. Like California. Or Hawaii. After all, he had plenty of money and no real roots. He was free to go wherever he chose.

Well, free to make the choice to leave.

He was far from unencumbered.

The ghosts of his love for A.J. haunted him, day and night, in the shadows and in the light. He thought of her all the time, almost to the point of obsession, trying to come to terms with what had separated them. He felt betrayed and sad. Beyond the pain he felt at her deception, he was still angry that she hadn't taken into account the risks she'd assumed. Competing with her arm in that kind of condition had been foolhardy. Dangerous. She could have been hurt even more seriously. She could have been—

Devlin shook his head. Enough, he told himself. He'd rehashed it all enough.

As he went back into the house, he shut the door behind him to keep the cold out. The fire he'd started at four a.m., when he'd been wandering around aimlessly, had died down though the embers were still throwing off heat. He sat down and watched their red glow, tossing the paper on the coffee table. After staring into space, he caught himself before his thoughts once more became too anguished. To distract himself, he cracked open the *Herald Globe*, trying to fill the empty daylight with something. Anything.

When he got to the sports pages, he sucked in a breath.

Staring up at him, out of a grainy photograph, was A.J.

He scanned the article with a hunger that pained him.

She'd decided not to sue the reporter whose flash had blinded the stallion. But that wasn't the shocker. She was selling Sabbath. And retiring from competition.

Devlin reread the text over and over. Competing was the most important thing in her life. And now she was just walking out?

He called Chester, who had followed the stallion over to Sutherland's. Apart from the fact he was the only groom Sabbath would let near him, there was, once again, no work at the McCloud Stables.

"Mornin'?"

"Ches, tell me she isn't really quitting," Devlin demanded. He just couldn't believe it was true. After everything they'd done with the stallion, all her progress. Everything she'd sacrificed. Like their relationship.

"So ya' read the article."

"Why is she doing this?"

"She's lost the drive."

"But she's good. I can't believe she's walking away. Is the arm not healing?"

"Arm's fine. She just doesn't have it in her anymore, so she says. She's stayin' on at Sutherland's, though. Stepbrother's moved on an' gone. She's runnin' the place but says she's not gettin' in a show ring ever again."

"But she loves to compete." Devlin was shaking his head, incredulous. "And the stallion. She loves Sabbath."

"The animal's heartbroken. He hasn't been eatin' well. It's a mess."

There was a long silence.

"Ches, if I went to her, do you think she'd talk to me?"

"Depends on whatcha got to say. Should I tell her you're goin' over?"

But Devlin had already hung up the phone.

A knock sounded at her office door and A.J. looked up from her desk.

Her office. Her desk.

The possessive pronoun still sounded foreign. It had been a couple of weeks but she was still getting used to her new job.

"Come on in," she called out.

One of the grooms stuck his head in. "When's the vet coming?"

"Tomorrow morning. What's up?"

"Sleeping Beauty's got colic again."

"You're kidding me."

"Didn't touch her feed and is walkin' in circles in the stall."

"Hell. Better call her owner. Is Johnson around?"

"He's in the ring on Juggernaut. He'll be done in a few."

"When he dismounts, tell him I need to talk with him. If Beauty's down for the count, we're going to have to change the hacking schedule this afternoon."

"Will do, boss."

"Thanks."

When the door shut, A.J. swiveled around and looked out of a window, seeing bare trees. Winter had arrived. There was frost on the ground when she came into work in the morning and she'd started wearing her parka around the stables. They were also using the indoor ring for training all the time.

Deciding to go find Johnson herself, she got out of her

chair and pulled her coat on. With her cast, dressing was an
awkward process and she didn't seem to be getting any better at it. Over the past four weeks, she'd learned to hate the
plaster deadweight and couldn't wait to get rid of the thing.
More than being a physical nuisance, it reminded her of
things she couldn't bear to think about.

Her hand was on the doorknob when another knock
rang out.

"Johnson, Beauty's off the hack schedule today. . . ."

As she opened the door, her breath caught in her throat.
"Devlin."

She thought he had to be a dream.

During the first weeks of their separation, she'd looked
for him in every knock, every phone ring, every truck that
pulled up to the stables. The letdowns had tortured her until finally, very recently, she'd given up. The loss of hope had
been a terrible blow but at least she didn't feel the agony of
rejection every moment of every day.

When she blinked and he was still standing in front of
her, she asked, "What are you doing here?"

Devlin didn't answer her right away. Instead, she felt
his eyes going over her as if he were memorizing her features.

"I hear you're selling Sabbath."

"I am."

"Why?"

"I don't ride anymore and he deserves to keep jumping."

"Why are you quitting?"

"Did you come over here just to interrogate me?"

She was praying the answer was no.

His response was a long time in coming.

"I came to change your mind because it's a waste of talent for you not to be in the ring. Now that I'm here,
though . . . there seems like so much more to say."

A.J. motioned for him to enter. She shut the door.

"Nice office," he said.

As Devlin looked around, she watched him with greed
while she waited for him to speak. He carried himself in
that way she found so attractive and she noticed he'd just
had a haircut. Remembering what it felt like to run her

hands deep into those dark waves hurt so much, she had to close her eyes against the pain.

"How's the arm?" he asked.

"Healing well."

"Any reason you can't ride when the cast comes off?"

"No, but it doesn't matter." She went around her desk. Sat in the chair. Fiddled with a pen to keep from telling him she loved him.

"How long until it's off?"

Frustration got the better of her.

"Look, Devlin, I'm not sure why you came but if you don't get to the point, I'm going to start screaming. It hurts too much to be in the same room with you and I'd just as soon get through this. Are you opening a door by showing up here or throwing more dirt on a grave?"

He turned slowly toward her.

"Competing was everything to you and now you're quitting. Why?"

"You can't compete without the burn."

"All your dreams—"

Pain made her lash out.

"What do you want? To hear how losing you has made me despise the sport I loved and everything I wanted to prove about myself through it? That I bitterly regret not telling you about this stupid arm? That I wish I could do the whole thing over again? Those things are all true, but I'm not inclined to run through the particulars, if you don't mind. I miss you. I wish you were still in my life but I'm moving on. Because that's all I can do." She shook her head sadly. "Look, I think you should go."

But Devlin didn't leave. He stood there, looking deeply into her eyes, his expression melting into a mixture of tension and grief. Her heart began to pound as she watched the change.

And then he came around to her. When he held his hand out, she looked at it curiously, unable to grapple with the gesture. Then he reached down and took her in an embrace, his arms wrapping around her and reminding her of a haven she missed so much. To feel his broad shoulders against her cheek, to smell the tang of his aftershave, to sense the strength in his body, it all overwhelmed her. Holding herself stiffly, she prayed she wouldn't break down and thought it was grossly unfair of him to get close. She tried to push him away.

"You've already ended things once," A.J. said in a broken voice. "Don't ask me to go through it again."

He mumbled something and held her tighter.

"Let me go."

"I can't," he said clearly.

A.J.'s heart stopped as she wondered if she'd heard him right. "What?"

"I can't let go. I can't let you go."

Fear and happiness warred inside of her. She was desperate to believe him. Terrified of being hurt more.

"Oh, God, I've missed you," Devlin said against her hair. "Trying to stay away has been unbearable. You've been in my dreams so I can't sleep. Everywhere I look around my house, I see your shadow. I put my stables on the market because the only way I could go on not seeing you was to move away." His laugh was strained. "Although I'm realizing now I wouldn't have been able to leave."

She forcibly pulled back. "Devlin, what exactly are you saying? I—I'm not strong enough to read between the lines. It hurts too much."

"When I read the newspaper this morning, I couldn't believe it. I know how much competing means to you, and suddenly, you're walking away? I was stunned. I thought I was coming over to change your mind but now I realize it was just a pretext." He reached out and took her hands in his. "After I learned that you'd kept your injury a secret from me, I was pissed, especially because you'd been hurt because of it. It made me wonder what else you were keeping from me. I felt like I didn't know what I could trust about you. Or us. For chrissakes, why didn't you just tell me how much you were hurting?"

She tried to explain in a halting voice. "When I went back to training after I fell that first time, and I realized the arm hadn't healed, I was afraid to tell you. I thought back to the fight we had over my going to the doctor. I was worried that you'd demand I pull out of the Qualifier."

He shook his head with regret. "I'm sorry I lost it at you that afternoon. I reacted emotionally and that was a mistake. I just couldn't bear to see you hurt."

"Devlin, it was stupid of me not to tell you the truth. I felt awful the whole time. I'm so very sorry. And I never lied about anything else. You've got to believe me."

She watched as his hand rose and then she felt the skin of his fingers stroke her cheek. "I do."

There was a long silence and then he said, "I don't want to be without you. I love you. I need you in my life."

Tears welled in A.J.'s eyes and she wasn't able to speak as they embraced. All she could do was hold on to him, and vow she would never let go. As they stood, chest to chest, hip to hip, she could feel the pound of his heart against her cheek, the warmth seeping from his body into hers, the sensation of his hands stroking her back and her hair. When the touch of his finger came under her chin, she lifted her lips for his kiss, a soft, gentle brush that was a declaration of love.

"Don't sell him," Devlin whispered.

She pulled back in surprise.

"Sabbath is your horse. No one else is going to be able to ride him like you can."

"You're saying I should go back in the ring?"

"It's what you love to do. What you were born to do."

"But how can you—"

Devlin kissed her, drowning out the words. This time his mouth was passionate as it moved over hers, his tongue coming inside and stroking hers with a demand she met feverishly.

When their lips parted, he said, "I want all of you. And that means the stallion and the eventing, too. I'm not saying we won't clash again but I know we can find a way to work anything out. Our love will be strong enough. This I know."

A.J. closed her eyes against the emotions that rushed over her. She felt gratitude, relief, happiness. When she looked up at him again, she brought his hand to her lips, kissing it before speaking.

"Losing you, and knowing I was responsible for it, has been the hardest thing I've ever faced in my life." She laughed ruefully. "I don't know. Maybe I got what I needed out of the Qualifier after all. Even though it didn't turn out as I expected or wanted, I feel like I've grown up. It isn't enough just to separate myself from my family or go into the ring on a flashy horse. If I want to be taken seriously, I've got to be more serious. Stop being so impulsive and reckless. Does that make any sense?"

"It does."

She warmed under the respect and love that shone in his eyes.

He said, "And I'm ready to train you in the ring, if you want. I think we make a great team."

"So do I," she replied as she pressed her lips to his.

They were married two weeks later in a small church deep in the Virginia hills. Chester, Devlin's best man, wore a tuxedo for the first time in his life. He liked it so much he declared he was going to throw out his overalls. Margaret said she loved him with or without the cummerbund. Carter Wessex, A.J.'s cousin, took tranquilizers to get on an airplane for the first time in ten years and flew in from her latest archaeological dig. The occasion was, she'd said, well worth the anxiety. And while Garrett walked his daughter down the aisle, his eyes were light even though his heart was heavy because he'd never missed her mother more.

Peter was a big surprise. After the accident, he'd quit his job, moved out of the mansion and taken up residence in a penthouse in New York City. He'd done it all in a matter of three days and, sooner than he had a working telephone, he'd signed on with an agent to represent him as an actor. Both the move and the agent had turned out to be good choices. He relished life in the big city and had just learned he'd been signed by a major soap opera to play a villain people would love to hate. When he shared the news with A.J., he said that playing Brock O'Rourke on *Wings of Fate* was going to be hard but, considering all he and A.J. had been through together, he had the character in the bag.

During the wedding, Peter sat in the front row of the church, and for the first time in anyone's memory, there was someone sitting by his side other than his mother. The woman he'd brought with him was a brunette, with a flashing smile and smart eyes. An investment banker who was also a socialite; he'd met her at an art exhibition. Regina had hated the woman on sight.

It was going to be, Peter told A.J., a fair fight.

After the festivities and a reception at the Borealis Club, A.J. and Devlin returned to the farmhouse. As he carried her over the threshold, he stepped around the boxes of her things, which had been delivered the day before, and then took her upstairs to their bedroom. There, he removed her veil and released, one by one, the hundred or so pearl buttons down the back of her mother's wedding dress. When he was finished, he slipped the acres of thick satin from her body and stripped his own clothes off so they were standing naked together.

"You're so beautiful," he told her softly, his lips caressing her collarbone. She felt his hands slip around her waist and pull her against him. His skin was soft, his body hard. "Now that you're my wife, I only need one more thing to be complete."

"What's that?" she asked breathlessly.

He pulled back, and began plucking pins from her hair, releasing the waves from the chignon. "What the hell does *A.J.* stand for?"

Laughter filled the room.

"Didn't you look at the marriage license?"

"I was too blinded by love. So?"

"You aren't going to believe it."

"Try me," he said, as the last pin fell to the floor. He buried his hands in her hair, shaking it out around her shoulders.

"The first is *Arlington*."

"Not bad. Better than a lot of other words that start with *A*." His smile was warm.

She cast him a dry look. "It was the city I was born in."

"Makes it easy to remember."

"The other is *Juniper*."

He froze in disbelief. "You're named after a bush?"

"It's a damn nice planting, a hearty shrub."

Devlin was laughing as he said, "And the connection is . . ."

"I think I might have been conceived under one."

"That's adventurous."

"I haven't asked a lot of questions."

"I can see why."

Devlin's eyes scanned her features with a hunger and a love she relished. When she felt his hand on the base of her neck, urging her forward to his lips, she went eagerly into his kiss. Passion flared as their bodies melted and their hearts hammered and their blood rushed.

When they were too breathless to continue, Devlin pulled back and murmured against her mouth, "Whatever the origins, I think A.J. suits you. It's a strong name, for a strong woman."

"I'm stronger with you," she said tenderly. His tongue slid into her mouth and she moaned, gripping onto his shoulders, scoring his skin with her nails. When he left her lips and began to lick his way down her neck, her head fell back and she mumbled, "To think this all happened because of a baseball cap."

Devlin shot her a puzzled look as he bent down and kissed the tip of her breast.

"If you hadn't picked up my hat at the auction, who knows. . . ." Her words were lost as he suckled a proud nipple.

"There's only one other thing," Devlin said, falling to his knees. His hands splayed over the small of her back and then the swell of her hips.

"Something else?" A.J. said breathlessly, as she felt his tongue go across her belly.

"We haven't figured out what to do for a honeymoon."

She pulled back, eyes sparkling with purpose.

"Oh, no," he groaned. "You've got that look again."

"What look?"

"What are you thinking?"

"Well, since you brought it up, there's an auction down in Florida and there's this mare I heard about—"

"Don't tell me her name is Babylon."

"No." A.J. tried to look innocent.

"Let me guess, she's a real handful."

"She may need a little work but she's got terrific—"

Devlin rose and silenced her with a powerful kiss, his tongue rushing into her mouth, his arms steel around her body. When he was finished, he said, "Wherever you want to go, whatever you want to do, I'm there for you. And that includes horse auctions in Florida."

A.J. sighed as he scooped her up in his arms and carried her over to the bed.

"Devlin?"

"Hmmm?" he said, as he laid her down.

"I think her name is Angel."

He shot her a wry look.

"And she and Sabbath would have the most fantastic colts. . . ."

Read on for a sneak peek of
another contemporary romance by
J. R. Ward writing as Jessica Bird

HEART OF GOLD

Available from Signet.

CARTER WESSEX straightened her shoulders, lifted the heavy brass door knocker and let it fall. As a thunderous noise rang out, she took a step back and regarded the grand entrance to the mansion with a jaundiced eye. The place could have been a luxury hotel.

But what else did she expect a billionaire corporate raider to live in?

While she waited for a response, she couldn't believe she was about to ask Nick Farrell for permission to dig on his land. After he'd just thrown off her competitor. Or rather, after one of his groundsmen had chased off her closest competitor with a shotgun.

She looked down at her running shoes and wondered with gallows humor whether she was about to put them to good use.

Of course, that rat Conrad Lyst hadn't asked first. He'd just gone up Farrell Mountain with his shovel and started making holes. Like a lot of other professional and amateur archaeologists. And one by one, they had all been removed. As a matter of fact, in archaeology circles, it was considered a rite of passage to get tossed off Farrell's property.

The site was considered a Holy Grail of American history because of what it might be hiding. The solution to one of the great Revolutionary War mysteries, as well as a fortune in gold, were probably buried in the man's soil but he refused to let people get anywhere near it.

Which only made Carter more determined.

When the door opened, Carter was surprised to find herself staring into the pleasant face of a sixty-year-old woman. She'd assumed only Lurch would answer that kind of knocker.

"I'm here to see Mr. Farrell."

"About?"

"I'm an archaeologist and I—"

"He doesn't like archaeologists much."

"So I've heard. I just want to ask him if I can dig up on the mount—"

"He doesn't like people digging up there."

"Heard that, too. But if I could just ask him—"

"He doesn't like being asked."

"Does the guy like anything? Or is he as bad-humored as his reputation suggests?"

Carter clamped her mouth shut. Great, she thought. She'd just managed to insult him to his staff while trying to wheedle a way in to see him. Way to win friends and influence people.

"Sorry about that crack," she muttered.

There was a long pause. She waited to hear how she was going to be summarily tossed off the property and wondered whether cops would be involved.

Instead, the woman smiled. "Tell you what. I'll give you twenty minutes to see for yourself if he's that awful. If you're crazy enough to want to give it a try, you might as well get the full experience. Besides, the way he'll throw you out will be a heck of a lot more interesting and inventive than anything I could do to you."

"Thanks," Carter said, dubiously.

Swallowing unexpected fear, she followed the leader through the house, taking in a host of spacious rooms. Every one was filled with antiques and had an atmosphere of elegant leisure, with freshly cut flowers adding to the sophistication and grace. When they came to a stout mahogany door, the woman paused and knocked.

"Do yourself a favor. Make it short and sweet. He likes things that way."

At the muffled reply, she opened the door and walked into an old-world study.

Nick Farrell looked up from an ornate desk and Carter's feet stopped working. The first thing she noticed was the unusual color of his eyes, a gray so pale that the irises were almost invisible. The next thing that registered was his extraordinary looks. He had dark hair that looked glossy and luxurious, a face that must have launched a thousand women's fantasies and she could tell he was tall, broad-shouldered, and imposing, even though he was sitting down.

The eyes meeting hers held frank appraisal and a hint of cruelty that somehow only added to his allure. It made her wonder if there was any softness in him at all and she imagined that women had driven themselves crazy trying to find it.

The man was a heartbreak waiting to happen.

Not for her, of course, she amended. But she pitied whoever fell for someone like him.

"This woman is here to see you," his housekeeper announced.

One dark eyebrow rose sardonically. "I don't recall asking to meet with any teenage girls."

His voice was a deep rumble and had a very sexy, smooth sound. She thought of dark chocolate. And then realized his words were meant as an insult.

"I can't speak to your appointment calendar," Carter replied. "But I've been out of my teens for a decade, thank you very much."

The eyebrow took flight again at her tone, which was every bit as commanding as his had been. Their eyes clashed. Busy assessing each other, neither heard the housekeeper leave.

"Maybe we should start over," Carter said, clearing her throat. "Mr. Farrell, I'm—"

"So what do you want?" she was asked.

"I'm an archaeologist and I—"

"No." Farrell started rifling through papers.

"Excuse me?"

"The answer is no."

"But I haven't asked for anything yet."

"The operant word being *yet*. Letting you chatter on before you get to the asking would only be a waste of our time."

She was stunned into silence and, for a moment, all she could do was watch his eyes trace over words on some document.

"You know, you don't have to be so rude," she told him. "And you could look at me while we're talking."

The arrogant brow arched. "I always knew Miss Manners came with a shovel. I just assumed it was for slinging drivel, not digging up other people's property."

"And it's hard for me to believe someone living in a place like this has the social skills of a cow."

"Fine." He put the papers down and leaned back in his chair. "Is this better? Tell you what. I'll even go one further and remember to say *please* when I ask you to leave. Will you *please* leave?"

"You can't just toss me out before I have a chance—"

"I can't? I've got a deed in the safe that says this is my land and I don't think there's any law which mandates the cheerful tolerance of trespassers."

"Lucky for you. I don't think you could pull off cheerful to save your soul."

Crossing his arms over that powerful chest, he looked her over again. "How old are you?"

"Twenty-seven—er, twenty-eight."

"Try eighteen." He glanced at her clothes. "You look like you could be a babysitter. Or even need one."

"It's hard to look mature in cutoffs and a T-shirt," she said indignantly.

"You pulled that getup out of a closet, not me."

"I had to go to an associate's dig before I came here."

"Hopefully not as an image consultant."

"I'm not here to talk about my clothes."

"You seem determined to talk about something. Since I'm not going to discuss your digging up my land, I figure clothes are a natural launching pad for inane conversation. Considering you're a woman."

She took a deep breath, trying not to lose her temper.

"Look, I know Conrad Lyst was just caught up on your mountain—"

"Perhaps I need to be more clear. I'm not discussing anybody's digging on my land. Your questionable taste in sportswear is still on the table, however."

"I didn't wear this for you!"

"Obviously."

Carter did her best to look at him calmly.

"Mr. Farrell, all I'm asking is for you to hear me out."

"Call me Nick and forget the speech. It won't improve your bargaining position any more than those shorts do."

"Are you always this nasty?"

"As a rule, yes. But sometimes I'm worse."

There was a long silence. She had the feeling she was amusing him.

"I'm a professional, Mr. Farrell, not an itinerant ditch-digger. You may have the answer to one of the great puzzles of the revolutionary era on your land. No one really knows what happened to the Winship party and the gold they were carrying. You owe it to posterity—"

"To let you come in and rescue the solution from my land? I've got news for you. I don't think it needs rescuing. As far as I'm concerned, the past is best left buried and posterity these days is far more interested in MTV and who's the next person to get kicked off the *Survivor* island. They couldn't care less about minutemen and redcoats or how this nation was forged."

"That's a pretty narrow view."

"I'm a narrow kind of man."

"I can tell."

He chuckled. "So Miss Manners is also a behaviorist?"

"No, it's the flashing *Royal Pain in the Ass* sign over your desk."

Nick Farrell tilted back his head and laughed. It was a rich, rolling sound.

In that moment, Carter found herself liking the man.

Just a bit.

When he focused on her again, he was smiling, and the grin lit up his austere face, cleaving years off him. He looked closer to thirty-five than forty-five.

He said, "Do you have any idea how many people come at me each spring asking to tear into Farrell Mountain?"

"No, but I don't care."

"You don't?"

"When you go after some company, do you worry about what all the other little raiders are doing?"

"Been doing a little research on my history?"

"You're pretty well-known."

He shrugged and then asked, "What would you do if I decided to let Lyst have a go of it?"

"I'd say good luck and good riddance to both of you." The words sounded like a straight answer but she knew the anger behind her voice gave her away.

"Something tells me," he said, getting to his feet, "you wouldn't be quite that phlegmatic."

She gave him a disparaging look.

"I'm wrong?" he asked.

"You think I'm underage because of my shorts. In my opinion, that doesn't give you a whole lot of clout in the judgment department."

Farrell came around the edge of his desk and approached her, stopping only when he was a foot away. Carter's heart started thumping. He was taller than her by at least a head and that was saying something, considering she was five-nine. As those arresting pale eyes of his traced her face and neck, she had to stop herself from stepping backward.

Across a desk, he was insulting and intimidating. Up close, she found him totally compelling.

Not exactly an improvement, Carter thought, running her tongue over her lips.

That was a mistake. Like a predator, he watched the movement, eyes sharpening on her mouth. The way he was looking at her made her body swell with something she was determined to think of as anxiety. Even if it felt more like hunger.

"What do you really want?" he asked.

"I don't understand." The words were garbled, like she was talking around marbles.

"Everyone has a hidden agenda. What else are you after?"

Carter knew he was speaking but the words were lost on her.

She decided she also had marbles in her brain.

"Look, Mr. Farrell, I don't know where you're going with this. I just want to dig."

Abruptly, he broke the eye contact with her lips and returned to his desk and his papers. His voice was offhand when he addressed her again.

"I think you should put your learner's permit to good use and drive yourself back to wherever you came from. You aren't going to get what you want here, either in the dirt or from me. However much I wish I could be ... accommodating."

"What are you talking about?"

"I like women, not schoolgirls."

Carter's mouth dropped open.

"Are you suggesting ..." She couldn't even finish the sentence.

"Shut the door on the way out," he commanded before drawling, *"Please."*

"You insufferable, egocentric—"

"There you go with the compliments, making me blush."

"I hope you rot in hell."

"See you there," he said cheerfully.

On the way out, Carter slammed the door as hard as she could.

Wincing, Nick lurched forward in his chair as the clap of wood reverberated through the room like a gunshot. His head was still tender from a migraine he'd had the day before and he massaged his temples, waiting for the sting to wear off.

That was one hell of a beautiful woman, he thought. The kind of beautiful that makes men do stupid things. Like believe in love and other fallacies.

He arched his neck and thought it was a good thing she'd left. Reeling in his impulses had been getting more difficult every time that kitten pink tongue of hers had come out for a lick of those sweet lips. Moves like that had been performed for him countless times before but, because they were calculated, he'd never been tantalized. The trouble with that archaeologist was he got the sense she didn't know how enticing she was.

But that couldn't be possible, he told himself.

One thing Nick knew about beautiful women was they were always willing to leverage their assets. Not that he faulted them for it. He'd made a fortune doing the same thing, only his bait was dollar bills, not the promise of sexual thrills, and his acquisitions were companies, not marriage licenses. In the romantic marketplace, no one had acquired him, of course, though it hadn't been for lack of trying. Futile as it always was for the other party, he enjoyed the bartering.

And that woman in the cutoffs could have been a real contender. If it hadn't been for the way she was affecting him, negotiations over how much she'd be willing to give of herself to get at Farrell Mountain would have been fun. Aside from her beauty, she had a keen intelligence and a heavy dose of wit. In all of Nick's life, his adopted son was the only one who dared to spar with him. Everyone else either wanted something or owed him money, neither of which were breeding grounds for resistance, even of the playful variety.

And that archaeologist had been captivating when she was angry, he thought. A flush on those high cheekbones, her breath coming in drumbeats, her mouth open, agape at his rudeness.

Delightful. Utterly delightful.

Too bad he wouldn't be seeing her again.

Read on for a sneak peek of
#1 *New York Times* bestselling author
J. R. Ward's Novel of the Fallen Angels

ENVY

Available from Signet.

Two houses down from Detective Thomas DelVecchio's, Internal Affairs Officer Sophia Reilly was behind the wheel of her unmarked and partially blinded.

"By all that is holy . . ." She rubbed her eyes. "Do you not believe in curtains?"

As she prayed for the image of a spectacularly naked colleague to fade from her retinas, she seriously rethought her decision to do the stakeout herself. She was exhausted, for one thing—or had been before she'd seen just about everything Veck had to offer.

Take out the *just*.

One bene was that she was really frickin' awake now, thank you very much—she might as well have licked two fingers and shoved them into a socket: a full-frontal like that was enough to give her the perm she'd wanted back when she was thirteen.

Muttering to herself, she dropped her hands into her lap again. And gee whiz, as she stared at the dash, all she saw . . . was everything she'd seen.

Yeah, wow, on some men, no clothes was so much more than just *naked*.

And to think she'd almost missed the show. She'd parked her sedan and just called in her position when the upstairs lights had gone on and she had gotten a gander at the vista of a bedroom. Easing back into her seat, it hadn't dawned on her exactly where the unobstructed view was going to take them both—she'd just been interested that it appeared to be nothing but a bald lightbulb on the ceiling of what had to be the master suite.

Then again, bachelor pad decorating tended to be either storage-unit crammed or Death Valley–barren.

Veck's was obviously the Death Valley variety.

Except suddenly she hadn't been thinking about interior decorating, because her suspect had stepped into the bathroom and flipped the switch.

Hellllllllo, big boy.

In too many ways to count.

"Stop thinking about it . . . stop thinking about—"

Closing her eyes again didn't help: If she'd reluctantly noticed before how well he filled out his clothes, now she knew exactly why. He was heavily muscled, and given that he didn't have any hair on his chest, there was nothing to obscure those hard pecs and that six-pack and the carved ridges that went over his hips.

Matter of fact, when it came to manscaping, all he had was a dark stripe that ran between his belly button and his . . .

You know, maybe size did matter, she thought.

"Oh, for chrissakes."

In an attempt to get her brain focused on something, anything more appropriate, she leaned forward and looked out the opposite window. As far as she could tell, the house directly across from him had privacy shades across every available view. Good move, assuming he paraded around like that every night.

Then again, maybe the husband had strung those puppies up so that his wife didn't get a case of the swoons.

Bracing herself, she glanced back at Veck's place. The lights were off upstairs and she had to hope now that he was dressed and on the first floor, he stayed that way.

God, what a night.

Was it possible Veck had torn apart that suspect? She didn't think so.

But he did—even though he couldn't remember a thing. Whatever, she was still waiting for any evidence that came from the scene, and there were coyotes in those woods. Bears. Cats of the non–Meow Mix variety. Chances were good that the suspect had come walking through there with the scent of dried blood on his clothes and something with four paws had viewed him as a Happy Meal. Veck could well have tried to step in and been shoved to the side. After all, he'd been rubbing his temples like he'd had pain there, and God knew head trauma had been known to cause short-term memory loss.

The lack of physical evidence on him supported the theory; that was for sure.

And yet . . .

God, that father of his. It was impossible not to factor him in even a little.

Like every criminal justice major, she'd studied Thomas DelVecchio Sr. as part of her courses — but she'd also spent considerable time on him in her deviant-psych classes. Veck's dad was your classic serial killer: smart, cunning, committed to his "craft," utterly remorseless. And yet, having watched videos of his interviews with police, he came across as handsome, compelling, and affable. Classy. Very non-monster.

But then again, like a lot of psychopaths, he'd cultivated an image and sustained it with care. He'd been very successful as a dealer of antiquities, although his establishment in that haughty, lofty world of money and privilege had been a complete self-invention. He'd come from absolutely nothing, but had had a knack for charming rich people — as well as a talent for going overseas and coming back with ancient artifacts and statues that were extremely marketable. It wasn't until the killings had started to surface that his business practices came under scrutiny, and to this day, no one had any idea where he'd found the stuff he had — it was almost as if he'd had a treasure trove somewhere in the Middle East. He certainly hadn't helped authorities sort things out, but what were they going to do to him? He was already on death row.

Not for much longer, though, evidently.

What had Veck's mother been like—

The knock on the window next to her head was like a shot ringing out, and she had her weapon palmed and pointed to the sound less than a heartbeat afterward.

Veck was standing in the street next to her car, his hands up, his wet hair glossy in the streetlights.

Lowering her weapon, she put her window down with a curse.

"Quick reflexes, Officer," he murmured.

"Do you want to get shot, Detective?"

"I said your name. Twice. You were deep in thought."

Thanks to what she'd seen in that bathroom, the flannel shirt and academy sweats he had on seemed eminently removable, the kind of duds that wouldn't resist a shove up or a pull down. But come on, like she hadn't seen every aisle in his grocery store already?

"You want my clothes now?" he said as he held up a trash bag.

"Yes, thank you." She accepted the load through her window and put the things down on the floor. "Boots, too?"

As he nodded, he said, "Can I bring you some coffee? I don't have much in my kitchen, but I think I can find a clean mug and I got instant."

"Thanks. I'm okay."

There was a pause. "There a reason you're not looking me in the eye, Officer?"

I just saw you buck naked, Detective. "Not at all." She pegged him right in the peepers. "You should get inside. It's chilly."

"The cold doesn't bother me. You going to be here all night?"

"Depends."

"On whether I am, right."

"Yup."

He nodded, and then glanced around casually like they were nothing but neighbors chatting about the weather. So calm. So confident. Just like his father.

"Can I be honest with you?" he said abruptly.

"You'd better be, Detective."

"I'm still surprised you let me go."

She ran her hands around the steering wheel. "May I be honest with you?"

"Yeah."

"I let you go because I really don't think you did it."

"I was at the scene and I had blood on me."

"You called nine-one-one, you didn't leave, and that kind of death is very messy to perpetrate."

"Maybe I cleaned up."

"There wasn't a shower in those woods as far as I saw."

Do. Not. Think. Of. Him. Naked.

When he started to shake his head like he was going to argue, Reilly cut him off. "Why are you trying to convince me I'm wrong?"

That shut him up. At least for a moment. Then he said in a low voice, "Are you going to feel safe tailing me."

"Why wouldn't I?"

For the first time, emotion bled through his cool expression, and her heart stopped: There was fear in his eyes, as if he didn't trust himself.

"Veck," she said softly, "is there anything I don't know."

He crossed his arms over that big chest of his and his weight went back and forth on his hips as if he were thinking. Then he hissed, and started rubbing his temple.

"I've got nothing," he muttered. "Listen, just do us I both a favor, Officer. Keep that gun close by."

He didn't look back as he turned and walked across the street.

He wasn't wearing any shoes, she realized.

Putting up the window, she watched him go into the house and shut the door. Then the lights in the house went out, except for the hallway on the second floor.

Settling in, she eased down in her seat and stared at all those windows. Shortly thereafter, a massive shadow walked into the living room—or rather, appeared to be dragging something? Like a couch?

Then Veck sat down and his head disappeared as if he were stretching out on something.

It was almost like they were sleeping side by side. Well, except for the walls of the house, the stretch of scruffy spring lawn, the sidewalk, the asphalt, and the steel cage of her Crown Victoria.

Reilly's lids drifted down, but that was a function of the angle of her head. She wasn't tired and she wasn't worried about falling asleep. She was wide-awake in the dark interior of the car.

And yet she reached over and hit the door-lock button. Just in case.